MW01689256

"Serena," he whispered.
"I never thought I'd touch you again."

His smooth, gloved knuckle ran down her cheek. "I'm not Serena," she murmured. But it was a weak denial, and they both knew it.

Slowly, he bent down, closer . . . she reached up and pressed her palm against his chest, not to push him away but to encourage him.

His lips brushed hers, once, twice, and then pressed gently. His arm wrapped around her waist, tugging her against the hardness of his body.

All of her restraint, all rational thought, melted away. She couldn't remember why she'd ever resisted him. She was completely enthralled, completely thrown into the moment, into the feeling of his strong arms, his supple lips. Nothing else mattered . . .

PRAISE FOR THE NOVELS OF JENNIFER HAYMORE

"Jennifer Haymore's books are sophisticated, deeply sensual, and emotionally complex."

—Elizabeth Hoyt, *New York Times* bestselling author

A HINT OF WICKED

"Full of suspense, mystery, romance, and erotica... I am looking forward to more from this author."

—Las Vegas Review-Journal

"A clever, provoking, and steamy story from an up-and-coming author to keep your eye out for!"

—BookPleasures.com

"Haymore is a shining star, and if *A Hint of Wicked* is any indication of what's to come, bring me more."

—FallenAngelReviews.com

"Debut author Haymore crafts a unique plot filled with powerful emotions and complex issues."

—RT Book Reviews

"A unique, heart-tugging story with sympathetic, larger-than-life characters, intriguing plot twists, and sensual love scenes."

—Nicole Jordan, *New York Times* bestselling author

"Complex, stirring, and written with a skillful hand, *A Hint of Wicked* is an evocative love story that will make a special place for itself in your heart."

—RomRevToday.com

"Jennifer Haymore is an up-and-coming new writer who displays a skillful touch in her erotic tale of a woman torn between two lovers."

—Shirlee Busbee, *New York Times* bestselling author of *Seduction Becomes Her*

"Recommended for readers who enjoy steamy Regency-era romance...there's a surprising lightness and tenderness to the love story."

—Historical Novels Review

"A story of life and death, revenge and true love... filled with passion, intrigue, and suspense...I look forward to reading much more historical romance from Jennifer Haymore."

—ArmchairInterviews.com

"Sweet and satisfying...refreshingly honest...a gripping read."

—LikesBooks.com

"A new take on a historical romance...complicated and original...the characters are well crafted... surprisingly satisfying."

—TheRomanceReadersConnection.com

"The characters in this book are easy to love...I can't wait to read the next book!"

—TheBookGirl.net

"What an extraordinary book this is!...What a future this author has!"

—RomanceReviewsMag.com

"Ms. Haymore's talent for storytelling shines throughout this book."

—Eye on Romance

A TOUCH OF SCANDAL

"Jennifer Haymore's books are sophisticated, deeply sensual, and emotionally complex. With a dead sexy hero, a sweetly practical heroine, and a love story that draws together two people from vastly different backgrounds, *A Touch of Scandal* is positively captivating!"

—ELIZABETH HOYT, *New York Times* bestselling author

"Sweep-you-off-your-feet historical romance! Jennifer Haymore sparkles!"

—Liz Carlyle, *New York Times* bestselling author

"Haymore discovers a second fascinating, powerful, and sensual novel that places her high on the must-read lists. She perfectly blends a strong plot that twists like a serpent and has unforgettable characters to create a book readers will remember and re-read."

—RT Book Reviews

"*A Touch of Scandal* is a wonderfully written historical romance. Ms. Haymore brings intrigue and romance together with strong complex characters to make this a keeper for any romance reader. Ms. Haymore is an author to watch and I'm looking forward to the next installment of this series."

—TheRomanceReadersConnection.com

"A deliciously emotional *Cinderella* tale of two people from backgrounds worlds apart, *A Touch of Scandal* addicts the reader from the first page and doesn't let go until the very last word. Hurdle after hurdle stand in the way of Kate and Garrett's love, inexorably pulling the reader along, supporting them each step of the way. *A Touch of Scandal* is a sure-fire win!"

—FallenAngelreviews.com

"A classic tale...Reading this story, I completely fell in love with the honorable servant girl and her esteemed duke. This is definitely a tale of excitement, hot, sizzling sex, and loads of mystery."

—FreshFiction.com

"These characters are just fantastic and endearing. I just couldn't wait to find out what happened on the next page."

—SingleTitles.com

"4 Stars! Kate and Garrett were wonderful characters who constantly tugged at my heartstrings. I found myself rooting for them the whole way through...If you like historical romances that engage your emotions and contain characters you cheer for, this is the book for you."

—TheRomanceDish.com

A SEASON OF SEDUCTION

"4½ stars! Haymore uses the Christmas season as an enhancing backdrop for a mystery/romance that is both original and fulfilling. Her fresh voice and ability to build sensual tension into lively love stories... makes this tale shine."

—RT Book Reviews

"Sizzling...an engaging historical tale."

—RomRevToday.com

"Each time Ms. Haymore writes a book in this series I think there is no way to top the one I just finished. I started this latest one and realized she has done just that and has proven to me how fresh this series can remain."

—The Reading Reviewer

"Jennifer Haymore strikes a good balance of strength, sensuality, drama, and intrigue in her characters...Becky is an independent, fearless woman except when it comes to opening her heart to another man. And Jack, while strong and passionate, shows great sensitivity under his 'rogue' persona."

—www.FictionVixen.com

Confessions of an Improper Bride

Also by Jennifer Haymore

A Hint of Wicked
A Touch of Scandal
A Season of Seduction

Confessions of an Improper Bride

JENNIFER HAYMORE

A Donovan Novel

FOREVER

NEW YORK BOSTON

This book is a work of fiction. Names, characters, places, and incidents are the product of the author's imagination or are used fictitiously. Any resemblance to actual events, locales, or persons, living or dead, is coincidental.

Book design by Giorgetta Bell McRee

Forever
Hachette Book Group
237 Park Avenue
New York, NY 10017

www.HachetteBookGroup.com

Forever is an imprint of Grand Central Publishing.
The Forever name and logo are trademarks of Hachette Book Group, Inc.

Printed in the United States of America

Walmart Edition: August 2011
First Edition: August 2011

10 9 8 7 6 5 4 3 2 1

To my husband, Lawrence, who does so much for me, it's impossible to list it all.
I love you.

Acknowledgments

To my agent, Barbara Poelle, and my editor, Selina McLemore, who have blown me away with their patience and support through the writing of this book. Thank you so much for everything.

To all the people who held my hand, drove me to appointments, or sent me messages, cards, dinners, or supported me in other ways during the summer of 2010. Knowing people care is an amazing, empowering thing, and it was all of you who kept me going through the most difficult time of my life.

And to all the people in the world who've ever lent a helping or supportive or understanding hand to a person suffering from cancer. You are so special. Thank you.

Confessions of an Improper Bride

Prologue

Off the coast of Antigua
1822

Serena Donovan had not slept well since the *Victory* had left Portsmouth. Usually, the roll of the ship would lull her into a fretful sleep after she'd lain awake for hours next to her slumbering twin. Her mind tumbled over the ways she could have managed everything differently, how she might have saved herself from becoming a pariah.

But tonight was different. It had started off the same, with her lying beside a sound-asleep Meg and thinking about Jonathan Dane, about what she might have done to counter the force of the magnetic pull between them. Sleep had never come, though, because a lookout had sighted land yesterday afternoon, and Serena and Meg would be home tomorrow. Home to their mother and younger sisters and bearing a letter from their aunt that detailed Serena's disgrace.

Meg shifted, then rolled over to face Serena, her brow furrowed, her gray eyes unfocused from sleep.

"Did I wake you?" Serena asked in a low voice.

Meg rubbed her eyes and twisted her body to stretch. "No, you didn't wake me," she said on a yawn. "Haven't you slept at all?"

When Serena didn't answer, her twin sighed. "Silly question. Of course you haven't."

Serena tried to smile. "It's near dawn. Will you walk with me before the sun rises? One last time?"

The sisters often rose early and strode along the deck before the ship awakened and the bulk of the crew made its appearance for morning mess. Arm in arm, talking in low voices and enjoying the peaceful beauty of dawn, the two young ladies would stroll along the wood planks of the deck, down the port side and up the starboard, pausing to watch the sun rise over the stern of the *Victory*.

What an inappropriate name, Serena thought, for the ship bearing her home as a failure and disgrace. She'd brought shame and humiliation to her entire family. *Rejection, Defeat,* or perhaps *Utter Disappointment* would serve as far better names for a vessel returning Serena to everlasting spinsterhood and dishonor.

Serena turned up the lantern and they dressed in silence. It wasn't necessary to speak—Serena could always trust her sister to know what she was thinking and vice versa. They'd slept in the same bedroom their entire lives, and they'd helped each other to dress since they began to walk.

After Serena slid the final button through the hole at the back of Meg's dress, she reached for their heavy woolen cloaks hanging on a peg and handed Meg hers. It was midsummer, but the mornings were still cool.

When they emerged on the *Victory*'s deck, Serena tilted her face up to the sky. Usually at this time, the stars cast a steady silver gleam over the ship, but not this morning. "It's overcast," she murmured.

Meg nodded. "Look at the sea. I thought I felt us tossing about rather more vigorously than usual."

The sea was near black without the stars to light it, but gray foam crested over every wave. On deck, the heightened pitch of the ship was more clearly defined.

"Do you think a storm is coming?"

"Perhaps." Meg shuddered. "I do hope we arrive home before it strikes."

"I'm certain we will." Serena wasn't concerned. They'd survived several squalls and a rather treacherous storm in the past weeks. She had faith that Captain Moscum could pilot this ship through a hurricane, if need be.

They approached a sailor coiling rope on the deck, his task bathed under the yellow glow of a lantern. Looking up, he tipped his cap at them, and Serena saw that it was young Mr. Rutger from Kent, who was on his fourth voyage with Captain Moscum. "Good morning, misses. Fine morning, ain't it?"

"Oh, good morning to you, too, Mr. Rutger." Meg smiled pleasantly at the seaman. Meg was always the friendly one. Everyone loved Meg. "But tell us the truth—do you think the weather will hold?"

"Aye," the sailor said, a grin splitting his wind-chapped cheeks. "Just a bit o' the overcast." He looked to the sky. "A splash o' rain, but nothin' more to it than that, I daresay."

Meg breathed a sigh of relief. "Oh, good."

Serena pulled her sister along. She probably would have tarried there all day talking to Mr. Rutger from Kent. It wasn't by chance that Serena knew that he had six sisters and a brother, and his father was a cobbler—it was because Meg had crouched on the deck and drawn his life story out of him one morning.

Perhaps it was selfish of her, but Serena wanted to be alone with her sister. Soon they would be at Cedar Place, everyone would be furious with her, and Mother and their younger sisters would divide Meg's attention.

Meg went along with her willingly enough. Meg understood—she always did. When they were out of earshot from Mr. Rutger, she squeezed Serena's arm. "You'll be all right, Serena," she said in a low voice. "I'll stand beside you. I'll do whatever I can to help you through this."

Why? Serena wanted to ask. She had always been the wicked daughter. She was the oldest of five girls, older than Meg by seventeen minutes, and from birth, she'd been the hellion, the bane of their mother's existence. Mother had thought a Season in London might cure her of her hoydenish ways; instead, it had proved her far worse than a hoyden.

"I know you will always be beside me, Meg." And thank God for that. Without Meg, she'd truly founder.

She and Meg were identical in looks but not in temperament. Meg was the angel. The helpful child, ladylike, demure, moral, and always unfailingly sweet. Yet every time Serena was caught hitching her skirts up and splashing at the seashore with the baker's son, Meg stood unflinchingly beside her. When all the other people in the world had given up on Serena, Meg remained steadfast, inexplicably convinced of her goodness despite all the wicked things she did.

Even now, when she'd committed the worst indiscretion of them all. When their long-awaited trip to England for their first Season had been cut sharply short by her stupidity.

"As long as you stand beside me," Serena said quietly, "I know I will survive it."

"Do you miss him?" Meg asked after a moment's pause.

"I despise him." Serena's voice hissed through the gloom. She blinked away the stinging moisture in her eyes.

Meg gave her a sidelong glance, the color of her eyes matching the mist that swirled up behind her. "You've said that over and over these past weeks, but I've yet to believe you."

Pressing her lips together, Serena merely shook her head. She would not get into this argument with her sister again. She hated Jonathan Dane. She hated him because her only other option was to fall victim to her broken heart and pine over him, and she wouldn't do that. She wouldn't sacrifice her pride for a man who had been a party to her ruin and then turned his back on her.

She'd never admit—not to anyone—that every time she looked over the stern of the *Victory,* she secretly hoped to see a ship following. And Jonathan would be on that ship, coming for her. She dreamed that it had all been an enormous mistake, that he really had loved her, that he'd never meant for any of this to happen.

She dragged her gaze to the bow of the ship. The lantern lashed to the forestay cast a gloomy light over the fog billowing up over the lip of the deck.

Smiling, she turned the tables on her sister. "You miss Commander Langley far more than I miss Jonathan, I assure you."

Meg didn't flinch. "I miss him very much," she murmured.

Of course, unlike her own affair, Serena's sister's had followed propriety to the letter. Serena doubted Commander Langley had touched her sister for anything more than a slight brush of lips over a gloved hand. They danced exactly twice at every assembly, and he'd come to formally call on Meg at their aunt's house three times a week for a month.

In the fall, Langley was headed to sea for a two-year assignment with the Navy, and he and Meg had agreed, with her family's blessing, to an extended courtship. He'd done everything to claim Meg as his own short of promising her marriage, and Langley wasn't the sort of gentleman who'd renege on his word.

Unlike Jonathan.

Serena groaned to herself. She *must* stop thinking about him.

She patted her sister's arm. "I wager you'll have a letter from him before summer's end."

Meg's gray eyes lit up in the dimness. "Oh, Serena, do you think so?"

"I do."

Meg sighed. "I feel terrible."

"Why?"

"Because it seems unfair that I should be so happy and you..." Meg's voice trailed off.

"And I am disgraced and ruined, and the man who promised he'd love me for all time has proved himself a liar," Serena finished in a dry voice. It hurt to say those words, though. The pain was a deep, sharp slice that seemed to cleave her heart in two. Even so, Serena hid the pain and kept her face expressionless.

Meg's arm slid from her own, and tears glistened in her eyes. It didn't matter that Serena struggled so valiantly to mask her feelings, Meg knew exactly what she felt. Meg always knew. She always understood. It was part of being a twin, Serena suspected.

Gently tugging Serena's arm to draw her to a stop, Meg turned to face her. "I'll do whatever I can . . . you know I will. There is someone out there for you, Serena. I know there is. I *know* it."

"Someone in Antigua?" Serena asked dubiously. Their aunt had made it quite clear that she would never again be welcome in London. And Meg knew as well as she did that there was nobody for either of them on the island they'd called home since they were twelve years old. Even if there were, she was a debauched woman now. No one would want her.

"Perhaps. Gentlemen visit the island all the time. It certainly could happen."

The mere idea made Serena's gut churn. First, to love someone other than Jonathan Dane. It was too soon to even allow such a thought to cross her mind, and every organ in her body rebelled against it. Second, to love anyone ever again, now that she was armed with the knowledge of how destructive love could be. Who would ever be so stupid?

"Oh, Meg. I've no need for love. I've tried it, and I've failed, through and through. A happy marriage and family is for you and Commander Langley. Me? I'll stay with Mother, and I will care for Cedar Place."

A future at Cedar Place wasn't something she'd been raised to imagine—from the moment they had stepped foot on the island, the Donovans had told one another that Antigua was a temporary stop, a place for the family to rebuild its fortune before they returned to England.

But now Cedar Place was all they had left, and it was falling into ruin. Long before her father had purchased the plantation and brought the family to live in Antigua six years ago, Cedar Place had been a beautiful, thriving plantation. Nine months after their arrival, Father died from malaria, leaving them deeply in debt with only their mother to manage everything. And Mother was a well-bred English lady ill equipped to take on the responsibilities of a plantation owner. Serena had doubts Cedar Place could ever be restored to its former glory, but it was the one and only place she could call home now, and she couldn't let it rot.

Meg sighed and shook her head. "I just think—oh!"

The ship dipped into the trough of a wave and a boom swung around, trailing ropes behind it. A rope caught Meg's shoulders, and as the boom continued its path to the other side of the deck, it yanked Meg to the edge of the deck and flipped her over the deck rail.

Serena stood frozen, watching the scene unfolding before her in open-mouthed disbelief. As if from far away, she heard a muffled splash.

With a cry of dismay, she jerked into action, lunging forward until her slippered toes hung over the edge of the deck and she clung to the forestay.

Far below, Meg flailed in the water, hardly visible

in the shadowy dark and wisping fog, her form growing smaller and finally slipping away as the ship blithely plowed onward.

After living for six years on a small island, Serena's sister knew how to swim, but the heavy garments she was wearing—oh, God, they would weigh her down. Serena tore off her cloak and ripped off her dress. Clad only in her chemise, she kicked off her shoes, scrambled over the deck rail, and threw herself into the sea.

A firm arm caught her in midair, hooking her about the waist and yanking her back onto the deck. "No, miss. Ye mustn't jump," a sailor rasped in her ear.

It was then that she became conscious of the shouts of the seamen and the creaking of the rigging as the ship was ordered to come around.

Serena tried to twist her body from the man's grasp, roaring, "Let me go! My sister is out there. She's…Let me go!"

But the man didn't let her go. In fact, another man grabbed her arm, making escape impossible. She strained to look back, but the ship was turning and she couldn't see anything but the dark curl of waves and whitecaps and the swirl of fog.

"Hush, miss. Leave this one to us, if ye please. We'll have 'er back on the ship in no time at all."

"Where is she?" Serena sprinted toward the stern, pushing past the men in her way, ignoring the pounding of sailors' feet behind her. When she reached the back of the ship, she tried to jump again, only to be caught once more, this time by Mr. Rutger.

She craned her neck, searching in vain over the choppy, dark water and leaning out as far over the rail as the sailor would allow, but she saw no hint of Meg.

"Never worry, miss," Mr. Rutger murmured. "We'll find your sister."

The crew of the *Victory* searched until the sun was high in the sky and burned through the fog, and the high seas receded into gentle swells, the ship circling the spot where Meg had fallen overboard again and again.

But they never found a trace of Serena's twin.

Chapter One

Portsmouth, England
Six years later

Serena hadn't been on a ship for six years. She'd had no desire to go near a ship. But she'd spent the past several, miserable weeks on the *Islington,* watching over her younger sister Phoebe with hawk's eyes, ensuring she kept safely away from the deck's edge.

Phoebe liked her freedom, and she was on the verge of wringing Serena's neck out of frustration, but Serena didn't care. It was far better to have a sulking sister than to have the unthinkable happen again. These weeks at sea had brought back so many memories of Meg. Each day had served as a painful reminder of the hole left in Serena's life.

Serena stood at the rail, keeping her back to her fate—a fate she hadn't asked for and had never wanted. Behind her, men scurried about and officers barked out orders. The pungent fishy tang of Portsmouth

Harbour washed over the decks of the *Islington,* and between the called-out orders and the "aye, sirs," the anchor chain rasped along the edge of the deck. The sailors were lowering the anchor into the dingy harbor waters.

Serena stared out toward the open sea. A lone ship was passing the round tower that marked the harbor entrance and making its way out to sea, its sails puffed full with wind. A part of Serena wished she were on that ship, headed away from England. Cedar Place was a safe haven, a refuge, a place where she could be herself. England was none of those things. Here, she'd be nothing but a fake. A poor replication of a priceless original.

Once she disembarked from the *Islington,* Serena would begin to spin a web of lies that would ensure her three living sisters' futures. A person who admired honesty above all else, she nevertheless intended to live a life of deceit.

How would she manage it? Especially in London, a place fraught with danger, with its society and parties and ladies with sharp eyes looking for an opportunity to spread any scathing bit of gossip. If she was caught, society would rip her to shreds.

Serena and Phoebe would be staying with their aunt Geraldine in St. James's Square. Aunt Geraldine was a viscountess, the widow of Lord Alcott, one of the most respected members of Parliament in his day. Serena knew from her last visit to London that her aunt was ruled by the expectations of society, and she bowed to its every whim.

When the sisters left in disgrace six years ago, Aunt Geraldine had loathed Serena and despised Meg by association. Even worse, she lived two houses down from the Earl of Stratford, Jonathan Dane's father. This time, Serena had begged her mother to arrange housing elsewhere, but they couldn't afford suitable lodgings in London. Aunt Geraldine was the only reasonable choice.

Serena squeezed her eyes shut. Jonathan Dane probably wouldn't be in London. Six years ago, his father had ambitions for him to take holy orders, and if that had happened, he'd be residing at his family seat in Sussex or at some other vicarage far away from Town. She fervently hoped Jonathan wasn't in London. If he was, he could only be a reminder of all the pain and heartache of the past, and of her willful deception of the present.

If he was in London, she would avoid him at all costs. Because, as much as she aspired to be more like Meg, she was still Serena. If she came face to face with Jonathan Dane, it was likely her claws would extend and tear him apart. If that happened, all would be lost.

She must remember that. There was more at stake here than just her reputation.

With shaking hands, Serena drew out the letter from the pocket of her pelisse. Careful to pin it tightly between her fingertips so the breeze wouldn't tear it from her grip, she read it for the hundredth time.

My dearest Meg,

I waited breathlessly for your last letter, and when it arrived, I tore it open right away. I cannot express the level of joy I experienced when I read your assurances of love. And my happiness only increased when I read that you will be returning to England, and that you have agreed, with your mother's blessing, to become my wife.

I'm equally delighted to hear that you and your sister, Phoebe, will come to London for the duration of the summer. It will give us an opportunity to plan our wedding, and to reacquaint ourselves in the flesh after so many lonely years of separation.

How I long to look on your sweet face again, my dearest. I shall come to Portsmouth the instant I hear of your arrival. I look much as I did the last time we met.

With my sincerest love,
Wm Langley

Carefully, Serena folded the letter and replaced it in her pocket. She returned her gaze to the horizon and the ship slowly slipping away through the waves, becoming smaller with every moment that passed.

She hated lying. She hated herself. She hated her mother. She hated England. She hated everything about this situation.

"This! This very moment is the most exciting moment of my whole, entire life!"

Serena turned to see nineteen-year-old Phoebe grinning at her, her face young and alive, and her expression bright with happiness.

More than anything, Meg would want to see Phoebe and their other sisters, Olivia and Jessica, well situated. All Serena wanted was their happiness. She couldn't stand it if anything horrible happened to them. She'd do anything to shield them from an experience like she'd had on her last visit to London.

She'd do this for her beautiful, innocent, lovely sisters. To insure their future.

"It is very exciting," she said to Phoebe, her voice grave. They had moved to the West Indies when Phoebe was only seven years old, and she hardly remembered England at all. The bustle of Portsmouth Harbour was nothing like the lazy, slow-paced English Harbour at Antigua. Portsmouth's sprawling waterfront held dense clusters of buildings, conveyances, and people—likely more buildings, people, and conveyances than populated their entire island.

Phoebe didn't perceive the sadness leaching into Serena's voice. With a pang, Serena remembered she'd never been able to hide such things from Meg. Now, though she possessed what most people would consider a tightly knit family in her mother and sisters, no one really knew her.

Nobody would ever really know her. It was too late for that. She'd sealed her fate in stone in the summer of 1822. From that point forward, she'd been the only person in the world to know her true self. Even after six years, the loneliness that thought provoked was nearly unbearable.

Blinking hard, she turned to gaze back out to sea. Looking in the opposite direction, Phoebe clapped her hands together and stood on her toes, craning to see through the thick lines of rigging blocking her view. "Oh, do look! There is a boat approaching. Can it be the one meant to bring us ashore?"

Serena looked over her shoulder in the direction her sister was pointing. The long boat, filled with empty seats, with abundant room in the stern holding area for their luggage, bobbed toward them, its rowers driving the oars through the murky water in long, precise draws. "I believe so."

"We should make certain we've packed everything, shouldn't we?"

"Yes." Serena didn't move, though. Rooted to the spot, she stared at the horizon, where the dark blue of the ocean faded through haze into the crystalline blue of the sky. She was about to become someone she'd despise. She was about to do something unforgivable.

What would Meg do?

That question had guided Serena's life for the past several years. She had grown calmer, and she gave far more forethought to her actions than she had before her sister's death. Phoebe was the one who'd taken over the role of hellion in their family.

For Phoebe's sake, she'd do this. For Olivia's and Jessica's sakes. If she betrayed her mother now, her sisters would be the ones to suffer. Mother was no fool—she knew exactly what drove Serena. She knew that Serena would never willingly cause pain to her sisters, and she knew exactly how to use that truth to manipulate her eldest daughter.

Yet if Serena succeeded with what Mother intended for her to do, it held far-reaching consequences. Consequences so life altering Serena could hardly fathom them. Soon, she'd be married to a handsome, rich gentleman, with more funds than she'd ever require at her disposal. Yet, she couldn't imagine spending her life with William Langley. The thought of marrying him had never even crossed her mind until a few weeks ago, when Mother had told her everything.

"Well?" Flicking a tendril of blond hair out of her face, Phoebe stamped her foot lightly on a deck plank. "Are you coming or aren't you?"

"I'll come down in a moment, Phoebe. You go ahead and make sure Flannery has gathered all our things, all right?"

Phoebe's brow creased, and she gave Serena a hard glare. "Are you feverish?"

She tried to smile. "Not at all."

"Humph. Very well, then." With a swing of her jewel-blue skirts, Phoebe turned and disappeared.

Squeezing her eyes shut, Serena curled her fingers around the deck rail. She didn't want to do this. She despised lying. Despised even more that she would aspire to standards she couldn't attain. She could never succeed in living up to Meg's goodness.

What would Meg do?

Meg wouldn't risk their sisters' reputations. Phoebe, Olivia, and Jessica needed freedom from their mother, and from Antigua, once and for all.

Serena's sisters needed to marry, and marry well. They could never do so if Captain William Langley discovered the truth and revealed it to the world.

Jonathan Dane, the Sixth Earl of Stratford, stared broodingly at his ale. The delicious brew at the Blue Bell Inn had lured him to Whitechapel tonight, and the smooth amber liquid shimmered in his glass.

No, he fooled himself. It wasn't the ale that had drawn him here. He'd been a frequent customer at the Blue Bell Inn for years, but he hadn't come for a while. And he knew damn well why he'd come tonight.

Meg Donovan.

She would arrive in England soon—within the

next day or two. Jonathan had little previous connection to the lady. The problem was that on the outside she was identical to her twin sister. Serena...the woman whose death he was responsible for. The woman he'd loved...and betrayed.

Meg would be in London. He'd undoubtedly see her often, considering the fact that Langley had asked him to be the best man at their wedding. And each time he looked at her beautiful lips or gray eyes or blond curls, he'd be reminded of Serena...of kissing those lips, of gazing into the depths of those eyes, of sifting those curls between his fingers.

Suppressing a groan, Jonathan thrust away the sudden flood of memories. This happened on occasion—just when he thought he was free of her, she swept through his memories, blazing a trail through his dark, cloudy mind and leaving a bright, glittering stream of happiness in her wake. After all these years, the memories served nothing but to remind him of how worthless he had become.

Jonathan took a healthy swallow of ale.

"Well, if it isn't the Earl of Stratford."

Jonathan jerked his head upward to see a voluptuous redhead dressed in a red and black dress, her bosom flowing over the bodice.

"Hullo, Maggie."

"Thought you'd disappeared into the ether, milord." She winked at him. "Haven't seen you in half a year."

"Haven't you?" Jonathan asked, frowning. Had it been that long?

She pursed her red-painted lips and shook her head. "I've missed you."

He chuckled. "Been busy."

The owner of the Blue Bell Inn had discovered Maggie in a Covent Garden whorehouse four years ago. He'd taken a powerful fancy to her and had married her. They worked as a team, Maggie flirting with the male customers and seducing them to return for more, and her husband in the back office, overseeing the inn's operation.

She winked at Jonathan. "Carousing elsewhere, I take it?"

He raised his glass of ale. "Exactly."

His face heated from the lie. *Carousing*. He hadn't done much of that lately. Yet it was well known that wherever Lord Stratford went, scandal and debauchery followed. Jonathan thrived on his poor reputation. He would go to his grave known for his wicked soul and black heart. Better, after all, than being remembered as a brainless coward. But lately the game had begun to bore him.

Maggie grinned. "Well, I'm right glad to see you back, then, milord. Can I fetch you something? More ale?" She looked dubiously at his nearly full glass.

"No, thank you."

Wishing him a good evening, she inclined her head and left, her red and black skirts swishing over her abundant backside as she strode away.

He sat staring at his ale. He'd accomplish nothing by sitting here and moping. It was time to summon his coachman and go home. With a deep sigh, he began to rise, but the dark shadow of a man loomed over him.

"I've been searching for you all evening. Suppose I shouldn't have been surprised you decided to come here, of all places."

Jonathan blinked at William Langley, Post Captain in His Majesty's Navy, as if he were viewing a ghostly apparition. The man standing at the end of the table was so strictly composed and so straight-laced, most people didn't hesitate to call him priggish. Jonathan knew otherwise. Langley wasn't priggish, he just had a strong sense of a man's moral duty. He was a good man, but a human one, through and through. Still, he wasn't one to go chasing after Jonathan at such a late hour. Something was wrong.

"Why are you here?" Jonathan asked, his senses going into full alert. "What has happened?"

"It's...well, it's Miss Donovan." Langley slid onto the bench across from him, his face twisted in consternation.

Jonathan's gut churned. He'd tried to be happy for Langley. Really tried. But every time his friend mentioned his betrothed, he felt the sour burn of jealousy scraping over his throat.

Langley had been his friend for many years, and he knew Jonathan far too well. Jonathan couldn't look him in the eye right now—his damned aching memories were probably written all over his face. And Langley would remember. He had gone through it with him, had been there in those miserable days after Jonathan had lost her. Before Langley had gone to sea that autumn, he and Jonathan had helped each other through the darkest time of their lives.

Langley placed his hands on the table and leaned forward. "I received word that her ship arrived in Portsmouth today. And, well, I thought I'd come find you."

"Seems you succeeded in that, at least." In one long draught, Jonathan finished his ale.

"I remembered this was the tavern where you... well..." Langley's voice trailed off. "It was just a guess."

Jonathan rubbed his thumb over a bead of condensation on his glass. "A good one."

Langley nodded.

Jonathan finally looked up at him. "So why are you here, Langley?"

Casting his gaze to the table, the other man adjusted his cravat. "I was wondering... well, you were acquainted with Miss Donovan."

Jonathan pressed his lips together. Unable to speak, he gave a slow nod. Indeed he had known Meg Donovan. Not nearly as well as he'd known her sister. Langley knew that. "Yes. I was acquainted with her."

"Well... will you accompany me? To Portsmouth, I mean. I'm to escort her and her sister to London."

"Accompany you," Jonathan repeated, enunciating each word carefully. "To Portsmouth." He stared hard at Langley. Was the man sotted? No, Langley rarely drank. But other than the deep gray circles beneath his eyes, he looked pale as death.

"Yes. Today. I've received word that her ship has arrived." Langley's Adam's apple moved as he swallowed. "I thought you might... you know... help. If it became... difficult between us. Awkward. If I say something—"

Jonathan raised his hand, stopping the man midsentence. "Let me see if I understand this correctly. You've sought me out *here,* at this hour, to ask me if I might travel with you to Portsmouth later today to meet your betrothed."

"Yes. That's right."

Jonathan stared at Langley incredulously. For Christ's sake, the man had been a captain in the Navy. Accustomed to barking out orders and having them obeyed without question. Accustomed to having the lives of hundreds of men under his control. Accustomed to leadership.

Yet he was deathly afraid of meeting his beloved after a six-year separation. Poor Langley.

Langley blew out a breath through his teeth. "What if I say something wrong? What if I... ?"

Jonathan shook his head. "By all accounts, the

lady is as besotted with you as you are with her. There's nothing you could possibly say that would offend her."

Langley gave him a baleful look.

As much as Jonathan could sympathize with the panic of a man about to face the shackles of marriage, there was no way in hell Jonathan would be going to Portsmouth. He knew he'd eventually come face to face with Serena Donovan's twin sister, but it wouldn't be today. He'd had months to prepare for the eventuality of seeing her, but he wasn't ready. Not yet.

He was a damn coward.

Well, he'd always known that, hadn't he? He'd been a coward six years ago. Nothing had changed.

Langley would have to face her eventually, just as Jonathan would. It was better for Langley to get it over with now, rather than have him leaning on Jonathan for support every time he saw her in the weeks to come.

"I can't go to Portsmouth today," he said in a kindly voice. "Sorry, old chap. I've a meeting with my solicitor, and it cannot be missed."

Langley's face fell. "Damn," he said under his breath.

Jonathan drew back a bit, unused to hearing Langley curse. "You'll do fine."

Langley grimaced. "I hope you're right."

"Of course I am right."

"But... you will come to the soiree?"

"Of course I'll be there." He didn't want to go to Langley's soiree, but he would. He'd promised Langley he would go. That would give him a full week to prepare for his reintroduction to Meg Donovan.

Langley stared at Jonathan's empty glass of ale, and Jonathan felt a surge of compassion for the man. Langley would be nervous tomorrow, and for very good reason. But it was for the best that Jonathan didn't go. His presence at Portsmouth wouldn't be good for any of them. Meg Donovan probably hated him, probably blamed him for her sister's death. As well she should.

He forced himself to smile at his friend. Langley understood exactly why Jonathan had become the man he was. Jonathan had lost his Donovan sister through his own cowardice and stupidity, while Langley had held on to his. And in three months, he would marry her.

One thing Jonathan was sure of: No matter what, Langley would remain loyal to Meg Donovan. He would love her forever. She was a lucky woman to have ensnared a man such as him.

"Let's retire, then," Jonathan said, keeping his voice gentle and even. "It's getting late, and I should be going home."

Langley sighed. "Yes, yes. I should as well. Forgive me for interrupting you—"

Jonathan gave a dismissive wave of his hand. "You interrupted nothing."

That was too true for comfort.

Sighing, he rose and escorted his friend out of the Blue Bell Inn.

Serena and Phoebe ate in the common room at the inn, where they were fed a heavy breakfast that made Serena feel weighted down and greasy. Neither of them was used to such lavishness, but Mother had scraped her pennies so Serena, Phoebe, and their new maid, Flannery, could spend one night in this particular inn. Even this breakfast had been an extravagance, and Serena's purse was uncomfortably light after her payment for it.

But of course they couldn't give the appearance of genteel poverty. That simply wouldn't do. Forget the fact that Mother couldn't afford the passage for herself and Serena's other two sisters, nor could they afford the proper stylish garments required by London society. Mother would never show her face in London if she couldn't look fashionable.

Today Serena wore her new cherry-striped silk with puffed sleeves and a satin-net trim on the skirt and cuffs. She hadn't worn it on the ship, per Mother's orders. She'd wanted Serena to reunite with William Langley in a spotless, crisp new gown.

Serena shouldn't have eaten, for the mix of her breakfast, her stays, and her nerves caused her stomach to twist and cramp. She hadn't even been hungry, so her only excuse was anxiety. She was about to meet Commander Langley—now Captain Langley—for the first time in six years.

"Are you ready?" Phoebe patted her coiffure. Of the five sisters, Serena and Meg had resembled Papa, with golden-streaked blond hair and gray eyes. The three younger girls looked more like their mother, with the same snapping blue eyes and a reddish gleam in their blond hair.

"I'm ready." Serena sighed. As ready as she'd ever be.

"I'm stuffed like a pig," Phoebe announced.

Serena's brows snapped together. "You should be happy Mother's not here," she said under her breath. "She'd whip you for that. Especially if you spoke that way in the presence of her sister."

Phoebe elevated her nose primly. "Which is exactly why I shall not speak so in Aunt Geraldine's presence. I'm sure Mother would hear of it immediately and fly all the way from Antigua like a rampaging dragon to punish me. I'm not stupid, you know."

"Don't be impertinent," Serena chastised mildly.

Phoebe probably didn't remember, but Serena had been equally impertinent before she and Meg had gone to London six years ago. Everything had changed when she'd returned without her sister at her side. She'd withdrawn into herself.

Mother had been devastated by Meg's death, but she had been somewhat gratified to learn that the bulk of Serena's rebelliousness had drowned along with Meg. Unfortunately, Serena still had a scandal of enormous proportions hanging over her head, ruining any chance whatsoever of a respectable gentleman asking for her hand in marriage.

Her rebelliousness hadn't drowned, though. Serena had just forced it to plunge below the surface. It threatened to emerge every day, but she kept it firmly concealed.

Serena and Phoebe retired to a sitting room where they pretended to sew while they spoke in muted tones and awaited Captain Langley's arrival. Eventually, a gentle knock sounded on the door, and Serena froze, needle poised.

"Come in," Phoebe called.

The door opened a crack to reveal a maid. "There's a gentleman come, miss. Says his name is Captain Langley and he's arrived to escort you to London."

This was it. This first meeting would decide once and for all whether Serena had the nerve to go through with this charade. Her heart thumped through her body, as loud as a clanging church bell. She was surprised no one else seemed to hear it.

Phoebe set her embroidery aside and rose, brushing her skirts straight, and Serena realized she was expected to do the same. Moving her limbs was like moving solid iron. It took every bit of strength her body contained.

Can I lie to this man? Can I be what—and who—he wants me to be?

How could she? This was all her mother's doing. Serena hadn't even known what was happening. She should end the ruse right now, before the lie spread through London, before it was too late.

Phoebe had already pasted a smile on her face, preparing herself to be introduced to Serena's betrothed.

Serena stood, straightened her spine, and nodded to the maid. She was glad she wore her new kid gloves, because nerves had soaked her hands with sweat. "Show him in, please."

It seemed like hours passed before Captain Langley appeared in the doorway. He was quite a handsome man, tall and lithe, with angular features and dark brown hair. He wore a stiff collar, a snow-white cravat, and a dark blue coat. His eyes were his most handsome feature, Serena thought. Meg had always spoken highly of his eyes. They were kind, expressive eyes, of a rich, deep brown.

"Captain Langley," she said in the smooth, cultured London accent she'd spent endless hours practicing under her mother's watchful eye. "It is so lovely to see you again."

"And you, Miss Donovan," the captain said. His voice was soft, but his bow was stiff. "I trust your voyage was comfortable?"

"Indeed it was. Please"—Serena gestured toward Phoebe—"allow me to introduce you to Miss Phoebe Donovan, my sister."

Phoebe bobbed a curtsy, and Langley gave another stiff bow. "Miss Phoebe."

When he turned back to her, hope and expectation brimming in his expression, tears surged up in Serena so powerfully and so quickly she almost couldn't contain them. She dipped her head so Langley wouldn't see the shine in her eyes.

How could she possibly meet his expectations?

She'd changed in the past six years. She'd grown slimmer and taller, her hair had grown a shade darker, and she'd lost the residual plumpness in her cheeks, stomach, and thighs. Physically, Meg would have changed similarly, she knew. She didn't know if Meg's eyes would have changed as her own had.

When she was little, Papa used to say that he could always tell Serena from Meg because Serena had the silver gleam of a sprite in her eyes, the spark that promised mischief. He'd always teased her about it.

He hadn't been there to see the change in her after Meg died, but Serena had seen the difference in the looking glass. The sprightly gleam faded into cloudy shadow, and her eyes had changed from sparkling silver to flat gray.

Langley strode forward and gathered her hands in his own. His hands were large, firm, and comforting.

"Miss Donovan." His breath hitched, and he squeezed her fingers tightly and shook his head, seemingly at a loss for words. Then he murmured, "Meg. I never thought you would come after…I mean, I hoped—I prayed—that I would see you again, that you would respond with an acceptance to my offer of marriage... But to have you here... my love—it is a dream come true."

As his words sank in, it struck Serena for the first time that her mother's lies had deeply affected another person outside the core of their family. This man truly did love Meg. He'd loved her for years. Captain Langley would be devastated if he learned the truth of what had happened that day on the *Victory.*

She looked up and stared into those deep brown eyes brimming with emotion. Langley was a good man, a respectable man. He was the man Meg had loved, and now Serena had the power to destroy him.

She squeezed his fingers in return. "I missed you," she whispered.

Chapter Two

A week later, Serena faced her official reintroduction to society as Miss Margaret Donovan, the future wife of Captain William Langley.

She played the part to the best of her ability—she smiled so hard and for so long that her cheeks hurt. She danced with gentlemen whose names she forgot seconds after the dances ended. She'd never been good with names, and after a while, Langley's friends, all of a similar age, half in somber Navy uniforms and the other half wearing dark tailcoats and sharp white cravats, began to look the same to her.

The dance ended, and Langley bowed formally and then offered his arm to lead her off the dance floor. She took his arm, and they strolled toward a woman whom he introduced as Lady Montgomery, a tiny woman with sleek dark hair and a smart gray dress.

Serena would have thought she looked like a stern governess if not for her warm smile.

"Are you happy to have returned to London after so long away, Miss Donovan?" she asked.

Serena hesitated. Should she tell the truth? What would Meg say?

"I'm gratified," she said slowly, "that my sister, Phoebe, will have the opportunity to be in London society for the first time. More than anything, I'm happy to finally see Captain Langley again."

She smiled at him, and he very appropriately blushed and excused himself. As he walked toward a group of Navy officers, Lady Montgomery smiled.

"Of course you are," she said quietly. "Captain Langley is a friend of mine, Miss Donovan, and he is a good man. He has missed you beyond measure in these past years. It brings him great happiness that you have accepted his offer of marriage."

Serena's face felt hot as a lobster dumped into a pot of boiling water, and she was sure she possessed the complexion to match. "Thank you."

She glanced at Langley, who was conversing in animated tones with a group of Navy officers. She wished he would speak in such a manner to her.

"Have you known Captain Langley for very long, my lady?"

Before Lady Montgomery could answer, she glanced toward the ballroom door and sucked in her breath. Serena followed her gaze. Her entire body stiffened.

Oh, God.

The world spun, driving away the smell of burning wax and the heavy perfumes of the guests. The sounds of the waltz and the laughter and discussions that had moments ago swelled into a crescendo around her seemed to have been sucked into a vacuum.

At the age of eighteen, when Serena had first seen him, she thought him the most handsome man in the world. Since then, she had dismissed those interpretations as the warped imaginings of an inexperienced and besotted mind. Since then, she had studied men from afar, and now believed she understood masculine allure.

She was wrong.

There was nothing, nobody. Except for the man standing across the room, shaking the hand of another guest Serena couldn't see at all.

The years had treated him well. Very well. His body appeared larger now than it had back then. He was heavier, but none of it was fat. From his shape, she knew it was all firmness and muscle and not the work of a man's corset. His hair was dark blond and thick but cut short, his fashionable sideburns trimmed close to his face.

He turned his head a little, and she gazed at his profile. Since she had last seen him, his face had roughened, its angles had become sharper and more defined. His face had always been beautiful, but the years had etched light lines around his mouth and eyes and given him character. His nose had a small bump along its ridge that hadn't been there before.

"Yes." Lady Montgomery's voice was like a feather tickling at Serena's consciousness. Serena jerked her head around to face the lady and saw the knowledge of her and Jonathan's past in Lady Montgomery's dark eyes. "That is the Earl of Stratford. I understand you and he were previously acquainted."

Serena blinked at the lady. The Earl of Stratford? What? Serena opened her mouth and then snapped it shut. Quickly, she gathered her fractured wits.

When she'd first met him, she'd learned his name as the Honourable Mr. Dane, a second son to an earl and to her young eyes, a very high personage indeed.

"Forgive me," she said carefully, "I wasn't aware that he'd inherited his father's title."

"Oh? Well, yes, he did, in fact. His older brother's death preceded his father's by a few months. Back in . . . twenty-three, I believe it was."

"I am very sorry to hear that." That meant Jonathan's father had died a year or so after her departure from London. Serena had never been told. If she'd lived in England, there would have been no way of keeping such news from her, but she'd been so far away, and the topic of Jonathan Dane was forbidden in their home. She wondered whether Mother had known. Probably.

Lady Montgomery studied her with eyes that

seemed to take in too much. "I would very much like to know you better, Miss Donovan," she said. "You must call on me soon."

"Oh, well yes," Serena said. She needed to escape this suddenly stifling place, these people she didn't know. Most of all, she needed to get away from Jonathan Dane, now the Earl of Stratford. But where could she go? She felt like a wild animal, trapped and caged, knowing it was no use to try to claw her way out. "I'd love to. If you'd excuse me, my lady, I believe I need some air."

Sympathy washed over Lady Montgomery's face. "Of course. Your constitution must be in rebellion. The stifling atmosphere in a London ballroom is probably nothing like the fresh open air of the West Indies."

"Quite true. Excuse me." Serena curtsied and then spun toward the double doors leading to an outside balcony, where escape, at least a temporary one, lay.

Gripping her champagne glass tightly, Serena made her way through Langley's guests, answering politely to those who acknowledged her as she passed. Since her betrothed's town house was too small for an event this large, a friend had given him the use of his family's grand Kensington home for the event.

The orchestra was playing the final notes of a waltz, and Serena glimpsed Phoebe dancing beneath the row of glittering chandeliers. Phoebe's partner, a handsome, dark-haired young man, was whisking her about the floor, and Phoebe was grinning and giggling at some joke he had just told her.

Despite herself, Serena smiled. Seeing Phoebe like this gave her hope that all this awful deception might be worth it after all.

The waltz ended, and laughter and pleasant chatter quickly drowned out the sudden silence. Serena reached for the door handle.

"There you are."

It was Langley's voice. With a sigh, Serena dropped her hand and turned. There he stood, not an arm's length away, with Jonathan Dane at his side.

Jonathan's wide, sensuous mouth hadn't changed in shape, but its turn seemed more cynical, more inclined to smirk rather than display the genuine, joyful smiles she remembered. His lips were parted, and she could see the hint of teeth behind them.

She remembered those lips. How often she'd kissed them, had run her tongue over those teeth.

"Good evening." Serena's voice emerged smooth and deep and contained no tremor. It reminded her of her voice when she was with Jonathan before, when she was aroused and could only think she wanted more, wanted him to take her to the pinnacle.

He had taken her to those heights, not only physically, but emotionally as well, and she had counted on it never to end. But ended it had, with an abruptness that had shattered her.

He gazed at her as if startled, a slight frown forming between his brows. "Serena?"

The cheerful roar of the ballroom faded to nothing behind the din of her shock. She glanced at Langley to see him blanch. Everyone standing nearby had turned to gape at them.

She stared up at Jonathan, unable to speak, to breathe.

He stared back at her, his eyes dilated in the shadows until they looked black. She remembered them, though. They were midnight blue, like the deepest ocean on a sunny day. They always appeared quite dark whenever there wasn't enough light to illuminate their true color. In broad daylight, his eyes were exotic, their dark cobalt sparks contrasting with the gold streaks in his hair and the broad slashes of his eyebrows. Such a handsome man.

Langley gave an awkward laugh and clapped Jonathan on the shoulder. "No, this is Meg, man. Meg Donovan, my betrothed."

Jonathan shook his head, as if flinging away a fog that had descended over him. He blinked hard, and seeming to come to his senses, he bowed. "Of course," he murmured. "Of course. Forgive me. Miss Donovan, it is a pleasure to see you again."

The low timbre of his voice made something within Serena clench. She had dreamed about that voice more times than she could count. His voice had whispered in her ear, caressed the most private parts of her body, told her wicked things she was certain she'd never hear again. The words he had uttered to her had made her first fall madly in love and later tremble in ecstasy.

It had nearly killed her when she learned all those words had been lies.

Was he still a liar?

Such characteristics were usually ingrained in a person by the time he reached adulthood. If a man was a liar at twenty-two, he probably was at twenty-eight as well.

Serena couldn't answer him. She simply stared. Langley gave her an apologetic look, as if asking for forgiveness that he hadn't warned her about the arrival of the man who had defiled her sister. Serena sucked in a steadying breath. Suddenly, she felt perilously close to bursting into tears.

Langley came to her rescue. "Were you going to take some air?"

She nodded dumbly.

He gave her a gentle smile. "May I accompany you?"

His kind words helped her find her voice, and she waved her hand. "No, no, please. It looked like you two were headed toward the punch bowl." She gave them a game smile. "I certainly wouldn't want to deprive two gentlemen of their punch."

Langley returned her smile and inclined his head. "But I won't have you outside alone." He clasped Jonathan's shoulder. "If you'll excuse—"

Just then, an arm slipped through hers. Lady Montgomery squeezed her wrist. "Oh, do come onto the terrace with me, Miss Donovan. I was just thinking about taking some air myself."

Serena swallowed hard, then smiled at her savior. "Thank you. I'd love to join you outside."

She gave a faltering, watery smile to Langley, silently thanking him for his thoughtfulness. The two men bowed, Langley looking understanding and Jonathan looking as bewildered as if he'd just been awakened from a yearlong sleep. They turned toward the punch bowl, Langley holding on to Jonathan's shoulder, guiding him away and across the room.

Keeping her arm tightly entwined about Serena's, Lady Montgomery flung open the door and led her toward freedom and the outside.

The day after Langley's soiree, Serena rose from bed and went through the motions of her morning routine. Bathed and dressed, she wandered downstairs. The breakfast room at the back corner of the house was unoccupied, and she went to the sideboard and collected a cup of coffee and a crescent-shaped roll.

Since Serena had last been in London, her aunt had hired a French cook, and she demanded a plate of fresh bread at the breakfast table every morning. Serena loved these fluffy concoctions—they were so different from the heavy breads she was accustomed to—and she'd taken to eating these wonderful, flaky rolls for her breakfast. Aunt Geraldine's permanently narrow frame hadn't widened from all this bread, but Serena knew her own would suffer if she ate too much, so she limited herself to one every morning.

Sitting at the end of the breakfast table closest to the window, she nibbled on the roll, sipped at her coffee, and gazed out the window looking onto Duke of York Street.

The sky was jewel blue and cloudless, and it would be simply lovely when she met with Langley for an afternoon drive later in the day. For now, the sun had half risen over the buildings on the opposite side of the street, casting a bright golden glow over them, making them look like they'd been touched by Midas.

She remembered the summer she'd met Jonathan. The weather then had been equally lovely. She'd think every summer in London was this beautiful if Aunt Geraldine didn't often proclaim that it was not. Sometimes it rained every day in June, her aunt assured her. Sometimes, frost still covered the ground this time of year. And sometimes, Aunt Geraldine said, London could be hotter than the depths of Hell.

As if summoned by her thoughts, the brisk tapping of heels over the wooden slats of the corridor outside heralded Aunt Geraldine's entrance. Her aunt, dressed in a dark red pelisse, strode into the breakfast room.

"Good morning, Aunt," Serena murmured.

"I doubt it." Aunt Geraldine didn't look at Serena; instead, she turned her attention to the sideboard.

Serena raised a brow at her aunt's straight, narrow back. "Why do you say that?"

Aunt Geraldine muttered something unintelligible. She turned and plunked her plate on the table opposite to where Serena sat, then deposited her slight body into the corresponding heavy wood chair. Her gaze settled on Serena, and she frowned. "Where is your sister?"

"Still in bed," Serena replied.

Aunt Geraldine's lips drew into a narrow, straight line. "She is a lazy chit."

Serena chuckled. She'd learned quickly that if she took offense to every slight her aunt offered to her or someone she loved, she'd be angry forevermore. So she shrugged away most of the older woman's smaller jabs.

"She's just nineteen," she murmured between nibbles of the delectable bread. "We were out very late last night, as you'll recall. In any case, people her age need more sleep than the rest of us."

So their mother had told everyone during those days after Serena had just returned to Antigua. Having lost her reputation, her love, and her sister, her spirits had sunk so low that she'd found it impossible to drag herself out of bed until long after noon almost every day. Mother had used that explanation on her younger sisters, and though it was mostly to protect her, Serena still believed there was some truth to it. It hadn't been until she was twenty that she'd been able to rise at a decent hour on a consistent basis.

Taking a bite of her roll, Aunt Geraldine stared at her. After she swallowed, she plopped the bread back down on her plate, pushed it away, and narrowed her eyes. "I must speak with you about something."

Oh, dear, what now? Serena gazed steadily at her aunt, but inwardly she braced herself.

"It is about my neighbor, the young Earl of Stratford." Aunt Geraldine gazed at her, studying her reaction.

Serena did her best to keep her face perfectly blank. "Oh. I wasn't aware that the new earl occupied his father's old London home."

"He does."

When her aunt didn't speak for several moments, Serena asked, "What about him do you wish to tell me?"

Aunt Geraldine's thin lips disappeared altogether. "I believe you have been sheltered since you were last in London, Meg. I know you have a forgiving nature—you always have—but hear me on this: That man is not to be trusted. I saw him speaking to you last night. I don't know what game he's trying to play by insinuating himself into your good graces."

"Goodness, Aunt. He's not in my good graces in the least, but since he appears to be the closest friend of my betrothed, what choice do I have but to be polite to him?"

"You have no concept of what that man is, Meg, and you should feel quite free to cut him if you wish to do so. Do whatever is necessary to discourage his attentions."

"But, Aunt... I cannot cut him. He..." Wildly, she racked her brain for a reason. "He's an earl."

"I might agree if you had a chance of becoming his countess." Aunt Geraldine sniffed, and Serena stared at her in astonishment. "Oh, don't look at me like that, Meg. He's an earl, for goodness' sake. It wouldn't matter if he were a three-foot-tall simpleton—if it were possible for one of my nieces to marry an earl, I'd do whatever I could to encourage it."

"Aunt..." Serena breathed.

"However, the wretched man has made it perfectly clear to the world that he shall never marry, and you"—picking up her bread, she pointed it at Serena—"are otherwise engaged. I can only see trouble when it comes to any association you establish with Stratford, earl or no."

"Why do you say that?" Serena asked. "You must understand that after... after what happened with Serena, I have no intention of establishing any association with him beyond as a friend of my future husband."

Her aunt made a low noise of distaste. "What he

did to your sister was wretched enough, but after you left London, he became the most insufferable of scoundrels."

Serena shook her head, confused. "How do you mean?"

Aunt Geraldine raised her coffee cup to her lips and took a long, fortifying swallow, wincing a bit at the scalding heat. She took a deep breath as she set the cup down. Serena's heart began to hammer against her chest. She couldn't fathom why. Whatever Aunt Geraldine was about to say, it had no bearing on her. It shouldn't matter at all.

"Stratford remained in London until we received word that your sister had perished by drowning. Upon hearing this dreadful news, the young man tore his father's home apart and then ran to Bath."

Under the table, Serena gripped her knees through her dress. "Why would he do such a thing?"

"Because he went mad, that's why. He was never entirely stable, you know."

Serena blinked at her aunt. "Aunt, instability is one thing, but I fail to see what this has to do with him being an insufferable scoundrel."

"Within a week, he'd cuckolded a curate in Bath and then fled back to London."

"Oh, goodness." Serena could virtually feel the cracks spreading over her heart. A week after he learned she'd died, he was tupping a curate's wife in Bath?

Serena took a slow, measured breath, willing her pattering heart to slow down. She'd wondered so often about what Jonathan had become. But she'd thought he'd been on the course of becoming a vicar. With that image so firmly entrenched in her mind, she couldn't picture him as a dissolute. But now it seemed as though she needed to reform her image of him.

Aunt Geraldine seemed not to notice her consternation. "He grew worse after that. He drank, he gambled, he cared nothing about anyone or anything. He took loose women into his bed, then turned them away, one after the other. He flaunted his mistresses at social functions at every opportunity. He did whatever he could to spit in the face of propriety, and he didn't care a whit what anyone thought about it. He still doesn't, though in recent months it seems he's become less of a topic of gossip."

Serena stared at her aunt, speechless.

How could it be true? Jonathan, the man who'd loved her with such passion, had turned into a cold, ruthless rake? A debauched seducer lacking in every scruple?

The first time he'd bedded Serena, in the stables behind her aunt's house, he'd been a virgin, too. They'd been equally overcome, equally nervous. That bedding was a fumbling, awkward thing, but so sweet. They'd lain in the fresh hay and held on to each other for hours afterward, sharing the pleasure of what they'd just experienced together.

Whenever she remembered that night, Serena's recollections contained nothing of the bitterness she held in every one of her other memories about Jonathan. Even after all that happened later, she believed in him that night. That had been the true Jonathan, layers peeled away, raw and sensitive, giving and taking, open to her as she'd been open to him.

She blinked hard, banishing that memory.

"It is quite for the best that he turned your sister away," Aunt Geraldine announced. "The man is a louse and would have made her miserable."

That was probably true. If, by some turn of fate, he'd ended up marrying her, he probably would have turned away from her as soon as he'd tired of her, just like he'd turned away from all those other ladies he'd bedded.

Aunt Geraldine made a growling noise. "God save us from the fools overrunning this society." She looked at Serena, her blue eyes speckled with yellow sparks from the glow of the sunlight flooding through the windows. "This is what we have become. Amoral, gambling, rutting . . . idiots."

Serena felt sick down to the marrow of her bones.

Aunt Geraldine frowned into her cup. "Of course, news of his exploits has done no irreparable damage to his reputation, though it should have. Every wretched thing he did just seemed to increase his popularity among his peers. He's admired." She shook her head in disgust. "He's fashionable."

What would Meg say?

"But Aunt, Captain Langley is the earl's close friend. Surely Captain Langley would not befriend him after all that, even if he is considered fashionable."

Aunt Geraldine sighed and took another swallow of her coffee. "Captain Langley is a kindhearted soul, and moral, too. Yet he was in Bath with Stratford, and he was the one who helped him escape after that incident with the curate. To what end, I've no idea. I've never understood why Langley, as proper as he is, as much of a gentleman as he is, remains such a staunch supporter of the earl."

Serena thought of the way Jonathan had cut her after they'd been discovered making love at the Dowager Duchess of Clayworth's ball. It had been enough—more than enough—that she'd been branded a brazen whore unworthy of London society. She'd felt so scared and alone, but she'd known Jonathan was close and she'd clung to the knowledge of his love.

But a few days later, she'd passed Jonathan in St. James's Square. She'd called his name, hoping, praying that he would have a solution for them both. That he'd say he didn't care and that they could run away and be married, to hell with the gossips. But that hadn't happened.

Instead, his eyes had turned an icy cobalt. He'd said, "I'm sorry, I've not had the honor of your acquaintance," in a frosty voice, then pressed his lips together and turned away.

Yes, he was capable of becoming a heartless rake. If he was capable of professing sweet, undying love to her and then treating her like so much rubbish, he was capable of anything.

Slowly, Serena removed her grip from her knees, thinking she'd surely bruised them. She reached for her bread and finished it, savoring the flaky layers and swallowing a sip of coffee before looking back to her aunt.

She tipped her lips up at her aunt in the semblance of a smile. "Never worry, Aunt. When I encounter him, I shall be polite but aloof, but I will never, *ever* forgive him for what he did to Serena."

Chapter Three

Meg Donovan had changed. When Jonathan had leaned toward her last night, he'd inhaled and caught the scent of fine ocean sand baked for hours in the sun. He'd glanced at her face, shocked, his heart pounding frantically against his breastbone. That wasn't Meg's scent at all. That was how Serena had smelled.

Then he'd opened his damned mouth and called her by the wrong name.

Jonathan took a sip of his morning coffee—despite the fact that it was after noon—and pushed away his copy of the *Times* so he could rest his elbows on his breakfast table.

Could she be Serena posing as Meg? Why would she do such a thing? Why would she deceive Langley?

Shaking his head, he chuckled into his coffee. Surely not. Ridiculous even to have considered it. Only his own scoundrel's soul could conceive such a thing.

Six years could certainly change a person. Meg had changed physically, too. Her hair had darkened to a golden blond, framing her face with waves he was certain were natural. She seemed thinner—no, that wasn't quite right. Her curves had developed—her waist had slimmed above flaring hips, and the tops of her breasts rounded over the edge of her bodice. Her skin was darker than most London ladies', no doubt due to the climate of the island where she lived, but it wasn't heathen dark. It was a subtle golden shade that complemented her hair.

Her gray, soulful eyes seemed larger, and sadder. Meg had never been as lively as her twin, but she'd glowed with happiness that summer so long ago, especially when Langley was near. Now, she didn't glow at all.

Jonathan understood that was probably because she'd lost a sister and her closest companion. He completely comprehended the tragedy of that, because not a day passed that he didn't think about Serena Donovan. But it had been six years, after all, and finally Meg was marrying the man she'd loved for a very long time. Shouldn't she be glowing?

This afternoon, Jonathan was going to Mayfair to call on the Duke of Calton, but afterward he was free. Meg Donovan was residing at her aunt's house, only two doors down from his own. He wanted to see her again. She reminded him so much of Serena. So much more than even he had expected.

A footman came in to offer Jonathan a tray of sliced ham, but Jonathan waved him away.

Meg had the bearing of a true lady, which probably surprised some of the soiree attendees who might expect her to be provincial and awkward, but it didn't surprise Jonathan. Serena had told him that her mother's life goal was to see her five daughters appropriately situated in London society, and that she'd spent years instructing the girls on how to behave like proper ladies.

He smiled slightly, remembering Serena's fiery blush as she'd admitted to him she'd always tried her best to ignore her mother's teachings. At the time, she hadn't seen any benefit in behaving like a lady. There was a wild edge in her that couldn't be tamed, and he didn't want it tamed. He'd loved her just the way she was.

"I'm glad you ignored your mama," he'd told her. "I don't want a perfect lady. I want you." Then he'd kissed her soundly, and all talk of her family was forgotten.

In the months they had known one another years ago, he'd found Meg to be so different from Serena. In temperament, she was the opposite of her sister. He'd always been amazed that so many people couldn't tell them apart. Yes, their features were identical, but to him, the two women were like night and day. From one glance at their eyes, he'd been able to tell one sister from the other.

But Meg had changed. In the six years since he'd last seen her, and in ways he couldn't properly define, she'd grown so much more like Serena.

For some reason, that terrified him.

That afternoon, the sisters sat in Serena's bedchamber, Serena composing letters home while Phoebe fidgeted with a book in her lap.

"It was a lovely party." With a soft smile curving her lips, Phoebe cast a dreamy look toward the window.

Aunt Geraldine had given Serena the room she'd shared with Meg on her last visit, a guest chamber decorated in crimson. Six years ago, Meg and Serena had giggled about how stern, how heavy this room had seemed, with its thick velvet drapes and bed curtains, mohair hangings, walnut bed with posts as thick as tree trunks, and opulent tables and dressers made of rich woods and covered with black-veined marble.

Now the place brought back memories of Meg. Serena stared into the heavy round looking glass of the dressing table, recalling how she'd wept in Meg's arms here after she'd been caught *in flagrante delicto* with Jonathan Dane.

Sighing, she laid down her pen and bent her head, pressing her fingertips to the bridge of her nose.

She wished she could agree with Phoebe and say it was a lovely party. Instead the soiree had unsettled her. If only Jonathan hadn't come, it wouldn't have been so bad. But his arrival had thrown her hard-won equilibrium into confusion. Images of Jonathan, past and present, had disrupted her sleep all night long, and she hadn't been able to stop thinking about him all day.

That surge of attraction, that rush of feeling when she'd first seen the earl, disconcerted her. She should not feel this way about someone who had proven himself the very worst breed of scoundrel, not only with her, but in all of his actions in the years following their separation. Where was her pride?

She must remember her hatred. On the ship that fateful morning, she'd told Meg that she despised him. She must hold on to that feeling. She must remember what he'd done to her, how he'd devastated her.

"Do you know I met twenty-three unmarried gentlemen?" Phoebe said.

Serena raised her brows. "You counted?"

"Of *course* I counted."

"How did you know they were all unmarried?"

Phoebe gave her a sly smile. "By the way they looked at me."

Serena considered telling her sister that the way a

man looked at a lady could mean nothing at all, for some married men were scoundrels, but then she thought better of it. A part of her wanted her sister to hang on to her sweet näiveté for as long as possible. Instead, she asked, "How many ladies did you meet?"

"Goodness! Why would I have counted the ladies?"

Serena eyed her. The gleam in Phoebe's eyes told her she wasn't revealing everything. And she wouldn't, if Serena didn't tread carefully. "Do you think there might have been a potential suitor for you among those twenty-three?"

"Hmm." Phoebe brought her fingers to her chin and tapped it thoughtfully. "Perhaps. I danced with Mr. Pultenoy twice. He is the grandson of a duke, you know, and very handsome."

"If I recall," Serena said dryly, "he is seventeen years old."

Phoebe shrugged. "That doesn't matter, does it? It is only two years younger than I am, after all."

Serena shook her head. "Ladies mature far faster than gentlemen, Phoebe. A lady at seventeen is ripening for marriage. A man, however, requires at least another ten years to reach that point."

"And how would you know?" Phoebe scoffed. "As if you can claim to know anything about men, *Meg*."

Serena pursed her lips. Phoebe knew of the scandal that Serena had caused, but not the details. She'd only been thirteen when Serena had returned to

Antigua, and the loss of Meg had taken the focus off Serena's disgrace.

Her three sisters did know that Serena had made a terrible, reprehensible mistake, one that would make her a pariah, and Mother had told them that the change of identity was an absolute necessity if any of them wanted any chance of being accepted by the ton. To Phoebe, that reasoning made logical sense, and that was all she required.

"I met another man of interest. I believe he is twenty-eight. Mature enough for you?"

Serena ignored her sister's sarcasm. "Maybe. Who was this gentleman?"

"Oh, he's more than a gentleman. He's an *earl*."

Serena stiffened. She knew of the presence of only one twenty-eight-year-old earl last night.

"But I daresay you would advise me to look elsewhere." Phoebe sighed, but there was a glint in her blue eyes.

Serena stared hard at her sister for a full minute, then decided, grudgingly, to play along. "Why would I advise you to look elsewhere?"

"Because... oh, goodness, the stories I heard about him last night..."

Serena's breath caught in her throat. Surely no one would tell Phoebe about her history with Jonathan Dane! "What kinds of stories?" she choked out.

Phoebe leaned forward and lowered her voice. "His name is the Earl of Stratford. He came in late, quite unfashionably so. Were you introduced to him?"

"Yes. I was."

"Well, I'm sure you saw that he's quite a dashing man, if you look very hard at him from certain angles, ignore his wrinkles, and pretend he's not quite as old as twenty-eight."

"Heavens, Phoebe. Twenty-eight isn't old at all."

Phoebe snorted. "Easy for you to say, considering that your betrothed is even older."

"You're speaking nonsense. Captain Langley is only six years older than I am. It's a perfect age difference."

"He's in his third decade. I shall always maintain that once you reach that advanced age, you are firmly on the shelf, whether you be man or woman."

Serena had to laugh. "Good heavens. Where do you get your ideas?"

Giving Serena a look she attempted to infuse with wisdom, Phoebe tapped her skull, and they both chuckled.

Phoebe took a sip of her tea, which must have been completely cold by now. "I met a young lady last night, a Miss Trumpet, who told me that Lord Stratford is the most dissolute rake in all of London. She says that despite his terrible reputation, he's still invited to the very best parties, but only because he is an earl."

"The most dissolute rake in *all* of London?"

Phoebe nodded, full of self-importance that she should be the imparter of such significant gossip. "Indeed. Miss Trumpet said it began years ago, when he ruined a poor young lady and then broke her heart. Since then, he's blazed a trail of broken hearts through England. And..." Phoebe's voice lowered to a whisper. "It's said he fathered a child out of wedlock five years ago. He keeps the child—a boy—living in the lap of luxury and occasionally uses the mother as his mistress."

Serena closed her eyes. It was too much. His presence at Langley's soiree and then her aunt's gossip had nearly undone her...but this news...She swallowed hard.

Jonathan had a child.

She had once wanted to be the woman who bore his children. In times of great weakness, she'd let herself dream.

It was over between her and the Earl of Stratford. It had been over for several years. She should not be affected at all by this news. This was common behavior for London aristocrats, after all—many of them had illegitimate children. Jonathan had become just like his forebears. Really, she shouldn't be surprised at all, especially after what he'd done to her. She knew what he was capable of.

Glancing at Phoebe, she saw that her sister's attention had turned to the window again. "What is it, Phoebe?"

"What? Oh, I thought I heard a carriage outside, that's all," Phoebe said absently.

Serena watched her, tapping her chin thoughtfully. Phoebe was keeping something from her. "So, which of the gentlemen made the strongest impression on you last night? Surely it wasn't this debauched earl."

Keeping her eyes averted, Phoebe sucked in her lower lip, hesitating.

"Tell me," Serena murmured.

"That would be... Well, that would have to be Mr. Harper."

"Mr. Harper," Serena repeated, trying to remember him.

"Yes. He is the younger brother of one of Captain Langley's Navy associates."

"Did you dance with him?" Serena asked.

"Three times."

Serena raised her brows. "Really?"

Once again, Phoebe's gaze darted away. "I was supposed to dance the waltz with Sir Sheffington..."

"But he twisted his ankle, of course." Serena remembered the poor man's whimpers of pain as a footman had helped him limp to a chair, where he had sat like a prince for the remainder of the night. Serena had checked on him often to make sure he was still enjoying himself despite his fall.

"Yes, so Mr. Harper asked me to waltz instead."

"I assume this didn't disappoint you," Serena said.

"Oh, no!" Phoebe grimaced as soon as the vehement words emerged from her mouth. Once again, her gaze flitted to Serena and then to the window. She made her voice light. "He was very kind."

"And handsome?" Serena asked.

"Yes," Phoebe confirmed. "*Very* handsome."

Phoebe's gaze met hers, and a jolt of unease ran through Serena. She'd seen that stubborn look in her sister's eyes before. But what could it mean in this circumstance? They'd just arrived in London. Surely Phoebe couldn't have set her sights on one gentleman after a single meeting.

Serena kept her tone mild and unconcerned. "You'll have to point him out to me when you see him next."

Phoebe stood, craning her neck to look down from the window. "There's a carriage parked in the front of the house. I think Captain Langley has arrived."

"Oh, dear," Serena muttered. "Is it four o'clock already?"

Last night, Langley had said that the day promised to be lovely—and it was—so perhaps she would like to go for a drive with him in Hyde Park. She'd said yes—it certainly wouldn't be proper to turn down such a request from one's betrothed.

That wasn't the only reason she'd agreed to go. She was feeling cooped up and restless as a chicken inside her aunt's house, and she craved the outdoors. And then there was Langley himself. She dreaded being in his presence, but that had nothing to do with him—it was all her own feelings of guilt and dread over what, or rather *who,* she had been forced to become. It was the lie she was too much of a coward to recant and almost too much of a coward to enact.

Serena had changed into her carriage dress earlier, a lavender gown of gros de Naples covered by silvery netting with sheer, long sleeves, their puffs contained at her elbows and wrists with silver ties, but had since forgotten all about the planned excursion.

She leaned down to give Phoebe a quick kiss and then she left the room. "Don't forget your hat," Phoebe called after her.

"Oh, drat. I forgot again." Serena made an abrupt turn toward her dressing room. She always forgot about her hat, which was all very well in Antigua where nobody cared and she was always running in and out of the house, but going out hatless would not be considered at all proper in London. Flannery met her inside her dressing room to help her don the wide-brimmed behemoth bedecked with a flower garden that felt like it weighed half a stone.

Finally, she hurried downstairs, girding herself for an afternoon with the man she must find a way to love as much as her sister had.

Jonathan stood at the door of Lady Alcott's house, unsure what exactly had driven him here. After leaving the Duke of Calton's house, he'd instructed his coachman to take him here, rather than his own residence, just two doors down St. James's Square.

He stared at the viscountess's door. What had he been thinking? Was he mad? The very last thing he wanted to do was poach on William Langley's territory. Langley was his friend, and the list of people who Jonathan could name as friends had grown very short in the past few years.

This couldn't be Serena, he reminded himself. It was Meg. He'd liked Meg well enough, but she wasn't the woman he'd loved.

Serena had died six years ago. She'd drowned on the way home to Antigua. Her disgrace and subsequent banishment had been his fault, so it followed that her drowning was his fault, too.

He turned and lifted a hand of dismissal. His coachman nodded, then flicked the reins, driving the team down the street, then turning the corner at Duke of York Street, where he'd take them to the stables behind Jonathan's house.

He raised the knocker and lowered it. Once, twice, three times, before he chastised himself for being a damn fool. Lady Alcott knew who he was, knew what he'd become. The woman had smiled and nodded at him last night as if she didn't hold him in contempt for what he'd done to her niece. But she did. The knowledge of it lurked deeply in her eyes, as did dislike. *This is the man who embarrassed my family, debauched my niece, and was the cause of her demise...*

He lowered the knocker for the fourth time and heard the sound echo through the house.

He wanted to lay eyes on Meg Donovan again. Hear her voice. If he spent any time pondering the reason for that, he'd only realize how absurd this notion was. So he stopped thinking about it and instead allowed that burning desire to see her again flow through him.

A butler answered the door, and Jonathan handed the man his card. "The Earl of Stratford here to see Miss Donovan."

The man bowed and promised to see whether the lady was at home. Jonathan translated that to, "I'll check with Lady Alcott to see whether you are an approved caller."

No doubt he was not.

The butler reopened the door and stepped away. Lady Alcott stood at the threshold, her arms crossed over her chest, her eyes glaring azure daggers at him.

"What are *you* doing here?"

Jonathan met the older woman's gaze, keeping his own steady. "Good afternoon, ma'am. I've come to see Miss Donovan."

"Why?"

Good question. One he honestly could not answer. So he gave her the response she was most likely to accept. "I should like to wish her felicitations on her upcoming marriage."

Lady Alcott's eyes narrowed. "I believe you were given the opportunity to do that last night."

"Indeed not," Jonathan said casually. "It was a crush, and as the honored guest, she was in high demand."

The lady's turquoise eyes were so narrow they appeared reptilian. "I don't believe you."

Jonathan widened his own eyes as if he were surprised. "Oh?"

"Have you plans to destroy her as you did her sister?"

Lady Alcott had nearly as much of a hand in Serena's destruction as he did, and she damn well knew it. "No, ma'am."

"Then what could you possibly want from my niece?"

"As I said—"

"No."

Jonathan raised a brow.

"She is not at home," Lady Alcott said stiffly.

Jonathan hid his seething annoyance. He hadn't expected anything less. He deserved to be cut by this woman and by her family.

He leaned forward. "Very well, my lady. I'll tell you the truth."

"Please do."

"I've come to apologize."

The woman's gaze narrowed. "Why?"

"I fear I embarrassed Miss Donovan last night. It was quite unintentional and I wish to tell her so."

A flash of silver caught his eye, and he looked past Lady Alcott's shoulder to see Serena—*Meg*—reeling to a halt on the black and white tiles of the entry hall. Beneath her fruit tree forest of a hat, she stared up at him, her gray eyes wide, her mouth opening to breathe a whispering, "Oh!"

He inclined his head. "Miss Donovan. Good afternoon."

She walked forward, slowly as if she were dragging herself through syrup. "Good afternoon, my lord."

Lady Alcott hissed out a breath, and for a moment, Jonathan was certain she'd slam the door in his face. But some sliver of propriety must have remained somewhere within her, because she relented. "The earl wishes to have a word with you, niece."

Those gray eyes widened even farther, as if to say, "Whatever for?" Instead she held firmly to ladylike politeness. "Oh? I will be going out shortly, but I might have a few moments."

"Come in, then," Lady Alcott said from between clenched teeth. She widened the door, giving Jonathan space to enter. Removing his hat, he stepped inside.

Both he and Meg turned to Lady Alcott.

"I'll be in the drawing room if you need me." She swiveled and strode down a corridor lined with enormous family portraits.

Serena—*Meg*—stood in silence until her aunt was out of sight, then the smile that she'd plastered on her face melted away.

"How can I help you, my lord?"

"Thank you for seeing me," he said, studying her. So, so much more like Serena than the Meg he remembered. Whenever the sisters had stood side by side, even motionless, he'd known which one of them was Serena. He'd been proud of his rare ability to distinguish between the two of them. Even Langley, who'd fallen in love with Meg, had confused Serena for his beloved once.

"I wished to apologize for my rude behavior last night."

"Your rude behavior?"

"For calling you by your sister's name," he explained.

Her eyelids fluttered in a quick blink. She gave him a tight smile. "Think nothing of it. It's a common mistake."

"Still...I...I know how close you were to your sister. How much you must mourn her."

Her tight smile didn't break. "I'd prefer it if we didn't discuss my sister, Lord Stratford. You will certainly understand."

He couldn't tell, not for certain. She looked like Serena, but she also looked like Meg. There were the subtle things, the turn of her lips, the flash in her eyes, that reminded him of Serena, but damn, six years was a long time. And no matter which sister this was, she would be changed from the last time he'd seen her. She'd lost the person closest to her.

"I do understand," he said softly. "Forgive me."

She nodded. "Of course." She hesitated. "I didn't expect to see you last night. I'd no idea you'd become such a good friend of Captain Langley's."

"We've been good friends since—" He broke off abruptly and revised his statement. "We've been acquainted for several years. He is a very good friend, and a good man."

Unlike me.

Her smile widened, but it did not reach her eyes. "Yes," she murmured.

"Indeed, Langley has asked me to be his best man for your wedding."

The smile dripped away, leaving her lips flat. A light line appeared between her brows. This news seemed to have angered her.

Well, he shouldn't be surprised, should he? After all, he'd been the cause of her sister's demise. Surely she hadn't forgotten that.

"You look very well, Meg," he said in a quiet voice.

She startled like a bird at that, realized he'd addressed her informally, then forced the return of her ever-present smile. "Thank you. And you as well."

He returned her smile, his body heating in a slow bloom from the inside out. He needed to leave this place before he did something he would regret. Like pull her into his arms, take her lips, and test once and for all who this woman was.

Langley. Think of Langley.

He did think of Langley. He thought of how much Langley had been through in the past six years. Most of that pain was rooted in Jonathan's wrongdoings, and Jonathan had no intention of wounding his friend yet again.

Taking a step backward, he returned his hat to his head. "Well, I know you're leaving. Thank you for seeing me, Miss Donovan."

"Thank you for your apology, Lord Stratford," she said, not exactly disingenuously, but the words were coated by a layer of brittle politeness.

He gave the lady a proper bow, said he hoped to see her again soon, and withdrew. He paused at the street corner as a phaeton driven by a familiar dark-haired man passed him, and then he turned to watch it halt at the Alcott residence. Langley hadn't seen Jonathan as he'd driven by. He unfolded his tall body from the conveyance, straightened his coat, then walked to the door and knocked. The door opened, and he was immediately granted entrance.

Fury surged in Jonathan, hard and hot. He raised his clenched hands and saw that his knuckles had whitened.

He forced himself to turn and walk away from the house, hating that Langley could see her, be close to her, speak with her all afternoon...*forever*...and he couldn't. Hating that, for the first time in six years, a woman had the ability to make him *feel.*

Chapter Four

Langley led Serena outside, where a sharp little phaeton waited. A man jumped from the perch and handed him the reins, and Langley helped Serena into the small, sleek carriage. Langley nodded at the man, dismissing him, and he turned on his heel in a military gesture and strode down St. James's, whistling.

"How lovely," Serena said, admiring the shiny carriage.

"I had it delivered just last month." Langley shrugged. "A bit of a splurge... but you deserve it."

Of course, he'd purchased this more for himself than for her, but she smiled at him. "It is beautiful."

He helped her into the bench seat and then settled beside her. Reins in hand, he gestured at the horses. "Meet Theseus and Aphrodite," he said as they set off at a brisk pace.

She gazed at the pair, the white one about a hand shorter than the black. Their names seemed mismatched—as far as she could remember, Theseus had very little to do with the goddess of love. He'd been rescued from the minotaur by the king's daughter, Ariadne. "Why did you not name the mare Ariadne?"

"Not Ariadne, not a partner he could lead around by the nose and then abandon. No, she wouldn't do at all. My Theseus needed someone to put him in his place. A goddess. Nothing less would do."

"I see," she murmured.

"See how companionable they are? She's got him conducting himself as if he were the most well-behaved gelding, when in fact he is a devil. With her, though, he is a docile creature."

Without smiling, he wove the carriage around the traffic and headed toward Hyde Park. "I'd like to take you driving every day this Season. If that suits you."

Why did their conversation feel so stilted? Why did he so rarely smile at her? He rarely smiled at all. Was he like this with Meg? She couldn't remember.

He was so stiff, so proper, Serena feared she'd never be able to delve into his head, never truly understand him. Surely Meg hadn't felt that way.

Langley looked at her expectantly, and she realized he was awaiting her response. "I'd like a daily drive in the park very much."

The phaeton seat was narrow, and Langley's thigh

pressed against hers as they negotiated the traffic on the way to Hyde Park. The day was bright and airy, cooler than Antigua ever was, but Serena was comfortable in her new carriage dress, heavy hat, and gloves. Langley was dressed smartly as usual, in a double-breasted wool coat and brown trousers.

"I wish to personally express my condolences for the death of your sister. I wrote to you about it, I know...but I wanted to say so in person." His voice was somber, his expression grave, and Serena did believe he was sorry, that he could look past the outward disgrace of "Serena" and truly sympathize with how it felt to lose someone so close.

How kind he was. She smiled at him, but it was a sad smile, a smile that didn't go beyond the upward tilt of her lips.

He stared straight ahead, and his voice was solemn. "What a terrible loss. I remember how devoted you were to her."

"Yes." Serena couldn't say any more without choking on the words. She thought of Meg all the time, thousands of times a day, but she rarely spoke of her. Even after all these years, the pain was too sharp.

Serena stared at the silvery silk netting of her dress on her lap. Too many emotions boiled together inside her.

Langley said no more, and for that Serena was profoundly grateful. Though he didn't speak, sympathy glimmered like an aura surrounding them. It was so strong she thought he might feel inclined to pull her into his arms and stroke her back, offering her physical comfort instead of this silent understanding. But that didn't happen. Someday, perhaps. When they were married.

She sat in silence for some time, her hands clasped tightly in her lap, and when the silence simply became too loud to bear, she said, "I enjoyed the soiree. I thought it was a wonderful success."

Keeping his focus on the busy road, he nodded. "As did I." He slid her a quick glance. "Everyone agreed that you were the loveliest lady there."

"Thank you." Serena wrenched her gaze from him and examined the enormous statue of Apollo as they entered the park.

"Your eyes are lovely." The bench squeaked as Langley shifted his weight. "Does that sound cliché? But it's true, you know. I have never seen such a shade of gray on anyone but you and your sister. They are as pale as the sky at sunrise."

She managed to arch her eyebrows. "Oh, goodness. Thank you. But you needn't flatter me."

"I disagree. Engaged couples flatter each other all the time."

She smiled at him. "Then I suppose I owe you some flattery as well."

"Well..." The heaviness in his dark eyes lightened a little. "I'd never take a little flattery amiss."

You are perfect, she wanted to say. *Too perfect, in fact. You are so perfect, you don't seem real. So why don't I feel the same with you as I once did with Jonathan?*

"You have very striking...cheekbones," she finally murmured.

He smiled, and it was the first real smile she'd seen from him. "Cheekbones? Well." Holding the reins in one hand, he brushed his fingers over his cheeks. "Here, you mean? And here?"

She nodded, feeling her own lips twitch. "I believe, in fact, they are the most finely shaped cheekbones I have ever seen."

"Truly? I believe they are the bones that form the face, therefore, if one is not blessed with well-shaped bones, one would have a deficient countenance indeed. So I thank you. I am much relieved."

"Were you never aware of your well-formed face?"

"I wasn't sure," he mused. "I have received my share of flattery but in more general terms. Nobody has ever dug to the bones of it, so to speak, prior to this moment."

She smiled freely then, not nearly so tense as she'd been a moment ago. "Well, then. I'm happy I was the first to get to the bones of the matter."

They spent the next several moments in companionable silence, listening to the sounds of life in the park: the breeze rustling through tree branches, clomps of horses' hooves, clatter of carriage wheels, and the murmurs of distant conversations.

"Ah, look, Lord Stratford is here." Langley directed the horses to swerve around a stationary carriage, and there he was.

Still dressed all in black, with his shining Wellington boots and the sleek top hat he'd doffed as he'd spoken to her in Aunt Geraldine's entry hall, Jonathan sat erect upon a beautiful bay. His coat defined his broad shoulders in a way that sent shivers of recognition cascading down Serena's spine.

Her breathing turned ragged—how had that happened? Clasping her hands tightly in her lap, she stared up at him. He met her eyes. His jaw tightened, and tension vibrated in his shoulders.

What was he thinking?

He tipped his hat. "Langley, good to see you." His blue gaze settled on Serena as he drew up alongside them on her side of the phaeton. The three horses took on a tranquil, side-by-side gait. "Miss Donovan."

There was a gruffness in his voice—she'd heard the same tone earlier, and was certain it was recognition. Panic welled in Serena's chest, but she flung it away. *No.* There was no way he could possibly know her identity.

"Lovely afternoon, isn't it?" Jonathan asked, seemingly intent upon engaging them in conversation.

Jonathan was an earl. She still couldn't fathom

it—he'd been so rebellious with his father, so anti-aristocracy. He'd been quite happy in his position as younger son. What did he think of his title? What kind of a man had he become, beneath his dastardly reputation?

"I hope the weather is a telling precursor of the remainder of the Season," Langley said.

"As do I," Jonathan said.

She didn't understand the way her body reacted to Jonathan. She hated him, she reminded herself. He was the man who'd betrayed her. And yet, how could she forget him? He was the last man—the only man—who'd ever touched her. She remembered those blue eyes that gazed at her now, but she remembered them dusky with longing, staring at her from across the Duchess of Clayworth's crowded ballroom. She remembered the words of love he whispered into her ear as she shattered in his arms.

She should forget. She should have forgotten all of that years ago.

Serena returned her gaze to her lap, her face hot to the tips of her ears. After a short, uncomfortable silence, Jonathan said, "Vauxhall Gardens opens for the season a week from Monday. I thought I might attend. Would you like to accompany me? If the weather holds, it promises to be a glorious evening."

She felt his stare acutely. It washed over her as it always had, in a bath of tingling warmth.

Had he followed them here?

Serena glanced up, and his hot blue gaze collided with hers. She almost flinched at the shock of it, but she kept those impulses controlled. It would do none of them any good if Langley knew anything about her roiling feelings regarding the Earl of Stratford.

She couldn't even sort out just how she felt about him. There was a visceral reaction to his nearness, but that had always been the case when they were physically close to each other. In the past, it had been mutual, but was he feeling it now? She couldn't be sure. On horseback, he held himself as stiffly as she sat on the phaeton seat.

How could he possibly have those physical reactions to her now? To *Meg*?

She ground her teeth. She was jealous of Jonathan feeling lust for Meg. But she *was* Meg. And she still despised him for what he'd done to her…even though a part of her, an undeniable part, was still hopelessly attracted to him. What a tangled mess.

Beyond all these feelings, however, there were so many other new, wary feelings that hadn't existed in her when she'd known Jonathan before. When she was eighteen years old, the world had seemed simple. Now she knew she'd been living in a world of childish dreams.

"Meg?"

It was Langley's quiet, questioning voice.

She blinked at him, then remembered the conversation. "Oh, yes," she said automatically. "Vauxhall Gardens sounds lovely."

Oh, Lord, had she just agreed to see him again? With Langley?

Jonathan smiled politely, but he narrowed his eyes as he studied her, his dark blue gaze seeming to drill right into her soul. "The past few years have changed you, Miss Donovan."

Serena's heart stopped, stuttered, and began beating again at a frenetic pace. The heat of the two men's stares burned into her. She cracked a smile through the ice coating her face and glanced at Langley. "I daresay we've all changed, haven't we? No one can be exactly the same person they were six years ago."

"Indeed not," Langley agreed firmly. "We are all older. And wiser," he added as an afterthought.

"Exactly." Serena pinned Jonathan with her own hot stare. "Much, *much* wiser."

"I am certain that is the case for you two," Jonathan said. A grimness edged into his tone as he added, "But I wouldn't say so for myself."

"I should hope you're wiser," Serena said darkly before she could stop herself.

"Ah, Stratford." Langley kept his voice light as he turned the horses around a bend in the path. "You're too modest. You've matured significantly since your days of youth. You just don't allow yourself to see it."

Jonathan smiled tightly at Langley, then glanced at Serena. "Do you see why your betrothed is one of my closest friends?" he asked her. "It's because he sees the good in me where no one else can…not even myself."

She nodded. It seemed Langley did have a way of seeing the good in people. But after all she'd been told Jonathan had done, she still didn't understand Langley's obvious affection for him.

"Well, then. I'll see you Monday next?"

"We'll look forward to it," Langley said.

Jonathan tipped his hat and wished them a good day. His back stiff and straight, he turned his horse and rode away.

Langley watched him go, and then he sighed. "I'm sorry," he said in a low voice.

Turning back to him, she frowned, confused. "Why?"

"That was uncomfortable for you."

She opened her mouth to speak and then closed it. She couldn't think of anything to say that wouldn't sound absolutely awful. It had been terribly uncomfortable, but not in the way Langley must imagine.

He fixed his gaze on the road. "I know you blame him for what happened to your sister."

Still, Serena couldn't speak.

"But he is my friend. He is a good man, despite what you might think after what happened to Serena. He has waged a strong inner battle in the past several years. At times I thought he was losing, but I do hold out hope." Langley drove for a few minutes in thoughtful silence. "Lately, he's seemed quite subdued. And Vauxhall Gardens. This is new. It is not the kind of place men like Stratford frequent."

She frowned at him. "I don't know what you mean."

He shook his head, then gave her a small smile. "I feel he's very close to being completely reformed."

"I see."

"I should like to remain his friend, Meg, so I hope you will find it within you to forgive him. It has been a long time since his association with your sister. He has changed since then."

"I... I'm not sure."

He nodded in understanding.

"I'll try," she added. Langley couldn't know how difficult his request would be. How could she forgive Jonathan? And if she did, would that not be risking falling in love with him again?

His lips tipped up in that not-quite smile, and he said, "I think you've already come far. You agreed to join him at the opening of Vauxhall Gardens."

"So I did," she said, her voice mild now. "You're right. I do hope we shall become friends someday."

What a lie that was.

He swung the horses off the thickly populated route onto a narrower trail. As they rode along, the tree-lined path turned along the edge of the Serpentine River. The crowd thinned here, and pale sunlight glistened off the rippled surface of the water. A single oarsman rowed a narrow boat near the far shore.

"It is peaceful out here."

"Compared to the crush on Rotten Row? Indeed," he agreed.

He pulled the horses short under a giant maple tree with budding leaves and turned to her.

"I wish you would call me Will," he said quietly. "As you did in your letters."

Serena gazed at the horses. Theseus shifted impatiently and snorted, and Aphrodite swung her head toward him, as if telling him to settle down. The gelding stilled instantly.

Slowly, Serena turned to Langley. "I'm sorry. Everything is so new, so different. And it has been so long since I have seen London—seen *you*."

Langley's thigh was very warm pressed against hers. Suddenly, he took her hand fervently in his own. "Please, Meg. Call me Will."

Suddenly, surprisingly, his lips descended on hers, soft, warm, and altogether...nice. Gasping, she jerked away, pressing her body back against the leather hood of the phaeton, not far from his seeking mouth.

"Forgive me." Stiffly, he turned away, took up the reins, and guided the horses away from the tree.

Serena squeezed her eyes shut, trying to calm the panicked, frenetic clanging of her heartbeat. She'd just ruined everything. Her reaction had been entirely wrong.

Body tense, face rigid, he drove her home in silence.

• • •

On the night of the soiree, Jonathan had been so overwrought from seeing his lover's sister again, he hadn't paid much attention to *her.* Yesterday had been different. He'd watched her closely at her aunt's house and at the park. He'd studied her, drunk her in. And he came to the conclusion that something was very wrong.

Something inside her was wound taut, like a ball of yarn. As if she were on the verge of unwinding, unraveling, revealing something horrible, something she fought diligently to hide from everyone. But what was it? In the years they'd been apart, had she fallen out of love with Langley? Had she developed a *tendre* for someone in Antigua? Was her mother forcing her to marry Langley now?

The way she looked at Jonathan—when she forgot to be demure and actually *looked* at him—there was something in those gray eyes he couldn't decipher. Did she hate him and seek vengeance for the death of her sister? Or was she attracted to him, as he was to her?

Or—God forbid—was it both?

He worried for her and whatever burden it was that she struggled so hard to bear. He worried for Langley and for his upcoming nuptials.

Most of all, Jonathan worried for himself. His reaction to her was not only improper, it was unnatural. It was wrong to have these confusing feelings for his beloved's sister, no matter how many traits the new Meg shared with the old Serena.

Overpowering his worry, however, was the craving that had awakened in him. The undeniable and irrational urge to learn more about Meg, what had changed her in the past six years, what drove her. Why he was drawn to *her,* when before it had been nothing more than a mild interest, and then only because she was Serena's identical twin?

He'd see her again at Vauxhall Gardens. There, he'd get to the bottom of the mystery of Meg Donovan.

June the second came, the night of the opening of Vauxhall Gardens. Jonathan had seen Langley earlier in the day, and they agreed that since Meg's aunt's house was two doors down from Jonathan's, he'd fetch her first, then go to Cavendish Square for Langley, and they'd all continue to Vauxhall together.

Jonathan had been anticipating the evening all day. He would have her alone, if only for a few moments. He would converse with her, drive out the truth of whatever it was that was tearing her apart.

He couldn't wait.

He ordered his coachman to take the most circuitous route possible to Cavendish Square. Meg was unfamiliar with London routes and would certainly remain ignorant that he'd deliberately lengthened their journey to Langley's house.

He walked the few steps to Lady Alcott's front door and knocked sharply. The unhappy-looking butler opened the door and invited Jonathan into the entry hall, where he was ordered to wait.

It was a step forward to be allowed a few feet into the house, Jonathan thought grimly, staring at the Oriental silk tapestry on the opposite wall. He turned to approaching footsteps and released a silent breath.

There she was. Meg, looking beautiful in a simple ivory silk. Beside her was her sister, Phoebe, whom he'd met at the soiree. The girl marched up to him and made a jerky curtsy.

"Good evening, my lord. I'm so looking forward to tonight!"

He cast a glance at Meg, and she gave him a soft smile. He remembered that smile. Serena had looked up at him once, her blond hair tousled and framed by hay, and smiled like that.

"Phoebe shall be my companion this evening," she murmured.

Of course. If he could, he'd slap himself across the back of his head for the stupid assumption he'd made. Of course a young, unmarried lady wouldn't attend the evening's entertainments without a female chaperone, even if she were to attend with her soon-to-be husband and his friend. That would be grossly improper.

He'd been too long separated from respectable company, he supposed.

"Of course. It's good to see you again, Miss Phoebe."

The girl's grin was infectious, and suddenly Jonathan was quite certain that while this young woman might have heard something of her eldest sister's disgrace, she wasn't aware that Serena's disgrace had anything to do with him.

He wondered whether Phoebe had been told about him. Warned about him. Then again, families of a certain status liked to keep their girls sheltered. And she'd been raised far away from the scandal and gossip of London.

Meg knew, though. She'd been there, and even now, the knowledge of what had happened so long ago lurked in her gray eyes.

Returning Phoebe's smile, he held out his arm. "Shall we?"

"Certainly!" the young woman agreed, and slipped her arm through his.

Was it his imagination, or did Meg's eyes narrow when her sister touched him? He must tread carefully here. He had no intention of flirting with Phoebe Donovan, and for God's sake, he didn't want Meg to believe he was. He'd already hurt one of her sisters. One sister was more than enough.

He helped Phoebe into the carriage, and then he held out his hand to Meg. When her gloves touched his and her fingers curled around his, he sucked in a breath. Her touch—it was so familiar; it brought back a flood of erotic memories he couldn't contain. Those fingers wrapped around him . . . stroking him . . .

Gritting his teeth, he covertly adjusted his trousers and took the back-facing seat across from the sisters. He watched them as the carriage began to rattle down St. James's Street. Phoebe was dressed in a bright yellow satin to complement her sunny personality. Meg's dress, while simple, appealed to him in a deep-seated way. There was an innocence about the white color, about the simple strand of pearls she wore about her neck, that made his gut clench.

Serena had been innocent when he'd first known her. Then again, so had he. Not anymore.

Phoebe squirmed restlessly. Clearly the girl was eager to be out of the carriage and exploring the gardens.

"Is it difficult being separated from your other sisters?" he asked her, trying to make conversation. One of the sisters he remembered being older than Phoebe. Why hadn't Meg brought that one instead?

"Oh, yes. I cannot wait until Jessica and Olivia come to London." Phoebe leaned toward him conspiratorially. "They plan to come as soon as Meg marries Captain Langley."

Jonathan raised his brows. "Do they?"

Phoebe nodded. "They hate Antigua, you see. We all do."

Jonathan turned to Meg. "Oh?"

"Hate is a very strong word, Phoebe," Meg said, a

mild chastising tone in her voice. "There are many factors involved in our desire to relocate to England."

Phoebe made a scoffing noise. "Mostly because we all hate the West Indies."

Meg sighed.

"But I do hope they all arrive before winter. You see, my lord, Olivia is very frail," Phoebe said, as if revealing a great secret. "Mother rarely allows her to go outside."

"Oh? I'm sorry to hear that."

"She has improved recently," Meg said. "And I think the climate in London will be better for her."

"Is that so?" Jonathan asked. "What, exactly, is her ailment?"

"When we first arrived in Antigua, she was only nine years old. She and our father contracted malaria. Olivia conquered the first fever, but Papa didn't." Meg stopped there, but Phoebe resumed where she had left off.

"But that awful disease left her with a much-weakened constitution. She is always very pale and easily exhausted and prone to fainting and terrible fevers."

Meg didn't look at him; instead, she stared out at the street. Sympathy welled up in Jonathan as he watched the crease deepen between her brows. "But Olivia is stronger than she looks. She will conquer this illness."

"I'm sure she will," Jonathan said, "with your strength behind her."

Her gray eyes flickered to him, and then away. God, he wanted to touch her. She was so beautiful. He wanted to taste her sweet flavor, kiss her fingers and arm, brush his lips across the sensitive skin inside her elbow and up to her neck. He wanted to explore the delicate spot behind her ear, sample her jawline, and make his way to her lips.

Those full, bow-shaped lips. She ran her tongue nervously over the lower one, and it sparkled from moisture he wanted to kiss away. He wanted to do more than taste those lips, though. He wanted to take them until she submitted and opened to him, and he could explore and then conquer her completely.

Just like he had, once upon a time, with Serena. They'd both been young and inexperienced, but she'd never been a passive observer to their love-making. She'd been present, exchanging power with him, making the experience about both of them rather than just himself. He'd searched for that ever since and had never found another partner willing to engage, willing to throw herself as completely into him as he had thrown himself into her.

He glanced at Meg. *She isn't Serena. She isn't Serena.* He repeated the chant dutifully in his head, again and again.

Hell if he understood any of this. From the way she made him feel, she couldn't be anyone *but*

Serena…But to think that she was impersonating Meg—that just didn't make any sense. Serena wasn't the sort of person who'd do such a thing. She'd been self-assured and confident. He couldn't imagine her voluntarily choosing to take on someone else's identity—even Meg's. *Especially* Meg's.

The air felt close and warm in the carriage, but Jonathan didn't want to be at Langley's house. Not yet.

Across from him, she turned to look out the window, drawing his gaze to the long, slender column of her golden neck. Jonathan closed his eyes in a long blink, imagining removing her dress. In the depths of his mind, he pictured his hands all over her, floating down her smooth neck, across her shoulders and lower. Touching her, learning how her body had changed in the past six years.

"And Olivia has my strength behind her, too," Phoebe piped up, yanking Jonathan out of the mire of his dissolute thoughts. Thank God.

What the hell had they been talking about? Oh, yes, their sister's illness.

He smiled at her. "And yours, too, of course, Miss Phoebe."

God, what was he doing here? With Meg Donovan sitting across from him, making his mind whirl and his body hot and hard all over?

He was dreaming if he thought anything could come of this. She was forbidden to him. She wasn't his—she was Langley's. And, damn it, she wasn't Serena!

He was making himself crazy over the impossible. Despite whatever dark secret she struggled to hide, it was clear she intended to marry William Langley. Langley was his friend.

And once she'd married him, what then? Jonathan would go back to the life he'd lived for the past six years. The debauchery, the "pleasure," the underlying sourness of it all.

She was a dream, an illusion in white silk and pearls. God, she was beautiful. Her beauty squeezed his chest so tight he could hardly breathe.

Why did Serena have to have a twin? Perhaps she was placed on this earth—two doors down from him, no less—simply to torment him. To remind him of what could have been had he not been so stupid and so weak.

"Why are we on the Strand?" she asked suddenly.

He glanced at the window. The hour was approaching ten o'clock, and it was pitch-dark outside except for the occasional glimmer of the streetlamps. "We're heading to Langley's."

She shook her head, frowning. "This isn't the most direct route to Cavendish Square, though."

He feigned surprise. "It isn't?"

"No." She glanced at him, and then her eyes darkened with understanding. She pursed her lips, giving him a hot stare. There it was again, that mixture of vengeful dislike and hot...*desire*. Jonathan shifted in his seat and tried to appear casual, even though his own body flared back to life in response.

"You're not from London," he said, keeping his voice even. "How could you know the most direct route from St. James's Square to Cavendish Square?"

"Oh, that's easy," Phoebe supplied. "Meg has spent hours studying every inch of our father's map of London."

Meg stared at him, her gaze a sizzling, brazen challenge that wended through him, heating him more.

His stomach twisted. As much as he'd grown tired of his own behavior of the past years, here he was, fantasizing about his friend's future wife. He was beyond redemption.

"I shall have you elucidate my coachman, then, Miss Donovan."

"I'll do that," she said coolly.

He held her gaze, refusing to be the first one to look away.

Several minutes later, the carriage jerked to a halt. Looking out the window, Jonathan saw Langley awaiting them on the curb-stone, his tall, dark form looming like a specter in the light filtering from the front window of his house.

This wasn't over. Jonathan needed to understand what drove this new Meg Donovan. He had to get her alone.

Chapter Five

It was settled. Serena was going to fail, utterly and completely, at this ridiculous attempt at deception. She simply could not control herself in front of Jonathan Dane.

When she'd first been wrenched away from Jonathan six years ago, she thought she might go mad for wanting him. She wanted him so badly that for many nights, she clutched her knees in her arms, rocking her body, trying to force it to forget.

She had dreamed of him coming for her; she had prayed for it late at night when everyone else was asleep and wouldn't hear her pleas. She'd hoped his snub had been some sort of terrible mistake.

But he had never come, of course. He had turned away from her in London, left her brokenhearted and wanting. He'd left her trapped in a loveless life, in a lonely body.

And then there was Will. He slid in across from her to sit beside Jonathan, all polite kindness, as usual. But she'd hurt him at the park last week with her horrid reaction to his kiss, and everything between them since had been nothing more than cool politeness.

At first she'd told herself that Meg would have reacted the same way to that kiss, because Meg was so modest and so innocent. But that was wrong. Meg had *loved* Will. Meg was always proper and reserved, but she would have melted into his kiss like butter. Serena, on the other hand, had jerked away like he was a venomous snake.

She'd spent the past several days trying to think of ways to make it up to him, but she'd drawn a blank. Even now, as he made polite conversation in the confines of the carriage, she saw the hurt of her rejection in his dark eyes.

She was awful. This situation was wretched. If she'd had any inkling that Jonathan and Will were close friends, she would have realized the impossibility of this scheme and have stopped this charade before it began. Now she was caught.

There could be no good resolution to this. She would be found out, and all her hopes for Jessica, Olivia, and Phoebe would be dashed.

The other occupants of the carriage exchanged niceties about the weather and about the exciting events of the upcoming evening while Serena's mind roiled. She remembered to smile at Will, though, and she kept her eyes diligently off Jonathan.

He'd looked surprised when Phoebe had joined them. And clearly he'd told his coachman to take an indirect route to Will's house. Had he planned to confront her?

Please, God, don't let him suspect the truth.

Serena took a deep breath, difficult given the tight constriction of her stays, and focused on the conversation.

"My aunt says that Vauxhall Gardens has become quite vulgar in the past few years, but she said as long as you're there to accompany us, Captain Langley, and since tonight's crowd won't be so vulgar as it will be for the remainder of the summer, she would allow us to attend tonight's opening," Phoebe said.

Serena knew Jonathan's presence tonight worried her aunt and truly regretted the whole plan as much as her aunt disliked it. Will had reassured Aunt Geraldine that Jonathan had turned a new leaf and was trying to regain some status in the realm of respectability. Not wanting to cause Will any undue disappointment, Aunt Geraldine had relented. Serena had reassured her aunt that she'd no intention of speaking beyond the basic necessities to the Earl of Stratford.

Will's gaze slipped to Jonathan and then back to Phoebe. "I haven't been to the pleasure gardens in many years myself, but I believe it to be a place everyone should see at least once."

"I cannot wait," Phoebe said. "There is absolutely nothing like it in all of the West Indies! I can promise you that without ever having been there."

"I'm sure you're right, Phoebe," Serena said. "I've never been to Vauxhall Gardens, either, but from what I've heard, it can be quite a spectacle."

She continued to chat with them about nothing, deliberately keeping her focus more on Will than on Jonathan, and by the time they arrived at the gardens, the tension in the carriage had seemed to dissipate a little.

She walked beside Will while Phoebe, who'd been ecstatic ever since she'd found out they were going to Vauxhall with the devilish earl, bounced alongside Jonathan, her blond curls escaping from her hat in wild coils, and they joined the throng passing through the gate.

Rows of circular lamps marked the way, their golden glow lighting the trail, and Jonathan led them down a great path lined with stately elm trees toward a square, where an orchestra, set in a Greek-style temple and illuminated by hundreds of twinkling lanterns, played the familiar strains of Handel.

He led them to one of the small apartments enclosed on three sides and opening toward the orchestra. They were served Vauxhall's famous thin-sliced ham, roasted chicken, baskets of biscuits and cakes, and a bottle of champagne.

Phoebe's blue eyes were round as saucers as she

alternated between gazing at the orchestra and the passing throngs of people. Serena halfheartedly picked at her ham and tried to ignore Jonathan.

One by one, ladies and young gentlemen emerged from the passing throng to dance. Serena watched in fascination as the number of dancers grew, until entire families held hands to dance on the expansive graveled area beside the orchestra.

Phoebe gazed at the dancing crowd with glowing eyes. She clasped her hands together at her chest. "Oh, I'd so love to dance."

Will glanced at Jonathan, who busied himself with taking a bite of spice-cake, leaving him free to ignore Phoebe's statement. Serena met Will's gaze. He frowned at her, a silent question. Will knew how she felt—correction, how *Meg* felt—about Jonathan. Even though her heart began to clang against her breastbone, Serena gave him a nod to say she'd be all right. With a nearly indecipherable sigh, Will turned to Phoebe and asked her if she would dance with him.

She sprang up from her chair and held out her hands. "Oh, yes, please!"

When they disappeared into the crowd, Serena gazed at the round lanterns strung from branch to branch of the tall elms. She studied the colorful dresses of the ladies, their feathered hats, the men dressed sharply in dark colors and tall hats. She watched the musicians and allowed the vibrant music to flow through her. She inhaled deeply the smells of earth and people mingling with fresh-baked meats and pastries.

She gazed at the sky. Far above the roof of the orchestra's Grecian temple, the stars winked at her, mocking. She blinked and looked down, her gaze colliding with Jonathan's.

The corner of his lips quirked up in a smile, but his expression was questioning.

She took a steadying breath and leaned toward him so he'd hear her over the sounds of the music and crowd. "Everything is so different here. It's a different world."

"There must be parties, balls, soirees, dinners, in Antigua. Events and people that link you to England."

She shrugged. "Yes, there are, and they do provide a link, but at times it seems very weak."

Jonathan's blue eyes remained steadily focused on her. As if nothing else existed besides her. It was how he had looked at her six years ago, when she'd thought he loved her. He'd made her feel like the only woman in the world. Powerful, but also sheltered and protected. Safe.

She released a cynical chuckle. How false those feelings had been. How silly. He probably made all women feel that way. She remembered how the other young ladies had whispered about him before. "He's soooo handsome," "Oh, he touched my wrist! I declare I shall not wash it for a month!"

And now . . . he was so much more. Women probably fell prostrate at his feet on a daily basis.

She swallowed down a feeling of disgust and turned away. She didn't know exactly what she was disgusted by. Perhaps it was the idea of other women being taken in by him as she had been. Perhaps it was the idea of herself being taken in by him all over again.

Still his eyes burned into her. She could feel their heated caress over her.

"Would you like to dance?" he asked as her gaze strayed once again to the crowd near the orchestra.

"No, thank you." Her voice was stiff. Uncomfortable.

"How about a short walk? We could return before they are finished."

"No. Thank you."

"You've made my friend a very happy man," he said.

Her gaze shot to his. "Have I?"

He nodded, his expression thoughtful as he continued to study her. "He wasn't certain. So much distance had separated the two of you, and for so long. When he received your acceptance of his proposal, he was the happiest I've ever seen him."

How could she answer that? She couldn't. She kept her mouth shut. It was her mother who had accepted Will's proposal, for God's sake. Not her.

"Did you write to Langley often in the past

years?" Jonathan's polite voice masked something deeper. He probed under her skin, hoping to pry out the truth. She wouldn't let him.

"I did. At least once a month." She knew that much, at least. Mother had locked herself in her bedchamber on the first day of every month, and for years Serena and her sisters had no idea what she did up there. Now she knew: she'd been penning love letters to William Langley in her dead daughter's name.

Jonathan nodded. "It's fascinating that you were able to remain so close for so long with such a vast geographical separation between the two of you."

"Captain Langley is an honorable man," Serena said quietly, not sure—and not caring—if he heard her. She remembered Meg with him. Serena had always approved of the match between her sister and Will—the two of them were so well suited, and she knew without a doubt that Will would make her sister happy.

Thinking Meg was alive and Serena was the one who'd died that day—the lie her mother had led all of England to believe—Will had devotedly written her a letter every month. Sometimes, Mother had said, they'd arrived in batches because he'd written to her at sea and months had passed before he could properly mail them. But write he had, and mail he had, until he sold his commission, returned to London, and was in a position to offer for her. Only a good man, a devoted man, would do such a thing.

How could Serena live up to that? How could she

expect Will to remain in love with a Meg who no longer existed? Meg, with her innate goodness, could inspire such devotion in a man without even trying. Serena, on the other hand, had never succeeded in inspiring devotion in anyone.

"Yes," Jonathan agreed. "He is perhaps the most honorable man I have ever known." He paused, then said, "He loves you, you know."

Serena drew back, shaken. "Does he?"

That was not a very Meg thing to say. *Control yourself, Serena!*

She held Jonathan's gaze for long, crackling moments. The hair on the back of her neck rose, and her skin prickled all over. It was hot within the confines of her dress, and she could hardly breathe.

"I love you, you know," Jonathan had whispered in her ear, just before he'd taken her for the first time. "I love you so much."

He was a liar.

Finally, he smiled, but the expression was a bitter one. "Yes, he does love you. As I loved your sister."

She jumped to her feet. The legs of her chair scraped over the ground as she pushed it back. In less than a second, he had risen, too.

"I did love her." His gaze met hers, burning hot, testing her.

Serena pressed her lips together. She didn't trust herself to speak. She gave a firm shake of her head and stared at him, denial burning in her eyes. *Liar.*

"I never forgot her."

She ground her teeth. "If you loved...my sister, you never would have hurt her."

Stark, icy pain crept over his features, crumpling them, and he closed his eyes for a long moment. When he opened them again, they were dark with regret. "I was young. I was weak. I believed I had no other choice."

Her lip curled, and she made a scoffing noise. Another gesture that wasn't Meg, but then again, Meg wasn't a weakling. If she stood here in Serena's place, Serena knew her sister would have stood up for her.

Jonathan leaned forward and placed his palms flat on the table. "My father threatened to disown me, and I was a coward. I hadn't the first idea what to do without the support of my family. I fought them, but they crushed me. My father swore he'd drag me to Sussex and lock me up until she was gone."

"That's all well and good," Serena said coldly. "But you cut her. Publicly. You destroyed her reputation. Her future."

He shook his head, and now his blue eyes had flattened, turned hard and cold. With anger at her, at himself, or at his family, she couldn't say. "I was stupid and foolish. I didn't understand what I was allowing to walk away from me. I didn't know what to do."

She stared at him, feeling the icy chill of her own expression enveloping her.

He almost spoke too quietly for her to hear. But

she did hear. She read it on his lips. "Until it was too late."

"Well, it *is* too late," she shot back. "Serena is gone forever."

And she realized she spoke of herself as well as her sister. Serena *was* gone forever. Her identity had been wiped clean, and she'd been given a new, albeit familiar, one. Serena had never really thought of it that way. But she *was* Meg now. She'd never be Serena Donovan again. Serena Donovan was dead.

Pain knotted her stomach, but she didn't break her gaze away from the Earl of Stratford.

"No," he said. "She won't come back. I'd do anything to change that."

"So would I."

He nodded.

"But it's too late," she said.

"I am sorry."

"So am I."

He claimed he'd loved her, that he'd never forgotten her. Should she believe him? Could she? It seemed far safer to continue hating him, to continue blaming him for all the pain he'd caused her. If she forgave him... then what?

She didn't dare trust him. She'd believed his protestations of love once, and look what had become of that. In any case, he hadn't taken long to mourn her loss. Just after her "death," he'd gone off to Bath to seduce someone else.

They stood there, locked in a silent battle of—well, Serena couldn't know exactly what—until a hand pressed gently on her shoulder.

"Meg?"

She jerked her head around. Will stood there, a look of concern etched on his handsome face.

"Are you all right?" He glanced at Jonathan, frowning.

She forcibly relaxed. "Yes, yes, of course I am. We were just standing..." Her voice dwindled. She couldn't think of a single reason they might be standing.

"...to get some oranges," Jonathan supplied. A glance at him revealed an easy smile and relaxed posture. How did he do that? Only a lack of caring, she decided, could allow him to pretend so easily that nothing had happened. "There's a vendor near the rotunda. Would you like one, Langley?"

Will stood beside her. Will was the man she was to marry. Will deserved none of this deceit, and she didn't want to hurt him. She certainly would not hurt him by being a fool about Jonathan Dane.

"Oh, an orange!" Phoebe exclaimed, rushing in behind Will and bouncing on her toes. "Oh, yes, please!"

As soon as Jonathan turned to go, Phoebe continued. "Meg, you absolutely must dance the next set! It's so much fun!"

Serena pressed her fingers to the bridge of her

nose and squeezed tightly. "Well—" she began, but then Phoebe cut her off with an exclamation of pleasure.

"Mr. Harper!"

Serena spun around to see a young gentleman approaching them, tall and dark, his eyes on Phoebe, who clasped her hands to her chest, her eyes shining in pleasure. "Oh, just when I thought nothing could be lovelier about tonight, you appear!"

Serena sucked in a sharp breath. Phoebe was outgoing and sometimes said embarrassingly improper things, but she'd never known her as a flirt.

The gentleman bowed, took Phoebe's hand, and pressed a kiss to her glove. "Miss Phoebe. The pleasure is all mine."

Will stiffened beside Serena, and a gush of affection swept through her. How noble he was to feel protective of her sister.

"Good evening, Harper." Will's voice was even, as always, but there was a warning edge to it that Serena had never heard before.

Mr. Harper jerked his head up. He looked blankly at them for a moment, as if he hadn't registered their presence before, and then he offered them a charming smile. "Ah, good evening, Langley. And Miss Donovan."

Serena inclined her head at the younger man. She remembered him from the soiree now, as one of the many gentlemen Will had introduced to her.

Sebastian Harper, brother to one of the lieutenants who'd worked under Will's command. Their family wasn't old and distinguished as Serena's mother's was, and they possessed no fortune. Sebastian Harper was a gentleman, but hardly—he stood several steps back from the fine line that divided the select few of the *haute ton* from the masses who made up the rest of the world.

He was young. Couldn't be a day over twenty-one. And clearly, from the way Phoebe looked at him, her cheeks flushed and her eyes gazing in rapture at his face, she was strongly affected by this man.

Serena wasn't sure what to think about that. Phoebe's first Season was planned for next year, when Mother would have the money—via Serena—to fund it. Then they intended to find Phoebe a wealthy and hopefully titled husband the proper way. Now was too early, and Serena knew her family would find such a man unworthy of Phoebe's beauty and connections, despite her lack of fortune.

An association between these two could only lead to scandal. And possibly heartbreak for poor Phoebe. Serena sighed.

Harper's gaze turned back to Phoebe. "Would you like to dance?"

The first chords of a waltz were playing, and Serena opened her mouth to say no.

"Oh, yes!" Phoebe exclaimed. "I'd love to!"

A slow grin spread over his features, and suddenly

Serena could see what her sister saw in him. He was extraordinarily handsome, in a surprising way. Serena had the feeling he could transform from gracious gentleman to lethal adversary in a matter of seconds.

Before she could utter a word, he said, "Let's go," and grasping on to Phoebe's hand, he tugged her away. The crowd closed around them, leaving Serena gazing after them openmouthed.

Will sighed, and Jonathan returned with four oranges, which he set down on the table. She took one of them and without sitting, began to tear the peel away, her eyes scanning the crowd.

"Would you like to dance, Meg?" Will asked.

"I..." She cast him an apologetic look. "I'm sorry, I'm not feeling well disposed to dancing tonight."

"Would you like to go for a walk instead?"

She looked into the crowd to see Mr. Harper and Phoebe waltzing, both of them looking as though they were having a wonderful time. She wouldn't stare at them the entire time like some old harridan of a chaperone.

"Yes," she said to Will, "that sounds nice."

Will glanced at Jonathan, who pressed his lips tightly together, no doubt remembering that she'd refused to walk with him.

"Miss Phoebe is dancing with Sebastian Harper," Will informed him.

Jonathan nodded, and Serena wasn't sure if it was her imagination that his eyes narrowed slightly.

"Will you keep an eye on them?" Will asked.

"Of course."

"We'll be back shortly," Serena promised.

Side by side, she and Will left the crowded dining area and strolled onto one of the wide paths. It was still very bright along here, with strings of round lanterns lighting their way.

"It is beautiful," she murmured, eating a slice of orange.

"It is a lovely night. But Vauxhall..."—he side-stepped a piece of trash littering the path and steered her clear of it—"it isn't what it used to be."

She looked up at him. "How do you remember Vauxhall Gardens?"

"When I was a boy, my parents brought me here once a week during the summer. My father—when he was in Town, which was seldom as he was also an officer in the Navy—would buy me treats, and I'd lick at my confections and watch the fireworks. It was different then. Hard to define exactly how."

"I think it's difficult to return to a place you've glorified in your mind for so long, only to realize it isn't quite as heavenly as your memory would have you believe." It reminded her of the first time she'd returned to London six years ago. It had seemed so changed from how she'd remembered it—so dirty, crowded, and loud. And the smells...

Will's lips curled in one of his half smiles. "That's probably true."

Her stomach began to settle. Out here with Will, she felt so much safer than she had moments earlier when she was alone with Jonathan.

"Were you all right with Stratford?" Will asked quietly. "He didn't say anything, did he?"

She flinched, then realized the truth couldn't be destructive, at least not in this case. "He apologized for what he did to Serena."

"Did he?" Will's gaze slanted toward her. "And do you forgive him?"

"I . . . I am trying."

"You looked angry."

She chewed on an orange slice thoughtfully and gazed at the path that stretched before them, glowing gold in the light of the lanterns. "I know. I was angry—a little. He was offering excuses when there can be no excuse for what he did to my sister. Yet he truly did seem remorseful."

"I believe he *is* remorseful."

Serena said nothing.

Will's voice was quiet. "I told you before that I'd like to remain his friend. But if you'd prefer, Meg, I can exclude him from our social sphere."

"Oh, no, Will, you mustn't do that."

He nodded somberly. "His friendship is important to me, and I think it's important to him, too. However, I wouldn't want my friendship with him to stand in the way of us."

"It won't," she reassured him. She didn't know

why she was so quick to reject his proposal, though. It would make it far easier for her if Will eliminated Jonathan from their lives forever. Perhaps it was guilt—she didn't want to disrupt Will's life any more than she already had.

They walked in silence for some time, finishing their oranges before they turned down another path, this one maze-like, with high shrubbery on both sides. They passed people every few moments, lovers and families with young children. Finally, deep in the gardens, the lights hung more sparsely and they were afforded a semblance of privacy. Music filtered through the trees and shrubs, but the sound was gentle, muted.

"Will?"

"Yes?"

"I'm so very sorry about how I behaved when you kissed me at Hyde Park last week."

"Think nothing of it." But his arm muscles contracted under her hand.

She took in a deep breath. In truth, she didn't know if Meg had ever kissed Will. She hadn't asked Meg, because she'd simply assumed they hadn't kissed. They were both such good, moral people, she couldn't imagine they had. After last week, though, she wasn't so certain.

"It's just that... it's been so long," she murmured. "I was caught off guard."

She looked up at him and took what must sound

like a steadying breath. A breath like one Meg would take in this situation. "It won't happen again."

"Please forgive me," he said stiffly. "It was rash of me to assume—"

"No!" She curled her fingers tightly around his arm. "It wasn't rash. We're to be married at the end of summer. It's altogether proper that we spend time together, that we learn more about each other. At least a little."

His forearm was like a stone beneath her hand.

She stopped walking, drawing him to a halt beside her. What she wanted to do was command him to forget this foolishness and kiss her now so that they could get past this moment of tension. But that wasn't how Meg would have said it. So instead, Serena looked up into his eyes and said, "Will . . . If you don't mind very much . . . I would like to try it again."

Chapter Six

Sebastian Harper was the most beautiful man Phoebe had ever met. He was tall and dark, with expressive, changeable hazel eyes that focused solely on her whenever she was near him. His body pressed up against hers as they waltzed, and it was hard all over. So masculine, so strong, it made her feel weak and delicate in comparison.

Nothing had ever made her feel weak or delicate before. It was rather shocking, really, to realize that she liked it.

As they danced, they gazed into each other's eyes, and suddenly, it struck her like a mallet. She was in love. Truly, deeply, *madly* in love.

He spun her around, and for a moment she focused on the steps so she didn't trip over his feet. She'd danced her share of waltzes back home in Antigua, but none of them were this fast. And none of them had been with a man who made her skin prickle and her heart flutter.

He slowed, and she felt the low rumble of laughter in his chest. "You're very good at this."

She raised a brow at him. "Waltzing? I don't think so!"

"But you are," he said. "I've waltzed with women before, but never..." He hesitated, then gifted her with a smile that made her heart tumble. "Never anyone like you."

She scrunched her brows together. "Are you flattering me, Mr. Harper?"

"I wish you'd call me Sebastian."

She absorbed his first name, took a moment to savor it, and then said, "Are you flattering me... Sebastian?"

He didn't take his eyes from hers. They remained steady on her, delectably intent. "No."

She smiled then, power surging in her chest as they maneuvered past another dancing couple. These feelings were so odd—power and delicacy, strength and weakness. They pulsed through her, confusing and heady. Beyond anything, they excited her.

He held her tightly against him, led her through the motions of the dance with sure, strong steps. He was much taller than her, and when he bent his head, his lips brushed the top of her ear.

"Come away from all these people with me."

"But I can't leave—"

"Just for a few minutes. I want to see you—talk to you—without all these bodies pressing in on us."

How could she refuse? She didn't want to refuse. She didn't care what Serena would think. Ever since Meg had died, Serena had been far too prim and proper for her own good.

Anyhow, she wasn't a little girl anymore, despite what her older sister might think. Serena would still be treating her like a child when she was thirty. She smiled up at him. "All right."

"This way."

He took her hand, and together they slipped through the crowd. At the edge of the dance floor, he led her down a narrow, dark path.

When they were far enough from the orchestra, and she was certain no one would bother them, he stopped and turned to her.

"What is it about you?" he murmured. He took off his black glove and moved the back of his hand down her face. It felt so good, she pressed her cheek against his touch.

"I should ask you the same."

They stared at each other, and she knew he felt it, too. That confounding, beautiful attraction, that invisible force drawing them together.

There it was: incontrovertible proof that love at first sight did exist. She knew very little of this man besides the fact that his brother had served in the

Navy with Captain Langley. But the feelings she had for him were inexplicably intense.

"We can't stay out here long, but I"—he swallowed hard—"I need—I want to see you again, Phoebe."

She fought a smile and tilted her head to look up at him. "I want to see you, too."

"Soon. Tomorrow." His dark eyes remained steady on her. It wasn't a question. He stated it as a fact, as if he knew she wouldn't deny him. As if he knew she didn't want to deny him.

"Yes." She allowed her smile to spread her lips wide. "Tomorrow."

"Meet me at midnight in the garden pavilion behind your aunt's house."

She nodded, her heartbeat surging in excitement along with the rising crescendo of music. Oh, she couldn't wait till tomorrow. Where would he take her? What would they do? Would he want to have carnal relations with her?

Something trembled inside her at that thought. Would she willingly give her body to this man?

Yes, she would. Because she'd never seen anyone more strikingly handsome than Sebastian Harper. Because she'd never been attracted to anyone even a tiny fraction as much as she was now attracted to him.

They smiled at each other, and Phoebe's heart surged in triumph. This was him. It had happened more quickly than she'd suspected, but she had chosen the one man in London she wanted.

After Meg and Langley left the supper box, Jonathan had sat for a while in brooding silence, staring after them and tossing back his champagne. If Meg had been avoiding him before, she was doubly avoiding him now.

And why the hell did he feel jealous that she'd gone off with Langley when she'd refused to walk with him? She was engaged to Langley, not to him. She was Meg Donovan, not Serena Donovan. They looked alike, but they had very distinct personalities. He kept telling himself that. He *knew* that.

After several minutes had passed, he realized he'd lost sight of Phoebe and that deuced youth, Harper, in the crowd. Jonathan's gaze sifted through the waltzing couples, searching for them. He hoped to hell Harper hadn't cast his net for Phoebe. The Donovan sisters didn't need the kind of trouble that would entail.

But his mind kept drifting back to Meg.

What was Langley saying to her? What was Langley *doing* to her?

The thought of Langley touching Meg made his blood boil. It made his whole body ache with a painful kind of rage, a hot poison that seeped into his muscles and burned. The thought of Langley putting his lips on that soft, sweet skin...

His fists curled at his side, tingling. Aching to punch something.

He'd take his fury out in the boxing ring tomorrow. For now... He stood and thrust himself into the crowd, looking for Phoebe and Harper in the swarm of bodies.

Such a fiery emotion had blazed in Meg's eyes after he'd mentioned his love for her sister. The way she spoke to him—it wasn't how he'd ever heard Meg speak.

Yes, six years could change a person, but could six years alter a person in such a drastic way? Jonathan didn't think so.

Seconds before Harper had appeared—the way she'd brought her thumb and forefinger to the bridge of her nose and squeezed—that was something Serena often did when she sought relief from stress.

Once, they'd been lying in the grass bemoaning the obstacles preventing them from staying together, and he had mentioned how his father wanted him to marry an aristocratic, titled lady. Serena hadn't spoken; instead, she'd closed her eyes and pinched the bridge of her nose. He'd drawn her hand away and kissed both sides of her nose where her fingers had left white spots because she'd pressed so hard.

"Why do you do that?" he'd asked, moving his lips down to graze hers.

"I don't know," she said, her breath feathering over his mouth as she spoke. "It helps me to think, I suppose."

"Is it a trait you share with your sister?" The similarities and differences between Meg and Serena fascinated him.

"I don't think so," she'd mused. "I've never seen her do it."

He nearly stumbled over one of the dancing couples. Quickly righting himself as the man saved the woman from a disastrous fall, he muttered, "Sorry," and turned away.

As impossible as it sounded, she *could* be Serena. All the signs said she was. But how could he be sure?

The waltz came to an end, and Jonathan found himself standing in the center of the crowd of dispersing dancers. Blinking himself back into the present, he turned slowly, looking for Serena. No...no, he was searching for Phoebe and Harper.

No sign of them. Where the hell had they gone?

The better question was, where would Harper take a girl like Phoebe? Somewhere quiet and dark, no doubt, where he could work his wiles on her.

He'd have to warn the man away from Phoebe, somehow.

He almost laughed aloud at that thought. What was he now, the protector of ladies' virtue? Ridiculous. He hardly knew Phoebe Donovan.

In any case, who was he to think ill of the places where he'd seen Harper? The activities in which he'd seen him engaging? Jonathan himself had been in those same places, doing the same things.

Langley knew about Harper, too. Why the hell had he allowed Phoebe to dance with him? He remembered seeing them dance at Langley's soiree, and he sighed. Langley tended to think the best of people. He should be more discerning in whom he chose to befriend. Then again, if he did that, he would have done away with Jonathan as a friend long ago.

Jonathan skirted the edge of the dancers, trying to think like a young man with a beautiful woman on his arm might think. He thought of the time he had been in a similar situation with Serena. The night they'd met, he'd been eager to speak to her privately. They'd watched a young lady performing on a pianoforte, but he'd barely paid attention to the girl.

When an intermission in the interminable performance finally came, he'd wrangled an introduction to Serena, then considered himself enormously fortunate to have the opportunity to speak to her alone. He'd led her out onto the balcony.

An earlier rain had cooled the air and left a slick of water on the balcony floor, an atmosphere unappealing to most of the attendees of the recital, but perfect for Jonathan and Serena. They'd stood there talking, their heads bent close and their breaths releasing in puffs of fog, until her aunt had stomped out and dragged her away.

She'd looked back over her shoulder at him as she'd left, and that look—a look of longing, interest, and desire—had smacked Jonathan square in the chest. He'd felt the same way. He would have given anything for her not to leave. He'd wanted to talk to her all night, then make love to her and wake up beside her the next morning.

He'd never felt emotions like that.

From that point onward, he'd pursued her relentlessly. When he finally possessed her completely, he thought he would lose interest, but it hadn't happened that way. Their first time had been on a vast lawn behind the stables of a Mayfair house, where they'd been attending a large assembly. After that, he'd only wanted her more. He'd been obsessed. So much so that he'd made that fatal mistake on the night of the Dowager Duchess of Clayworth's ball.

Jonathan took one of the narrower, more private-looking paths off the Great Walk. He passed a few strolling couples, but as he progressed deeper into the gardens, the path grew quieter and lonelier, the crunch of gravel beneath his feet seeming loud over the distant strains of the orchestra.

He saw them. A couple paused at the edge of the path as it swerved sharply to the right, deep in conversation. He breathed out a sigh of relief, but then the lady moved and recognition shot through him.

The lady was wearing white, not yellow, and her hair was a shade darker than Phoebe Donovan's. The man was dark haired like Sebastian Harper, but he was taller and leaner. Older.

Every muscle in Jonathan's body snapped into

stiff outrage. This wasn't Phoebe and Sebastian leaning toward each other like lovers.

It was Langley and his affianced bride... and for God's sake, Jonathan could swear that was Serena Donovan and not Meg.

Serena stared at Will. His hesitation was palpable. Had she already ruined things with him? Did he want to call off the wedding? Had she botched it so badly that in the space of just a few days, he'd already fallen out of love with Meg?

Then she saw the sheen of sweat at his temple, however and he took her hand between his own and squeezed tight.

"I don't want to hurt you, Meg. Or frighten you."

"You won't hurt me. And I'm not afraid." She was afraid, mind-numbingly so. But not in the way he thought.

Deep inside, Serena knew she had nothing to fear from Will Langley. He was an honest man, a good man. He wouldn't harm her.

He shook his head, but then he bent closer and his lips touched hers. Soft, gentle, the slightest brush. It was nice, even nicer than the last time. So nice she didn't exactly know how to respond.

This was not how she'd been kissed in the past. It was not the voracious, hungry kiss of Jonathan Dane, who'd kissed her as though a viper had filled his body with deadly venom and her lips were the only antidote.

Will Langley's kiss was hesitant and sweet, but Serena sensed a great, throbbing tension behind it. Something told her that beyond all this restraint, Will possessed just as much sensual power as Jonathan had.

Did Jonathan still kiss like that?

She slipped her arms around Will and pushed away the awful thought. How wicked to think of another man when the man who was kissing you was doing such a...*nice* job of it.

She parted her lips slightly, moving them over his, so warm and soft in the chill of the evening.

The tension in her shoulders eased. If she could forget her horrid deception and focus on Will, on his kindness and gentleness, and stop worrying about everything else, then perhaps this could work.

A life with Will would be safe and comfortable. Since Meg had died, she'd felt neither safe nor comfortable, and there was a great appeal in both.

If she could stay in Meg's skin, work on being more like Meg...perhaps she could be happy. Perhaps she could make Will happy, too. After six years spent wooing a ghost, he deserved a little happiness.

Someone close behind her cleared his throat harshly, and Will jerked away from her. She leaped back, her cheeks heating, and turned slowly, hoping it wasn't a family with a half dozen children all staring openmouthed at her and Will.

It wasn't a family. It was worse: Jonathan Dane, his features tight, his mouth set, his eyes narrow.

His gaze clashed with hers, and Serena's flush deepened. He stared at her for a long moment, his jaw twitching and his shoulders radiating tension beneath his fine wool coat.

Finally he spoke in a stiff voice. "Forgive me for interrupting, Miss Donovan. Langley." He nodded in Will's direction but kept his focus entirely on Serena. "But you must come right away. Your sister is missing."

With a beautiful scowl Jonathan could never have attributed to the Meg he'd known, she lifted her skirts and marched back toward the orchestra. He and Langley followed just behind. Once they arrived at the still empty supper box, she stood outside, hands on hips, surveying the even more crowded dancing area.

She turned back to the two men. "I'll search the crowd. Lord Stratford, if you could investigate the area back there?" She gestured toward the vicinity behind the supper boxes.

"Of course," Jonathan said.

"And Will, would you please inspect the paths leading off the Great Walk?"

Langley nodded his agreement.

"Good," she said, her gaze already scanning the throng. "I shall meet with you here in a quarter of an hour."

As Meg strode into the crowd, Jonathan rounded

the corner of the supper box. Back here the grounds were more densely wooded, and it took a few moments for his eyes to adjust to the relative dimness.

Jonathan's fists balled at his sides as he surveyed the area. Damn it. He regretted suggesting this outing. There were far too many places in Vauxhall Gardens to compromise a young lady. Langley and Meg had left him responsible, and if that deuced Harper had ruined Serena's sister…

He spied a dark, empty path between two elms. It looked like a service path rather than a path meant for visitors strolling. At the end of it there might be a storehouse or something of the sort.

Here. If he was young and pursuing Serena, he'd bring her here. Somewhere quiet, dark, unobtrusive.

With a grim smile, he strode down the path, and sure enough, in a few moments, he heard the tinkle of Phoebe's laughter.

He rounded a bend in the path and reeled to a halt. Harper and Phoebe were standing head to head, laughing, touching nowhere but at their entwined hands. Both looked up in surprise at his approach, the smiles slipping from their faces.

Anger, sadness, and regret twisted into a hard knot in his gut. He scowled at them, feeling as ancient as the chestnut tree they stood beneath. The expressions on their faces reminded him so much of himself and Serena six years ago.

He focused on Phoebe. He'd deal with the eager pup later. Harper must know that a lady like Phoebe was beyond his scope.

"Your sister asked me to keep an eye on you. You worried me, Miss Phoebe."

She had the grace to flush, and she glanced guiltily at Harper. "Sorry, my lord."

He gave her a stern nod. "Let us return, then. Your sister is distraught. She and Captain Langley are searching the whole of the gardens for you."

"Yes, of course." Tucking her lower lip between her teeth, she untangled her fingers from Harper's.

Jonathan swiveled on his heel in military fashion and led the two lovers back down the path and to the supper box. Within a few moments, Langley joined them, and then Meg—*or Serena*—arrived, her cheeks flushed with concern.

Jonathan glanced back at Phoebe and Harper, pasting a disapproving frown over his features.

Phoebe surged forward to allay her sister's worries, and Harper tried to follow, but Jonathan grabbed his arm and held him back. Remembering the lad's famous temper, he bit back his own.

Harper looked from his arm to Jonathan's face, one dark brow raised.

"Stay away from her," Jonathan murmured, low enough that Langley couldn't hear.

"No."

Jonathan tightened his fingers over the man's arm.

"She's a lady. Different from the women you usually associate with."

Harper's lips twisted. "And from the women you usually associate with, my lord."

True as that was, it was none of this boy's business, and Jonathan narrowed his eyes. "Don't push me."

"I'm not afraid of you, Stratford."

Jonathan knew that was true. The stupid pup wasn't afraid of anyone. He dropped his hand. "Just stay away from her." He spoke just loudly enough to be heard over the booming music of the orchestra. "I say this not only for her virtue, but for your sanity. Whatever happens, it will not end well. I guarantee it."

With a scoff, Harper turned away and went to join Phoebe and the others.

Jonathan took a few seconds to compose himself, and then he followed. Harper was making his adieus, but Jonathan hardly paid attention. How could he when Meg-or-Serena Donovan was standing inches away from him, diligently keeping her attention focused on Langley? Why did she try so hard?

Jonathan curled his fingers into fists. As soon as he could get the oldest living Donovan sister alone, he was going to prove his theory.

Chapter Seven

A few nights after the excursion to Vauxhall Gardens, Jonathan decided to make an overdue visit to his club. Afterward, he'd make his monthly appearance at Stone's gambling hell.

He had no interest in engaging in his usual activities in either place, really, but if he kept himself locked in his house, people would begin to talk. And as of late, Jonathan was loath to draw attention to himself. Tonight, he would be home by midnight, and he'd be sober.

He handed his hat, gloves, and cane to the porter and mounted the stairs to the first-floor gaming room at White's. The room, brightly lit with wall sconces and two glittering chandeliers, smelled of cheroot smoke and hummed with conversation. After a long moment of picking through dark-colored tailcoats, Jonathan spotted Langley sprawling in an armchair.

Langley didn't see him at first, and Jonathan considered turning around, slipping out the door, and offering some excuse later. The last thing Jonathan wanted to do was discuss his suspicions regarding Meg Donovan with Langley, or anyone else for that matter.

Hell. Just thinking about Serena—about her soft breasts, her creamy skin, her sweet voice—made him hard all over.

Langley would kill him if he knew Jonathan was having these thoughts.

Hell, he wished he *weren't* having these thoughts. Of all the men in the world, Langley was the least worthy of Jonathan's betrayal. After all Jonathan and Langley had been through together in the past years, Jonathan was an ass to be thinking about Langley's betrothed in such a scandalous way, regardless of her true identity. Langley deserved far better from his best friend.

Langley spotted him, spoke to someone obscured by a pillar, and beckoned him over, smiling.

Steeling himself, he crossed to Langley, pinching a glass of port from a tray on the way.

"Welcome back." Langley rose from his chair to clasp Jonathan's shoulder. "Haven't seen you here in weeks."

"I haven't been much in the mood to drink or gamble," Jonathan said mildly. "I've been staying quietly at home, for the most part."

Recognizing Franklin Kincaid as the form hiding behind the pillar, Jonathan greeted him. Kincaid was a man with whom Jonathan had caroused often, but he'd recently developed a fondness for Jonathan's widowed cousin, Jane, Lady Montgomery, and they'd been exclusive lovers for several months now.

Kincaid gazed at Jonathan with an inscrutable expression, then held out his hand. "It's been a while, Stratford. Have you abandoned all your old haunting grounds?"

Jonathan shrugged as he took the other man's hand. "Kincaid." He didn't answer the question.

"Allow me to guess." Kincaid's silvery brows drew together, and he gripped Jonathan's hand tightly, not letting go. "Ah, I've got it. You've developed a *tendre* for some innocent society miss, and we're doomed to lose you to the shackles as we've lost Langley here." He grinned at Langley.

Jonathan met Langley's eyes for a second and then looked away. "Don't be ridiculous. You are well aware that I intend to remain a bachelor forever."

"Ah, indeed. The famous vow made to your father on his deathbed." Kincaid chuckled.

Jonathan managed to stop a wince before he revealed it to the men. He pulled his hand away from Kincaid's. "Indeed."

"Let's register a wager in the book tonight, eh? It's been months."

"What kind of wager?" Jonathan asked.

"I wager you'll marry within the year. A thousand guineas. What say you?" Kincaid's black eyes twinkled.

Jonathan sighed. Not agreeing to the wager meant that he'd be admitting to the possibility that he planned to marry. Still... "No, thank you."

Kincaid laughed, a raspy, rough sound. "So who's the lucky lady, Stratford?"

Jonathan looked him in the eye. "As I said. No one. I've just had no taste for wagering of late."

"What? The insatiable Stratford has finally had his fill?"

"It seems so."

Langley laid a hand on Kincaid's arm. "There now, Kincaid. Don't push the poor man."

Kincaid turned his attention on Langley. "And what about you, Langley? How goes it with your lovely betrothed?"

"Very well, thank you."

Jonathan knew Langley wouldn't be overtly open with a man like Kincaid, yet the stiffness behind the clipped words surprised him.

"However," Langley continued, some of the tension melting from his shoulders, "I've hardly seen her—I've been called to my offices every day this week."

"What for?" Jonathan asked. Usually Langley's businesses ran smoothly enough while he remained a background figure.

"We're having trouble with Siam—one of our officers refused to be bodily searched upon his ship's arrival into port, and now the king won't allow our ships entry into any of their harbors. We are trying to negotiate a diplomatic solution."

"What happened to the officer?"

Langley sighed. "He's been imprisoned. We are negotiating his release, as well."

The talk moved to Langley's business dealings and to the state of trade in general, and Jonathan sat on a leather settee and engaged himself in the conversation, more than happy to veer away from the topics of marriage and women.

Within two hours, Jonathan escaped White's and walked to Stone's gambling hell in Spring Gardens. The hell wasn't a place he felt forced to pretend to be someone he wasn't, and he'd come like clockwork every month for the past two years.

Today he didn't visit for the usual reasons. He had no plans to drink himself into a stupor or gamble away another few thousand pounds. He came because he had a few items of unfinished business to attend to.

Stone met him at the door. He was a heavyset beaming man with a tall top hat and a thick waistcoat of burgundy heavily embroidered in gold thread.

"A pleasure as always, my lord," he said.

Jonathan gave Stone a nod. "I should like to wrap up my account with you tonight."

"Of course, of course." Stone led him into his office, a poorly ventilated hold of a room, and with a flourish of his puffy hand offered him the only chair. Jonathan declined and withdrew a bank draft from his tailcoat pocket, which he slid across the weathered surface of the desk toward Stone. "This should cover everything I owe."

Stone glanced down at the draft, his eyes dilating when he saw the number written on the draft. Jonathan had owed quite a sum, and he'd paid the entire amount. Stone kept everything on his account and had never questioned him, as if he'd always known Jonathan could be trusted. He'd given the man a few pounds now and then, but usually he was too sotted when he left to remember to pay his bill.

Stone's hell was located in a small, nondescript town house that looked like a well-kept residence from the outside. Inside, it was furnished in dark tones with heavy draperies. The man ran a tight ship that was open seven days a week—there was no need to sacrifice the potential for profit on the Sabbath—and he managed with aplomb the wide variety of sorts that circulated through his doors.

Jonathan left Stone and ascended the stairs to the gaming room. Men packed the vast room, many of them sitting around card tables, focused on their games. A small number of servants milled about, offering drinks; other men stood in clusters, talking in low voices. A few lanterns gave off scarcely enough yellow light for the men to see their cards and their bets.

Jonathan's gaze skimmed over the players. He was acquainted with the vast majority of them. Sebastian Harper was here—this was where he'd first been introduced to the young man months ago. He sat in a seat by the window, playing a fast game of *Rouge et Noir*—a stupid game based purely on chance with the odds heavily in favor of the house. Jonathan had never liked it.

He took a snifter of brandy from a servant and sat alone by the fire. He didn't touch the drink—just rotated his glass and watched the fire sparkle like amber jewels through the liquid.

He remembered Serena underneath him, her hair damp with sweat and peeking out of the edges of a lacy hat. Serena walking with him through the park on a spring day, stealing touches so that her sister and aunt wouldn't see, laughing with him, her bonnet strings dangling from her fingertips and swinging in time to their step. Serena on top of him, the second time they had joined in the loft of her aunt's stable in the middle of the night, her teeth clamped over her lip so she wouldn't cry out as she shuddered in his arms.

A figure lowered himself into the leather chair across from him, drawing Jonathan's attention away from his memories.

"Evening, Stratford. There's a new game of hazard forming. Care to play?" Ralph Charles, a man

Jonathan had seen here often and was on friendly terms with, nervously twirled the edge of his mustache around his finger. It was a habit he often resorted to after a few hours of drinking and losing.

"Ah, good evening, Charles. As for hazard..." Jonathan nearly groaned. There was no use staying here tonight. Jonathan had no interest in drinking, gaming, or even conversation with men he didn't really know. "No, thank you. I was just about to head home for the evening."

A few minutes later, Jonathan had finished his brandy and rose to leave, but when his hand was on the door handle, a loud crash stopped him cold.

"I told you, I'm finished!"

Jonathan turned, keeping his fingers wrapped around the door handle. Harper had turned over the *Rouge et Noir* table, and coins had scattered everywhere. Jonathan sighed, resigned.

"And we said you're not finished until the hand is completed," snapped one of the men who'd been sitting at the table, now rising to his feet. He must be the bank keeper, for he was dressed in the green tailcoat worn by all of Stone's employees.

"I'm late as it is," Harper growled.

Hell, a round of *Rouge et Noir* lasted all of thirty seconds. What was the boy's sudden rush?

The other men scrambled to retrieve the money that had fallen. Harper took no part in the dash to secure his funds—Jonathan could see the note he'd crumpled in his hand. He'd probably snatched up his bet after the round had already begun.

"Not only that," the bank keeper said mildly, "but you cannot leave, for you still owe the bank eighty pounds."

That was a huge sum for Harper, Jonathan knew.

"Deuce it!" Harper growled, thrusting a hand through his black hair. "The bastard knows I'm good for it."

"Mr. Stone insists you pay before you leave us tonight," the bank keeper said. Two other employees now flanked Harper, and another coming in pushed past Jonathan at the door.

Harper glanced around at the other occupants of the room, his face flushed and his dark eyes narrowed. All playing had ceased, and everyone watched the proceedings with interest. Damn it. Jonathan knew the man well enough to understand what his expression meant.

Jonathan discreetly unbuttoned his tailcoat and waistcoat but left them on. The tailcoat was tailored so well it fit like a second skin while allowing him free movement of his arms. His valet should feel gratified later when he explained that he'd taken precautions not to tear off all the buttons.

Harper reeled around as if to march away, but one of Stone's men grabbed his arm. Mistake, Jonathan thought as Harper whipped back and laid his fist into the poor fellow's meaty face.

Chaos erupted. Men leaped into the fray, and Jonathan couldn't tell who was fighting whom. The red embroidery of Harper's tailcoat tumbled beneath a much larger hell employee. Harper wasn't beneath him for long, even though the man must have outweighed him by four stone.

Harper flipped over, straddled the bigger man, and began to pummel him.

For many years now, Jonathan had resorted to hammering out his aggressions in the boxing ring. Today, however, intuition told him brains would serve him better than brawn. Time to drag Harper out of here.

Jonathan plucked him off the larger man and hauled him to his feet. When Harper turned on him, fists raised, he pushed his nose into the younger man's face.

"It's Stratford," he growled. "Watch yourself. You said you wanted to leave. Now is the time. Follow me."

Using the back of his hand to wipe a line of blood away from his nose, Harper nodded. With Jonathan leading the way, they pushed through the open door, leaped downstairs, and burst out the door and onto the street.

It wasn't far from Spring Gardens to St. James's Square. At this time of night during this time of year, Jonathan preferred to walk, and he turned toward home and began to stride down the street. Harper matched his pace, and Jonathan raised a brow at him. "You live in the opposite direction, Harper."

Harper shrugged. "I'll walk you home, my lord."

Seeing a line of blood trickling from Harper's nose, Jonathan passed him his handkerchief. He'd left his hat, gloves, and cane at Stone's, damn it. They'd have to stay—he had no desire to return to the place, and probably wouldn't be welcome after tonight. His valet would be displeased, despite the precautions he'd taken to save his tailcoat and waistcoat.

"Thanks," Harper said. "For your help in there. The bastards said—"

Jonathan raised his hand, stopping the younger man from saying more. He wasn't interested in hearing excuses, anyhow. "You're a friend of a friend. Though you brought that trouble on yourself."

A muscle twitched in Harper's jaw, but he didn't respond. It was odd that he had chosen to walk Jonathan home after he'd caused such a ruckus over a thirty-second game because he'd suddenly realized he was late for something. Jonathan had to admit he was walking faster than the pace Jonathan would have preferred to keep, but unless his business was in St. James's Square...

Jonathan cast an assessing glance at Harper, who dabbed the handkerchief to his nose with one hand while brushing his shoulder-length black hair back with the other.

Interesting.

Harper left Jonathan with a good-bye and another brusque thanks. After Jonathan closed his door behind him, he waited ten beats inside his entry hall before slipping out again in just enough time to see Harper turning down Duke of York Street and passing Lady Alcott's residence, which stood at the corner.

Jonathan followed, keeping close to the wrought iron railings that separated his house, Lady Alcott's, and the house between them from the pavement. After Harper passed Lady Alcott's house, he slipped into the alleyway separating it from the mews. Jonathan followed. At the end of the alley, he paused. Behind Lady Alcott's house, voices murmured in urgent tones, one of them distinctly female.

Jonathan tensed, prepared to stop this illicit meeting. But Harper's expression stopped him. Instead, he flattened his back against the corner of the house and listened.

Sebastian was late. Five minutes late.

Gnawing on her lip, Phoebe turned from the clock on the drawing room mantel and slipped out the back door once again, anxiety rising like a tide within her. What had kept him? Was something wrong? He'd never been late before.

Since the night at Vauxhall Gardens, they'd met seven times. He came to her every other night. The first night, they'd walked, skirting the edge of St. James's Park. She'd seen things she'd never thought to see before—disreputable people making questionable transactions in the dark, loose women selling their wares. But Sebastian had slipped his arm around her and held her close, and even in such surroundings, she'd never felt safer.

Soon she'd forgotten what was happening around her and was sucked into conversation with the man beside her. By the time he brought her home, it was four o'clock in the morning, but it seemed like only moments had passed.

The second time they'd met, he'd taken her to a tavern, where they ate cherry pie and drank ale and again passed away hours deep in conversation. She learned all about his past, about his brothers and his family. His father was a minor landowner in Lancashire, and his four older brothers had purchased commissions in the Navy as soon as they'd come of age. That hadn't appealed to Sebastian, though, so he'd gone instead to London to make something of himself. He was twenty-one now and still undecided about how to spend his life. It wasn't possible, he'd explained to her, for him to be a gentleman of leisure—he simply wasn't a rich man.

She'd told him of her sisters, her mother, and the failure of her father's investment in the plantation at Cedar Place. She told him all about her father's death, Olivia's weakened state from the malaria, and her youngest sister Jessica—the great beauty of the family. Finally, she told him about her mother's failure to manage the plantation and her obsession with her daughters marrying into the aristocracy.

When Phoebe had told him that, he'd looked concerned, and her heart had fluttered. Could he be thinking of marriage? Was his attraction to her more than she'd hoped?

He'd kissed her that night after they'd returned to the garden pavilion. The kiss was tender, romantic, so unlike she'd imagined it would be. So much better. They'd sat on the pavilion steps between two of the Ionic pillars, kissing and whispering, exploring each other through their layers of clothing until the first hint of a gray dawn lit the sky and he urged her to go inside before they were discovered. She'd fallen into her bed, fantasized about him taking off her clothes and touching her… and more.

The third time they'd met, he'd taken her back to Vauxhall Gardens. That night proved to be more raucous than the opening night, with tightrope walkers, trained monkeys, and acrobats performing for a much more boisterous crowd.

He'd bought her an ice and they'd strolled through the gardens, again falling into easy conversation. He'd been solicitous and gentle with her, the same as every one of their prior meetings.

Their liaison wasn't how Phoebe had imagined it would be. She'd imagined a torrid love affair that wouldn't last. This courtship was so much better. It was passionate, but not in the way she'd anticipated. It was subtle, deeper, more contained. He was pursuing her with gentleness and regard she hadn't thought such a demanding, impulsive man would be capable of.

Each time she saw him, her love at first sight transformed into a love born of knowing someone, of respecting and admiring him.

Phoebe hated being separated from Sebastian. She hated the nights they spent apart. After meeting him seven times in total, she knew without a doubt that she wanted to be with him forever.

The sound of footsteps returned her to the present, and she jumped to her feet.

"Sebastian!" She ran into his welcoming arms but pulled back instantly, her hand clapping over her mouth. Blood trickled from his nose, and the flesh around his eye was swollen. "Oh, no! What happened to you?"

"I was in a fight."

"What?" With her stomach churning, she led him to sit on the steps of the garden pavilion. "What happened?"

"I was at a gambling club—a hell."

This came as no surprise. He'd told her he gambled. "What happened?"

"They tried to swindle me." Leaning forward, he rested his elbows on his knees and pressed fingers to his temples. "The bastards were cheating." He took a breath. "I didn't want to drink tonight, because I knew I was coming to see you and I wanted to be sober, and I watched them carefully. They were manipulating the deck so the house would win—I'm sure of it."

"Did you accuse them?"

"No, I just wanted to leave and never return. I grabbed my money and stood, but they said I couldn't go until the hand was finished. Then"—he frowned—"they said I couldn't leave until I paid off my account."

"Did you pay them?"

"No." His brow furrowed. "I don't remember owing anything—I thought I'd paid my debt to them. But I was too angry to argue, and I wanted nothing but to get out of there and come to you. But when I started to leave, one of them grabbed my arm..."

"And...?"

"And all hell broke loose." He groaned softly and lowered his face into his hands.

She slid her arm over his shoulder and squeezed gently. "Can I do anything?"

"Can we...just sit for a while?"

"Yes. But will you be all right?"

"If I'm with you, I'll be more than all right." His expression softened as he looked at her. "You're tired, love."

A thrill sparkled through her. He'd called her

"love." Without even trying to contain her smile, she said, "Aunt Geraldine rouses me from bed at noon, and—" Her heart was always racing when she left him, and she'd found it impossible to fall asleep until late in the morning. She shrugged. "I just miss you when you're not with me."

"I miss you, too." He shook his head and slipped his hand into hers. "Just sit with me for a while, Phoebe. But I'll leave early and you must promise me to get some sleep." He brushed a finger over the tender skin beneath her eye. "I hate to see those dark shadows."

"I promise," she said gravely. And she leaned into his kiss.

Chapter Eight

A few nights later, Serena stood before the mirror, her knees locked, her hands clasped over the back of a chair. Flannery stood behind her, tugging on the laces of her long stays. She held her breath and studied the evening gown that hung from the door of the armoire.

A primrose band covered with tiny embossed pink rosebuds garnished the sleeves and dotted the band around the hem of the pearly silk skirts. The little flowers shimmered in the failing sunlight.

Before they'd left Antigua, Mother had sold most of their furniture so she could order dresses straight from Paris for Phoebe and Serena for the Season. Nothing but the best was sufficient. Mother was the daughter of an earl, and though she'd married lower than her station, she wouldn't advertise the fact that they hardly had enough money to keep food on the table, much less purchase the latest fashions from Paris. She was far too proud.

The gown was the richest thing Serena owned, and she was thankful to have it. She'd been commanded to wear it wisely and guard it with her life. Mother had promised that she'd come to England and whip her to ribbons if she stained it.

Serena couldn't really blame her. Mother had sacrificed so much for this summer, and if everything went as planned, all her hopes for her daughters would soon fall into place.

"Just a little tighter, miss, and we'll get you into that lovely gown," Flannery said cheerfully. She tugged, yanked, and tightened until the stays squeezed Serena from breast to belly button. Goodness. Perhaps she'd been eating too many of those melt-in-the-mouth French rolls.

As the maid finished tying the knot at the base of Serena's spine, the door opened to reveal Phoebe in her special evening dress, a peach silk with a crepe overdress. Not as expensive as Serena's, but far dearer than any of their other dresses.

"Oh, Phoebe, you look lovely!" she said as Phoebe preened.

Serena straightened for Flannery to button her into her dress, eyeing her sister closely in the mirror. Phoebe had been complaining of headaches and exhaustion for the past fortnight, and Serena had been worried about her. She'd even written to Mother about her concerns about her sister's health. "You're looking less tired."

With a mumbled acknowledgment, Phoebe turned away to fetch Serena's bandeau from the dressing table, and with the help of the maid, she fit it on Serena's head. As Flannery worked to shape the curling strands of hair that escaped from the band of the headdress, Phoebe plopped down onto Serena's bed.

"Must we go?" She gave a long-suffering sigh. "You know how I detest everything about Shakespeare."

Serena shrugged. "It wasn't really a choice."

Aunt Geraldine had ordered them to join her at the theater this evening. They were to attend a rendition of *Othello* at the King's Theatre. Unlike her sister, Serena enjoyed Shakespeare, but tonight it seemed rather daunting. Mostly because she'd have to guard her dress for four long hours, making sure nothing dripped on it, she didn't sweat too much, no one stepped on the train...

A sharp knock sounded at the door. It was Aunt Geraldine's housekeeper, Mrs. Waite.

"Lady Alcott wishes to express her concern that you shall be late." Mrs. Waite paused pointedly. "Lady Alcott despises being tardy to any event."

"Even to an hours-long rendition of a play she's no doubt seen dozens of times?" Phoebe shot back, but Serena held up her hand.

"Hush, Phoebe." She turned to Mrs. Waite. "We'll be down in three minutes."

Mrs. Waite nodded sharply. "Very well. I'll have the carriage brought round."

Serena turned to her sister when the older woman left. "Phoebe, you must learn to be more polite."

"Oh, that woman is a virago. Why should I be polite to her?"

Taking a deep breath, Serena adjusted her curls in the mirror, then stood, thanked Flannery, and led Phoebe downstairs. The two young women retrieved their reticules and their shawls and joined Aunt Geraldine, who awaited them in the carriage.

"You are late," their aunt announced when the carriage door clicked shut.

"No, Aunt," Serena corrected politely, sitting on the rear-facing seat across from her aunt. "We've an hour before the play begins. And it isn't far from here, is it?"

The tips of Aunt Geraldine's lips curled downward. "I enjoy seeing the opening production, you know."

Well, they'd certainly miss most of that. Serena closed her mouth and didn't speak for the remainder of the trip as Phoebe fidgeted next to her. Since infancy, Phoebe had never been able to sit still.

They met with some traffic—a fruit cart had overturned in Piccadilly, and by the time they arrived, they had only a quarter of an hour until *Othello* started. A scowling Aunt Geraldine stomped up to her box, but once they were inside, the surroundings distracted Serena from her aunt's poor temper.

The inside of the King's Theatre was blazing with lights. Far below, people crowded the cheap seats, laughing and talking, occasionally pointing up to some personage in the boxes. Aunt Geraldine's box was in the top row center, giving Serena a good view of the aristocratic patrons in the other boxes. Some boxes were empty; others were crowded with chattering people, their jewels and gold embroidery glittering in the gaslight. Serena recognized Lady Montgomery seated in one of them, laughing as she conversed in animated tones with a silver-haired gentleman.

Will arrived just before the performance began. He hardly had enough time to kiss Serena's hand and bow to her aunt and Phoebe before the actors came onto the stage, and he settled into a chair behind them.

The novelty of being at the theater nearly made Serena forget about Will's gaze boring into her back, but it couldn't stop her from remembering the last time—the only other time—she'd been to the theater.

It was the first time she'd ever laid eyes on Jonathan. She'd sat in this very box, which offered an excellent view of him and his family sitting in a lushly appointed box a row higher up and directly opposite Serena and her family.

He'd stared at Serena throughout the performance,

and she hadn't been able to resist staring right back until her aunt had slapped her hand and admonished her for being vulgar.

Now Will stared at her. She could not see his eyes, but she felt them warming her back. Occasionally she heard him speaking in low tones to gentlemen friends of his, who had been wandering in and out of the box since the start of the performance.

She watched *Othello,* and though she could recite some parts of the play along with the players, she sat quiet and still, as Meg would have. Occasionally, she reached to touch Phoebe's knee to settle her sister's incessant squirming.

When intermission came, Aunt Geraldine nudged her and whispered, "Prepare yourself, girl. Here they come."

This, Serena knew, was her true reintroduction to society. Far from those generous people who'd been invited to Will's soiree, tonight there would be gossipmongers looking for some "similarity" between her and the disgraced, deceased Serena, searching for something to criticize.

Suddenly, the box crowded with people, some of whom looked vaguely familiar to Serena, all eyeing her with blatant curiosity. Phoebe disappeared within a group of girls, adding to Serena's discomfort, but Aunt Geraldine moved to one side of her and Will to the other, and together the three of them faced the crowd head-on.

"And who is this lovely creature?" one elderly man asked, nostril hairs quivering as he eyed Serena up and down through a quizzing glass.

Aunt Geraldine and Will made the proper introductions repeatedly until their throats must have scraped raw. Serena fidgeted in her satin slippers—Mother must have sent the shoemaker the wrong sizing for these, for they were too small and pinched her toes. She smiled and curtsied through the pain, however, and did her best to offer pleasant tidbits of conversation.

Until the crowd parted for an elderly woman.

That harsh face, with its beak nose and angry eyes, had etched itself into Serena's mind long ago. She gripped the back of the chair closest to her and watched in mounting horror as the Dowager Duchess of Clayworth approached.

She dragged in a breath, as deep as her restrictive clothing would allow, and willed herself to remain calm. She'd never fainted in her life, but the combination of the tight lacing of her stays and the appearance of the woman who'd brought her life to a grinding halt was enough to bring her perilously close.

Gazing at Serena through eyes the color of storm clouds, the dowager pursed her lips until they were barely visible. She flung her hand back imperiously. "My spectacles, Rae Ann."

The duchess's companion, a young and pretty

woman with vibrant red hair and green eyes that currently looked rather alarmed, handed her a pair of spectacles. The duchess perched them on her nose and inspected Serena.

Will stood beside her, tall and straight as a pillar, and she was relieved. If she fainted, he might be able to catch her.

Aunt Geraldine curtsied with a pleasant, "Good evening, Your Grace," and began to introduce Serena as Meg, but the dowager raised her hand.

"I already know this *lady*." Her emphasis on "lady" informed everyone present she did not think the term appropriate for Serena. "You see, Rae Ann. It *is* her. Just as I told you."

The dowager's companion stared at Serena with wide green eyes.

Serena dropped her gaze, curtsied, and managed a few steady words. "How lovely to see you again, Your Grace. You are looking very well." She smiled at the old woman's companion. "It is very nice to meet you, Miss . . . ?"

"Miss Parker," the young woman said with a smile. "It's nice—"

But the duchess cut her off before she could say another word. "Explain to me why you are standing in a box at the theater. You're dead. You've been dead for years."

"Miss Donovan looks well enough to me, Your Grace," Will said smoothly. "Perhaps you mistake her for someone else?" His expression was perfectly flat—devoid of expression.

"Oh, no, Your Grace," Aunt Geraldine reassured the old woman. "That was her twin sister, Serena, who suffered the unfortunate accident. This is the younger of the twins, Margaret."

"Indeed it is not. I remember Margaret very well, and this is not Margaret."

The world began to undulate all around Serena. Good Lord, she couldn't faint. This was madness! How could it be that a single, rheumy-eyed woman was the one to see through her deception?

Miss Parker whispered in the duchess's ear just loudly enough for Serena to hear. "It has been a long night, Your Grace. Perhaps we ought to return home?"

Home to the dowager duchess was a grand house near Kensington Palace, where Serena and Jonathan had last made love. When the duchess had come upon them, she had screeched loudly enough to summon a crowd of people. Serena jumped off Jonathan, he leaped to the wall, his hands frantically working the buttons on his trousers. It was obvious to everyone what they had been doing. Serena's hair had fallen halfway out of its chignon. Her gown was crumpled, her hat askew. She remembered the looks of shock on the people's faces, and in the center stood the Dowager Duchess of Clayworth, her wiry frame shaking from top to bottom with fury.

Serena's face was so hot it must be purple. She hardly caught the tail end of what the old woman was saying.

"—not going home. I shall watch this spectacle to the end, despite all the vile, vulgar people in attendance here tonight."

Finally, the signal sounded the warning for the end of intermission, and a flurry of activity ensued as people returned to their seats. As Miss Parker tugged her away, the dowager duchess threw a scowl over her shoulder. "You have no place in the ton, young woman. I shall see you are shunned by every drawing room in London!"

"She has lost her wits," Aunt Geraldine murmured as she led Serena back to her chair. She shook her head mournfully. "It is a wonder the family still allows her to show her face in Town."

Serena sat quietly, her fists clamped in her lap, watching people wander back toward their seats. A few moments later, Will came up behind her. "Are you all right, Meg? Can I fetch you something? A glass of claret, perhaps?" he asked.

She smiled at him. His face still had that void, flat expression. "Oh, no, Will. Thank you."

He reached down, took her hand, and squeezed it. "Forgive me," he said quietly. "But they need me at the offices."

"At this hour? Oh, Will."

"I'm so sorry. But it's another emergency and

Rogers is here for me." He glanced at the door, where one of his managers hesitated at the threshold.

"All right," she murmured. "Will I see you tomorrow for our afternoon ride?"

He kissed the back of her hand. "Of course."

He took his leave as the actors walked onstage to open the scene. Serena clenched her hands to stop them from shaking. Pinpricks of sweat beaded her forehead.

Feeling hot and out of sorts, she glanced around for Phoebe. Her sister was nowhere to be seen. Panic tightened her throat, and she surged to her feet.

"Where's Phoebe?"

"Well..." Aunt Geraldine looked around, frowning as if she'd forgotten all about Serena's younger sister. "I don't know."

"I must go look for her."

"No, you mustn't—"

But Serena had already lurched to the door and opened it. She closed it against her aunt's protestations and paused, breathing heavily, looking up and down the corridor. She wished she could rip off her stays and inhale deeply. Why had Flannery pulled the strings so tight tonight?

When she finally caught her breath, she strode down the corridors and checked all the retiring rooms for Phoebe. The repercussions of being seen alone and without a chaperone did not scare Serena tonight. What could society do? Shun her? Eliminate the opportunity for her to find a suitable mate? She was engaged to a respectable man. Will would not fault her for wanting to find her sister.

She descended the stairs and slipped through the crowded lobby until she saw the doors that led outside. She rushed toward one of them, thrust it open, and burst into the street. Cool night air seeped through her gown and she shivered, but she took great, gulping breaths of the clean night air, looking to the right and left for any sign of her sister. Carriages rattled down the street in rapid succession, and one that looked like Will's turned the corner, heading in the direction of his offices.

The crowd was thinner out here, but there was no sign of Phoebe.

"Meg?" Jonathan's voice swept over her like a bath of soft, warm water. "You're shaking. Here, take my coat."

Before she could protest, he'd laid his coat over her shoulders. Turning, she looked up at him. Those deep eyes, cobalt blue, stared back at her.

In recognition. *Serena,* they said. But he'd called her Meg.

She shuddered harder, remembering what Aunt Geraldine had told her about him. Remembering the gossip Phoebe had told her, too.

"What is it?" he asked her, his voice gentle, concerned.

There was so much to say to him, she was

overwhelmed by it all. So she went directly to the matter at hand. She looked beyond his shoulder at the last of the people filtering into the theater. "I'm looking for Phoebe. She vanished at the beginning of the intermission and I haven't seen her since."

"I saw her a few minutes ago." After a heavy pause, he added, "She was with Sebastian Harper."

"He came tonight? I didn't know that."

"Neither did I," Jonathan said dryly. He opened his mouth to say something more, then seemed to think better of it. "They were descending the steps from the gallery together when I saw them."

Jonathan held out his arm for her, and she stared at it for a long moment before he dropped it. She glanced at his face to see the slightest tinge of pink staining his cheeks.

"I'll help you find her," he said quietly.

In silence, they explored the area fronting the theater, then reentered. The crowd had thinned, so it took only a few minutes to explore the inside arcade and galleries. Serena grew more concerned by the second.

"Where could she be?" Serena muttered, ignoring yet another narrow-eyed glance by one of the patrons still wandering the halls. She didn't care what they thought of her walking with the dissolute earl. She was far more concerned about finding Phoebe and Mr. Harper, and no one but Jonathan seemed willing to offer help.

Serena bit her lower lip, trying not to mince her steps. Later, she would burn these slippers.

"They aren't in the gallery," Jonathan murmured, "nor in the arcade, nor outside. They . . ."

She looked sharply at him. "What?"

"Well, they could be hiding from prying eyes somewhere. Or . . ."

She narrowed her eyes. "Or?"

"Or they might have gone somewhere else."

Serena huffed. "Certainly not."

As impetuous as Phoebe was, she wouldn't dare leave the theater with anyone besides Serena and their aunt.

Jonathan slowed his step, then stopped fully. They stood in the long upstairs arcade near the staircase leading to the boxes. He turned to her, the expression on his face hidden in shadows. "Perhaps she has slipped past you, then. Returned to your aunt's box."

"I hope so. I'll check there." She shrugged out of his coat and handed it to him. "I'm warm enough now. Thank you."

Turning away, she began to walk, but he caught her arm and pulled her close enough that she breathed him in, his nearness sparking a shower of memories. Tumbling, rolling in the sun, the grass, him above her, laughing down at her . . .

"There's something I must speak with you about," he said in a low voice. "I have some essential information for you."

Several younger ladies passed them, chattering happily.

"Not here," he added.

She gave a firm shake of her head, but her heartbeat surged. Would he finally accuse her of pretending to be Meg? Would he tell Will?

"I've nothing to say to you, Lord Stratford."

His expression darkened. "I understand why you don't think you have anything to say to me." He hesitated. "But I've information of great consequence about…your sister. It's something you'll wish to know."

Which sister, she wondered. Meg? Serena? Phoebe?

This was ridiculous. "I must find Phoebe." She tried to pull her arm out of his grip, but he held firm.

"Tomorrow. Meet me at the servants' entrance at the back of my house at noon."

"Meet with you alone at midday, in plain sight?" She huffed. "I think not."

"At midnight, then," he murmured in a low voice to make sure only she could hear. "Meet me at midnight, and no one but you and I will be the wiser."

She stared at him, memories slamming through her, hard and fast. They'd met behind his house and Aunt Geraldine's house at night before. But that was six years ago, and she'd been a different person then. So had he.

She yanked her arm away from his grasp. "How dare you."

"It's important. Please, trust me." He gazed at her, his expression so guileless she nearly faltered. He'd worked his wiles on her before, and she could never forget what had come of that.

Pressing her fingers to the bridge of her nose, she turned away from him. "Good-bye, Lord Stratford."

She marched away and up the stairs, then down the long corridor leading to Aunt Geraldine's box. She knew he followed; she sensed his soft footsteps close behind her. She refused to acknowledge them. She reached the box and thrust the door open. Phoebe jumped to her feet, and Serena groaned.

"Phoebe! Where have you been?" She kept her voice low so she wouldn't disturb the patrons in the neighboring boxes.

Phoebe rushed to her and took both her hands. "Oh, Meg, I didn't know you were searching for me! It was so stifling in here, and when Miss Trumpet came in, I went downstairs with her to take some air."

Despite herself, Serena glanced back at Jonathan. He shrugged, Phoebe saw him for the first time and curtsied, and Aunt Geraldine glanced toward the door to scowl at them all.

Serena squeezed her sister's hands. "I'm glad you're here, Phoebe. You scared me half to death, though. Don't do that again without telling me where you are going, please."

"I won't, Meg. I promise."

They looked over to Jonathan, who gave them all a formal bow and then retreated with a final meaningful glance at Serena.

"It's important," he'd said. What could possibly be so important?

Why on earth was she dying to find out?

Serena knew that if she arrived at his servants' entrance at midnight tomorrow, he'd be there, waiting for her. Something deep inside her screamed that she must go.

She'd deny that voice.

Still grasping her sister's hand, Serena returned to her seat and finished watching the tragedy of *Othello.*

Jonathan knocked on the door to Kincaid's box and was granted entrance immediately. Everyone turned to see who the latecomer was—and Jonathan gave tight smiles to Kincaid and Jane and the other occupants of the box seats.

Kincaid and Jane stood to welcome him, and Jonathan kissed his cousin on the cheek. Kincaid asked him to sit with them for the remainder of the performance.

Jonathan hesitated, his desire to escape this place warring with his knowledge that Meg Donovan was still here, and Kincaid's box offered a good view of Lady Alcott's.

"Thank you," Jonathan said. There were no available seats, but Jonathan was content to stand in the back of the box.

The fashionable ladies and gentlemen sitting in the seats in front of him paid little attention to the play—instead the men were engaging in a heated conversation about George IV's failing eyesight and general health, and making bets on the number of months the monarch had to live. The women were using opera glasses to observe who had accompanied whom to the performance this evening, and gossiping in whispers among themselves.

Jonathan accepted a pair of tiny opera glasses from Kincaid and made a show of leisurely scanning the theater. He didn't look at the stage, where Iago was doing his best to work Othello into an enraged frenzy over his wife's alleged unfaithfulness, but at the audience, where he finally caught sight of Lady Alcott, Phoebe, and Serena.

She sat still, hands in her lap, eyes trained on the stage, lips moving slightly. It looked like she was reciting Othello's lines along with him: *"Lie on her! We say lie on her when they belie her..."*

Hell, he was making assumptions again. He wasn't positive she was Serena. It was only a strong hunch—an intangible sense. Only hope, perhaps. Nevertheless, it was a feeling he needed to either prove or disprove before his tangled thoughts drove him to madness.

Tomorrow at midnight. He hoped she'd come.

Kincaid nudged him, and he jerked the opera glasses, losing sight of her.

"See something of interest?" Kincaid murmured.

Jonathan gave a noncommittal grunt and gave a sweeping look over the boxes, catching a glimpse of a beautiful, laughing, dark-haired creature. Stunning, even in simple white muslin.

Jonathan sucked in his breath. There was no mistaking that wide smiling mouth, that dark waterfall of hair, that slender frame.

What was Eliza Anderson doing in London?

Chapter Nine

The following night, Jonathan slipped out of his servants' entrance at quarter to midnight. His pulse pounded at his neck, and sweat beaded at his nape.

At the end of the night, he'd know her identity for certain. That was, if she appeared. He wasn't sure she would, even considering the note he'd sent to her this afternoon with a cryptic explanation as to why he needed to speak with her.

After all he'd done, he shouldn't expect anything from her. He didn't deserve anything from her.

Pushing off from his position leaning on the servants' entrance door, he glanced over at the darkened garden pavilion behind Lady Alcott's house. No sign of Phoebe and Harper. He wondered if they planned to meet tonight.

He'd meant to stop Harper when he'd witnessed

his meeting with Phoebe Donovan. The minute he'd seen the man approaching Phoebe, he'd lunged forward, prepared to stop their meeting before it began. But then she'd leaned toward Harper, true concern etched on her face, and Harper's anger had instantly simmered and then disappeared altogether. Jonathan had stopped and stood in the shadows, uncertain.

Phoebe and Harper had talked in low tones, hers soothing, his anguished at first but soon taking on a more relaxed quality. Jonathan knew he should have separated them instantly, but ultimately he couldn't bring himself to. He'd watched the entire assignation, though, and he was surprised to see Harper behaving far more the gentleman than he ever would have suspected. Moreover, when it had ended, Harper was the one to urge Phoebe to return to the house and get some rest.

The couple reminded him of himself and Serena. He and Serena had met in the garden pavilion several times. On the last of those meetings, he'd been sitting between two of the pillars, elbows on knees and head in hands, feeling hopeless about everything. About his father, who was demanding he join the clergy. About Serena's dismissal as unworthy by both his parents. He'd been bold enough to suggest a permanent match between himself and Serena, and his father had laughed at him—no, he'd *guffawed* as if Jonathan had been telling him a hilarious joke.

Serena had sat beside Jonathan, gathered him in

her arms, and held him. She didn't speak—she didn't need to. She'd understood.

He sighed, resting his head back against the brick wall and staring through the tree limbs at the night sky. Only a few tenacious stars shone with enough brightness to pierce through the London haze. Their glow was blurred and muted, not the sharp, crisp pin-pricks of light clearly visible in the country's night sky.

The sound of footsteps jerked his head around.

She approached, dressed in a dark, hooded cape as if in disguise, as if she didn't want to be seen with him. Understandable, he supposed. It was always this way between them, meeting in secret in dark shadows, with hoods and other costumes to conceal who they were and what they were doing. Six years ago, it had been in an ultimately vain attempt to hide their love affair. Now it was because he was the man who'd ruined her sister, and she was engaged to Langley.

She was engaged to Langley. Jonathan swallowed the sickness that soured his throat at the thought.

Her head swung from side to side as she studied their surroundings. No doubt she searched for a sign of someone lurking in the shadows. Finding no one, she hurried up to him and spoke in hushed, urgent tones. "Tell me what it is you have to say, Lord Stratford. Please do it quickly. I've no desire to be seen here with you."

He didn't answer right away. His tongue seemed to

be twisted into knots. She was so beautiful. Her cape was a deep gray, a shade darker than the luminous eyes that stared at him. Blond hair curled around her face. He remembered sifting it through his fingers, tracing her hairline until his fingers met at her pointed little chin, and kissing her there…

"Lord Stratford," she snapped. "What is it?" She shifted her stance, impatient. "Your note said it had something to do with Phoebe."

He took a breath. "Phoebe. Right."

She arched her brows. "Well?"

He gestured at the door to his servants' entrance. "Won't you come inside? We can sit at the kitchen table and talk there."

She narrowed her eyes in suspicion.

"Please, Miss Donovan. You have my word as a gentleman—" She made a scoffing noise, but he ignored it and continued. "I'll allow no harm to come to you in my kitchen."

When she continued to hesitate, he added in a low voice, "I assure you, there's a far smaller chance of someone discovering us together in my kitchen than there is out here in the open."

With a frustrated sigh, she relented and followed him inside. Jonathan would have preferred speaking with her in his drawing room, but he knew when not to push. The kitchen would be considered a more neutral territory than his drawing room.

At the worn wooden table where his servants

dined, he pulled out one of the chairs and waited until she sat before he circled around to the other side and took the seat across from her.

She sat stiffly, her hands in her lap. "What do you have to tell me about my sister?"

"I think you must have an idea."

Not meeting his gaze, she flinched. "Just tell me."

He took a breath. As much as he sympathized with the couple, he knew well what would happen should they be discovered by someone other than himself or Phoebe's sister.

"She and Sebastian Harper are lovers."

Staring at a point on the wall beyond his shoulder, she didn't move. After a long moment had passed, she asked, "How do you know this?"

He told her, from beginning to end, the story of what had happened the night of the fight, leaving out no detail and ending with the two young people saying their good-byes.

Her gaze moved from the wall to him, and she listened to him, unmoving, taking it all in without speaking. There was another silence after he finished, and her focus shifted away from him again to study the ovens, the stove, the shelves lined with rows of well-organized stores. Finally, her gaze once again settled on him.

"Thank you for telling me." Her voice was low, rich, and smooth. Serena's voice, just as he remembered it.

"What will you do?" he asked.

She didn't hesitate. "I must stop it, of course."

He gave a slow nod. "Of course." And she was correct—as "perfect" as their affair appeared on the outside, Phoebe and Harper could not continue as they were. Her family would never allow such a match, and not only was Harper dangerously in debt, but he also possessed a marked lack of control. Though Phoebe appeared to soothe him, that might be only temporary.

"Might I suggest..." He hesitated.

She raised a brow until it was a perfect dark blond peak above her eye. "What do you wish to suggest, my lord?"

She clearly thought it was none of his business to offer a suggestion in how to manage her younger sister, and she was right. Yet he couldn't seem to stop himself.

"I would suggest not being too harsh when you speak to her." He leaned forward, studying her in earnest as he spoke. "I don't think he's using her, and I don't think the opposite is true, either. I believe their affection for each other is mutual and honest."

She stiffened visibly, the sheen of her eyes hardening and growing steely cold.

"That hardly matters," she said.

"Doesn't it?"

She shook her head, and the motion was stiff, as if it hurt her neck to move it. "Not at all. They must understand that nothing can come of this."

Sadness swept through him at her words. He knew she was right, but he had to ask. "Do you believe that? Honestly?"

"I do." So stiff, so cold, the way she stared at him. "My mother and aunt have already planned her Season next year. They are hoping to find a good husband for her, then, with my example..." She hesitated, took a breath, and continued. "I am to be married to Captain Langley, and Phoebe is lovely—witty and beautiful. We all harbor high hopes that she'll do even better than I have."

Her words brought such a rush of bile to his throat it took him several moments to recover. Serena never would have said such a thing—those words did not represent anything of what she had valued. Perhaps she wasn't his Serena after all.

He spoke quietly. "Serena always believed that love matches—despite the disparate ranks of those involved—were possible. Even ideal."

Her eyes narrowed at him and her lips thinned until the line of her teeth shone in the candlelight. "Do not speak of Serena to me. I've already asked you not to."

"But what if I wish to speak of her?"

"You wish to cause me pain. Is that it?"

"No. Never." He leaned forward. "Tell me, Meg. Does me speaking of Serena truly cause you pain?"

"Yes," she said through clenched teeth.

"Why is that?" Each word he was able to draw out

of her lured him in more, made him hotter, made his heartbeat ratchet upward.

She stared at him, her eyes cold and hard as gray stone. "It reminds me of how you behaved toward her. How you betrayed her."

"Does it remind you of what happened between me and Serena prior to that betrayal?"

If possible, her eyes hardened further. "No," she said firmly. "There's nothing I recall beyond that moment."

"Which moment, exactly?"

"When she turned to you for support…for *love*. And you made it clear that she was nothing to you. You cut her."

"I don't recall you being there at that moment, Meg."

Her lip curled. "I wasn't. Serena told me about it. She was my twin, if you recall."

"Oh, I recall. But if you'll also recall, I was one of the few people who could tell the two of you apart."

She pressed her lips together, saying nothing.

"Quite identical, you were. But in appearance only, wasn't it? In every other way, you were very different."

She shook her head, slowly, from side to side.

"I remember," he murmured, leaning forward even more. "I remember what Serena sounded like. What she smelled like. The placement of each tiny freckle across her nose—she had a few more than

Meg, because she was drawn to the outdoors and often forgot to wear her bonnet, much to her mother's annoyance. I remember her little habits, the twists of her lips, the expressions deep in her eyes. I remember everything."

She rose warily from her seat, the chair legs scraping the flagstones. "I believe you've said everything you wanted to say, my lord."

He rose, too, keeping nose to nose with her. He kept his voice low. He captured her gaze with his own and wouldn't let go. "You may think you've changed. You may even think you're Meg. But do you know what I think?"

She swallowed hard but stared at him with steely eyes.

"I think it wasn't Serena who died on that ship. I think it was Meg. And for some reason, Serena has decided to change her identity. To fool the world into thinking she's Meg."

"I do believe you've gone mad, Lord Stratford."

"Oh, I don't think so. I think you know exactly what I'm talking about, don't you, Serena?"

"Don't call me that. Don't you dare."

Keeping her trapped within his gaze, he slowly made his way around the table until he stood beside her. She looked up at him, and he could see it clearly now—the panic flaring in her eyes, the deep crimson flush spreading across her cheekbones.

"I always knew the difference between you and

your twin," he murmured, staring down at her. "You knew that. How could you think you'd fool me now?"

She tried to patch her disintegrating nerves back together. He could see her near-palpable struggle to do it, to try to appear strong before him. "You're mistaken, my lord." Her voice shook as she spoke. "Serena and I were very much alike, and not just in appearance. I have changed in the past several years. Become more like her."

"No," he said quietly. "No. You haven't. You are just as I remember you."

She turned as if to go, but he snagged her around the waist with his arm, and before she could gather her wits to protest, he pressed his lips to hers.

Serena's sweet taste, her essence, her soft lips, the curve of her waist under his arm.

His blood sang with the knowledge. It poured through him from their point of contact.

There was no longer any doubt in his mind. This *was* Serena. The woman he'd thought dead for six years. The woman he'd loved with all his soul but had been stupid and thrown it all away.

Happiness. Love. Contentment. With her gone, his life had become hell.

Desperately, he held on to her, kissed her with all the passion he'd bottled up so long, with all the depth of understanding that he'd finally found the woman he'd thought lost to him forever.

His Serena was alive. She'd been alive all

this time. His mind wrapped around the fact and rejoiced.

You're alive. My God, you're alive...

He was shaking. Trembling from head to foot, except his arm, which was curved around her like iron, never wanting to let her go, never wanting to release her out of his sight where he might lose her again.

But she wrapped her fingers around his upper arms and thrust him away. He opened his eyes, surprised until he saw the look of devastation marring her beautiful face. A tear crested the lower lid of her left eye and trickled down her cheek.

He shook his head at her. Her lips had transferred an electric feeling into him, buzzing through his limbs and into his fingertips.

She stared at him wide-eyed, her fingers brushing over her lips. Was she feeling the same hum resonating through her body?

He shook his head slowly. "You're not... I can't let you..."

"No," she said, her voice strong.

"Langley... I..."

She winced at the sound of her betrothed's name.

"I can't allow anyone to hurt him. Not again."

She straightened at that, growing taller, stronger, more determined than ever. Her eyes snapped silver sparks at him. "I've no intention of hurting him. Ever."

"But you will..."

"I *won't.* He is an honorable man. I'll do whatever is necessary to make him happy."

"If he learns the truth..."

"There is no truth. I am who I say I am, Jonathan."

It was the first time she'd called him by his Christian name, and the way she said it...Oh, she was Serena, all right.

She leaned forward. "You will not spread lies about my identity. You will not put Will's happiness in jeopardy. Do you understand?"

He shook his head. Didn't she understand that if Will learned the truth after their marriage, it would be a million times worse than him discovering it now?

"I've nothing more to say to you, my lord." She made to turn away, but he caught her wrist.

"No," he whispered. "No...Please don't—"

She wrenched away from him, whirled around, and flung her body toward the door. He was too shaken, too overcome, to stop her. He stood there, immobile, as she fled, slamming the door behind her, leaving him alone in the kitchen.

Serena Donovan wasn't his at all. Not anymore. She was betrothed to William Langley, and she meant to go through with marrying him.

It had started to rain. Serena sprinted through the downpour across the stable yard, kicking up mud in her wake. She entered through the back door of Aunt Geraldine's house, only slowing when she was safely inside. She toed off her soiled shoes—she'd find a way to explain them tomorrow—and on tiptoe so she wouldn't wake anyone, she hurried upstairs and slipped into her bedchamber. Leaning against the door, she sank to the floor and clutched her wet, muddied knees in her arms.

Oh, God, Jonathan knew her. Without a doubt, he knew her, and after he'd kissed her, his mind would not be changed.

Why had she allowed it? She'd known that kiss was coming. What devil had compelled her to tilt her head up in anticipation instead of run when she had the chance?

He'd tell Will. They were good friends, and by all accounts, Jonathan possessed no scruples. He wouldn't hesitate to tell Will the truth. He'd ruin her, her sisters...

Furthermore, it was her fault, wasn't it? She'd betrayed Will with Jonathan. She'd cowered from Will, yet she'd allowed Jonathan to kiss her.

She breathed fast and hard, gasping for air. Leaning forward, she pressed her forehead to her knees and tried to control her inhalations and gather her wits.

She'd deny it. It was all she could do. Aunt Geraldine truly believed she was Meg, and she'd defend her. Even if Aunt Geraldine did know the truth, Serena thought she'd stake her reputation on her surviving niece being Meg. No matter what, her aunt would never admit to keeping an impostor under her roof.

Serena hugged her arms around her knees and rocked back and forth, her determination growing. Jonathan's reputation was in tatters among the upright members of society. Despite his elevated rank, they would not—could not—believe him. Meg's reputation was still intact, and with Aunt Geraldine behind her, the "truth" could not be denied.

A soft creak sounded in the corridor, and Serena jerked her head up, her chest seizing in panic. *Jonathan!* But then she heard the soft snick of the door across from her own, and her chest tightened. Phoebe. Surely it was Phoebe.

She'd just come in, which left no question as to where she'd been, especially after Jonathan's earlier revelation.

Serena took a few more moments to calm herself and turn her attention to the other crisis at hand. Shakily she rose from the floor and removed her cloak. With jerky movements, she hung it on a peg. Then she stripped off her muddied clothing, and clad only in her chemise, she turned back to the door.

She left her room, crossed the corridor, and knocked gently on her sister's door. "Phoebe? It's me."

"Meg?"

"May I come in?"

"Uhm... just a moment."

Serena shifted from foot to foot, her annoyance rising. How stupid Phoebe was, to be meeting with a young man at night. What on earth was she thinking?

Be gentle with her, Jonathan had said, and he was right. From past experience, Serena knew that Phoebe closed herself tight the moment someone spoke harshly to her. In fact, that was the way to get Phoebe to do exactly the opposite of what she'd been commanded to do. So as tempting as it would be to do so, Serena wouldn't be wise to march in and order her sister to never speak to Sebastian Harper again.

Finally, Phoebe murmured, "Come in."

Serena opened the door. Phoebe's bedchamber was decorated in neutral tones, with ivory silk and light brown hangings and a lovely Aubusson carpet covering the wood floor. Unlike the bed in Serena's room, Phoebe's had no curtains; instead, four tall, carved, mahogany posts adorned its corners.

Phoebe was under the covers, the silk counterpane tucked beneath her chin. "It's late," she announced, blinking sleepily at Serena.

Serena glanced at the telltale water droplets scattered over the light-colored carpet and forced her scoff to emerge as a sigh. Closing the door behind her, she crossed the room and perched on the edge of the bed.

"I heard you come in just now, Phoebe."

"Come in?" Phoebe's brow furrowed. "Oh...I was down in the kitchen. I poured myself some wine in the hope that it would help me to sleep."

"No," Serena said patiently, "you weren't in the kitchen. I know because I was just in the kitchen myself, and you weren't there."

Phoebe was silent, but Serena recognized the mulish set in her sister's jaw.

"I know you were with Sebastian Harper." Serena kept her voice low and deliberately devoid of judgment.

"I don't know—" Phoebe snapped her lips shut, as if thinking better of what she'd been about to say.

"You're lovers," Serena announced.

Phoebe gave her an owlish blink.

"Let's not beat about the bush, Phoebe. I know what you've been doing. I know you've been sneaking out at night to meet with him."

Phoebe said nothing. The only hint of the emotion boiling inside her was the tight set of her mouth.

"Phoebe." Serena laid a hand on her sister's shoulder. Phoebe's blue eyes slid toward the unwelcome touch, but Serena didn't move away. "This cannot continue. It's not a good match for you and could destroy your hopes of making a good match at all. You can do far better than Sebastian Harper. He's a young rake with no fortune, and it will be many years before he's in a position to settle down and marry. Even when he does, you know Mother and Aunt

Geraldine hope to match you with someone much more worthy."

"You haven't the faintest idea what you're talking about, Serena." Phoebe's voice shot out like a whip, and Serena nearly reeled backward. Phoebe hadn't called her by her real name since the day before they'd boarded the ship for England.

"On the contrary." Her own voice was firm. "I know *exactly* what I'm talking about."

Phoebe knew only a sketch of Serena's disgrace. She knew nothing of the man Serena had suffered that disgrace with, nothing of how the gap in their ranks had affected it. In this case it was Phoebe who was in the superior social position in the affair, but that didn't matter. It was all the same.

She didn't want Phoebe to suffer through what she had. They'd been in London for only a little over a month. Surely Phoebe couldn't have gone as far with Sebastian Harper as Serena had with Jonathan so long ago. If they broke it off now, privately, it would be so much easier, so much more bearable, than what Serena had had to endure.

"I love him." Phoebe's eyes shot off defiant sparks. "Nothing will change that."

Something in Serena's chest tightened and pulled. "Phoebe, it will never work. It can't."

"Why not?" Phoebe tore her gaze away from Serena to stare up at the recessed ceiling. "He loves me, too."

"Even if he does, it's simply impossible for there to be anything between you." Serena remembered Jonathan, how she'd felt about him. God, she'd been even younger than Phoebe. She'd loved him with the fierce passion and power of the young and unjaded. Nothing and no one could have stopped her from loving him.

Except Jonathan himself. That moment he'd cut her shattered everything, leaving herself—and her twin—to try to glue the pieces back together on their return journey across the Atlantic.

"Why is it impossible?" Phoebe demanded.

Serena pressed the bridge of her nose between two fingers. "You're too different from each other. Mother and Aunt Geraldine believe that with your beauty and education, you could win a gentleman with a title—"

"I don't care about titles!"

"—and even Captain Langley is eager to help us find a suitable bridegroom for you."

Phoebe scrambled up to a seated position, and Serena saw that she hadn't yet removed her petticoat or stays. She hoped fervently that Harper hadn't removed them earlier.

"Sebastian is suitable for me. No one else is. I know this in my heart, Serena, can't you see?"

"No, I don't see." But she did. More than she'd ever reveal. She gazed down at her sister and said in a low voice, "You must stop calling me Serena."

Phoebe jerked her head away.

"Don't make me tell Aunt Geraldine about this," Serena warned. It was an empty threat, though, because she'd never dare tell Aunt Geraldine. She remembered too well what had happened when Aunt Geraldine had found out about her affair with Jonathan, and she'd never subject Phoebe to that.

"You wouldn't," Phoebe breathed, an edge of fear in her voice.

"Truly," Serena said gently, "where do you see this going with Mr. Harper?"

"He wants me. I know he does."

Serena narrowed her eyes at her sister. "You haven't... given yourself to him, then?"

"No."

Serena's shoulders slumped in relief.

"Not yet," Phoebe said, staring at her through slitted cat's eyes. "But I will."

"Oh, Phoebe." Serena groaned. "You mustn't. Please trust me. Remember the terrible mistake I made the last time I was in London? I don't want you to suffer like I did. Like I still am."

"That was different," Phoebe said. "The man you fell in love with didn't love you back."

Serena squeezed her eyes shut as pain sliced through her.

"I already told you," Phoebe said impatiently, "Sebastian loves me. This is very different from what happened between you and that horrid man."

"Has he told you that he loves you?"

"Not yet, but he will."

"I thought..." Serena's voice shook, but she didn't stop it. "I thought he loved me, too. He even told me he loved me, and I believed in his love with all my heart. And then..." Her voice dwindled. She took a moment to steady herself and tried again. "He refuted me. Pretended he had never known me and had no desire to. He said to my face, before a crowd of people, that he'd never seen me before. He fooled me completely, Phoebe. All he wanted was to use my body, so he seduced me, and then when it became known we were lovers, he cast me aside. I was meaningless to him, and I'd utterly deluded myself into thinking otherwise."

"Sebastian's not like that!" It was almost a shout, and Serena glanced toward the door. All they needed was to have a servant listen in on this conversation and report it to their aunt. Phoebe clearly recognized this, for when she spoke again, her voice was much quieter. "He doesn't want to take advantage of me, Seren—Meg. I *know* he doesn't. I know it! He's so sweet with me, so gentlemanly..."

"Oh, God." Serena's voice was hollow. *Sweet, gentlemanly.* Just like Jonathan had been. "Oh, please, Phoebe. Please, I beg you. Don't be stupid."

Her eyes welling with tears, Phoebe shook her head. "I'm not stupid. It's the truth. I don't know what happened to you all those years ago, but I promise you, it's different. Believe me." She hesitated, then leaned forward, hope shining behind the tears. "Help me. Please, help us. If we help him, then I'm sure he can prove to Aunt Geraldine, Mother, Captain Langley—everyone—that he is suitable for me. He's so brave, so intelligent, and so strong. Really, he is. And he'll want me. I know he will."

Serena shook her head. "Has he mentioned marriage?"

Phoebe shifted uncomfortably. "Well…no. But there's so much he's concerned about right now. I think he doesn't believe it would be proper to broach that topic until he works it out."

Serena frowned. "What, exactly, is his trouble?"

Phoebe shook her head. "I don't know. Gambling debt, maybe? Whatever it is, it hurts him terribly. He has such powerful misgivings. I can see it when he looks at me. He's such a sad look in his eyes, such a look of regret." She hugged her arms over her chest.

"Phoebe, you must never see him again."

Phoebe's unblinking gaze met Serena's. "But I will, Serena. I must."

"You are too young to understand the trouble this might cause for us, Phoebe. For our family. You've been too long away from London…"

Phoebe shrugged. "None of that matters."

"Don't be selfish."

"I don't care! I will see him again, whether you or Mother or Aunt Geraldine like it or not."

"*No,* Phoebe. I…forbid it." Serena winced. She'd

never disciplined her siblings—in fact she was the one most likely to need the disciplining for most of her life—and she wasn't accustomed to it. She feared she was doing a rather poor job of it.

"You cannot *forbid* me to do anything. You're not Mother."

"Mother passed your care into my hands."

Phoebe's lips twisted. "Hardly. She doesn't trust you at all, and you know it. She's passed my care into Aunt Geraldine's hands, but I'm nineteen years old and perfectly capable of making my own decisions."

"Neither I nor Mother nor Aunt Geraldine would agree."

"Then you're all stupid."

"Phoebe!"

"I don't care what you think. It's true. You don't understand."

"So since Aunt Geraldine is responsible for you, you're saying I must tell her about you and Mr. Harper?"

Phoebe gave her a look searing with challenge and shrugged. "Go ahead, *Meg,* tell everyone my secrets. And if you do so, I just might feel inclined to tell everyone yours."

"Oh, for heaven's sake. You wouldn't do any such thing." Still, Serena's insides twisted.

"It doesn't matter anyway," her sister said mulishly. "Nothing anyone says to me will make me look differently at Sebastian. I *love* him."

Serena bowed her head, knowing she'd in no way be able to draw out a promise from her sister to never see Sebastian Harper again. "Please listen to me. You two aren't suited—"

"Oh, indeed we *are* suited," Phoebe snapped. "And we'll prove it to the world, I promise you."

Chapter Ten

Serena survived the next few days in a haze of panic, waiting for someone to come barreling in to tell her the ruse was over, that everyone knew she wasn't Meg. She feared the worst: that she would be sent back to Antigua, exiled for good this time.

On top of the fear, guilt racked her. How could kissing Jonathan feel so right when she knew—she *knew*—how wrong it was?

Again and again, she went through the motions of the routine she'd established since her return to London: spending the mornings with Phoebe and Aunt Geraldine, taking her afternoon ride with Will, and engaging in various social events in the evenings. She managed to maintain a calm façade, though her insides felt tossed like a ship in a hurricane, and she couldn't eat much without feeling sick to her stomach. She pretended to eat, and nobody—not even Phoebe—seemed to notice her consternation. Meg would have noticed instantly.

Will seemed distant. He'd had to cancel several of their rides in the park due to business obligations, but even when they were together, he hardly spoke. When he did engage in conversation with her, he mostly spoke of his infant trading business, which was suffering from growing pains. He never said so, but Serena had the distinct feeling that he wished he were captaining one of the ships instead of being trapped, helpless for the most part, in his London offices.

A week after her midnight meeting with Jonathan, Serena and Will decided to forgo their usual ride and instead strolled down a well-maintained path in Hyde Park. Serena couldn't talk to Will regarding her worries about Jonathan; instead, she disclosed her concern over Phoebe's liaison with Harper. When he responded by giving a stony glare to the curving path, she instantly regretted her decision to confide in him.

"I wish I'd never said it would be acceptable for him to attend the soiree," Will blurted after a long silence.

She glanced at him to see dagger-like glints shooting from his eyes into the gravel. "What do you mean? I thought you'd invited him."

"No, I did not. I invited his brother, Manfred Harper, who was a lieutenant on my ship. Manfred had told me his younger brother Sebastian was in Town and he was trying to keep him out of trouble, that night specifically, as some scoundrels were after him to pay a gambling debt. Manfred begged me to extend the invitation to him."

"And you did." Of course he would.

"I did. I wish I hadn't," Will said in a clipped voice.

Something twisted in Serena's stomach. "But, Will," she murmured, "you always see the good in people."

"Not him," he said flatly.

"Well, I agree that he and Phoebe aren't suitable for each other. But he seems a decent enough young man."

It was early, and the bulk of people hadn't yet arrived for their daylight promenades, but the path was far from empty. People rode and strode, dodging puddles from the recent rains. Beyond a nearby tree, a boy scampered over a mound of grass, trying to launch a kite with long streamers.

Will squeezed her arm. "I don't believe he's decent at all. I beg you to keep your sister away from him. I've no wish to see Mr. Harper damage your sister in any way."

She frowned at him, pretending ignorance. "How could he damage Phoebe?"

"I wouldn't be surprised if he did everything in his power to destroy her reputation and then take on no responsibility for doing so."

"I can't quite imagine him doing that!" she exclaimed. "Surely he'd behave like any gentleman, at least." Although if he was a gentleman, he'd never have encouraged Phoebe to meet with him at night.

"He's a gambler, and though he possessed little money to begin with, he has gambled himself deep into debt. Like many young men of his status, he's been unable—or unwilling—to choose a profession. He refused to take up a commission in the Navy like his father and brothers, and he dislikes anything to do with the clergy. Law was an option, and indeed he began the schooling for it, but he abandoned it just a few weeks in."

"Surely he must enjoy something," Serena murmured.

"Besides gambling and debauchery?" Will asked sardonically, then at her silence he retreated a little. "I've heard he enjoys rendering plans for gardens and houses and the like."

"So, he is an architect?"

Will shrugged. "He has apparently shown some aptitude for it, but he has made no attempt to seek out the proper training."

"Why not, if he enjoys it?"

"Laziness," Will said tightly. "He could pursue the profession, but he possesses none of the drive. He came to London believing it would be more exciting to take his chances at the gaming tables. According to Manfred, he's lost everything but the shirt on his back and the small house and plot of land he owns near Prescot."

A pang of discomfort shot through Serena. "Perhaps he will mature with time."

Will shrugged. "I'm ten years older than him, Meg, and many men my age haven't matured. There's a slow-growing canker in society, and it is fed by men and women alike who squander their fortunes and destroy the legacies of those who came before them, those who labored so arduously to build their estates and fortunes."

He paused, his lips turning down at their edges, his expression reminding her of Aunt Geraldine. "Harper is worse than most, though. He didn't have much to begin with, and instead of taking that little and building upon it, as he was clearly capable of doing, given some moral character and a little drive, he has destroyed it. And his penchant for debauchery and gambling isn't all there is to it."

Serena frowned deeper. "What more could there be?"

"The man has the devil's own temper. He hasn't been in London long, but he's been banned from several hells already, and Manfred says he has lost count of the number of times he's brawled."

They walked along in silence for several minutes as they turned down the path that traveled along the Serpentine, its waters glinting amethyst blue under the bright afternoon sun. As they approached, a mother duck squawked at them, then turned away, angrily herding her ducklings around a bend into the safety of a pool hidden by overgrown bushes along the bank.

"You must order your sister to stay away from him. Lock her in the house if she refuses."

Serena jerked her head up to Will.

"I truly fear what he will do to her." There was a rare edge of vehemence in his voice. "He very well might destroy her reputation, as Serena's was once destroyed."

"Do you equate Mr. Harper to the Earl of Stratford?" Serena asked.

"I—" The furrows in his brow deepened, and he shook his head. "No. Stratford is my friend, and I believe his motivations with your sister were… different."

"Different? How?"

"I cannot trust Harper's motivations in the least. Stratford, however"—he glanced at her, then continued—"I believe Stratford possessed a very strong feeling for your sister."

A tremor jerked through Serena's body, and she blew out a hissing breath. "He cast her aside," she croaked. It felt like a garrote was wrapped around her throat. "He cut her. He shunned her publicly."

Will hesitated, then in a gentle voice he said, "He had obligations to consider—"

Serena often didn't completely concur with certain statements Will made. The old Serena would have challenged him when she didn't agree with his assessment of things, but Meg would never have argued with him, so Serena didn't, either. Still, it was against her basic nature to remain quiet, and every time she held her tongue with Will, it felt like a tiny flame inside her died.

This time, though, she couldn't keep her thoughts to herself.

"Obligations," she spat, truly angry now. "How can the significance of any obligation surpass the destruction of a woman's life?"

Will winced. Reaching with his free hand, he squeezed her forearm. "I know how protective you are of your sister. And I know you will always find it difficult to forgive him for what he did. But he was a young man, and the pressures his family—especially his father—had placed on him were extremely high. He wanted Serena, but the earl threatened to pull his very existence out from under him. He had no choice. And then when he heard of her death..." His voice dwindled.

"What?" Serena asked in a choked voice. "What did he do when he heard of her death?" Surely Will wouldn't tell her about his escapades in Bath!

Will's hand slipped off her arm. "He struck out on a path of self-destruction that was difficult to witness."

Her lips felt tight and awkward. "So, I am supposed to forgive him because not only did he cast my sister off, but he then fashioned himself into a dissolute?"

Will closed his eyes in a long blink and drew her to a slow stop in the middle of the path. A couple brushed by them, chatting about the fashion in headwear this summer, as Will turned to her. "I remember you as being more forgiving."

The chastisement in his tone was mild, but it was there. Furthermore, he was right—Meg had possessed such a forgiving, gentle soul. After all that he had done, however, could she have forgiven Jonathan?

Yes.

She tore her eyes away from Will so he couldn't see the expression on her face, and stared out over the glassy waters of the Serpentine. "I'm sorry. You're right, of course. Forgiveness is a virtue I seemed to have forgone in the past six years." She turned back to him, trying her best to offer a reassuring smile. "I'll try, Will, truly I will."

He patted her hand. "Good, my darling."

He commenced walking again, his pull on her arm gentle but commanding, and she followed at a sedate pace, though her mind whirled.

My darling.

Stratford possessed strong feelings for your sister.

He wanted Serena…

My darling.

She was Will Langley's counterfeit darling. Oh, God. She looked up into Will's serious face. The urge to tell him the truth, tell him everything, nearly overpowered her.

But how could Serena destroy all her sisters' potential and hopes for the future with a few little words? How could she dash William Langley's hopes right along with her sisters'?

She couldn't.

She squeezed Will's arm and noticed that he was watching her closely. "It is gallant of you to feel protective of Phoebe," she murmured. Then she sighed. "You're right, of course, about her and Mr. Harper. She cannot be allowed to see him again."

She would limit Phoebe's independence, make certain that her sister knew it would mean dire consequences if she met with Mr. Harper again. Phoebe would be devastated, but not as devastated as she'd be if the truth were revealed about Serena and they were sent back to Antigua in disgrace—of that, Serena was certain.

"Well," Will said in a low voice, turning toward an intersecting path. "Look who's here."

Awareness slammed like a lead ball right into Serena's solar plexus. Jonathan Dane sauntered toward them. Beside him the elegant and slender Jane, Lady Montgomery, seemed to glide over the path.

After she'd seen Lady Montgomery at the theater, Serena had gone to the lady's house for tea one afternoon and had promised to return soon. Serena had liked Lady Montgomery a great deal and thought her to potentially be her first real friend, but now, seeing her beside Jonathan, with her arm linked through his, hot, green jealousy shot through Serena. Was the lady Jonathan's current conquest?

Instantly, she felt her cheeks heat, partly from being in Jonathan's presence again after that searing kiss, partly from being so appalled at herself for feeling jealous of whomever Jonathan's current conquest might be.

Jonathan's gaze met Serena for a fraction of a second, and the blue in his eyes winked at her before he smiled, and with a little bow, said, "Good afternoon, Miss Donovan. Langley. A fine day for a stroll in the park, to be sure, especially after yesterday's rain."

"Very fine indeed," Will said in his grave voice.

Lady Montgomery gave Serena and Will a warm smile. Jonathan shook Will's hand and clapped his back like they were old school chums who hadn't seen each other in years.

Serena's hands were clammy, and her heart beat a dull, heavy throb in her chest. She could hardly bear watching the obvious affection between the two men. She had lived in such a state of fear for the past several days. Would Jonathan betray her yet again—use his knowledge of her identity to bring about her downfall? Why hadn't he done so already? Why had he waited so long?

She'd ask him in person, but she was far too much of a coward to meet with him again. She didn't trust him. Worse, she didn't trust herself to be unaccompanied with him.

Even out in the open, Jonathan's essence of fresh-cut grass filled her senses, as much as she tried to thrust it away. Every time she inhaled the scent of cut grass, she was reminded of that first time they'd joined together, and of the fresh heat of their kiss last week.

Had Lady Montgomery been a willing recipient of those desperate, warm kisses? Serena's stomach jolted in harsh revolt to that thought, and she resisted pressing her hand against it.

"It is so fortunate we encountered you today," Lady Montgomery said. "I had planned to send a formal invitation, but I daresay it's better to ask you in person. I'd like to invite all three of you—and your sister, of course, Miss Donovan—to my house for an intimate dinner party next Wednesday evening. Another friend will be there as well." She looked to the men. "You both know Franklin Kincaid."

"Indeed," Will said.

Jonathan turned to Serena, his brows raised in question.

Serena, whose cheeks had been burning, her stomach boiling, now blanched as Lady Montgomery and Will turned their gazes to her as well. With the weight of their stares pressing in on her, she couldn't invent an adequate excuse to avoid the evening. She tried her best not to grimace. "Phoebe and I will be delighted to attend," she said. "Thank you so much for the invitation, my lady."

Both men seemed to exhale a breath of relief, but Lady Montgomery clapped her gloved hands. "Excellent! I shall look forward to seeing you there. And I assume that means you'll attend as well, Captain?"

Will inclined his head. "Of course."

Lady Montgomery turned to Jonathan. "And you, my lord?"

Jonathan gave her a tight smile. "Trust me, Jane. I wouldn't miss it for the world."

Jonathan and Lady Montgomery were on a first-name basis. That meant they shared a certain level of intimacy. They could be lovers.

Serena ground her teeth. If they were, it was none of her concern.

She glanced at Will in a silent plea, and he squeezed her arm. "It was good seeing you both, but I'm afraid I've promised to return Miss Donovan home by half past three." Turning to her, Will smiled—actually smiled. Will was truly a handsome man, a good man. She wanted so badly to make him happy. "I've been informed that Meg has some shopping to do."

Her flush returned, the heat of it crawling from her neck to her jaw. Aunt Geraldine was taking her to a dressmaker this afternoon to be fitted for her wedding gown.

Jonathan gave her a brittle smile and tipped his hat. "Well then. I'm so glad we were able to wish you a good afternoon before you returned home, Miss Donovan."

"I shall look forward to seeing you both next week," Lady Montgomery said. They turned and drifted away, again arm in arm.

Serena released a slow, measured breath. Jonathan's relationship with Lady Montgomery didn't matter. All that mattered was that Jonathan hadn't betrayed her identity to Will. Not today, at least.

Even now she was flushed. Her skin prickled. Jonathan's presence confounded her beyond belief, and there was so much complexity in the way he made her feel—everything along the spectrum from bitter hatred to a mad, dangerous craving for him to touch her rather than the elegant lady at his side.

Chapter Eleven

On the first of July, Jonathan followed Langley and Kincaid into Jane's drawing room.

It had been a week since he'd last seen Serena. She'd been avoiding him, deliberately keeping herself sequestered indoors, declining social events at which she knew he'd be in attendance. But she'd already said yes to Jane's invitation, so she'd have to endure seeing him tonight.

He wasn't looking forward to watching her with Langley yet again. That didn't stop him from going to his cousin's intimate dinner party, though. He was dying to see Serena again, and that was what mattered most.

Candlelight blazed from the gilded wall sconces of Jane's drawing room as the gentlemen were announced. The three ladies rose to greet them.

Jonathan kept his gaze on Serena. She greeted Langley, who'd entered first, and then turned to him, her expression stony.

It was just like the last time he'd seen her at Hyde Park. Hell, he didn't want her to feel this way. Surely by now she understood that he had no intention of revealing her secret. That would be devastating to both her and her family. He wouldn't hurt her, or any of them, again.

She curtsied, and he gave her a formal bow. "A pleasure as always, Miss Donovan." He turned to her sister, who stood at her side. "Miss Phoebe."

"Oh, my lord," the younger woman chirped. "It is so lovely to see you again."

With a forced nod, Serena turned back to Langley, who took her hands in his. Trying not to react, Jonathan managed a few polite words of greeting to their hostess.

The conversation was light but with an underlying tension Jonathan was sure was due to his presence. Fortunately, only a few minutes passed before the announcement that dinner was served.

Jonathan was seated with Phoebe to his left and Serena to his right. Jane sat across from him, flanked by the other two men.

After the soup was served, he turned to the right and asked, "Are you enjoying the London weather this summer, Miss Donovan?"

"Oh, yes," Serena said, perhaps only out of necessary

politeness. "It is so much more palatable than the summers at home."

"What is it like in the West Indies this time of year?"

She spoke of the humidity and heat in Antigua, apparently finding the mundane topic somewhat of a relief. This caused Kincaid, who was sitting across from her, to question her further, and the dinner proceeded along in this fashion—everyone talking about matters that ultimately meant nothing.

But Serena sat at Jonathan's right, and even as the discussion turned to the improvements being made to the streetlamps in various neighborhoods in Town, he drank her in. Below the strong smells of oyster, roasted goose, duckling, and *au jus* sauce, he breathed in the scents of a sandy beach and salty air. He felt her warmth. When she smiled, a rare gift, his heart pounded; when she spoke, he sank into the words.

With Serena beside him, he could forget about everything else. Even her upcoming marriage to William Langley.

After dinner, Serena sat stiffly on the edge of a lime-green sofa, watching Lady Montgomery and Phoebe play a duet. Phoebe's blond hair shimmered in the golden light of the chandelier while Lady Montgomery's matched the gleaming mahogany of the pianoforte.

Mr. Kincaid gazed at them in rapt concentration from his position near the pianoforte. Jonathan sat on a nearby chair. Tension swirled between him and Serena. Surely Will, standing behind her with his fingers resting on the back of the sofa, must sense it.

Serena clenched her hands in her lap, feeling at odds with this situation, with the people surrounding her.

From the corner of her eye, she saw that Jonathan sat rigidly, his shoulders tense as he watched the performers. She wondered what he thought about as he watched Lady Montgomery play, his gaze focused solidly upon her. Compared to her hostess, Serena felt like a buxom milkmaid, with her pink, freckled cheeks and flyaway hair. With her smooth coiffure, angular features, and elegant stature, Lady Montgomery appeared older and more refined than Serena could ever dream of being.

Despite all the horrid things she'd learned about Jonathan, a part of her ached to sit beside him again, longed to ask him what it was he saw in Lady Montgomery—she was beautiful, yes, but in a remote kind of way, and so different from the kind of woman she'd imagine Jonathan to develop that kind of affection for.

Her skin remembered the touch of his firm, warm skin. She remembered staring at him all night, into his sapphire eyes. She had never seen anyone else with eyes as alluring as his, eyes so easy to fall into.

Phoebe and Lady Montgomery finished the song with a flourish, came to their feet, and bowed.

Mr. Kincaid, who Serena had just met this evening, rose, clapping. "Bravo! Well done! Excellent! So very talented, if I may say so."

Phoebe's cheeks flushed pink at his admiration, and she looked to Lady Montgomery, who gallantly took the reins. "Thank you. We ought to allow you to think it is true talent, but to be quite honest, it is one of the few songs I can play on the pianoforte with any competence at all. Thank goodness I had Miss Phoebe to lead me through the difficult parts."

"Oh," Phoebe exclaimed, "you are too modest! Indeed, you are quite skilled, my lady."

Jonathan rose. "Truly delightful, ladies." He turned to Serena. "Do you play, Miss Donovan?"

Serena flushed and lowered her gaze to her lap. Jonathan knew very well that she didn't play the pianoforte. "Very poorly, I'm afraid."

"Do you sing, then?" Will asked.

Jonathan also knew that she didn't sing, but it surprised her that Will wasn't aware of this very basic information about her.

"No, unfortunately I don't sing, either. Serena and I took lessons as girls, but we were told we possessed no talent."

"What about you, Miss Phoebe? Do you sing?" Will asked.

All eyes returned to Phoebe, and Serena released a relieved breath, thankful to have the attention diverted from her.

"I have heard Miss Phoebe possesses a lovely soprano voice," Jonathan said.

Of course. Serena had told him about her sister's talent years ago. She could hardly believe he remembered.

Phoebe's eyes twinkled. "Dare I ask how you might have heard such a rumor, my lord?"

"Ah..." Jonathan's glance flicked toward Serena. "Your sister told me at dinner."

"Do regale us with something, Miss Phoebe," Will said.

"Very well, then." Phoebe turned to Lady Montgomery, who nodded and, with a rustle of silk, lowered herself onto the bench.

Serena settled back on the sofa, wishing with all her heart that Phoebe and Lady Montgomery would play and sing the night away so she wouldn't have to talk about herself—or Serena—anymore.

The red velvet ribbons trimming Phoebe's satin gown brought out the soft strawberry tones in her hair. As she began to sing, she rested one small hand on the top of the pianoforte, her billowing sleeves confined at the wrists with more ribbons. Her voice was soft, high, and pure, and she filled every word with delicate emotion.

When Phoebe finished the song, everyone clapped, the gentlemen lavished her with compliments, and Lady Montgomery called for coffee and tea.

Serena took a cup of tea, covertly watching Jonathan's fingers curling around his coffee cup as he conversed with their hostess. A memory shot through her. Those long fingers cupping her breast, closing over her nipple as his mouth lowered and his lips brushed over a sensitive nub.

Lady Montgomery settled down beside her, jerking Serena's gaze away from Jonathan.

The lady smiled, then took a sip of tea. As she lowered her cup, she said, "I'd like to ask you something, Meg. May I call you Meg?"

"Of course," Serena said quickly.

"And you must call me Jane."

"I'll do that." She returned the other woman's smile.

"I have a question for you."

"Please ask it."

Jane frowned. "It is rather forward, and above all, I'd despise offending you."

Serena rubbed her thumb over the delicate edges of her China cup. "Forwardness happens to be a trait I admire in my friends."

Jane's smile appeared to be genuine, and her brown eyes sparkled. "I'm happy to hear that." She tapped her fingers on her knee. "I couldn't help but notice when Lord Stratford and I encountered you and Captain Langley in the park yesterday, the looks you were casting in his direction."

Oh, God. Serena's face went up in flames. "The... looks?"

Jane nodded. "Yes. You were throwing the same look at Stratford just now."

"Oh," Serena breathed.

"I've witnessed your attempts to be polite to him, but I've heard the story of what happened to your twin sister when you were last in London. It's no surprise you've such a deep aversion to seeing the man responsible for her disgrace."

Serena swallowed hard. "I..." She couldn't finish the sentence. She'd expected some accusation regarding her true feelings for Jonathan—not this at all. But of course, this made much more sense.

Serena glanced at Jonathan. He, Will, Kincaid, and Phoebe were over by the pianoforte sifting through a portfolio of music and discussing Mozart and Haydn.

Jane leaned forward. "You see, the earl is my first cousin. Our families lived in different parts of England, but we visited each other often as children. I know him well—perhaps better than anyone else."

His cousin? Serena held her hands clasped tightly in her lap, though they twitched to fly to cover her burning face. She'd been jealous about Jonathan and his *cousin*? She was such an idiot.

"I see," she said in a near whisper.

Jane took another sip of her tea. "After you and your sister left England, Stratford went through a very difficult period. I didn't see him often during that time, but I heard about his exploits." She sighed.

"From time to time, I believed he was deliberately killing himself."

Serena stared into the depths of her tea as Jane continued in a low voice. "The worst of it was that not only did he destroy himself, but he brought his friends down with him."

Serena looked up. "But why are you telling me this?"

"Because he's changed."

Serena gave her a doubtful look, and Jane raised her hand in capitulation. "Nothing he can ever do or say can make your sister come back, and Stratford knows this, Meg. For the first few years after her death, he couldn't stand that. But now—well, I believe he finally comprehends that debauchery and dissolution cannot clear a man's conscience. He has slowly been turning away from his previous exploits, become more thoughtful and sedate, and has chosen to spend more time with those of his friends who are true gentlemen."

"Like Will," Serena murmured.

Jane's smile grew wide. "Exactly. Like Captain Langley. And Mr. Kincaid."

Serena tilted her head. "How is it that you know Mr. Kincaid? You seem very close. Is he a cousin, too?"

Jane laughed, a bright tinkle that sounded like the fall of diamonds. "Oh, no, not at all." She leaned a bit closer. "Kincaid and I were friends when my husband was alive, but now..." Her voice trailed off as she glanced up at Kincaid, whose back was turned toward them as he bent over a sheet of music. "Now we are much more."

As Serena began to understand the implication, Kincaid turned, holding the music toward Jane. "Will you gift us with this one, my lady?"

"Oh, what is it?"

"A Haydn sonata."

With a small chuckle, Jane rose, took the pages from Kincaid, sat at the bench, and proceeded to prove that she'd been grossly misrepresenting her talent when she'd said she only knew how to play a few songs on the pianoforte.

Serena had heard this song once before—at the recital where she'd met Jonathan for the first time. He'd been sitting in front of her and had kept glancing back over his shoulder at her through the song, and Serena had been blushing and wondering what his name was, and hoping beyond hope that they would somehow be introduced.

When the song was over an intermission was called, and as she and her aunt and sister had stood conversing with an older lady, he'd approached them. He'd greeted the other woman—Serena had forgotten her name—and then, the woman introduced them. Serena remembered the thrill that his smile had sent through her, the way hearing her name on his lips had sent a shiver over her skin.

Serena glanced up at a movement in the corner

of her eye. Will's gaze caught hers and held. He tilted his head in a silent greeting and lowered himself beside her on the sofa, his own teacup held in one hand. He leaned toward her, his voice little more than a whisper. "One cannot help but to wonder what you are thinking, Meg, when your eyes travel so far away and the color moves across your cheeks just here."

He reached up and brushed the flat of his thumb near her cheek, not touching her skin, but close enough that she could feel the warmth of his.

For a long moment, she froze, uncertain of what to do or say. She felt Jonathan's gaze prickle over them as Jane stopped playing, laughing that she'd rather engage in conversation with her guests than sit all alone at a pianoforte. Kincaid helped her rise from the bench, easily acquiescing.

"What are you thinking, Meg?"

Turning back to Will, Serena spoke tightly. "I was thinking of the . . . fowl."

"The fowl?" Will frowned. "At dinner? The duckling or the goose?"

Oh, this was terrible. "The goose."

She was a goose.

"Ah, the goose. It was delicious, wasn't it?"

"Superb. I have never had such . . . such finely roasted goose."

"You must ask Lady Montgomery if her cook would share the recipe with our cook."

Our cook? The goose curdled in Serena's stomach. She'd met Will's cook—a stout, competent-looking woman—once. Soon, she supposed, she'd be Serena's cook as well, and Serena, as the lady of the household, would be her employer.

Across the room, Mr. Kincaid and Jane fell into an impassioned debate about a viscountess who'd left her husband and fled to the continent with her groomsman. Jane claimed the woman had good reason, for the husband was abusive, but Kincaid argued there could be no reason good enough for a woman to betray a spouse. Jonathan joined in the debate, and Phoebe listened to the scandalous topic with rapt attention. Will leaned closer to Serena and lowered his voice. "You look beautiful tonight, Meg."

"Thank you." She gazed down at her hands clasped in her lap.

After a lengthy pause, Will whispered, "I wish we were alone."

Serena's head jerked up, and her eyes met Jonathan's across from her. He'd turned away from the conversation and had been watching Serena and Will.

Every cell in Serena's body froze. This was it. He would tell everyone her true identity now. Will would cast her aside, and she would be ruined. Again.

She stared at Jonathan, not moving, not breathing, frozen in her panic.

Then the flame in his eyes banked to a low simmer,

and he made an effort to smile, though there was a grimness to it Serena prayed no one else could see.

He approached, addressing Will. "Looks like you're eager for your wedding day, old friend." Jonathan had infused lightness into his tone, but it was edged by the same heat that burned in his gaze.

Will lifted her free hand and kissed it. "I am, indeed."

Oh, good God. She cast Jonathan a pleading look. *Stop this. Please.*

But he didn't stop. "Are the plans in order for the blessed event?"

"Almost there," Will said proudly.

How disconcerting. She felt warm and jittery, like she'd just swallowed a gallon of tea, but she looked into her cup and saw that she'd barely taken a sip.

Will squeezed her hand, beaming at her as if to say how proud he was of her for accepting Jonathan into their lives after all that had happened between him and Serena.

"I'm looking forward to standing beside you on your wedding day," Jonathan told Will.

Serena tried to hide her shudder. How would she endure reciting her marital vows with Jonathan, the man she'd once loved, once dreamed of marrying, standing beside her husband-to-be?

She'd endure it. She had no choice, after all.

Chapter Twelve

After the pleasant but uninspiring night at Lady Montgomery's house, Phoebe came down with a terrible cold.

It was a lie, of course. Phoebe didn't have a cold at all. It had been a grand—and very successful—show for the past several days that had not only allowed her to catch up on some much-needed sleep, but had also made it possible for her to see Sebastian nearly every night.

Sebastian's company was something to look forward to far more than any mildly entertaining evening with her sister's crowd. Phoebe liked Captain Langley and Lady Montgomery, and she especially liked the scandalous, mysterious Lord Stratford, but being with them for an entire night wasn't nearly as exciting as being with Sebastian for one minute.

Phoebe slipped her hand through Sebastian's and stared up at the starry sky, then slanted her gaze toward him. Her beloved was edgy tonight, like a tiger with hackles raised and claws distended, ready to pounce on some unsuspecting prey.

His fingers curled around her hand, though, tight and secure.

"Are you frustrated because we must always meet in secret?" she asked in a low voice.

He looked at her, a frown furrowing his brows. "No, that's not it. I expected your family to forbid you to see me."

She gritted her teeth to prevent herself from blurting yet again how much she despised Serena for making that ruthless, thoughtless commandment. She'd thought her sister had some sense, but no, she was just as cruel as Mother and Aunt Geraldine.

"Oh, love. I wish..." He looked away, clearly frustrated.

They walked along the border between Hyde Park and Mayfair, and Phoebe was well aware that someone she knew could drive by and see her with Sebastian. She didn't care one bit, though. Let them see her!

But a tiny part of her shivered at that notion. If Aunt Geraldine thrust her onto a ship back to Antigua...

Well, she'd simply jump overboard and swim back to London and Sebastian, that's what she'd do.

"I wish it didn't have to be this way," Sebastian murmured.

She glanced at him sharply, reeling to a halt when she saw the glistening sheen in his eyes.

"It doesn't," she said.

He blinked at her.

"Come away with me," she whispered. "Let's go to Scotland. Let's get married. To the devil with all of them!" She flung her arm out in a wide, all-encompassing gesture.

He blinked again, harder this time. "Phoebe..."

"Why not?" she demanded. "I don't care about anything. About anyone but you, Sebastian. I..." She hesitated, then swallowed down the sudden lump in her throat and whispered, "I don't want to be without you."

He reached up and stroked a knuckle down her cheek. "This is my fault," he murmured. Pain clouded his eyes. "I want you so much, but..."

His voice dwindled as a carriage passed on the nearby street, its wheels rattling over the pavement and breaking the peace of the night. Phoebe ignored it.

"No, it's not your fault. Don't you see? It's *their* fault."

He shook his head. "No. It is mine. I destroyed any chance I ever had at success before I was even given it. I've lost what little I have, I've no profession and no hopes for one." His big palms curled over her shoulders. "Don't you see, love? Now that I've finally been given a reason to do well for myself, it might be too late."

"No!" she exclaimed, then leaned into him, pressing her face against his chest. "No, Sebastian." She kissed his breastbone through his coat, not caring a whit if anyone saw her. "No. We can do anything. You are so young. You can become anything. It's not too late."

His arms slipped around her, so gentle, so comforting. He was so much more to her than she could have ever imagined. She believed in him. He was intelligent, perceptive, thoughtful. He could do anything he set his mind to. He could conquer the world.

He cupped her cheeks in his big, warm hands and tilted her head up until she looked into his eyes. "I want to take you home," he whispered, blinking away the sheen in his eyes. "Will you come home with me, Phoebe?"

A thrill ran through her. She knew exactly what this meant. Finally, *finally,* he would make her his.

"Yes, Sebastian. Take me home."

Serena closed her book, turned down her lamp, and glanced at the door, wondering whether to go check on Phoebe. No, she didn't dare risk waking her sister. She'd had a bad cold and needed her rest. Sighing, she went to her heavily draped bed and slipped under the chilly covers.

She inhaled deeply and caught a wisp of Jonathan's scent. Dry grass in the sun. She and Will had encountered him in the park today—yet again—but why could she still smell him?

She remembered how he had laid her on a bed of summer grass and caressed her with his hands, lips, and body, and whispered heated, passionate words into her ear.

After everything that happened later, she never believed he'd planned to seduce her and then turn her away. It might make her naïve, or even stupid, but she truly believed that at the beginning, he had been as much a slave to their passion as she had.

For a long while, she lay on her back staring upward, seeing only the blurred, shadowy outlines of the ceiling molding.

After several meetings with him in Will's presence, she'd finally come to the conclusion that Jonathan didn't plan to tell Will about discovering her identity.

But why? What were Jonathan's real intentions? She understood why he'd kissed her—because he'd believed it had been a way to find out if she truly was Meg. But what did he plan to do with the knowledge? If he considered himself such close friends with Will, why hadn't he exposed her already?

It was horrible and it was sinful, and she felt like she was deceiving everyone, even herself. But after all these years, she still wanted Jonathan. So badly her body ached with it. His kiss, his lips—she had forgotten what they could do to her until he'd kissed her in his kitchen. Those kisses melted every iota of her resistance as swiftly as the sun melted snow in the summertime. Falling, spinning deep into his caress, it had taken long moments—too many moments—for her to come to her senses and realize the wickedness of her actions.

She stretched her limbs, reaching to grasp the headboard and point her toes to the foot of the bed, then flipped herself over, embracing the frigid sheets like a lover.

She and Jonathan had not planned to rendezvous that night at the dowager duchess's ball. They'd spotted each other across the ballroom. After they'd exchanged a series of glances and gestures, he'd led her into an alcove at the top of the stairs surrounded by heavy velvet curtains. Like a balcony at the theater, the alcove looked over the ballroom below. The danger of it had excited her, made her shameless, reckless.

She had wasted no time. As soon as he sat on a plush velvet armchair, she unbuttoned the falls of his breeches, then lifted her skirts, straddled him, and set herself over him. She'd felt such exquisite pleasure at that moment, knowing they were surrounded and that if she made one small noise, many people would hear it.

Serena hiked up her night rail and slid her hand

between the bed and her body, cupping her palm over the soft curls. How he had filled her there. Deep within her, his energy permeated every inch of her body, made her feel full and alive. Happy.

She tightened her buttocks and thrust her body into her palm, into the bed. He had held her by the hips, pumping inside her to the lively music. She squeezed her eyes shut. The sounds of the quadrille resonated in her mind. She thrust to that same rhythm now.

She had reserved the dance for someone else. The idea that she'd jilted another gentleman to be with Jonathan instead, and the gentleman would likely be searching for her, that the risk of what she and Jonathan were doing was very great indeed, opened her wider. The thrill of danger made her slick between her legs, made her nipples tighten to the point of pain, made her shudder from head to toe.

To feel that way again…oh, how she wanted it. She'd never felt so free before that moment, or since.

The way he had moved beneath her had rubbed against her most sensitive spot. Now, she slipped two fingers deep inside herself, then out, touching that place Jonathan had stroked over and over with his body.

The sudden sound of laughter just beyond the curtains had racked her with spasms, and lust had torn her apart, made her lose herself, made her cry out.

Serena muffled her cry into her pillow now as the

muscles in her body tightened and then released in a flood, and her sex pulsed around her drenched fingers.

It was then that the dowager duchess had found them.

Slowly, Serena relaxed, sinking deep into the bed. After that night, shame, scandal. Jonathan had not offered for her as she'd believed he would. He had not saved her from disgrace. Instead, he'd turned away from her. He'd given her the direct cut.

Aunt Geraldine told her that she was a weak, odious creature, a stupid, amoral slut and that Jonathan had never wanted her. Soon thereafter, Serena had left London in shame.

"Why?" She asked it aloud. Why did it have to be this way?

She rolled onto her side, tucked her knees into her chest, and stared at the door, sick with the unfairness of it all.

Sebastian rented rooms in a part of London Phoebe hadn't yet visited. The streets were busy in this area, but they were narrower, the houses smaller and in various states of disrepair, tucked close together. Savory steam wafted out from the sealed windows of pie shops closed for the evening, and spring flowers bloomed in window boxes, but these pleasant smells mixed with the rank odors of fetid water and smoke.

Sebastian stopped at a tall, narrow door set right

up against the pavement. He held her close against him, his fingers squeezing over hers while he fumbled with the key in his other hand. She watched him out of the corner of her eye.

He was nervous, and that gave her a flush of pleasure. She knew he was an experienced lover—he'd told her he was, and it didn't surprise her, what with him being a young buck about Town. But he was anxious this time, because it was her, Phoebe Donovan, and he cared for her.

He went inside and drew her into the dark, closing the door and leaving them in utter blackness.

"Wait here. I'll light a candle."

She did as she was told, tugging off her gloves as shuffling footsteps moved away from her and she heard the sounds of him fumbling about. Light flickered and blazed to life, revealing him by a table in the small room beyond the tiny entry hall. He smiled at her, his handsome face bathed in a yellow glow, and she smiled back.

"It's nothing like Lady Alcott's house," he said, apologetic.

She shook her head. "How could you think I would care about such a thing?"

A fine line appeared between his brows as his smile faded. "Everyone does, Phoebe."

She could see it: the pain in his expression—the hurt that stemmed from the fact that some stupid, arbitrary line had been drawn between him and his "betters."

"Not me," she said. "I don't care one bit."

He reached out his hand, and she went to him. He enveloped her in his arms, drawing her hood off and burying his face in her hair. "I'm not good enough for them," he murmured. "I'm not good enough for you."

She pulled away to frown up at him. "You cannot be serious."

His nod was tiny, but there it was, and all at once she understood his hesitation with her, his insistence on treating her like a piece of glass.

"My family is poor," she said. Probably poorer than his, when all was said and done.

"But aristocratic. Your uncle was a viscount. Your grandfather was a earl."

"My father was nobody."

"He was of noble birth."

"Noble *Irish* birth," she corrected in a low voice. "To most of the English, that is a few steps *below* nobody."

He looked at her, and she rested her cheek against his shoulder. "I'm just a person, Sebastian. Just a woman, like any woman you've ever known. A woman who"—she hesitated, then swallowed hard—"loves you."

"But why me?" he whispered.

"I could ask the same question of you." And she had asked it of herself, night after night, since she'd met him. With his dark, sleek good looks, women must clamor to be in his bed. Yet he'd chosen her.

He pulled her away from his body and framed her face with his hands, tilting her head up so she faced him. "You're different from the others. You understand me like no one else. I can be myself with you." He hesitated, and the look in his eyes melted a spot deep inside her. "You soothe me, Phoebe. You siphon away all the rage I feel at the world and leave only calmness and peace."

His voice was so soft it reminded her of a leather saddle her father had owned, so used and worn she would go into the stables and rub her hand over it again and again, loving the supple feel of it against her palm.

That was long ago. Before they'd sold the horses. She wondered what had happened to that saddle.

"Yes," she whispered. "I feel the same way about you."

The truth of it stroked through her, like his voice, like the leather of the saddle, softening every bit of her from head to toe. She'd never felt more comfortable, more herself, with anyone.

Sebastian was *special.* No matter what Serena said, what *anyone* said, she wouldn't let him go.

He lowered his lips to hers, gentle, loving, caring, and she slipped her arms around him and moved her lips against his in a slow dance as old as time. A dance he'd begun to teach her but had stopped again and again before it was properly finished. Tonight, they'd take the dance all the way to completion, and she couldn't wait.

"Make me yours, Sebastian," she whispered against his mouth.

His arms tightened around her, and his hand moved to her neck to untie the strings of her cloak. Fabric puddled at her feet, but she hardly noticed. She was fumbling with his cravat. Finally managing to untie the long tails of stiff white fabric, she pushed it away and began to work on the buttons of his waistcoat. She pulled the woolen edges open, and he shrugged, allowing his coat and waistcoat to fall to the floor.

There it was. His shirt, white and billowing, freed from the constraints of his coats. She ran her hand down the front, fascinated by the feel of linen under her hand, hardly noticing that he'd gone to work on the buttons at the back of her dress.

She'd worn only her simplest dress and cloak over her chemise tonight. No petticoat, no stays. When he parted the material of her dress and drew it down over her shoulders, she looked up at him.

"I've never done this before." Her voice was breathless.

"I know you haven't." His hands stilled, cupping her shoulder blades. "Do you want me to stop?"

"You know I don't. I want you. I've wanted you from the beginning."

He stared at her. "I know it hurts the first time, Phoebe. I'll try..." His Adam's apple bobbed as he swallowed hard. "I'll try my damndest not to hurt you, but..."

"It's all right," she whispered, pressing two fingers over his lips.

He shook his head. "No, it's not. I don't want to hurt you."

"I know."

"If I must stop, tell me. Tell me anytime, and I'll stop."

"I trust you, Sebastian."

When her dress slid down, snagging on her hips, she pushed it the rest of the way off and stepped out of it, leaving a pile of her clothing on the floor.

The room was tiny, with a small table to one side and a tidy sofa near a compact fireplace. A closed door stood between the sofa and the table, and Sebastian took her hand and opened the door.

"No one comes here." He glanced over his shoulder at her while he led her into the bedchamber. "Nobody but me has been in this place since I first came to London."

She didn't need to ask him why. It was because he had wanted to portray the image that he was better than this small dwelling. He wanted people to imagine that perhaps he lived in a house as grand as Aunt Geraldine's.

"I'm glad you brought me here," she said. Though it was plain, it was tidy and homey, with a neat stack of newspapers in a pile near the sofa and a fresh loaf of bread and square of butter on a plate on the well-worn table. The bed was narrow but neatly made, and Sebastian's clothes lay crisply folded on the parallel rows of shelves nearby.

Even though the place was small and simple, he treated it with care, and that showed her something about his character she'd already suspected—he respected simple things. Ultimately, Sebastian was a simple, good man trying to live in a world in which he didn't belong.

Phoebe studied his face, suddenly feeling to her soul that she understood him in a way that he himself had only recently come to terms with. How could that be? He'd lived in his own skin for twenty-one years, and she'd only known him for a few weeks.

He smiled down at her, and she gazed up at him, allowing all her desperate longing—*caring*—for him to show in her face.

Tension tightened his cheeks, and need flared in his eyes. "I love you, Phoebe Donovan," he whispered, and he kissed her again.

This kiss wasn't as gentle as the last. It was possessive and thorough. A rush of passion, of desire, soft as warm water yet with all the force of a flood. Phoebe wrapped her arms around him, tugging his shirt up from the waist of his trousers and sliding her hands beneath, gliding them over the smooth furnace of his skin.

His lips moved down her neck, and then his fingers were fumbling with the strings of her chemise. Likewise, her hands traveled to the ties at his neck. They untied each other's strings simultaneously, and they dropped their arms to grab handfuls of material to pull over their heads. Phoebe lifted her chemise, yanked it off, and tossed it aside, leaving only her drawers, shoes, and stockings on. At the same time, he threw his shirt over his shoulder, and her breath caught in her throat.

His bare torso, shining gold in the lamplight streaking in from the adjacent room. How beautiful he was—all slender, manly muscle. She blinked hard at the planes of his chest and then looked up in his face just in time to see a similar awe crossing his features as his gaze took in the swell of her breasts, the pucker of her nipples.

She hesitated then, staring at him, keeping her muscles from forcing her to lurch toward him, from obeying the compulsion to touch him all over, to drink him in.

"So…beautiful," he choked out. He curled his fingers around her waist, his skin rasping over hers as he drew her upward and forward. Tenderly, he cupped her breast in his palm and then bent down and pressed his lips to the tip.

It was as if something connected his lips to her breast to her very insides. Sharp, prickling sensation buzzed through her so powerfully, her knees threatened to buckle. She reached up, grabbing his shoulders as his free hand slid around her back and drew her closer to him, supporting her. She gasped. Goodness, what pleasure! What power could be transferred in just the simple press of his mouth to her breast!

He moved to the other side, his lips soft, questing, and she looped her arms around his waist, her palms flat on the warm skin of his back, murmuring into the thick black mass of his hair.

He drew back from her breast. "Go to the bed."

His voice contained the soft lilt of a question in it. She complied readily, lowering herself onto its edge and then swinging her legs over and tucking herself against the wall, making room for him to crawl in beside her.

The narrowness of the bed pressed them together by necessity, but Phoebe didn't care. Her heart pattered with excitement, her flesh felt hot and prickly, and a strange, empty ache resided between her legs.

"Touch me, Phoebe."

He guided her hand until her fingers brushed the length of his manhood. She sucked in a breath, looking at him with wide eyes. He released her hand, and she gave him an experimental swipe, fascinated by the ridges and bumps, the steel of muscle beneath the silky layer of skin.

She watched him in curiosity, studying the way his lips parted and his eyelids grew heavy. "Does it feel good when I touch you here?"

"Ah... Yes."

She frowned. She wanted to know what to do,

how to please him. She wanted to make him groan like she'd groaned when he'd kissed her breasts.

"But . . . tell me how."

"You're doing very well."

She moved her hand away slightly. "I want to know what feels best."

He moved his hand down again and cupped it over hers, pushing her fingers so they curled over his shaft and she gripped him gently in her fist.

He nodded on a sigh of pleasure, his eyes half-lidded. "That's right. Now . . . stroke me. Gently. Up and down."

She did as he said, concentrating on the feel of him, his length, girth, softness, and hardness.

"Very . . . very . . . good."

"I've always been a fast learner." She gave him a wicked smile, and he set his lips on hers, his own hand insinuating between her dampened thighs, touching her, stroking her, until she squirmed and gasped.

"Enough." He jerked away from her, pulling himself from her grasp and removing his hand from her body.

Phoebe's eyes popped open, and, yanked out of pleasure, she stared at him stupidly. "What—?"

But he rolled her onto her back and he moved over her, pinning her wrists against the bed, his sex heavy against her thigh.

He stared down at her, his eyes sparkling obsidian in the meager light of the candle.

"Are you ready for me?"

She looked at him, at his narrow, beautiful face, strong bones, the strand of thick dark hair falling haphazardly over one eye, and she knew, without a doubt, that she was his. There would be no one else for her. Ever.

"Yes, Sebastian, I'm ready."

There was pain, in the beginning. At first sharp, then subduing to a dull throb, drowning beneath the tide of pleasure that swept between her thighs and through her body. Sebastian gazed down into her eyes as he moved deep within her, and she whispered his name with every breath she took.

"Sebastian. Sebastian. Sebastian."

This would never end. This was where she was meant to be, in Sebastian Harper's arms, forever. She gripped his shoulders and looked up at him, and something powerful flowed between them, so strong that she was unaware of anything but their connection and their love.

Suddenly, he jerked out of her. Gathering her quickly into his arms, his body tightened and shuddered. And then he was still.

Phoebe was confused. After a long silence in which Sebastian didn't move, she asked, "What just happened?"

He raised his head as slowly and heavily as if it were solid iron. And he stared at her, a frown puckering the skin between his brows. "What?"

"You pulled away," she whispered. "And then you...stopped."

He blinked, stared at her for a few more seconds, and then all the tension seemed to drain from his body. Sighing, he rolled off her, then tucked her up against him, stroking her hair as she nuzzled against his chest.

"How much do you know about when a man and woman join together, Phoebe?"

She stiffened, just a little. "Why, I know quite a lot. I should say I do, since I am now rather experienced in the matter."

She cringed at the offended huff in her voice. She was confused, certainly, but of course no one had ever bothered to walk her through the steps of lovemaking. Still, she wasn't an idiot. It wasn't her fault she wasn't sure about the intricacies of the act.

His fingers sifted through the strands of her hair again, and his chest rose against her cheek as he took a breath. Now that it was all over, she could feel the ache of his penetration filling her between her legs.

"When a man comes...finishes," he corrected, "he releases his seed into the woman."

"I know that." But he hadn't done that...at least, she didn't think he had.

"But it wouldn't be right for me to get you with child," he murmured, his fingers stilling, wrapped within strands of her hair. "So just before I finished, I pulled out of your body." He seemed to hesitate for a moment. "It doesn't guarantee anything, but it can help to prevent conception."

She pulled her head off his chest to look up at him. "Oh, Sebastian, I don't care about that!"

His eyes darkened. "You should."

"But I don't!"

"Surely you know what would become of your reputation should I get you with child."

She blew out a frustrated breath and turned away from him. Her voice was ragged when she spoke. "I don't care about my damned reputation. I care about you."

"God, Phoebe. I care about you, too. Don't you see? You're *all* I care about. I don't want to hurt you."

"You won't hurt me."

"If I were to get you with child—" He stopped talking and simply shook his head.

She scrambled around to face him again. "Then let's go away from London. I want to be with you. I don't care about anything else, either. I just want you. Just you!"

He gazed at her, the planes of his face flickering gold in the candlelight. "You could do better than me. You know that, don't you?"

"No," she whispered. "You're the best man for me, Sebastian. I feel it. Here." She reached down, took his hand, and pressed it against her heart.

"I feel it, too . . . but . . ."

"Believe it," she said. "Believe in us."

He looked at her for long moments, his hand pressing against her wildly beating heart.

"Yes," he finally agreed. "Just you. And me. I'll take care of you if it kills me. There's nothing more important."

He sucked in a breath, closed his eyes, and then opened them again in a long blink. "Phoebe Donovan, will you come away with me?"

Joy surged through her, so powerful that for a long moment, she couldn't speak. And then she said, in a solemn whisper, "Yes, Sebastian Harper. I'll come away with you."

And with that, they began to plan their escape.

Chapter Thirteen

"Going somewhere?"

Serena whipped her head around. The gloom of the stable lay thick and heavy, and the man who'd spoken was only a shadowy silhouette in the doorway, but Serena would know that shape, that voice, anywhere. *Jonathan.* He must have seen the servants preparing for her departure.

In the past two weeks, Jonathan had been ever-present, but not in an invasive kind of way. He was simply *there,* and she'd given up trying to avoid him. He often rode in the park during Will and Serena's daily rides and always engaged in pleasant conversation with them on the path. He attended nearly every evening gathering Serena did, and late at night, he filled her fantasies.

Everyone except Serena had grown accustomed to

his constant presence. She'd learned not to show her discomfiture when he was near. She'd made certain to never get herself into a situation in which she'd be alone with him. In public, she kept either Phoebe or Will with her at all times. Even if he'd tried, Jonathan wouldn't have been able to catch her alone.

She wondered if he'd tried. The wicked part of her hoped he had, but every day she was getting better at quelling that wickedness.

Nevertheless, he'd caught her now. Last week, she and Phoebe had accepted an invitation from Jane to visit her house in Bath. They were to depart this morning, but Serena had been ready to go for some time, so she'd come into the stables for a few moments of quiet. Mostly to think, to debate the idea of not going at all, and to ruminate over the problem of Phoebe.

"Yes, I am going somewhere." Her voice sounded unnaturally loud in the enclosed space of the stable. The horse she'd been brushing shifted its feet, and its nostrils flared. She laid a calming hand over its flank. Ever since they'd lost the horses in Antigua, she'd missed having them. Even though she wasn't a great rider, simply being near the animals calmed her. "Didn't Lady Montgomery tell you?"

"I haven't seen her."

"We're off to her house in Bath. We'll be gone two or three weeks, I expect."

It was meant to be a summer adventure for Jane, Phoebe, and her. A few weeks of fun before they returned to London to celebrate Meg and Will's marriage.

Now, however, Serena wasn't sure she should go. Her sister had upset everyone's plans.

In the dimness, she saw Jonathan's features tighten. "Is Langley going?"

She gazed at him, keeping her expression perfectly flat. "He had hoped to, but he was called to work at his offices."

"Ah."

Was that a trick of light, or was it a flicker of relief passing over his face?

She'd been excited about the trip, thrilled to get out of London for a while to enjoy herself far away from the searching, questioning, consuming blue eyes of the Earl of Stratford. Perhaps if she were away from him, she could think more clearly about her tangled feelings.

That disconcerting gaze probed her now. "Two or three weeks is a long while."

"It will seem to be rather a short while, I expect." She kept her voice light. "Jane wanted us to stay longer, but we must return to London to—" She broke off. The reason they had to come back so quickly was to have some time to finish preparations for the wedding, but she didn't want to talk to Jonathan about her wedding. "To attend to some business," she finished clumsily.

"I see."

"I was here"—she gestured around the stable—"thinking about whether I should go to Bath at all."

She supposed if there was anyone she could speak freely with about this problem, it was Jonathan. Brushing her hands together, she stepped out of the stall and drew closer to him until she could see the finer details of his expression in the stable's gloom.

"Phoebe has taken ill. *Again.* She has a headache and says she can scarcely sit up in bed without feeling like she's going to vomit. She claims that she cannot tolerate a carriage." Serena crossed her arms over her chest. "Phoebe is prone to severe headaches on occasion. But this time I fear she is lying."

"Why?"

"I assure you, I have followed your advice. I have tried not to be overbearing or dictatorial. Despite forbidding her to see Mr. Harper, I've given her a great deal of freedom here in London. Yet, I have this foreboding feeling…I'm afraid she's attempting to take advantage of the opportunity to seek out Mr. Harper while I'm away."

"Ah, I see." Jonathan leaned against the door frame, his casual stance drawing her attention to the snugness of his coat over his broad shoulders. "Well, then, I suppose it's good that I found you. I can allay your fears. Harper is no longer in town. He's been called away to Prescot—he owns a small parcel of land and a house there. I saw him three nights ago settling a debt in anticipation of leaving Town the following morning."

"Really?" Phoebe hadn't mentioned that, but perhaps she didn't know. She hadn't received any messages from Mr. Harper—and Serena had kept a strict eye open for any sign of communication between the two young people.

"He's gone. In fact, he told me he's given up the lease he had on his town house. He doesn't plan to return to London for some time."

Relief washed through her. "Do you think he left Town because he realized his suit for Phoebe was destined for failure?"

Jonathan fixed his gaze on the stall beyond her shoulder. A horse whickered, and she heard the sound of stirring straw, but she didn't turn to look. "He didn't say so, Serena, but I believe that might be at the core of it."

A little thrill buzzed through her when she heard her real name. From Jonathan's lips, it seemed even more wicked than it should.

She wouldn't have to worry about Phoebe now, but she felt an unexpected sympathy for both Mr. Harper and her sister. Perhaps if Mr. Harper truly loved Phoebe, he'd change his life, make something of himself, and then renew his suit in a few years when he could prove his worthiness.

Serena's lips twisted. The chances of that were nil. After all she'd learned from her own experiences, how could such romantic, impossible thoughts enter her mind?

"Well, that's good then." All the tension brought on by Phoebe's claim of illness this morning drained away. "I'm so relieved to hear I've been worried over nothing. Thank you for telling me."

Jonathan shrugged. "It's best for them this way, isn't it?"

"Yes," Serena said firmly. "It is."

Poor Phoebe really was ill. Serena had been impatient and brusque with her this morning, not really believing that her headache was as bad as her sister said. Now, guilt washed over her.

She looked up at him. "Would you—would you mind checking on her once or twice while I am gone?"

He smiled. "Of course. I'll watch over her like a brother."

Surprisingly, Serena believed him. For the first time since she'd come back to London, she genuinely returned one of his smiles. They stood there, a few feet away from each other, smiling, and it felt natural. It felt honest and real, like a connection she could share with him and no one else. She was smiling at him as herself. Everyone else she smiled at, she did it as Meg.

If only she could slice away this moment and freeze it forever. In this moment, she was herself, and Jonathan was himself, and they *knew* each other.

He stepped forward, raising his hand. A smooth, gloved knuckle ran down her cheek. She stared at him, trapped by the lure of his eyes.

"Serena." It was a whisper of sound, spoken with reverence. He shook his head, gazed at her in wonder. "I never thought I'd be able to touch you again."

"I'm not Serena," she murmured, but it was a weak denial, and they both knew it.

Slowly, he bent down, closer, until she breathed him in. Her eyelids drifted shut as every inch of her body reached for him, shoving all rational thought into the background, leaving them squirming to be heard but helpless to stop her.

She reached up and pressed her palm against his chest, not to push him away but to encourage him to come closer. Through the layers of fabric, she could feel his heart, a steady, powerful throb against her hand.

She tilted her head up, reaching, seeking, and when his lips touched hers in the softest, lightest caress, her skin came to life and sizzled with awareness.

His lips brushed hers, once, twice, and then pressed gently. His arm, strong and sturdy, wrapped around her waist, keeping her flush against the hardness of his body.

All of Serena's restraint, all rational thought, melted away into a puddle at her feet. She couldn't remember why she'd ever resisted Jonathan's touch, his kiss. She was completely enthralled, completely thrown into the moment, into the feeling of his strong arms, his supple lips. Nothing else mattered.

The sound of footsteps crunching on nearby gravel made them jerk away from each other. Jonathan's gaze swung to the shadows, and his features relaxed as he saw someone round the stable's corner. "Yes?"

"Oh, forgive me, sir." Serena recognized the voice as belonging to one of the maids. "I was looking for Miss Donovan."

Jonathan stepped to the edge of the door and gestured into the stable. "She's here."

The girl's round, sun-pinked face came into view. "Pardon me, miss," she said, "but Lady Montgomery has arrived."

"Thank you. I'll be right out."

The maid left, and Serena looked up at Jonathan.

Not breaking his gaze from her face, he murmured, "I'll miss you, Serena."

"I'll see you in a few weeks." Blinking hard, she walked past him and toward the house and Jane, torn between begging him to stay with her and help her find some solution to the mire of her life, and escaping from him forever.

Ten days later, Jane led Serena toward the marble pump at the Pump Room in Bath. Serena took a glass of the waters from the attendant, but Jane declined.

Serena sipped the hot liquid, swirling it around in her mouth like a fine wine before swallowing.

"Well, what do you think?"

Serena took another sip, considering. "I like it."

A shudder rippled across Jane's thin shoulders. "Not me. I think it rather tastes like someone has boiled a rotten egg in it."

Serena smiled, her gaze wandering through the vast room. She'd always hoped to come to the famous town. "I'm glad we came, despite your dislike of the waters."

"It is quiet today," Jane observed. "Though we certainly aren't here at the fashionable hour."

"I prefer the quietness of it, I think."

Both women had dressed warmly, for there had been a chill in the air—Serena wore a dark pink walking dress of corded Italian silk with a black velvet bonnet and pelisse and a high, matching velvet collar. Jane's dress was darker and sterner—a slate-colored silk. They'd come inside to escape the stiff breeze that had assaulted them as they were shopping.

The pump room was airy and bright, a glorious place. Recessed windows surrounded the fireplaces flanking the pump, and the wall opposite the pump consisted more of glass than plaster. White Corinthian columns separated the windows, which were tall and rectangular, topped with molding and oval windows above. The building provided a sheltered haven from the wind and amassing clouds but almost gave the impression of being outdoors.

"The crowds will arrive soon." Jane gestured at the platform built into one end of the room where several men were setting up their musical instruments. "They're preparing for the afternoon concert."

Side by side, Serena and Jane began a slow promenade, walking along the outer edges of the room, their heels clacking on the wood floor. The murmurs of the sparse crowd added to the serene calm of the place. Serena gazed out the tall windows as they passed. The clouds had gathered into a dense mass of grays, and now a light rain sprinkled over the city of Bath.

She handed her empty glass to a serving girl and wondered if it was raining in London. Whether Jonathan was caught out in it.

Why was she thinking of him? Again?

She brushed her fingers over her lips, which still seemed to tingle from his last kiss. She couldn't stop herself. She was in the city Jonathan had run to after he'd heard of her "death." This was the city where he'd cuckolded a man of God.

Every day, she walked the streets and imagined Jonathan having passed over those same stretches of pavement and dirt years before. Had he been thinking about her? About the look on her face when he'd turned his back on her?

She didn't understand her own feelings. For so many years, the possibility of her forgiving Jonathan for what he'd done had been as remote as the stars. And now . . .

Jane laid a hand on her arm. "Would you like us to return to London sooner than planned? Do you miss

Captain Langley terribly? And I know you've been concerned about leaving your sister all alone in London."

She gave Jane a firm smile. She'd had two letters from her sister, who seemed fully recovered and quite bored without her in London. "Not at all, Jane. My aunt is looking after Phoebe. And Will is very busy. And in any case, we've only a few more days here."

"I'll do my best to ascertain that the next few days fly by," Jane promised.

The days had already passed so quickly that Serena found it difficult to believe their time in Bath had almost come to an end. She smiled at her friend. "I've no doubt of that."

Jane drew her to a stop, and the two women gazed at a marble statue that occupied the alcove at the eastern end of the building.

"This is Beau Nash," Jane said. "Bath would be nothing but another provincial town without Nash. He brought society, fashion, and architecture here. But alas, he was a fool."

"A fool? Why?"

"His genius was overcome by his disease."

Serena frowned. She didn't know as much as she should about British notables, she supposed. "What disease?"

"Gambling. He lost all at the gaming tables."

"You speak of gambling as if it were a bona fide illness."

"Well," Jane said slowly, "I do believe it can be.

One need only observe all the men and women in recent history who have succumbed to it. Just like any fatal disease, once a person reaches a certain point, there is no turning back, no recovery."

Gazing at the sleek lines of the marble statue, Serena frowned. She wondered about Sebastian Harper. Had he gone that far? She was glad he'd come to his senses and left London before it was too late.

And what about Jonathan? He seemed so calm, so logical. She couldn't imagine him being overcome by such a disease.

They began their promenade again. "Jane," Serena asked after a moment, "your cousin, Lord Stratford..."

Jane looked up at her. "Yes?"

"Well, I've heard rumors..."

"About his gambling?"

"Well, yes. That, among other things."

"I see," Jane murmured. "Well, Meg, you mustn't believe everything you hear, especially when it comes to my cousin. Stratford is no saint by any stretch of the imagination, but he's no devil, either—at least not as much of one as people might have you believe."

Serena frowned, and Jane leaned closer. "What, exactly, have you heard about him?"

If there was anyone who'd give her a straight answer, it was Jane. The words rushed out of her. "I heard that after my sister died, he cuckolded a clergyman here in Bath. I've heard that he compromised many women after that one...and that he's fathered a child born out of wedlock."

Jane nodded, her face tightening almost imperceptibly. "And you wish to know if there's any truth behind these accusations?"

"Yes."

"But why?"

Serena gave a jerk of a shrug. "Curiosity, I suppose. You see, my sister...Serena...well, she fell victim to Lord Stratford's charms. She took his dismissal very poorly."

Jane's face softened into compassion, and she squeezed Serena's hand. "Of course. I understand."

"I suppose I just wonder...what became of him," she said awkwardly.

"Well, most of what you said is true, unfortunately. Stratford did escape to Bath after hearing of your sister's death. When he returned to London, he became someone I could hardly endure. He was a different person—dedicated to making his parents as miserable as he possibly could. When his brother Gervase died, it only became worse."

"How?"

"It seemed like his singular goal was to make the world think the absolute worst of him. Women, drink, gambling...He engaged in nearly every vice you could imagine, and he did so with gusto. He broke many women's hearts, ruined debutantes, engaged in liaisons with married women. I thought at times that he provoked gossip about himself only to enhance his poor reputation, and yet I saw some of his debauchery with my own eyes."

"I see," Serena said. The waters seemed to have solidified in her stomach. But Jane hadn't directly answered to the accusation about the child born out of wedlock, and Serena was curious. "What about the child he was alleged to have fathered?"

Jane glanced at her and then looked away. "I believe that is one of the false rumors," she murmured.

Good, she wanted to say. She couldn't pinpoint why, but she hated the idea of Jonathan having a child.

Jane patted her hand. "None of it is important, though. It's over, isn't it? It's all in the past. Stratford has moved on, and you have, too."

Serena tried to smile. "Yes."

"And in the last few months, it seems my cousin's thirst for dissolution has finally been quenched. I can only hope that he'll find a good lady soon to settle down with and marry."

"Yes," Serena agreed, though the thought of Jonathan marrying some conceited aristocratic beauty made her ache all over.

"Even though he always promised not to," Jane continued.

Serena tilted her head in question.

"Oh, yes, after your sister left, Stratford was furious with his parents, and that fury lasted until his father's death. When the old earl was on his deathbed, Stratford promised him that he'd never marry." Jane chuckled, but the sound held little humor. "A servant heard and spread the rumor—it was quite a scandal for some time after the earl died."

"But why was he so angry?" Serena asked. She'd known how annoyed Jonathan had been with his parents while they were together, but those had just seemed to be the frustrations of a young man whose parents were making unwanted limitations on him.

"I believe he partly blamed them for your sister's death. They had forbidden him to acknowledge her, and when she left, he was inconsolable."

"And when she died..." Serena's voice trailed off.

"...He became someone else entirely," Jane finished.

Serena and Jane had reached the doors, which one of the attendants held open for them. They stepped out into the blustery day. The rain had stopped, but cold washed over Serena's face, harsh and chapping. Still, she was so grateful for Jane's willingness to show her Bath.

"I've always longed to come here," Serena said as they turned toward Jane's waiting carriage. "Thank you so much for inviting me to join you—this might be my last chance to visit Bath."

Jane's thin brows snapped together. "Why's that?"

"Will's homes are in Northumberland and London.

He plans for us to reside in London for the most part, due to his business, and also because he plans to help with my sisters' Seasons for the next few years, but I think we'll make frequent trips to the country."

"And he'll never travel anywhere else?"

Serena smiled. "Will is highly organized and eminently rational, and he rarely strays from his plans. I doubt he'll find any reason for us to travel to Bath."

"But you've come now," Jane pointed out.

"Ah, but we're not married yet. I decided to come independent of whether he chose to. Once I'm his wife, it'll be different."

The coachman opened the carriage door and lowered the step, then reached for Serena's hand.

Jane pressed her lips together. "It shouldn't be that way, Meg."

"But it is," Serena said, her voice mild as she took the coachman's hand and slid across the seat, making room for Jane. She'd made peace with her future limitations as the summer days had gone by and she'd grown more familiar with Will's ways. Meg wouldn't mind. She'd want to be by her husband's side and follow his well-planned agenda.

Meg would be happy living like that.

Chapter Fourteen

Serena woke to an incessant banging. It seemed like it had been going on for hours. She covered her face with her pillow in hopes of muffling the noise, but it did no good. *Thump, bang, bang… Thump, bang, bang…*

She threw off the pillow and swung her legs off the side of her bed, moving her toes around until they found the floor. She climbed down and gingerly felt her way to pull open the curtains. Moonlight streamed through the window, and she flung her robe over her shoulders and made her way to the door. She cracked the door open and looked into the corridor to see the silhouette of a figure already descending the stairs, candle in hand. *Jane.*

Hearing the sound of her footsteps, Jane looked over her shoulder and nodded at Serena, who thrust her arms into her robe as she followed her friend down the stairs.

"What is it?" Serena whispered.

"I've no idea. Let's see for ourselves."

At the bottom of the stairs, they turned and passed through the arched doorway leading to the entry hall. The butler, wearing a night shirt and a drooping night cap, was speaking to a dark-clad figure at the door.

"I beg you, sir, please return at a more tolerable hour—"

"No. I must see her *now.*"

"Stratford?" Jane exclaimed, rushing forward. "What on earth—?"

Swallowing hard, Serena moved to Jane's side. "What is it? Has something happened to Phoebe?"

Seeing the two ladies for the first time, Jonathan doffed his hat. He looked directly at Serena. "I must speak with you."

"What has happened?" she asked, choked by sudden fear. Why on earth had he come to Bath, and at this hour?

Jonathan's gaze slid to his cousin, to the butler, and back to Serena. "Alone," he clarified.

Beside her, Jane let out a harsh breath. "This is most uncivilized."

Jonathan kept his focus on Serena, not breaking her gaze to look at his cousin. "Please."

She gave him a tight nod and turned to Jane. "It's all right."

Frowning, Jane turned to her. “Are you certain?”

“Yes.”

Looking bewildered, Jane led them to the parlor and ordered the servant to stoke the fire and light the lanterns. After a few moments, the man had finished and was dismissed, and with a wary look at Serena and Jonathan, Jane followed, closing the door behind her with a light click.

After the door shut, Jonathan’s and Serena’s gazes swung toward each other.

“What is it?” Serena asked, breathless.

“It’s about your sister.”

Serena went stiff all over, more from the tightness in his expression than from his words.

“She left London day before yesterday. I went to your aunt’s house last evening to check on her, and Lady Alcott said you had summoned Phoebe to Bath. Did you?”

Serena took a moment to digest this. “No.”

“I thought not. I was certain if you had, you’d have made me aware of it.”

“Oh, God.” A hard ball of panic materialized in Serena’s gut. “She’s run off with Sebastian Harper, hasn’t she?”

“That seems to be the most likely scenario.”

She clenched her fists at her sides and glared at him, accusation burning hot in her eyes. “You said he left London.”

"He told me he was leaving London. That doesn't mean he actually did."

"He lied to you."

"That's highly probable."

Serena ground her teeth. "The two of them planned this."

Jonathan shifted uncomfortably. "When I asked your aunt where Phoebe had gone, she told me that a carriage arrived from Bath bearing a letter from you. In the letter, you stated that the carriage was borrowed from Lady Montgomery and that you wanted Phoebe to come to Bath now that her health had improved."

"And Aunt Geraldine believed her, but you didn't."

Jonathan nodded. "Your aunt sent Phoebe and her maid off in the carriage..."

"...Which didn't bring her here but took her to Sebastian Harper instead," Serena finished with a groan.

"It seems so," Jonathan said. "I'm sorry, Serena."

Serena gave a long blink, her mind calculating rapidly. "Do you know where they've gone?"

"I imagine there are only two places they could go: Harper's house in Prescot or Gretna Green."

"Is his house anywhere near the road between here and Gretna?"

"Not too far. A few hours' drive, at most."

Serena heaved a breath. She didn't want the world to know about this. Aunt Geraldine, Will, Mother—

if any of them found out, there would be disastrous consequences. She had no choice but to ask Jonathan for help. Again. "Can you take me there?"

"You shouldn't even feel compelled to ask. You know I will."

"If anyone discovers that we traveled alone, there will be an enormous scandal. My reputation—*Meg's* reputation—would be destroyed. And if Will found out…" She closed her eyes, then opened them to stare at Jonathan, trying to discern his true motivation. He held her gaze evenly.

Why did her gut tell her to trust him when she had no reason to believe she should? "We must take extreme measures to ensure that Will doesn't hear about this. That no one does." She studied him. "Do you agree?"

He responded quietly. "The rest of the world can rot, as far as I'm concerned, but as for Langley…" He let the word trail off, grimacing a little as he shook his head. "We'll settle the problem of him later. However, if you don't wish for him to hear about us chasing after your sister, then I'll do whatever I can to prevent it, Serena."

"Stop calling me Serena."

"No."

"I'm not Serena anymore," she pushed out. "I'm Meg now. I have to be."

"But you're not."

It was hopeless. She hated the idea of traveling

with Jonathan. Of spending time with him. But he was the one person who understood, who could help her save her sister.

"We'll leave right away. Tonight. But I must inform Jane."

His brow furrowed. "Are you certain you wish to confide in her?"

"You don't trust your own cousin?"

He tilted his head. "*I* trust her. But can you?"

"Yes," she said firmly. "I can't just vanish. She is my friend. She'll be of assistance in explaining this to my aunt and to Will. Without Jane's help, I might as well give it all up and reserve passage for Phoebe and me on the next ship to the West Indies."

He reached down, taking her hand and holding it between both of his own. Heat transferred from his palm to hers. "I'm going to help you. Trust me, Serena. I'll do whatever I can."

Facial hair darkened the curve of his jaw. Long ago, she had once held his jaw cupped in both her hands and stared into his eyes for several long moments. Just stared at him, drinking him in. His jawbone had melded against her, the beginnings of a beard rasped her skin, and she had the feeling of something very powerful, something hardly contained, lying beneath her hand. She'd felt euphoric, because he had made her believe that she could rein that power, bring it into herself.

But in the end, he had misled her. Just as he had likely misled countless others.

She jerked her gaze away from him, hearing a noise, then realizing it was herself, sighing. "I know about you," she murmured. "I know everything."

Jonathan looked up to the ceiling as if begging for holy deliverance. Then, very slowly, he lowered his chin and met her eyes. "My past—the past six years, in any case—is irrelevant."

She winced. She really didn't want to talk about this—not right now. She had to think of Phoebe. "Forgive me. I shouldn't have said anything. You owe me no explanation. You had no connection to me at the time."

"I thought you were dead."

She hadn't expected his loyalty in the past six years. She'd expected him to have married some high-and-mighty lady and have a brood of little lordly Jonathans by now. Truly, she had. Then why was it that on top of her disgust at his despicable behavior, she felt such bitter jealousy when she thought of him with all those other women?

She shook her head. "I—we can't talk about this right now. I must go fetch Jane."

She turned her back on him and hurried out of the parlor, where she found Jane waiting for them in the entry hall.

"Jane?" Serena asked, her whisper sounding loud in the nighttime hush of the household.

Jane turned toward her, frowning. "Is everything all right?"

"I need to speak to you about something. Would you mind joining Lord Stratford and me in the parlor?"

Worry lines creased Jane's forehead. "Of course, Meg."

Serena followed her friend into the parlor, praying that the three of them would be able to devise a good excuse for her and Phoebe's disappearance for the next several days.

Jonathan sat in Jane's parlor, listening in silence as his cousin and Serena planned the trip north. As Serena had predicted, Jane was more than helpful. He'd known Jane since they were both in swaddling clothes, and he'd hadn't seen this caring, protective side of her for many years. Yet here she was, devising elaborate lies to tell Langley and Serena's relatives about her whereabouts.

His cousin and Serena had become good friends, for certain. But even Jane didn't know Serena's true identity. He felt an odd kind of satisfaction in that. He was the only one outside of her immediate family who knew. He was one of the privileged few.

Jane hardly looked at him, and he was glad for that. Finally, though, when Serena went upstairs to dress and gather a few items for their journey, his cousin turned to him, dark scarlet dashes highlighting her cheeks.

"If you dare compromise that woman in any way,

I'll have your hide," she snapped as soon as Serena had closed the door.

He didn't doubt her. Still, he managed to look affronted. "What?"

"I know what you're about, Stratford. I've watched you every time I've been in the same room with the two of you over the past several weeks. I don't like the way you look at her."

He almost laughed. How little she understood. "Meg is mature and confident enough to make her own decisions," he said, keeping his voice mild.

"Don't you dare."

He shook his head. This was a useless conversation. "There is no subterfuge here, cousin. She needs my help to find her sister. There's nothing beyond that."

Of course he was lying. There was so much more.

"I don't believe you." Jane crossed her arms over her chest as she glared at him. She reminded him of a blond panther, sleek and dangerous, and ready to pounce. She had bared her claws and pounced on him once or twice in their childhood, and he bore the scratch marks to prove it. He didn't wish to repeat the experience tonight.

"You've developed quite a strong friendship with Miss Donovan in a very short amount of time," he observed.

"I like her."

That was enough, he supposed. Jane was discriminate in choosing her friends, but once she chose someone for an ally, that was all that was required to form a powerful bond.

"Don't stare at me like that," he said. "You know as well as I do that Meg is perfectly capable of taking care of herself."

"Don't do it, Stratford."

He looked away.

"She is engaged to Captain Langley, and he is a good man. If you compromise that—" Jane faltered, then stiffened her spine and continued. "Surely, you wouldn't. I've told her that you've been improving, and I believe that. Even four years ago, in the midst of all that debauchery, you would not have been so low. You wouldn't have dared do such a thing after what you did to her twin."

Ah, but would he have? She *was* her twin, after all.

No. He couldn't. He couldn't betray Langley. After Serena's "death," Langley had proved that he was one of Jonathan's very few true friends, and he couldn't destroy that—not now.

Half an hour later, Jonathan and Serena were northward bound in a borrowed carriage. Jane would remain in Bath for the duration of their planned stay and then stay as long as necessary either for Serena to return with Phoebe or until she had heard otherwise from them. Serena had supplied letters for her aunt and Langley. She'd written to them that since Phoebe had arrived, they'd decided to extend their stay so that Phoebe could experience all the pleasures of Bath.

Jonathan and Serena traveled out of the town in relative silence, but he watched her covertly. She rested her chin on her palm and stared out the window into the graying dawn.

His heart still pounded in her proximity. That part of him continued to pulse in awe that she was alive, whispering her name, a syllable with every slow, heavy beat: *Serena. Serena. Serena.*

He'd liked Meg, and her loss was devastating for many reasons. But it was Serena he'd loved. Serena he'd wanted. Serena he'd mourned all these years.

And it was Serena he'd turned away from. Hurt beyond measure. It was her whose reputation he'd left in tatters. It was her whose life he'd ruined, and it was probably ultimately because of him that she'd been forced to perform this strange switch of identity.

The more he thought about it, the more certain he became that the ruse had something to do with him.

"Why?" he asked out loud.

She turned to him. "Why what?"

"Why did you engage in this deception?" he asked in a low voice. And suddenly, he realized there was no reason to be quiet. They were alone, in total privacy, for the first time in years.

She blew out a breath, and her gaze returned to

the window. "My mother was determined to make something out of me. Redeem me, though it was quite impossible for Serena Donovan to be redeemed after..." Her voice dwindled.

Watching a blush suffuse her cheeks, it struck him, not for the first time, how differently men and women were regarded. To be a rake was something a man could enjoy. Yes, a rake still endured whispers and gossip, but in some ways, his exploits made him more popular, more accomplished, more accepted by other men of his class.

Jonathan had enjoyed the scandals that surrounded his name. They were little jabs he could throw into his father's grave. But those were nothing compared to what a woman in the same situation would be forced to endure. She would be irrevocably labeled as an outcast and a whore.

"Your mother was always determined to make something of you, wasn't she?" he murmured. Serena had told him how Mrs. Donovan's single-minded goal had been to make fine ladies of all five of her daughters, to ensure they married someone of fortune and title, and how she'd been insistent that they not make any mistake similar to the one she had in marrying a near-penniless Irishman.

Serena made a small sound of agreement. "Always. But, happily for her, she had twins. And right away, she realized that while I had ruined myself beyond repair, Meg hadn't. Unbeknownst to me, the scheme began the very day Meg died. The day she read the letter from my aunt that detailed my disgrace."

Jonathan nodded, his throat suddenly feeling very dry.

"Almost immediately, she started to pen letters to Will in which she pretended to be Meg. My younger sisters and I knew nothing of this. Nor did we know that the obituary she'd sent back to London contained my name and not Meg's." A cloud of pain darkened her face before she turned away again, focusing on the shadowy trees rolling by outside. "I wasn't aware of what my mother was doing, but I knew she hated me for what I'd done to myself. How I'd destroyed not only my own reputation, but hers and my sisters' by association."

He couldn't answer that. What was there to say? Except that he was the one who should have been held responsible. Not her.

She spoke without turning to him, her voice so quiet he had to strain to hear. "Sometimes—often—I wished it was me who'd died instead of Meg. A part of me knew that my mother wished it, too. She'd wished so hard that it became the truth. The world believes I died out on the Atlantic Ocean, and so I suppose I did."

"No, Serena. You didn't. You're here." God, no. Now that he knew she was alive, he couldn't imagine her any other way. He couldn't—wouldn't—lose her again.

Jonathan stared at her profile, drinking in her creamy complexion disrupted only by the row of freckles across her cheekbones almost invisible to the naked eye. He probably wouldn't have seen them unless he'd remembered them. Remembered counting them—thirteen on one side and seventeen on the other—and kissing each of them one by one. He wondered if there were still thirty or whether some of them had faded away. It looked like they'd faded. She must be remembering to don her sunbonnets before going outside.

"I keep thinking that this must all be a dream," he said in a low voice, "like so many of the dreams I've had through the years, and you'll fade away like you always do."

Slowly, she turned to face him. Her eyes shone silver in the dim light of the carriage. "Did you dream of me?"

"All the time."

She tilted her head, probing him with her shining stare. "Why?"

He blew out his breath. He'd ruined himself a thousand times over in the past six years, and she knew it. If he told her it was because he loved her, because he'd never stopped loving her, because his devotion to her had never died, she wouldn't believe him for a second.

"I never forgot you," he said instead. "I never forgave myself for what I'd done to you."

She gave a small, bitter laugh. "It's far too late for such regrets."

"If I'd known you were alive..." His voice faded. What would he have done if he'd known she was alive?

Everything would have been different.

He'd have boarded a ship bound for Antigua the day after his father died, that's what he'd have done.

The day he'd been forced to cut her, the day he'd turned away from her despite the desperate longing in her eyes, his mind had been frantically at work, conjuring ways for them to be together. He had been too damned cowardly to defy his father by accepting her publicly, but he'd still been searching for some way to escape his family and be with her.

"I wanted to apologize to you." Jonathan ached to reach out and touch her softly rounded cheek, to brush his knuckle over that silky skin, but she was stiff, wedging herself between the soft velvet squabs and the window. Cold and rigid, unwelcoming of his touch. "But it was too late. I didn't know you'd be sent back to the West Indies so quickly. By the time I had an opportunity to come to you, you had already left London."

She didn't respond. Obviously, words were not enough. A simple, "Well, I meant to apologize" could not make up for being forced into years of grief and inadequacy. He understood that. But God, how he wanted her forgiveness.

"After you left, I would dream of finding you somewhere, and I'd tell you I was sorry. I'd ask for your forgiveness."

"And did I grant it?"

"Never," he said, his lips curling. "You would just stare at me, then fade into the mist."

Serena made a small sound, halfway between a smirk and a laugh.

"You haven't asked me to forgive you," she said. "Dreams don't count, since I was never actually present in any of them."

And now, it wasn't for only his behavior six years ago that he wanted her forgiveness. It was for his behavior after she'd left him.

Jonathan had made a shambles of his life. He'd done it deliberately, thinking of her every day. He'd been on a singular, determined path of self-destruction. But she wouldn't want the weight of any of that on her shoulders, and he couldn't blame her for it. It was his own fault.

"No, I haven't asked your forgiveness," he agreed. "Will you?"

"If I do, will you grant it?"

She gave him a cynical look. "Are you brave enough to ask me to find out? I don't see why you need a preemptive answer. That rather destroys the purpose of the apology, doesn't it?"

"Serena," he murmured, fighting against capturing her hand with his own, "if I ask your forgiveness now, you won't grant it."

"And you think you know that?"

"I do know it." And he did. She wasn't ready to forgive him. Not yet. "I learned you'd been lost at sea a month after the first dream I had about you." That was when the true self-destruction had flared to life... when he'd gone to Bath and made an even bigger shambles of things.

Her expression crumpled, but the break in her façade lasted for only the merest of seconds before she rebuilt her features into stiffness. "I know the demands your family placed on you were very great, Jonathan."

"And yet..."

"And yet, how can I possibly forgive you? Not only for what you did to me, but for what you've done during the past six years?"

He could feel the pain in her voice, like shards of glass raking over his skin. Why hadn't he stopped them? His father and his brother? Society as a whole, who mocked her for what he'd done to her? If only he could have sheltered her from all that. He had been so young, so green. If it happened now, it would be different.

The day after that old shrew had discovered them making love in her ballroom, Jonathan's father and brother had summoned him. Despite his acute embarrassment from the night before, Jonathan had sauntered into his father's study in high spirits, for he'd wanted to marry Serena since the first time he'd bedded her, and now he knew he had no choice but to marry her—and quickly. He assumed his father and brother intended to discuss wedding plans, but instead, his father announced, "You are not to see that little wanton again."

Shocked, Jonathan had frozen in place. So many

arguments crowded his thoughts, he hadn't known where to begin. *What of my responsibility to her? What of propriety? She's not a wanton, she's a gently bred lady. And I love her. I will see her again, no matter what you say.*

"And you, you wayward young buck, are for Stratford House," his father continued. "I've no desire to see you until this storm has passed. Perhaps you may return to London next year, but until then you are banished from Town."

Well, he certainly could respond to that. "I won't go. Not without her."

His older brother, Gervase, leaned negligently against the wall behind their father. "C'mon, Jon. She's a pretty piece, but you're a Dane, for Christ's sakes. Surely someone like her is hardly worthy of your distress."

Jonathan glared at Gervase, then returned his attention to his father. "I intend to marry her. I want her. It is the right thing to do."

His father burst out in laughter. "Do you even know who the girl is? She's Charles Donovan's daughter. You didn't know him, of course—you wouldn't have. The man was an Irish lout. Penniless. Her dowry wouldn't add up to a week's worth of your allowance."

"I don't give a damn," Jonathan ground out.

Gervase smiled smugly. "You will once you're living in poverty."

Jonathan clenched his fists at his sides. "I said I

won't leave London without her. I won't abandon her to be slurred by the gossips and scandalmongers."

His father seemed unperturbed. "If you don't leave, if you dare speak to that piece again, I shall see that she is known for what she really is—a whore. And then the gossips and scandalmongers will have their day."

"You are only feeling this way because she's your first." Gervase pushed away from the wall. "You'll find plenty of accommodating flesh to tumble in Sussex. Trust me, you will forget all about her. She's a mere slut, Jon, just like all the others."

Slowly, Jonathan swung his head to his brother. Gervase had insulted Jonathan's beloved. He'd insulted Serena. And Jonathan was going to wipe that damned pompous look off his fat face.

Overcome by blinding rage, Jonathan had advanced on him, aiming to kill. But Gervase had beaten him soundly, breaking his nose in the process.

That was the year Jonathan had begun to box.

He looked at Serena now, six years older, but even prettier than she'd been at the age of eighteen. Even more alluring to him now. Many women had baited him, but none had the effect on him that the Serena of six years ago had. And now . . . how could it be stronger?

"I cut you for no other reason than stupidity," he said in a low voice. "I was young; I was inexperienced; I was immature. I was cowed by my elders, but in the end I cannot blame anyone but myself."

"Jonathan," she said, her voice infused with a

sadness compounded by many years, "please tell me the truth. Was everything you said to me a lie?"

"Oh, God, no. They weren't lies," he said. "Not one of them. The only lie I ever said to you was when I turned away from you on that day and said I didn't know you. And that lie..." It had destroyed him. Worse, it had destroyed *her.*

"But they must have been lies. I just can't understand how you could treat a woman so coldly after saying such things to her."

After he'd fought Gervase, his father rescinded the order of exile, but persisted in the decree that he not see Serena. He'd come across her in St. James's Square, and with his father looking on, he'd cut her. Then, a few days later, he'd discovered that she'd left London. Determined to follow her to the West Indies, he secretly began to hoard money from his allowance.

After the closing of the autumn session of Parliament that year, he'd received a summons to the Blue Bell Inn in Whitechapel by his brother, to whom he hadn't spoken in several weeks.

By then, he'd nearly saved enough. He'd planned to leave for Antigua in the spring, and he decided it was time to make amends with Gervase. He might never see his older brother again, after all.

It was a blustery day, unseasonably warm. As Jonathan rode to the Blue Bell, he carried a letter to Serena in his pocket. He'd never been much of a writer, and it had taken him hours to compose it. He found it difficult to express thoughts and feelings on paper, and his thoughts and feelings for Serena were so powerful, it seemed impossible to turn them into letters and words. This was the first letter he'd managed to write to her since she'd gone. He'd finally completed it that morning, and he was anxious to send it.

He had stared at the single sheet of paper for many days afterward until he finally tossed it, crumpled and stained, into the fire. Even now, he remembered it verbatim:

Dearest Serena,

I hope this letter finds you well and prospering. Our last meeting did not go well, I am afraid, and it is my fault, so I must apologize for my grossly ungentlemanly behavior. My family is determined to keep me from you, but they will not succeed. It is my fondest desire and wish to make you my companion for the whole of my future life. Take this to heart and wait, for I will be with you this summer. I can only hope to remain seated firmly within your affections until then.

Believe me,
Dearest Serena,
Your most affectionate and devoted lover,
Jonathan

He had burst into the inn, sweating despite the bite in the air, slapping his gloves in his hand. Gervase rose hastily as he approached their table, and Jonathan stopped short at his brother's expression. His face was a deathly shade of yellow, and his frame so drawn, it appeared he had lost a stone since Jonathan had last seen him. Little did he know, his brother was already suffering from the sickness that would take his life a few months later.

"What's wrong with you, man?" Jonathan asked.

Gervase gestured to a chair. "Sit down, Jon."

Jonathan sat. Without another word, his brother slid a sheet of newspaper across the table. Jonathan scanned the page. When he reached the center, he stopped cold.

Serena Donovan of Antigua,
dau. of Chas. Donovan, drowned at sea
on the 27th day of August, aged 18.

He'd looked at his brother, whose face had finally taken on a bit of purplish color. The bastard had been smiling.

He succumbed to consumption in eight months, unmarried and childless, leaving Jonathan heir to the earldom. Jonathan's father followed Gervase a few months later with an apoplexy. At his father's deathbed, Jonathan had stared coldly into the earl's eyes and presented his revenge. He announced that he would never marry, never father an heir, that he would spend his life gambling away his fortune and living in debauchery, and in the end, terminate his father's line.

The dying earl begged for Jonathan to see reason, but Jonathan was finished with his sire and determined to end his days without becoming leg shackled to some strange woman he could never love.

So far, Jonathan had kept his word.

Now, he wished he had kept that letter to Serena, wished he could give it to her right now. He wished she could have been in the Blue Bell Inn and seen the expression on his face the day he'd learned about her death. He wished she could have been at his father's bedside when Jonathan had told him he'd never love another woman but her.

If she'd been in any of those places, it would have left no doubt in her mind as to his feelings for her. But how could he convey all of that now, after so long, after he'd done so much? It seemed impossible.

He shook his head. "I cannot force you to believe me."

"No," she said tightly, turning to the window again. "You cannot."

Chapter Fifteen

They spent the night at an inn near Gloucester. Jonathan took on the unoriginal false name of Mr. Smith and introduced Serena as his wife.

She'd turned hot with annoyance, but then he'd glanced at her and given the innkeeper a sheepish grin. "My wife cannot abide my snoring, sir, so I must beg you for separate rooms."

The innkeeper, seeing Jonathan's rich clothing and fat purse, complied instantly, and they were given adjoining rooms, of course "the best rooms in the establishment."

After a fawning servant had left them in the simple but thankfully clean sitting area separating the two bedchambers, Serena went into the bedchamber assigned to her to remove her traveling cloak.

As she reentered the sitting room a few minutes

later, Jonathan was seated in an upholstered chair near the simple fireplace, his fingers wrapped around an untouched glass of brandy. He wore bone-colored skintight trousers and a billowing white shirt with a V-neck. A sardonic tilt lingered about his lips as he stared into his glass.

Jonathan was such a handsome man, appealing in a roguish, permanently windswept sort of way. She fought the compulsion to flee before it was too late. He was far too alluring for such a weak-willed woman as herself.

He raised his head, but he didn't speak. His body bristled with a familiar wariness.

Serena scowled at him. "You didn't have to say all that to the innkeeper."

He raised a blond brow. "Didn't I? I believe you earlier had expressed some concern about your reputation. About Langley potentially learning of this adventure."

She didn't like the way he said Will's name. As if it were a piece of bad meat that he needed to spit out.

"We already discussed this. It's best he doesn't hear anything about our trip."

Rising, he advanced on her. "Is it? I don't know, Serena. It seems like everything that comes out of your mouth in Langley's presence must be a lie."

Her cheeks heated once again. "That's not true."

"The foundation of your engagement has been built on an untruth, hasn't it?"

She blinked hard. She would not—could not—allow Jonathan to make her feel guiltier for what she had done. She felt horrible enough without his judgment.

"Will is a good man."

He recoiled a little. Despite his reaction, she knew he agreed with that simple truth.

"I won't hurt him," she continued. "I *refuse* to hurt him."

Reaching up, Jonathan stroked a finger down her cheek. She fought with all her strength not to lean into his touch. She tried not to look at his lips, to think of his kiss.

But she did remember the feel of his skin against hers, and her traitorous body flared in instant recognition from the memory, and from his nearness. She squared her shoulders. Feeling her tension, he dropped his hand.

"I don't want to hurt Langley, either," he said. "He is a good man. My friend. But—"

She raised her hand to stop whatever he was going to say. "Then that is all there is to it. I am very grateful that you're taking me to my sister. But beyond that, there cannot be anything between us. After this is finished, we must do our best to stay away from each other." She hesitated and then added in a low voice, "It's too dangerous."

His lips twitched at that, and a flash of victory shone in his eyes. "Is it?"

She jerked her gaze away from him, crossing her arms over her chest and staring at the plain white plaster of the wall beyond. Her mouth was suddenly very dry. "Lord." There was a tinge of desperation in her voice. "It hasn't faded, has it?"

"Whatever it was that started everything between us? No."

She turned back to him, suddenly feeling utterly helpless. Why couldn't she feel this pull toward Will Langley instead of Jonathan Dane? Will was the better man, the *safer* man. Even Jonathan wouldn't dispute that.

"It's too late, Jonathan."

He gazed at her, his eyes probing. "Is it? Are you sure?"

In that moment, she looked deep into those blue orbs, and inside them, she saw the truth: He wanted her back. A fiery thrill ran through her, but she gritted her teeth and squelched it.

"Yes. I'm engaged to Will. To renege on the promise I made to him..." Her voice dwindled. If she were to break off her engagement to Will, it would prove to the world that she was truly the wicked sister. The one who should have died in the cold waters of the Atlantic, but hadn't.

"You aren't promised to anyone." Jonathan's voice was gentle. "Meg is. And as you said yourself, your mother made that promise. Not you."

And she'd gone on all summer perpetuating the

untruth. Pretending. Lying. She shook her head, despairing inside but trying so hard not to show it. "No. No, I cannot..." She couldn't. For Will's sake. For her sisters'.

"Is that what Meg would have wanted?"

She surged backward until her knees hit the sofa cushion. "Don't. Don't you dare make an assumption as to what Meg would have wanted."

But, oh, God, could he be right? In trying to be more like Meg, had she forgotten to consider what Meg's wishes might have been? Yes, Meg would want their sisters to be safe. But would Meg have wanted her to marry Will?

No. Of course she wouldn't. Meg knew Serena could never love Will as she had.

Yet, it was too late. She couldn't go back now. She was to be married in a month's time!

Her breathing had turned ragged—how had that happened? She fisted her hands at her sides. Jonathan specialized in seducing women with his words, with his masculine charms. He would lie to her and whisper how beautiful she was, then he would wheedle something from her. Something Will had already claimed and she wasn't at liberty to give.

"Come here, Serena." Jonathan's voice was low, settling squarely between command and pleading.

No, she wouldn't go near him. To do so would be to betray herself. To betray Will. She wouldn't take one step closer.

A long silence ensued. Serena clutched her arms around her. She saw the stiffness in his jaw, the tension in his shoulders. What was he really thinking?

"It has been so long," he rasped. "So long since I touched you."

That soft kiss in Aunt Geraldine's stables, the one that had made her float for hours afterward, hadn't been that long ago. It seemed like yesterday. "You touched me eleven days ago."

Well, that statement made it clear that she'd been counting. She tried to keep her face expressionless, but like Meg, Jonathan could see through her masks. It was so odd that he was the only person besides Meg who could read into her true emotions.

"Too long ago," he murmured. "And it wasn't enough."

"It was too much."

He blew out a breath. "I've missed you, Serena."

"Stop."

"It's the truth."

"You won't seduce me, Jonathan. I won't allow it."

A muscle moved in his jaw, and he leaned toward her, his eyes narrowing to slits. "Do you think that's what this is? A seduction? Do you think I want to betray Langley? Do you think I want to be in this position? Want you in this position?"

"If you don't want to be here, then you must stop. Go away. Go to your room, and I'll go to mine. We needn't speak of this." She turned toward her bedchamber, but he caught her arm and jerked her around to face him.

"I want you, Serena. I've always wanted you."

"You no longer know me." Her voice was cold. She certainly didn't know him, either. Not after what he'd become in her absence.

"Oh, but I do." His hand was firm on her arm. "You haven't changed."

She stared at him in disbelief. He couldn't be more wrong. "I've changed immeasurably, my lord. I'm not the same naïve innocent you fooled into loving you."

He flinched visibly at that.

Tears pricked at her eyes, but she held them at bay. "You've changed, too. You are no longer the young gentleman I trusted with all my soul."

Why, after all the pain he had caused her, did every inch of her traitorous skin cry out for his touch?

"I never meant to hurt anyone. Especially you."

"But you did. And not only me, Jonathan. I've heard so many things—wicked things—about you." She sucked in a breath. "Jane said it was untrue, but I've even heard you had a child out of wedlock."

She wanted him to deny it. To hear his denial would once and for all close the book on that topic.

He closed his eyes and bowed his head, his chest rising and falling with deep breaths. "I've never fathered a child, Serena."

Her knees felt weak with relief.

"But that doesn't matter," he continued. "None of

it matters. Not now. You're right. I did become someone different after I lost you. But you came back. And you brought those parts of me I thought I'd lost forever deep in the Atlantic along with the woman I'd always love."

This was not at all what she had expected when she'd returned to London. She had thought she'd already overcome her desperate, unrequited love for Jonathan. She'd recovered from her heartbreak. She had truly believed she had moved on and could make a good wife to Will.

She had been wrong, so wrong. She still wanted Jonathan Dane. Desperately. Madly. Coming to London had been a terrible mistake. She'd thought she was doing it for her sisters, but she'd lied to herself and to everyone else. She'd done it for herself. She'd done it because she wanted to leave Antigua. Serena had grasped on and clung to the only reason she could find to return to London and learn what had become of the man she'd once loved.

His voice was low, steady and earnest, as earnest as it had been when he'd held her in his arms so many years ago. "I always wanted you, Serena. Only you. You're the only woman for me."

Serena's breath caught and her lips tingled. The wanton woman deep within her clawed for release, but she fought it with all her strength. He stood before her, still and tense. The air surrounding them seemed to crackle.

Before she knew what she was doing, she lunged forward. Placing one hand behind his head, she pulled him forward and pressed her lips to his. Despite the chill in the room, his lips scorched her. Her chest tightened. Her heart surged against her rib-cage, banging out the message she had suppressed for so long.

You need this.

You need him.

You always have.

He pressed closer to her, opening to her kiss. When his tongue touched her lip, searching, seeking, a loud knock sounded on the door.

She jerked back.

For several torturous moments, they stared at each other. She broke the eye contact first, yanking her gaze to the floor.

The knock sounded again, impatient.

Sighing, Jonathan went to open the door. It was a serving maid to the rescue, bearing a tray with their dinner. The girl placed dishes on the small round walnut table, and then curtsied and left. Neither Jonathan nor Serena had moved a muscle while she'd been in the room.

Why had she done that? Why had she touched him? Why, why, why?

She was mad, she was insane, she was stupid. How could she reveal her weakness?

Serena had known from the beginning the man

was a danger. She almost wished he'd live up to his reputation in her presence. Perhaps she could have encouraged him to find some barmaid from the tavern downstairs to bring back to their rooms. If she actually saw his debauchery in action rather than hearing about it, then surely she'd be able to control her wicked urges in his presence.

But he had behaved like a gentleman. A gentleman who'd cared for her and her family, was deeply sorry for the mistakes he'd made, and who'd never stopped wanting her. He was behaving like a gentleman who wanted her back.

No. She thought she'd read it in his expression, but he hadn't actually *said* that. Perhaps he merely wanted to tumble her again to see what it would be like after all these years.

Serena walked to the table and looked down at the plates that had been placed there. It appeared to be a roasted bird with a side dish of some gelled substance she couldn't identify.

Jonathan pulled out the chair across from her and sat slowly, as if every move he made took great effort. He bowed his head over his food as if in prayer. When he looked up at her again, his blue eyes were bright as sapphires.

"Was there anyone else?" he whispered. "Before Langley, I mean. Was there someone in Antigua?"

She'd thought she couldn't get any stiffer, but she'd been wrong. "That's none of your business."

"Tell me. Please, Serena. I need to know."

She took the seat across from him and violently stabbed a piece of partridge with her fork. "No," she snapped. "There was no one in Antigua. There was no one . . . ever."

He inhaled sharply, and something resembling a groan resonated in his throat. "Is that true?"

"It is."

"Not even Langley?"

She didn't want to answer that. She shouldn't answer that. But she did. "No. Not even Langley."

"How can that be? You are so . . . surely many men have asked for you."

"You are the only one. First . . . and last."

Admitting this to him was a simultaneous relief and pain. Some part of her, some demon, wanted to say she'd had as many men as he'd had women. Then she could rub his face in it.

"I am not so virtuous as you, I am sorry to say." Was it her imagination, or did color tint his cheeks?

"I've been aware of that for some time now," she said dryly.

"And you despise me for it."

Yes. As long as she held on to her self-respect, she must despise him for it.

"Can we talk about something else?" she asked. "Please? I'm tired of rehashing the past."

"I agree. Let's talk about something neutral."

They sat in silence for long minutes, both of them

busying themselves with eating. Finally, she looked across the small space at him, trying to give a light laugh that instead sounded bitter. "So, I suppose we have nothing to talk about anymore."

Everything had changed. Before, they'd talked and talked. They'd conversed for hours on end, each of them fascinated by whatever it was the other had to say. Now it was all discomfort and tension between them.

"I doubt that," he said.

She looked up at him, challenging him with her eyes.

"Tell me about something pleasant that you've done since we last knew each other," he said. "Something unrelated to what happened between us. And then I will tell you something I've done."

"All right." She paused, racking her brain for a good memory from home unrelated to Jonathan, and then relaxed a little as she remembered a small happy part of her life in Antigua. "My father kept Guinea sheep, and we bred them after he died. Occasionally the mothers die when the lambs are born. I built a nursery for them in our barn, to foster them and care for them until they were big enough to go out on their own. Sometimes I slept out there with the babies to help them stay warm and feed them when they grew hungry."

He smiled. "You built a nursery for them with your own hands?"

"I did." Servants and slaves had been in short supply by then.

"I can easily picture the Serena I knew building nurseries and fostering lambs." After a short silence he said, "My memory was about a baby, too."

Spearing a piece of partridge, she raised her brows. "Was it?"

He nodded. "About two years ago, on one of my mandatory visits to see my mother at the ancestral pile in Sussex, I encountered a wagon with a broken axle on the side of the road. A man was bent over a figure lying there—it was his wife. At first I thought she was dead, that the crash had killed her. But in fact, she was laboring with child, and they had been in pursuit of the midwife, who had gone that morning to one of the neighboring villages. It was too late for me to take my horse to fetch the midwife myself. The babe was ready to make its appearance."

"Goodness. What on earth did you do?"

"Well, I thought I'd try to ride for help even so, but then the lady let out a particularly bloodcurdling scream and the husband fainted dead away. I couldn't leave her alone."

She stared at him, wide-eyed. "What happened?"

"I delivered the babe myself. A healthy girl." He laughed. "The husband didn't wake until the child was squalling in her mama's arms."

"Jonathan..." Serena was speechless.

He shook his head, smiling wryly. "I was with

strangers and yet it was a singularly beautiful moment in my life. I will never forget it."

"That's a wonderful story."

"The family lives at Stratford House now. Turned out the man had skill in gardening, and I hired him on when our old gardener died. I'm the child's godfather. Her name is Abigail. I try to see them every time I find myself forced to visit the place."

"You must be very proud."

He grinned. "Well, I suppose it was rather fortunate for them that I turned up at that moment. But it could have been anyone, really. I did nothing special."

The last part of the statement was said with no guile, and Serena thought he truly believed anyone would have done what he'd done. But he'd probably saved the child's life as well as her mother's, then he'd given the family a position on his estate.

"That was good for me to hear," she said softly.

His lips twisted. "Why is that? Have tales of my wickedness and debauchery been the only news you've heard of me?"

"I am sorry to say it...but other than Jane and Will saying that you've changed in recent weeks, yes."

Jonathan met her gaze evenly. "It is how I wanted to be known."

"Why, Jonathan? Why on earth would a man want to be known as an unscrupulous rakehell?"

"I haven't cared about anything or anyone. I haven't wanted to care. When you died, or when I thought you died, rather, you took everything that was good in me with you."

"No, I didn't. I couldn't have." She flung out a hand. "Look at how you helped your gardener and his wife. There obviously was a deep well of goodness left in you."

"Perhaps you are right." He took in a deep breath. "But when you died, Serena, it felt like a piece of me was destroyed and a devil took over part of my soul."

"And where is that devil now?"

"Gone."

She shook her head. "It can't be so simple."

He stared down at his food. "Everything has changed. The world has turned upside down. I don't know who I am anymore. All I know is..."

Serena slid to the edge of her seat. "What?" she asked breathlessly.

"I still want you." His voice broke to a whisper, and he looked up at her, his eyes pleading and haunted. "I want you near to me, to talk to you. To touch you. To *be* with you." He reached his hand across the table. "Come closer."

Unable to resist the command, she rose and stepped around the table until her gown brushed against his knees.

He kept his gaze steady on hers. "Do you remember? Our walks in the park? Our long talks? Remember how we used to trade books? Our letters? I kept them all."

"Yes." She remembered it all, and more. She remembered how she couldn't keep her hands off him. How each brush of his skin had driven her wild. Had that changed?

She lifted her hand and stroked her finger down the bridge of his nose. It was a different shape now, slightly crooked, with a small bump in the center. "What happened to your nose?"

"Broken."

"How?"

"In . . . in a fight."

"Did it hurt?" she asked.

He shuddered, whether from her touch or from a memory of the fight, she didn't know. "It did."

She threaded her fingers through his hair. Like fluid silk, it sifted between her fingers as she drew a lock of it away from his forehead.

She studied him carefully as she smoothed his hair back. He sat frozen, bringing to her mind a statue of Apollo, marble white and pale lipped, but with supple, living hair.

"Serena," he groaned. "Please stay with me. Be with me."

"I . . . I . . ." How she wanted to feel his lips against hers once again.

He lunged up, the chair legs scraping the floor as he rose. He closed the small gap between them and captured her mouth with his. His lips caressed hers, then his tongue nudged her mouth, forcing it to open. She moved her hand to cup the back of his head, dragged him closer, and deepened the kiss into something hot and demanding.

She thought she'd comprehended her own limits, the depth of her own need, but she'd misjudged. Her need was fed by his, and his was a tidal wave. He didn't kiss her with sweetness and adoration. He kissed her with raging desire, almost frightening in its intensity.

His tongue swept inside her mouth, claiming, demanding. She opened to him but didn't submit. Instead, she staked her own claim, made her own demands. Together, linked, they gave and took, and Serena sank into the drugging pleasure of Jonathan's kiss. The world faded away, until there was only Jonathan and her, their need, their hot, singular connection.

His mouth moved over her lips, then across her jaw, and heat wisped over her ear as he kissed her lobe, murmuring, "Do you want me, Serena? Please tell me you want me."

She closed her eyes. She wanted him so badly—*so* badly.

But it was wrong.

She dragged herself back to reality. She doggedly thought of Will. Of her betrothed. The man she was to marry. The good, honest man. The man she couldn't bear to hurt.

She tore away from Jonathan. Blood roared past her ears. Tremors swept through her body. For a long moment, she stood with her head bent, forcing herself to breathe, forcing her rubbery limbs to hold her upright.

Jonathan gasped for breath, too. It was as if their kiss had sucked the air from the room.

"Let me touch you." He reached out to her with his voice. "Let me see you again. Please. Let me have you."

She wanted to. She could unfasten his trousers and take him now, just as she had taken him at the dowager duchess's ball so many years ago. Her body tightened with heat, with longing.

No.

"I cannot," she managed between gasps.

"Serena..."

"No! I just can't." She staggered back to her chair and sank into it, looking up at him with all the hopelessness, desperation, guilt, and confusion swirling through her.

He bowed his head. "I should say I can't, either. God knows I don't want him hurt. I don't want you hurt. I should stay away from you. But God, Serena..." He gazed back at her, his own expression mirroring hers. "Being with you, seeing you, remembering you. Talking to you. It's...I think it's better than before." He shook his head. "I must stay away from you. But I don't know if I can."

Serena pressed her lips together and gazed down

at her congealing food. "You can," she murmured. "So can I. There is no other choice." She looked up at him. "Sit down, Jonathan, and let's finish dinner."

He squeezed his eyes closed, and she watched him struggle with the decision.

"For Will," she whispered.

Racked with guilt, indecision, and other emotions she didn't dare name, he thrust his hand through his hair. Finally, his eyes met hers. She'd won, for now. No, it wasn't her. It was the guilt that had won.

He sat, pulled his chair in, and stared down at his food.

They choked down the remainder of the cold partridge in silence.

After dinner, Serena bade Jonathan a polite good night and then retired into her bedchamber, feeling his blue eyes burning a hole into her back before she shut the door to his probing gaze. A few moments later, she heard the opening and closing of the door to the outside corridor.

She padded to the window, pulled aside the chintz drape, and leaned against the wooden sill.

A new mixture of anxiety and fear competed somewhere deep within her. Most disturbingly, she recognized in herself a familiar recklessness threading through it all.

The combination of recklessness and desire, she knew from experience, could prove fatal.

She gazed outside. The early moon's light sifted through an ominous layer of clouds and skittered across the grounds, sprinkling silver light over the wet grass. The drive to the stables and the path to the inn's back entrance cut through the ground in broad, black strokes. The stables had been shut tight for the night, and the kitchen was closed, with no smoke curling from its chimney.

For the past several years, she had repressed her rash and irrepressible nature and displayed herself as the model of propriety. Even after years of perfect behavior, society recalled every detail about her shocking past. She would never erase the stain on her. Unless she became Meg.

In the hustle and bustle of London she felt somewhat cleaner as Meg than she had in Antigua as Serena. But not clean enough—she could never be clean enough. And there was that new stain, black and ominous. The stain of her lies to William Langley.

If she revealed the truth, however, it might be far worse. The memory of her shame, the constant presence of it in her life, would keep her sensible.

Serena released a long breath and closed her eyes, remembering lying in the crook of Jonathan's arm, staring up at the stars shimmering in a cloudless sky. It had been a beautiful spring in London that year, and promised to be an even more splendid summer. Serena had been determined to stay there, just like that, in his arms, forever.

She dropped her forehead onto the windowsill. She hadn't touched a man for six years. Not until Will had surprised her by kissing her in the park. But six years ago, Jonathan had touched her in places she never dreamed a woman could be touched. And ever since, she had remembered—and, yes, she could no longer deny it—she longed for more.

After Serena had closed her door against him, Jonathan had gone down to the tavern. The serving girl, a pretty wench with reddish-brown hair, gave him a bawdy wink and leaned forward, showing off her ample bosom as she served him his ale.

"You look lonely, sir." Her voice was crisp and sweet, at odds with her behavior. He'd looked up at her in surprise. She was right. He *was* lonely. Seemed like he'd been lonely forever, but he knew exactly how long it had been. Six years and fifteen days.

The girl batted her eyes at him. "You needn't be lonely tonight, sir."

He blinked back at her. Really, he had no idea what she meant. Did she mean he should go to Serena? Talk to her? Try to convince her that she was the one for him?

Oh, hell. He was clearly distracted, obsessed with the woman upstairs, and missing this girl's obvious signals. "Ah . . . no, thank you."

She gave him a sweet smile. "My name's Maisie, sir. If you change your mind." Without waiting for a response, she ambled away, heavy skirts swishing as she went.

Jonathan hadn't changed his mind. He had finished his food quickly and gone back upstairs. In the sitting room, he'd gone to Serena's door and hesitated there for a few seconds, resting his palm on the painted wood. Then he'd sighed and turned away. He couldn't press her. Not tonight.

Jonathan returned to his bedchamber, stripped off his clothes, and climbed beneath the cold sheets.

He wanted her, desperately, madly, and yet he hesitated. Because of Langley.

No, there was more to it than that.

Less than a month after her "death," he'd left London bound for Bath, where he'd met up with Langley and a few of their other comrades from Eton. His friends had taken mere moments to assess his state, then had made it their goal to make Jonathan forget his grief. Jonathan had plunged into the depraved sea of drink, gambling, and women.

That was a wild time. Even Langley, depressed by Meg's absence, had succumbed momentarily. His wits had returned rapidly, though. Jonathan and Langley had saved each other from their misadventures in Bath, had stowed away at Langley's house in Northumberland for a short time, and then they'd gone back to London.

Langley had been determined to make something of himself in the Navy before proposing to Meg. But when Jonathan had returned to London, friends had dragged him from tavern to inn to brothel to boudoir, on many occasions narrowly avoiding mishaps—Jonathan's family connections and his friends' wealth had come to their rescue more than once.

And, in his drink-sodden state, Jonathan *had* forgotten. Sometimes.

The Serena he had once loved would never forgive him for all his transgressions against her. Even if she did prove to be enough of the girl he had once known, it was hopeless to think there could ever be something between them. He had ruined himself for her.

A new emotion solidified somewhere deep within him, and he considered it from all angles, as if studying the facets of a gem, before he was able to identify it. When the word came to mind, he drew back physically to separate himself from it, but it came along with him, hard and clear and irrevocably attached.

Shame.

Chapter Sixteen

Sebastian Harper owned a modest home on the outskirts of the town of Prescot. It was a white, box-shaped dwelling, in need of fresh paint but not unattractive. Lilies bloomed in bunches of white and scarlet near the front door, and the overall impression was one of simple cheerfulness. It was not how Serena would have imagined a house owned by a young London rake to look.

She'd been in close proximity to Jonathan for three days. His presence had made her insides turn molten and her skin prickle with an endless heat, yet she held herself stiff and aloof. She'd fallen into several conversations with him, but she kept herself on guard and didn't allow herself—or him—to talk about the past, about the two of them, about Will. If she dropped her guard for one instant when it came to those topics, she might just ignite.

Serena believed they'd find Harper and Phoebe at Harper's house, but a very small, very wicked part of her wished they wouldn't find the young couple. Wished that she and Jonathan could stay together, riding in this carriage for days on end, until this unbearable tension between them snapped.

She couldn't imagine what would happen when it did. Either she would attack him with her fists or fall into his arms. Either would be preferable to this purgatory.

Serena stood beside the carriage and gazed at Harper's house. It was early in the evening, and the sun was setting behind the trees crowding the edges of the path circling the house, dappling golden light over the shrubbery. There were signs of recent habitation—footprints in the dirt path leading to the front door—but the place itself was quiet as could be.

Jonathan came to her side. "Let's see if they're inside."

She nodded and stepped forward, Jonathan at her elbow. She reached the front door and rapped her knuckles on it.

She stopped, hand still raised, cocking her head to listen. She heard the faintest movement coming from inside. "They're here."

Jonathan cocked a brow at the door, which still hadn't opened. "Shall I break it down?"

She stifled a laugh. "No, I don't think so."

"What then?"

She took a breath. "Phoebe?" she called out. "Phoebe, it's me . . . Ser—Meg."

She wondered if her sister had told Harper about her identity switch. She didn't think Phoebe would reveal such a secret, even if she had threatened to a few weeks earlier. Then again, Serena hadn't thought her sister would run off with a man, either.

No response from inside. The muffled noises had stopped. Serena sighed. "Phoebe, you open this door right now, or Lord Stratford will be taking an axe to it!"

Jonathan frowned at her. "I don't have an axe."

"Well, then, find one," she hissed.

Raising his fist, he pounded on the door. "Open up, Harper. *Now.*"

Footsteps sounded, approaching the door, stopping just beyond the thick slab of wood.

"Don't do anything foolish." It was Phoebe's voice.

Serena's mouth dropped open. Was her sister joking? She begged Serena not to do anything foolish when she was the one who'd run off and was living with a man she wasn't married to?

Jonathan answered for her. "We just want to talk to you and Harper, Phoebe."

It was Serena's turn to raise a brow at him. He gave her a sheepish grin and shrugged. In the carriage he'd talked freely about his intentions of tanning Harper's hide. Serena had done nothing to try to convince him not to take that course of action—she had a rather strong desire to tan the man's hide herself.

The door handle turned, and the door opened a scant inch. Phoebe poked her nose out, rather like a cautious rabbit sniffing for danger.

"Meg?"

"Just let me in." Impatient, she shoved the door open to Phoebe's squeak of dismay.

Then she pulled it shut just as quickly, turning at the same time to block Jonathan from seeing her sister. "For heaven's sake, Phoebe," she tossed over her shoulder, "put some clothes on."

Phoebe was wearing nothing but a transparent chemise. Crossing her arms over her chest and tapping her foot impatiently on the stoop, Serena waited. "God grant me patience," she said under her breath.

Finally, the door opened again. This time it was Harper in shirtsleeves and unbelted trousers, looking tight-lipped.

"Planning to keep us out on the stoop all night?" Serena asked crossly.

"Er...no." He opened the door wider, warily granting them entrance, and she brushed past him, taking in the small, clean but unkempt parlor.

"Where is Phoebe?"

"Ah...in the bedroom." He gestured toward a narrow set of stairs.

Leaving Jonathan to manage Harper, Serena lifted her skirts and marched up the steps, her heels clacking on the wood slats of the staircase. There were two closed doors at the top of the landing, and she chose the one on the right, pushing it open without knocking.

Phoebe stood in the middle of the room, her back to the door. Her spine stiffened as Serena entered.

"The buttons are difficult to manage alone," Phoebe murmured. "Sorry."

Sighing, Serena went to help her finish fastening the buttons at the back of her white muslin. She didn't speak. When she lowered her hands, Phoebe slowly turned.

"Oh, Serena. Don't be angry with me."

She stared at her younger sister, aghast. "Have you gone mad?"

"No!"

Serena merely shook her head.

Phoebe's hands worked together. "Why have you come here?"

"What did you expect, Phoebe? Did you truly think I'd say, 'Oh, my, Phoebe has run away,' and continue merrily along with my life without you? Certainly you must've expected me to chase after you, to end this madness!"

"How did you—" Phoebe stopped suddenly, her mouth pinched. "Never mind. It was Lord Stratford, wasn't it? He ran to Bath to tattle on me."

Serena narrowed her eyes. "I asked him to look after you."

"I am fully grown, Serena. I needn't be looked after by anyone."

"Don't be stupid."

Releasing a harsh breath, Phoebe turned and stomped to the window. She placed her hands on the ledge and stared out for a long moment. Serena waited, her hands on her hips. Finally, Phoebe turned to face her again. "I love him. I want to be with him."

"We've been through this before, Phoebe. It's impossible."

Phoebe shook her head, a humorless grin quirking her lips. "Too late for impossible, wouldn't you say?"

"Not at all. Only Jonathan—Lord Stratford—and a few others know about this. Aunt Geraldine believes you are with me. If I bring you home now and you promise to never see Mr. Harper again, no one will ever know anything is amiss."

"Oh, Serena." Phoebe shook her head, sighing. "I think you are the one who is mad."

With that, she brushed past Serena and swept down the stairs. Scowling, Serena followed her into the parlor, where Jonathan had taken Harper by the scruff of the neck.

"No!" Phoebe cried, rushing forward.

Serena fought a satisfied smile. It was rather heartening to see Harper flailing wildly in Jonathan's .dlock.

Jonathan's eyes met hers, and she couldn't help it. She did smile.

He loosened his hold on the younger man but held him aloft as Phoebe batted ineffectively at him.

"Should I kill him?" he asked Serena mildly.

She considered it. "Well, he has debauched my innocent sister, ruined her, destroyed her reputation and put that of her family at risk, and sent us on a merry chase—"

It was true, all of it. The lightness in her voice faded. The man truly should be punished. Then again, Phoebe was clearly just as responsible as Harper in this disaster—maybe more so.

Serena sighed. "No, don't kill him. Not yet."

If she didn't know about his gambling and his lack of ambition, she would have no qualms with a match between Phoebe and Harper. Well, except for the fact that Phoebe was so very young. Many women were married at nineteen, but still . . . surely no one could be so sure of her mind at that age.

Serena had been sure of her mind at an even younger age, though. She'd known, to her bones, that she was meant to be with Jonathan. She hadn't doubted it for a second. Until . . .

Something jerked in her gut at the realization. Phoebe was so much like the Serena of six years ago. Before Jonathan spurned her, before Meg's death. Serena, like Phoebe, had always been a girl who knew her mind.

Nevertheless, she couldn't allow Phoebe to put herself at such risk, not with a man as unpredictable as Harper. Serena turned to him and said in a very quiet voice, "Phoebe and I are returning to London."

"No!" Phoebe's and Harper's voices rang out in simultaneous, stentorian denial.

"It isn't your choice," she told them. "Phoebe is only nineteen, not of legal age to marry without her guardian's permission—"

"We intend to go to Scotland," Phoebe said.

"I am responsible for you. I promised Mother I'd look out for you. We will return to London, continue with our lives, and forget this ever happened."

"No," Phoebe said again.

"You cannot refuse me, Phoebe. If I have to ask Lord Stratford to carry you, kicking and screaming, over his shoulder, then I shall do so."

Phoebe shot a desperate look at her lover, who gave a helpless shrug as if to say, "She's your sister, you must manage her." He had his own hands full trying to wrest himself free from Jonathan.

"I'm hungry," Jonathan suddenly announced. Three sets of eyes swiveled to him. He set Harper down with a plunk. "Have you anything to eat here?"

Harper stared at Jonathan in astonishment, rubbing at his sore neck.

"It's the maid's day off," Phoebe said sullenly. "We have cold pie for our supper."

"Enough to go round?"

"Probably," Phoebe said frostily, clearly not wanting to share what had promised to be a quiet, romantic dinner between her and Harper.

"Excellent!" Jonathan looked between the three of them. "Shall we eat?"

After Jonathan had tended the horses in Harper's small stable and had the coachman settled, Harper, Serena, and Jonathan sat at the table. Phoebe grudgingly served each of them a slice of mutton pie and a tankard of country ale. For long minutes, Serena enthusiastically attacked her food and drink in silence. The pie was delicious after days of bland, tasteless inn food.

She met Jonathan's smiling eyes over the rim of her ale cup and wondered what it would have been like if Will had accompanied her on this trip instead of Jonathan. She couldn't imagine it. There was a closeness, an understanding, that she innately felt when she was with Jonathan that was never present with Will.

It struck her like an anvil: When she was with Will, she didn't feel good enough. It was like she had to prove herself, prove she was as good as Meg had been. And the way he looked at her—behind the extreme politeness and gentleness, maybe there was something there that told him she *wasn't* as good as Meg. That she wasn't Meg and never could be.

She lowered her ale, giving Jonathan a faint smile before she took another bite of mutton.

Harper suddenly dropped his fork with a clatter. He clenched his fists on either side of his plate and looked Serena directly in the eye.

"I know you think I'm not good enough for your sister."

She didn't argue.

"But I will do right by her. I promise you that." His voice was very low, very certain. Shockingly mature.

Still, Serena shook her head. "How can I believe that, Mr. Harper?" She tried to keep her voice gentle. "You've nothing to offer her."

"He has himself," Phoebe said. Serena glanced at her sister to see her gaze lingering lovingly on Harper. "And that's all I could ever want."

"When I'm with Phoebe..." He swallowed hard. "Well, it's difficult to say, Miss Donovan." He shook his head, took a deep breath, and tried again. "She is my salvation."

"Salvation from what?" Jonathan asked him.

"From myself, my lord. She's saved me. When I'm with her...she makes me feel like a man at peace. She...calms me. I've never experienced that before...with any woman." He gazed across the table at Phoebe. "There is no one like her. No one in this world. I've found the woman I wish to be with forever."

Reaching across the table, he clasped Phoebe's hands in his own.

Serena sighed, trying not to soften at his words, though they did much to placate her as to his intentions. "That's all well and good, Mr. Harper. But by all accounts you are penniless. What little fortune you did possess you lost in gambling and women."

He flinched visibly. "I assure you, I'm finished with gambling and women. It feels like"—he frowned as if trying to formulate his thoughts into words—"like I wasted my life away, waiting for something. And now I know what I was waiting for."

"But how on earth will you care for her?" Serena asked.

His shoulders seemed to sag a little, but then he squared them once again, not taking his eyes from Serena's sister. "I'll find a way." His voice was firm.

Phoebe smiled at him. It was a reassuring smile, a smile that said, "We can do this, and we will. Together."

Despite herself, Serena was quickly softening toward them both. She didn't want to be soft. She mustn't be soft, for the sake of her family and their reputation, for the sake of Phoebe herself. But she looked at Phoebe and Harper and studied the way they gazed at each other, and she couldn't help but believe them.

She cast Jonathan a frustrated glance, and his expression stopped her short. There was understanding there, too. And something passed between him and her, something that reminded Serena that what Phoebe and Harper had was remarkably like what she and Jonathan had once had. What if their families hadn't torn them apart? What if the old earl had welcomed the match with open arms? Would Jonathan have betrayed her later on, or would his love have remained constant for the past six years? What would a life with Jonathan be like? Would they have children by now?

Jonathan would make beautiful babies.

Good Lord. Her eyes stinging, she jerked her gaze away from him. This was madness. She was thinking of making babies with Jonathan Dane. *The Earl of Stratford.* After everything that had happened between them. She was fairly certain she was the stupidest woman in the history of the world.

She found herself looking at Harper, whose gaze was still affixed on her sister. "If you truly desire to be together, it's best to prove that first. Wait a few years. Demonstrate your worthiness to my family."

Harper made a scoffing noise. "What are the chances of that, Miss Donovan? Phoebe has already told me that your aunt and mother are sniffing after a title for her. I'm about as far removed from a title as China is from England."

Jonathan sighed audibly and thrust a hand through his hair. "Pity I can't offer you mine."

"Sebastian is right, you know," Phoebe said, lowering her own fork. "Mother and Aunt Geraldine will never approve of my being with him, no matter what he does to 'prove' himself to them." She lifted a shoulder. "And I don't care one teeny, tiny bit. I don't give a tuppence about what they think. It's my life, and I know what's best for me."

Serena took another healthy swallow of ale. "Do you, Phoebe? Can you? And you are very young, too, Mr. Harper. Surely you have many years left to sow your wild oats before you settle down and marry."

"I'm old enough to know my mind," Harper said.

Phoebe's voice was mild, but defiant sparks lit her eyes. "I will not return to London with you. I simply won't."

"It's not your decision," Serena said.

"Oh, yes it is."

"Oh, Phoebe. Don't behave like an infant."

Phoebe's lips twisted sardonically. She glanced down at her plate, then back up at them. "Understand me when I say this," she said, her voice quiet but strong as steel. "I will remain with Sebastian. It doesn't matter what anyone says or does, not now."

Serena opened her mouth to speak, but Phoebe raised her hand to stop her.

"Sebastian and I shall marry as soon as possible," she announced. "We must, you see. For I am with child."

Later that night, Jonathan sat outside on a bench placed against the brick wall at the back side of Harper's house, enjoying the cool evening air, when the sound of footsteps turned his head.

It was Serena. Drawing her cloak tight around her body, she settled on the bench beside him, then tilted her head to gaze up at the sky. His skin reacted to her nearness, prickling all over.

"It's cold out here," she murmured.

Then hold me, Serena. We can make each other warm again. He couldn't bring himself to say that, though. He had shown her some of his desperation a few nights ago at the first inn and it had driven her away. He didn't comprehend her intentions, her feelings, what was happening between them. He had no idea how this could possibly play out in a way that wasn't devastating to both of them.

"Yes, it is a little chilly." He raised his glass, showing the amber liquid inside. "This is keeping me passably warm, though. Would you like some?"

"Yes, please."

He handed her the glass, and she took a sip.

"Ah!" She slapped a hand to her chest. "It's like fire. What is that stuff?"

"Brandy." He grinned at her. "Do you like it?"

She met his gaze over the rim of the glass. "Love it." She took another swallow that left her panting, and he refilled the glass from the decanter at his other side. He took a fortifying swallow and then offered her the glass again.

Taking it, she inched closer. For propriety's sake alone, he didn't wrap his arm around her and draw her closer, though he desperately wanted to.

"You are so warm," she murmured.

He wanted to stroke her skin, her face, her arms, shoulders. He ached to lift her skirts and touch her legs through her stockings. To kiss her in her warmest place, something he had never done but had dreamed of after her "death." He remembered how he had awakened from those dreams, his cock spent, his skin cold, his cheeks wet.

He wanted to be the first to kiss her between her legs. The first, and the last.

Get me through this, he prayed. *Keep her with me, and I will never forsake you again.*

God probably believed his promises empty. God had no reason to believe him, after all. More likely, God hated him for betraying Langley like this.

They sat quietly for a time, not touching.

"You did well tonight," he finally said.

She'd been magnificent. Mature. Composed in the face of adversity. She'd remained calm when her sister had tossed that news at them all.

Harper had been the most anguished—until Phoebe had left her chair and gone to comfort him, convincing him as Serena and Jonathan watched that if they faced this together, they would prevail. Her actions had solidified Jonathan's opinion that she was good for Harper. Something about the strength of her personality settled him, strengthened him, made him more of a man than the tempestuous youth he'd been ever since Jonathan had known him.

"Do you think so?" Serena asked, her voice musing. "I wish I could have thought of something better to do. I'm so worried about her. About them both."

"You couldn't have done anything better."

"I just don't know," Serena said, squeezing the ridge of her nose between her thumb and index finger. She had agreed to take them to Gretna Green so they could be married at once—the marriage laws of Scotland allowed them to marry without parental approval.

"It was the only way for your sister to retain any hope of maintaining some status in society."

"I know, but—"

"And it will save your other sisters from future embarrassment if they should ever come to London."

"They plan to," she said, "once I am . . . married."

Jonathan nodded, finding it difficult to speak past the sudden lump in his throat. Langley's absence made it easy to pretend he didn't exist. But he did exist, and he was at this moment awaiting his bride in London.

He turned to Serena, studying the outline of her face in the dim starlight. "Can you do it, do you think?"

"I don't know," she whispered. Her words jolted through him. Finally she'd admitted to her conflicted feelings about Langley. Her eyes met his, shining silver orbs in this light. "I really don't know, Jonathan. I know I should. I must. But . . ."

"You don't want him to know who you are," he finished for her.

"No, I don't. Will is a good man. Such a good man." Each word that emerged from her sounded like a groan. "But I am betraying him. My true identity betrays him. He'd be so devastated to learn about me. About Meg..."

Jonathan nodded. It was the truth. And he understood the conflict of her fears combating with her need to follow through with her promises and her desire to save herself and her family from certain ruin.

"There is no good answer," she said. "Either I marry Will and try to survive, be happy, make him happy, all the while knowing that I am living a lie. Or I don't marry him and suffer the consequences. The worst of which will be hurting him."

"What about me?"

She recoiled a little. "What about you?"

He chose his words carefully. If he revealed his true thoughts, they would more likely than not chase her away, like his kisses the other night. He needed to tread lightly.

"I told you I never stopped caring for you," he said.

"Yet your actions betrayed the falsehood of that." She didn't sound angry, but a bone-deep sadness permeated her tone.

He curled his fists tightly, refraining from punching the house's brick siding. He was responsible for that tone, for all she'd suffered through since he'd spurned her.

"I wanted you more than anything, even then, Serena. Even though I behaved like an ass. And I still want you. You know I do."

She stiffened. "Let's speak of something else. I can't do this, I can't..."

"We can't keep changing the subject. We can't avoid this forever." He wished he could touch her, comfort her. Reassure her that everything would be all right. But how could it be?

He bent his head and brushed his lips over her cheek. The contact sent a shock through his limbs.

Her cheek was supple, smooth, and sweet. He moved his lips over her skin again. There it was, that current just beneath the surface, resonating outward from the place they made contact. She must have felt it, too, because her breath hitched and she shifted away.

His chest tightened. He couldn't draw breath. He wanted her so much, it hurt.

Yet he couldn't demand anything from her. He wasn't about to foist himself upon her until she wanted it, until she begged him to take her. His logical mind told him it would not be anytime soon. If what she said was true, and he knew that it was, she was green compared to most of the women he knew. Despite their liaison years ago, she was still very inexperienced. Then, he had been a fumbling, ardent youth. He would love her much differently now.

If she would ever accept him.

"You're the same woman I knew years ago," he said, "loyal, loving, committed to your causes with all your heart, always thinking of others, sometimes at your own peril. Yet, you have changed. You're more mature. You're stronger. Braver."

Serena touched him inquisitively, the merest whisper of a touch, her fingertip skimming along his brow. He sat very still. Her warm fingers skittered over his eyebrow, down the side of his face, across his jaw and chin. There they paused, and then delicately traced over his bottom lip.

He froze.

"Different, but the same." Her fingers caressed the other side of his face. "You, too, Jonathan. You've changed, too, inside and out. You know, I envisioned your face, your lips, in my mind sometimes. In my dreams. They are the same, just as I remember, but stronger somehow, more rugged."

She shifted on the bench, and her lips glanced over his brow, forging the same path her hands had just taken.

When her lips reached his, he couldn't bear to be still any longer. He kissed her back. She yielded, followed his lead. She tasted sweet, like nobody else. Like *Serena*. Together, their mouths simmered.

He broke the kiss and pressed his lips over her

cheeks, her nose, her eyes, her brow. A journey of rediscovery.

"Different, but the same." He brushed his lips over her forehead. "The shape of your face has changed. It is sharper, more refined. Still Serena, but even more beautiful."

The energy between them built. He could almost hear it, a droning buzz in the air between them that snapped and sparked wherever they made contact.

"Let me touch you, Serena. I swear I will not harm you, not this time."

"I can't," she whispered.

His spirits sank. He knew why. Her reasons were the same as his own.

She paused, then made a small sound in her throat, and kissed him, slipping her hands under his shirt, spreading the hot sparks to his torso. Lower.

He groaned and kissed her deeply, holding her against him. He willed her to stay with him a moment longer, or an hour, or all night, or forever.

She held his arms, and as he kissed her, her grip tightened until he knew she would leave her marks on him. He didn't care. He drank in her sweetness and drew strength from her touch.

She gave a deep shudder and a low groan, then pulled away and pressed her forehead against his shoulder.

Still, she didn't let him go. He held her tightly until they shifted on the seat, and both of them gazed silently into the night until Phoebe came outside hunting for her sister.

Serena stood in front of the mirror in her night rail, clutched her arms about her body, and rocked on her heels. Simple lust. That was all this was. A reawakening of the desires she'd experienced long ago.

Please, please let it be true.

Jonathan's hold on her was an iron band, encircling her heart like a shackle. Only constant reminders to herself of her duty to Will gave her the strength to stop before she went too far.

Still, guilt flooded through her.

She'd kissed him. Yet again. Did that make her an adulteress even before she was married? If nothing else, it proved her wicked nature. If Will had seen that kiss…

She gritted her teeth and clenched her fists at her sides.

Soon, it would be finished. She and Jonathan would go their separate ways in London, and she wouldn't see him except on brief social occasions. She could manage that. It was being with him day in and day out, talking to him, touching him, that was driving her to madness. To recklessness.

They'd accompany Sebastian and Phoebe to Gretna Green. They'd witness their marriage and take them back to Prescot. Serena would return to London to manage her aunt's wrath and write to her mother about what had happened with Phoebe. And then she'd marry Will like everyone expected her to.

Unlike her experience with him six years ago, this time she truly knew Jonathan. For so many reasons, nothing between them could last.

She crawled into bed and lay there, awake, until dawn.

Chapter Seventeen

Gretna Green at this time of year was the color advertised by its name. Every shade of green prevailed in the sweep of the landscape beneath a seemingly permanent drizzle misting from the low, gray clouds overhead.

The marriage between Phoebe and Sebastian was a simple affair. They arrived at the inn at Gretna at noon, and a Mr. Elliott married the young couple at three o'clock in the afternoon.

Once the rings—cheap bands purchased at a roadside shop—were exchanged, Mr. Elliott had handed over the marriage certificate with a beatific smile plastered on his pale, wide face. Then he clasped his hands at his chest and looked to Serena and Jonathan. "Perhaps the young couple will require a nuptial chamber for immediate consummation of the marriage?"

Serena stared at him blankly, while Jonathan coughed into his hand.

"In the event that there should be a pursuer who takes exception to their newly formed bond," Mr. Elliott hastened to explain.

"No thank you, sir," Serena said primly. "We neither expect pursuit nor require a nuptial chamber, but we'll be spending the night at the inn and should like to reserve four rooms."

Phoebe laughed out loud. "Oh, don't be so missish, Serena. Three rooms will be perfectly acceptable. I'm a married woman now, and no one on earth can tell me I'm not to sleep in my husband's bed on my wedding night."

With a sigh, Serena relented. She'd have to stop thinking of Phoebe as a child who needed caring for. Phoebe was a married woman with a child on the way, and the duty of caring for her rested on Sebastian Harper's shoulders now. From the way he gazed at Phoebe with such adoration, it appeared he looked forward to the task with enthusiasm.

After midnight, a knock sounded at her door, and Serena, who'd been brushing her hair in preparation for sleep, stiffened. It was too late for a maid, and Phoebe had ignored her all evening. From the touches Serena witnessed the couple sharing all afternoon, she had no doubt her new brother-in-law and Phoebe were in the throes of connubial bliss at this very moment.

"It's just me," Jonathan murmured from the corridor.

Laying down her brush, she unlatched the door and opened it, not even bothering to feign surprise. "Is something wrong?"

He stood there hesitating, looking for all the world like he wanted to reach out for her and enfold her in his arms.

God help her, she wanted him to.

"Nothing is wrong. I just wanted to see you. Make sure all was well."

"I'm fine."

"You seemed out of sorts today."

"It's simple," she said quietly. "She's my sister, and I love her very much. I'm afraid for her."

"I know. But I think they will suit."

"I hope you're right."

Framed by the wood of the door frame, wearing buff trousers and a cambric shirt, Jonathan studied her, an unreadable expression on his face.

Why had he come, really? Was it in response to the silent call that seemed to emanate from her flesh, summoning him to come to her, to relieve the ache she'd held on to for so long?

Her arm rose of its own volition, seduced, fingertips aching to touch him. She clenched her hand and forced it to her side.

A sense of foreboding swelled from somewhere deep inside her. She teetered on the precipice that promised doom, and she was slipping rapidly, unable to cling to its crumbling edge.

Jonathan closed the door and stepped inside. He cocked his head, gazing at her as if trying to read her thoughts. "What is it?" he asked softly.

"I..." She couldn't finish. How could she explain all the emotions and desires swirling within her?

Raising his hand, he cupped her chin in his palm and tilted her face up to his. "You... what?"

She turned her face, extricating her jaw from his gentle grip. "You should go."

His stare was so unnerving. So *knowing*. His gaze made her skin prickle with awareness, with heat.

"We need to talk, Serena."

"Well, I'd invite you to sit, but—" Chuckling uncomfortably, she gestured to the bed, the only piece of furniture in the room other than the tiny table, currently littered with the remains of her dinner along with her hairpins and jewelry. The bed was an antique monstrosity, high enough to require steps, with heavy brown silk and damask draperies.

They both gazed at the bed. Finally, Jonathan shrugged. "We'll use it like a sofa." He toed off his shoes, then mounted the steps and settled atop the counterpane, leaning against the headboard in demonstration. "You see? It works well enough."

She smiled. "I suppose." From the corner of her eye, she saw the open bottle of wine left over from her dinner sitting on her dinner tray. "Would you like some wine?"

"I would."

Serena took up the bottle and poured a drink, then she climbed the steps to the bed and crawled beside him, handing him the glass as she did so.

They drank in comfortable silence for long moments, trading the single glass back and forth, refilling it until the bottle was nearly empty. The wine asserted itself through Serena's body, loosening the stiffness in her muscles.

Finally, she said, "You know, I'm beginning to trust you again. I think. Well... sometimes." She gave a small laugh. It was true. After all that had happened since he'd first witnessed Phoebe with Sebastian, not the least of which was the fact that he'd protected her identity all this time, she'd learned that she could trust Jonathan in many ways.

His lips quirked upward. "I'll take that as progress."

"It was very kind of you to escort me all over the country in pursuit of my sister."

He shrugged. "Anyone would have done it."

"No." She drummed her fingers on the glass. "Not anyone. Will, for example? He wouldn't have approved of my traveling in this fashion. He'd never have approved of the match between Phoebe and Sebastian. And if he'd learned that Phoebe was with child before they'd even left London..."

Serena shuddered to think of how Will might have reacted. Not that he'd have resorted to violence—he'd simply disapprove of it all, to his core.

"Langley doesn't mean to condemn anyone. He wants what's best for your sister, just as you do."

Serena's lips twisted. "And now you defend him."

"He's my friend. I know he means well."

Handing Jonathan the wineglass, Serena settled back against the headboard. Being beside him brought back memories of them lying on the grass and staring up at the sky so many years ago.

"We were very young six years ago, weren't we?" she asked softly. "I thought we could rule the world. But clearly, we cannot."

"No," he agreed. "We can't."

She didn't turn to him. "There are so many things I wish you hadn't done. *We* hadn't done."

"I know. Me, too."

"But we were young."

"Yes."

"But later... all the women... the carousing..." she said thoughtfully, "I think learning about all that hurt as much as when you cast me aside, if that's possible."

"Serena..." His voice dwindled, and she turned her head to look at him, questioning him with her gaze. "Believe me," he continued, nearly in a whisper, "if I could take it all back to erase that look from your face and the pain from your eyes, I would."

"Would you?" She shrugged, trying to lighten her voice. "But men carouse, don't they? You were simply behaving like every other young man of your class."

"Maybe I was, but it wasn't what I intended to do

with my life." He released a long breath, and he rubbed his thumb against the side of the wineglass. He gazed at the red liquid inside, his jaw clenched tight. "You see..." He looked up at her, his eyes gleaming. "I wanted to die."

She blinked at him.

"I wanted to ruin my life. End it by drowning, as you had drowned. I thought to inundate myself in debauchery, vice, decadence. I wanted it to stifle me, snuff out my heart until it was incapable of feeling."

"Why?"

His eyelids sank shut. "I turned away from you, Serena. I cut you, and I killed you, didn't I? I'd murdered the only person in my life who really mattered. I hated myself for it. I couldn't forgive myself."

Something inside her squeezed tight, like a fist in her gut.

"But before you came to London, it was... Well, it was worse. It took me years to realize that my plan wasn't working. Here I was, lying with women I didn't even like, engaging in pursuits I felt no enjoyment for, throwing away my fortune, leaving my title and responsibilities by the wayside. But none of it had cured me of your loss."

He raised his hand and pressed his palm against her cheek, turning her to face him. "I never wanted to live without you. I never stopped loving you."

She believed him. The expression on his face, the depth in his eyes, and the sincerity in his voice wiped away her doubts. He had loved her. He had mourned her death. Grief and regret had crippled him for six long years.

Very slowly, he lowered his mouth to hers and kissed her. His lips pressed against hers, stroking, soft, warm, comforting. Like coming home.

She remembered that fateful night, the night of the Duchess of Clayworth's ball. How she had wanted him. But then she was in love and thought the world to be in the palm of her hand. Now she knew that could never be the case.

"I'm so afraid, Jonathan," she whispered against his lips. "So afraid of marrying Will. So afraid of loving you. Nothing I do is right... No choice I make is acceptable. Whatever I do, I'm to be the wicked woman who destroys everything she touches."

She didn't want to be wicked. She'd tried, tried so very hard, to be good. Still, she'd been perceived as the wicked Donovan sister for her whole life, even after Meg had died and she'd dedicated her life to becoming more like her twin. She'd never be Meg, not really.

"It's my fault," Jonathan whispered. "I hate that it's because of me people have made you feel that way. I hated hurting you, more than anything in my life. I won't do it again. I promise to do whatever I can to make you happy. I will give you pleasure. You remember how much happiness, how much pleasure we gave each other, don't you?"

She had recalled it every day of her life since.

"Do you remember that last moment we were together, right before the dowager duchess walked in? I can make that happen again."

Could he? Tremors of sensation licked through her belly and up through her chest. *Yes*. She knew he could.

Her heart began a deep, fast thud against her ribs.

This was it. It had finally come. She had always known it would, eventually.

She wanted him desperately, completely. She'd never stopped wanting him. Even after he'd spurned her, she'd secretly dreamed he'd come back to her, that it had all been some giant mistake, that he'd ride into Cedar Place like a gallant knight to sweep her away from all the misery she'd endured since the day he'd turned away from her.

She clenched the bed sheet in her hand, blinking hard against the mist that frosted over her eyes. "I've wanted...I want so badly to remember what it was like...to be with you." She drew in a shaky breath. "It's driving me mad."

He didn't speak, didn't move, just stared at her from behind half-lowered lids. But then his lips tilted up, as if in victory. Unbidden memories flooded through Serena. He smiled down at her while they walked together; he smiled at her across the theater; he smiled at her over a book; he smiled at her before he kissed her. She had always loved his smile. Raising his hand, he traced the curve of her lip with one finger.

"I won't push you," he murmured. "I'm yours, Serena. Yours to do with as you will, whether you choose to offer me punishment or pleasure. Always."

But she didn't want to punish him. The mere thought of punishing him made her stomach twist.

This time, it was Serena who leaned forward and pressed her lips to his. The contact sent a jolt through her body. She jerked back.

"Again," he commanded, his fingers sliding behind her neck and tugging her to him.

She kissed him. Her nerves jumped and quivered as she focused on the soft swirl of his tongue in her mouth, the taste of wine on his lips. Moving to his jaw, the strong jaw that fascinated her so much, she ran gentle, open-mouthed kisses along it.

"Touch me," he murmured into her hair.

She took the wineglass from his hands and set it on the high table beside the bed. Then she turned back to him, and with her heart hammering hard enough to burst out of her chest, she slowly pushed his shirt up, watching the ridges of his torso come into view. She'd seen statues before, but never the real living flesh of a man. Every time she and Jonathan had been together, they had remained fully clothed except over those parts required to accomplish the deed.

She ran her hands over his skin. He sat upright, leaning against the headboard, his hands fisted at his sides. His powerful muscles, hard and hot, quivered under her hands. She studied his flat male nipples, then circled them with her fingertips and pinched them lightly between her thumb and forefinger. He released a harsh breath.

She flattened her hands over them, feeling them stiffen beneath her palms. "Did I hurt you?"

"Yes. No. In a... good way." He smiled tightly.

Allowing his shirt to fall back over his chest, she traced the light trail of hair down the center of his abdomen until her fingers caught on the waistband of his trousers.

She stared at him for a long, silent moment, then let her fingers drift lower. He sat still, his jaw stiff, his teeth clenched. Tension rippled from his body. He seemed not to be breathing.

She explored the contours of him through the buttery fabric. She stroked his granite length, marveling at his size and strength, his sheer masculinity. This was the part of him that had been her undoing so many years ago. She released a breath through pursed lips and forced her hand upward again, stroking his torso beneath his shirt.

He held back, keeping his fists closed at his sides, allowing her to explore him.

With her fingers and lips, she took full advantage of his stillness, for an occasional ripple of muscle beneath his skin and twitch of his fingers told her in no uncertain terms that his lack of aggression would be temporary.

Serena ran her hands through his hair. She kissed

his jaw, his lips, his nose and forehead. She feathered kisses down his neck. She stroked down his arms, feeling the curves and sinews of his shape through the cambric.

Each touch heated her from the inside out. Each stroke of her lips made them ache for more. He smelled like soap and musk and male, so alluring that she wanted to press her lips against every part of him, to taste him, to love him everywhere.

Nibbling on the tips of his fingers, she dragged a low groan from the depths of his chest. She moved back up the lean muscular surface of his outstretched arm and down the hard, trembling flesh of his torso, bunching his shirt up, reveling in the contour of muscle on the sides of his body, stroking, licking, kissing, discovering.

So this was what a man tasted like, felt like under her tongue, fingers, and lips. This was Jonathan, all of him, something she'd never before been able to experience.

He breathed raggedly now, and she dragged her lips back to his, falling into a kiss so deep, she thought she might drown. The kiss eclipsed everything outside of this moment, apart from Jonathan. Nothing else existed.

She ran her hands over his chest, over his jaw, through his hair.

Jonathan slid down so that she lay on top of him. His hard, male body pressed up against her from top to bottom. And then he flipped them both so that he lay over her.

He licked across her chin, down her throat. Using his teeth, he pulled loose the ribbon tie of her chemise. He tugged it over her shoulders and down her body, following the trail of the fabric with the soft caress of his lips. When he drew the chemise over her breasts, he kissed her nipples, making her draw in short, sharp breaths.

Taking his time, he moved lower, kissing her stomach, running his hands over the curves of her hips. She lifted her bottom from the bed so he could pull her chemise all the way down. She wore nothing beneath, but she lay very still as he paused to stare down at her, refusing to squirm beneath his scrutiny.

"You're so beautiful," he murmured. "Like an angel. So perfect."

She gazed up at him, taking in the expression of sheer awe on his face, knowing that this moment would be forever imprinted in her memory.

He sat up and divested himself of his shirt, trousers, and smallclothes. Seeing him completely naked for the first time ever, the hard contours of his body so different from her own soft curves, she shivered.

"Are you cold?"

"No," she breathed. "Not cold. Overwhelmed...I think."

He lay beside her and gathered her close. She had been cool if not cold, but his scorching skin quickly warmed her, sinking deep beneath her flesh and spreading through her muscles. Soon enough, she squirmed from the heat.

He touched her again, moving his hands and mouth over her. She wanted to touch him, too, to continue her exploration of his newly revealed flesh. To be together with him in a way she never had with anyone.

They'd come together before. But those times had been rushed and furtive. Now, they had the time to really be together. This was somehow . . . more.

They traded caresses and kisses for so long, Serena lost track of time. He was over her once again, his sideburn rough against her cheek as he sampled her jaw with his lips. Her hands were threaded through his silky blond hair. Their chests were fused together, his solid and warm over her, but he held his weight on his forearms so he didn't crush her. The steel length of his erection lay like a hot brand against her thigh.

His hand moved down, and her legs opened for his touch before she realized what they were doing. But when his fingers pressed against her intimate flesh, she gasped, her whole body jerking in reaction.

"Oh! That tickles!"

He smiled and touched her again, the callus on his fingertip rubbing over her most sensitive spot. This time, she managed to stay quiet and still, but the touch resonated through her, a shock of sweet sensation.

"No," she breathed. "I was wrong."

"It doesn't tickle?"

"Not... exactly."

His lips brushed over hers as he stroked her again. His shaft grew larger and harder against her thigh as he used his fingers to ramp up the pleasure and the sensation.

"Jonathan," she whispered. "Jonathan."

She clutched his arms, her fingers molding over his strong biceps.

"Beautiful Serena. God, you're so damn beautiful."

She wanted nothing but to be here at this moment, with Jonathan touching her so intimately, watching her closely, learning how best to pleasure her. This was heaven.

"Oh... I..."

"Come for me, Serena," he urged gently. "I can feel that you're close."

His fingers slipped inside and pumped, stroking her inside while his thumb pressed gently over the spot on her body that made her feel more brazen and wild than she'd ever imagined she could be. Her legs began to tremble, and she pressed herself more firmly against his hand.

Suddenly, the wave crested and broke in a warm wash that encompassed her entire body. She lost awareness of everything but the exquisite feel of the motion, taking her up and tumbling her deep within a foamy bliss.

She didn't know how long it was before he gently pulled his hand away from her. She opened her eyes to see him staring down at her, the tenderness of earlier now replaced by stark need.

"I can't wait," he said simply.

His leg moved between hers, his knee sliding up the inside of her thigh, pressing it outward. She could feel him move over her, through her highly sensitized flesh until he found the notch of her womanhood. His eyes met hers again, and he hesitated.

They stared at each other, each taking short, panting breaths. She could feel her heartbeat—or was it his?—pounding between them.

"Are you ready?"

"Yes, Jonathan." She pulled his face down toward hers, giving him a deep kiss of gratitude, of love. She was ready for him. She wanted nothing more than for him to take her, to reestablish that she was his—had never been and never would be anyone else's.

Slowly, he pushed inside her. She arched up with a gasp, forcing him in quicker and deeper than he'd intended, but he didn't complain. Instead, he pressed deeper in with a low groan. "God, you're tight. I'm not hurting you?"

"No... on the... contrary... the opposite."

"Good," he gasped. "Thank God."

"Don't... stop..."

With a low groan, he pulled partway out before thrusting inside her once again. She arched up to meet him even as the strength of his thrust forced the air from her lungs.

And then he began a steady, solid velvety deep rhythm of pleasure, his hands cupping her head as he kissed her. She wrapped her arms around him, savoring the flex of his muscles beneath her hands.

His tempo increased and so did the sensation. She met his every thrust with one of her own, straining once again toward that sweet release. He seemed to understand this, and he ground against her, rubbing over that spot once more. When she came, it was sudden and surprising. Like an explosion in the night sky, booming into bright flares of heat and color and light.

He expanded within her, tightening all over in response to her orgasm. And then he stiffened and shuddered in her arms, and she felt the pulse of his release deep inside her.

Fearing that he might collapse and crush her delicate body beneath him, Jonathan forced his body to slump beside her. He drew her into his arms and buried his face into her sweet-smelling hair as the tendrils of pleasure still detonated through him.

She nuzzled his neck, his jaw, and finally, his mouth. He kissed her fiercely, straining to show the extent of his feeling, his gratitude.

She broke the kiss and pulled back, the smooth curve of her waist utterly feminine, utterly lovely under his palm. She clasped her arm over her chest, but the pale curve of her breasts rounded above her forearm. Dark blond curls cascaded over her shoulders.

Six years had formed her into a woman. He remembered her as a beautiful girl—lightly freckled, pink cheeked and smiling—a splash of sunlight but with so much depth inside. The years had turned her gray eyes thoughtful and softened her ruddy complexion to peaches and cream.

"God," was all he could utter. He stared wordlessly at the red, glistening bow of her lips.

Her brow furrowed. "Was it that bad?"

"Oh, God, no, Serena. It was better... better than I ever dreamed."

She smiled, the creases in her forehead smoothing. "You dreamed about this?"

"Oh, yes. All the time."

"So did I," she whispered, and tilted her head, studying him. Then she raised her hand and traced his eyebrow with her fingertip. "I have so many memories of your eyes. I dreamed of them so many times. They're exactly the same."

"Are they?" He frowned. The last he'd closely observed himself in the looking glass, he had seen the beginnings of a series of most unflattering crow's feet at their outside edges. His vanity had been wounded and he'd gone out and... done something he now regretted.

"Yes, exactly the same," she said. "They are such a dark blue, they appear black in this light. Your lashes are . . . impossibly thick and dark. Just like they were back then."

She leaned forward and kissed him softly on the lips. Her breast brushed against his chest, and desire stirred his cock back to life.

Curling her soft, warm body against him, she drew the blankets over them. Wrapping his arms around her, he watched her, unable to drag his gaze away. He wanted to stare at her all night long.

Soon, her long, deep breaths told him she was asleep. Jonathan couldn't remember the last time a woman had slept in his arms, pressed against his body, in the same bed as him.

One of her soft curls tickled his chest.

It was over. As much as he hated what they must do to Langley, Jonathan wouldn't let this woman walk away from him again.

Chapter Eighteen

Serena woke from a dream sometime in the early hours of morning. Muted light leached through the curtains, but she could not see the details of the chamber, only faint outlines.

She had dreamed of straddling Jonathan, of red velvet curtains, of the sounds of the quadrille, of his seed pumping into her.

She couldn't believe she had fallen asleep so soon after they had joined. But when she had tucked herself into his body and rested her head on his shoulder, nothing had seemed more natural than closing her eyes and sinking into peaceful oblivion.

Jonathan's hard length pressed against her skin from head to toe. A flush of warmth infused her body. She stroked down his chest and slipped her hand between his legs. He was hard. Ready.

Drunk with sleep and lust, she wondered idly if he was even awake. No matter. He would be soon.

She rose to her knees and straddled his body. She took him in her hand and positioned him so the tip of his shaft touched the cleft between her legs. Then, inch by inch, she lowered herself.

He moaned, then opened his eyes.

Her passage was taut, but smooth and slick. She slowly rocked herself down over him, gasping as her body stretched and filled with the intoxicating combined sensations of pleasure and pain.

She splayed her hands over his chest and began to ride him slowly, grinding herself against him.

"Yes," she whispered, vibrating with pleasure.

This was what she needed. What she had needed for so long. Just this.

"Serena..."

He moved beneath her, thrust upward into her, speared her. His eyes glittered, sparkled in the growing light.

Her pace increased. She knelt forward, bracing her hands on either side of his head. Her nipples brushed against his chest, but all she could feel was Jonathan inside her, gliding against her sensitive inner walls. The sensations rushed through her, connecting her mind and her loins and her limbs. He flowed through her entire body and they were truly one—she a part of him as much as he was a part of her. Their harsh breaths came in unison, sweat smoothed the contact between their bodies, and every one of their muscles quavered and tensed.

It happened more quickly than she anticipated. She floated high above herself, high above the room, and then spiraled downward in a flush, a waterfall, a slick dive into a warm pool. All her nerves tightened and froze, and then they released in a sweet sensation that poured through her body. She could no longer support her own weight. She slumped down over him, burying her face into his neck, shuddering.

He kissed her ear, her temple. "I love you. I love you."

She squeezed her eyes shut. He had said he loved her before.

He rotated his hips, moving gently, and she responded to meet him. She couldn't stop herself. It was as natural as breathing.

Once again, she gave in to the sensations, the exquisite friction between their bodies. Even their moans seemed synchronous. She leaned forward, her lips caressing his neck, his ear, his shoulder as they moved together.

She slowly lifted herself until they were connected by a mere sliver of flesh and then pushed herself down. Hard.

And then she came apart once more, the white heat at her core exploded, and she shattered, closed around him, and arched her back as spasms overtook her. He thrust up into her, and she could feel every movement, every pulse, every tremor. Every part of his body that touched her so deeply. With a shout that seemed to emerge from the very depths of his soul, he surrendered, pulsing deep inside her.

She sank onto his shoulder, breathing heavily, feeling his heartbeat beneath her breast. She turned her head to watch him in the increasing daylight. He gazed at her with midnight-blue eyes, a soft smile tilting his lips.

She stared back at him until a shaft of sunlight pierced through the crack in the curtains and slashed a golden line across his face.

There would be hell to pay when they returned to London.

Gathering every bit of strength she possessed, she forced herself to climb off him and swing her legs over the side of the bed. Clenching her teeth, she leaned over to retrieve her chemise, which had landed on the bed stairs when he'd tossed it away last night.

She tugged it over her head, trying not to think of what she'd done, what her future would hold, all that she must face.

"Lie with me for a while," he said softly. She kept her back to him, but she felt him watching her, studying her. He probably saw the tremor in her hands.

"I cannot." Her voice sounded brusque, even though she didn't mean for it to. "You should return to your room. We're leaving in a few hours."

She knew they must talk about what had happened,

about what must be done. But not now. She couldn't bear to—not yet.

He rose and dressed in silence as she watched. As he tied the string of his shirt, he turned to face her. "I want to be with you, Serena."

She flinched at his words.

"We'll speak to Langley. Tell him—"

She raised her hand, stopping his speech. "No. *I* must speak to him. That responsibility is mine to bear." She licked her lips. "I'm...sorry. I'm still so afraid. Everything has changed. I'm trying, but I'm not sure if I can continue with..." Her arm flailed out helplessly. Common sense warred with emotion, hope warred with experience. If she set herself free with Jonathan, if she gave him everything he asked for, the past just might repeat itself. She was older now, and stronger, but even so, she didn't know if she could bear it all happening again.

"Even after last night? This morning?"

It hurt to say the words. "Even then." She stared down at her hands, twisting together in front of her. "You've a history of lying to women, Jonathan. Even though I want to trust you, even though you say I must trust you, in the end, how can I?"

His eyes narrowed. "I didn't lie to you. I never have."

It was possible that he'd set a velvet trap for her, just as he had six years ago. Soft, comfortable, and so alluring. And once he had ensnared her, he would grind her beneath his heel. He would turn away from her. Again.

"I won't relinquish you easily. I'll fight for you. With everything I possess."

"Please. Can we speak of this later?" She turned away so he wouldn't see the pain and fear that must be clearly marked all over her face. "We've a long day of travel ahead of us."

His lips so tight their edges turned white, he nodded. "Very well. I'll see you downstairs in half an hour."

He turned his back to her, unlatched the door, and stepped over the threshold. The door closed firmly behind him.

His words resonated within her. *I'll fight for you. With everything I possess.*

In the following days of travel, Serena managed to avoid discussion of the night she'd spent with Jonathan. She tucked what had happened deep inside her and focused on her sister. She would be separated from Phoebe soon, and she wanted nothing more than to make the most of these final days with her. Jonathan seemed to understand, for he didn't press. But he was always there, watching, bathing her with silent understanding.

When they arrived at Sebastian's small house in Prescot, an ornate carriage bearing the Alcott crest was parked in the drive.

Phoebe met Serena's eyes. "Oh, dear."

Jonathan sighed. "The three of you stay here. I'll speak with your aunt."

"I think not." Sebastian straightened, a look of defiance in his eyes. "This is my house, after all, and Phoebe is my wife."

Serena gave an inward smile. Few dared stand up to Aunt Geraldine, and she respected those who did.

The carriage stopped, and the men opened their doors and headed toward the house in long strides.

"Oh, dear," Phoebe said again, wringing her hands. "Do you think Aunt Geraldine will be very angry with me?"

"Of course she'll be angry. Surely you considered her reaction before you ran off?" Serena grimaced. "She'd have discovered the truth about your marriage sooner or later. I suppose it's best that we're far from London and won't have to face the ammunition of society directly behind her."

Phoebe pursed her lips.

"Come along, then. You're going to have to face her sometime."

Serena hopped down from the carriage before the coachman had time to place the step, and lifting her skirts, she hurried toward the front door. Just as she reached it, an enraged shout emerged from inside. "How *dare* you compromise my niece, you black-hearted villain!"

"Oh, heavens." Serena strode through the door, Phoebe following closely behind.

Sebastian and Aunt Geraldine stood within an arm's reach of each other. The only thing preventing Aunt Geraldine from charging at Sebastian like a rampaging bull was Jonathan's arm wrapped solidly around her waist.

Sebastian's face was flushed red with fury or embarrassment—Serena couldn't quite say—while her aunt's fists were tight balls trying to swipe around Jonathan to pummel her target.

"Oh, for goodness' sakes," Serena said irritably, hands on her hips. "What's done is done, Aunt. It's a little late to fight it."

Phoebe ran to Sebastian and flung her arms around him.

"How dare you!" Aunt Geraldine growled at the young man. "You insolent swine—"

"Now, now, Lady Alcott," Jonathan admonished mildly.

Sebastian had already stepped away and was speaking in low, gentle tones to Phoebe. His new wife, evidently, was a soft breeze to his flame.

Husband and wife turned to face Aunt Geraldine, side by side and standing tall. "We're married, Aunt," Phoebe announced.

"If that's so, I shall have it annulled. You're too young—"

Phoebe raised her hand. "We married in Scotland.

Furthermore, ma'am, I am with child." She glanced up at Sebastian, a light flush infusing her cheeks. "Sebastian's child. We are together now. Forever."

Even this didn't satisfy Aunt Geraldine. She flung Jonathan's arm away and leaned toward Sebastian, her arms rigid, her fists curling at her sides. "And how do you intend to support my niece?"

Sebastian looked to Jonathan who smiled knowingly. "Are you familiar with that pile of rubble I own out in Sussex, my lady?"

Aunt Geraldine swung her gaze to Jonathan, looking at him as if he were mad. "Stratford House? What of it?"

"Mr. Harper is said to be quite a skilled architect. I've hired him to redesign and rebuild it for me. I imagine the project will take several years, at least, but"—he grinned at Sebastian—"we've negotiated a fair price. And through the duration, Mr. and Mrs. Harper will have the use of one of the houses on my property. If his work earns him any acclaim—and I'm certain it will—I feel sure that he won't have to worry in the least about supporting his wife in the future."

Serena stared at Jonathan, aghast. When had he and Sebastian negotiated all this? Relief poured through her. If this truly came to pass, then Phoebe would be safe. Her future was assured.

Just then, Jonathan's gaze caught hers, and the corners of his lips tilted in acknowledgment of her silent "thank you."

Aunt Geraldine was less impressed. She sneered at Jonathan. "You must be mad. This man is a brawling, no good, debauching gambler—"

"Ah, yes," Jonathan murmured. "Just like me?"

"Indeed," Aunt Geraldine said haughtily.

"And yet I'd wager you'd allow your niece to marry me."

"You have a title," Aunt Geraldine sniffed.

"Yes, of course. The title and the fact that I have more blunt than Harper, to boot. However, those are the only things that separate our two breeds, aren't they, my lady? I daresay far more goes into the making of men than money and titles. And after closely observing Harper with your niece, I can say without a doubt that he'd lay down his life for her in an instant."

Aunt Geraldine gave a frustrated, "Humph." Crossing her arms over her chest, she turned to pace the room as everyone else watched her. Serena allowed her smile to curl the edges of her lips.

Jonathan had won.

While Phoebe and Sebastian remained in Prescot to honeymoon until autumn, at which time Sebastian would begin the work on Jonathan's estate, Serena and Jonathan returned to London with Aunt Geraldine.

In the carriage, Aunt Geraldine explained how she had come to know they were in Prescot. When Phoebe had left London in the carriage claiming to be headed to Bath, Aunt Geraldine had engaged a footman to follow her. The man had returned a few days later, bearing the news that Phoebe wasn't in Bath but in Prescot with a young rogue named Sebastian Harper. Without causing a scandal by telling anyone, and with Serena too far away to contact, Aunt Geraldine had decided to pursue them on her own.

"I've not the endurance for traveling I had when I was young," she sniffed. "I can only manage a few hours in a carriage every day." Still, due to Phoebe's pregnancy, Serena was certain that the end result would have been the same even if her aunt had arrived days earlier.

Dividing their time between the carriage and traveling inns with Aunt Geraldine, neither Serena nor Jonathan had an opportunity to discuss their future. Which was perfectly fine with Serena, because it gave her time to contemplate it on her own.

Regardless of the situation with Jonathan, Serena could no longer lie to Will. No matter what the future held, she needed to tell Will the truth. She needed to break the engagement and sever their connection once and for all. She couldn't be the wife Will wanted and deserved. She could never be Meg. And, most important, Meg wouldn't want this for either of them.

She would ask for Will's forgiveness, for his understanding, but she wouldn't blame him if he hated her. She'd accept that, and she'd accept with her head held high any public scorn and scandal that resulted from his anger.

Serena couldn't entirely predict what the next few days held for her, so as the carriage ate the miles between Prescot and London, a lump of trepidation grew solid within her. But a glimmer of hope softened that fear—a hope that she and Jonathan would somehow find a way to be together.

At least Phoebe was happy and had been properly settled. After days of witnessing the relationship between her sister and Sebastian, Serena knew they possessed a powerful admiration for each other. She could only hope that it lasted. Further, Serena had no doubt that even if things didn't work out between herself and Jonathan, he'd look after Phoebe and make sure she was well cared for.

"The final moments of our journey," Jonathan murmured under his breath as they negotiated the traffic leading toward St. James's Square, four long days after they'd left Prescot.

"Indeed." Serena glanced at her aunt who was dozing on a silk-covered pillow she'd placed against her window.

"Was it a successful one, would you say?"

She smiled at him. So much was still undecided. They were plunging back in the mire that was London, and she still had no firm idea as to how she was going to claw her way out of it.

"I think," she finally said, "Phoebe and Mr. Harper are ideal for each other, in spite of their relative youth." The disparity in their social ranks? Meaningless, as far as Serena was concerned. It had always been meaningless to her, she realized; she had merely been acquiescing to society's expectations. She regretted that now. She should have trusted Phoebe, seen at once the strong attraction shared between her younger sister and Sebastian.

They turned the corner onto St. James's Square.

"Aunt Geraldine," Serena said in a low voice, gently touching her aunt's shoulder.

Aunt Geraldine popped out of sleep with a jolt. "Eh?"

"We're home," Serena explained.

Aunt Geraldine blinked, then patted the wisps of hair that had escaped her coiffure and searched around for her reticule, which had fallen on the floor. Serena handed the small bag to her aunt.

The carriage drew to a halt, and the three of them withdrew, twisting their backs and stretching from the long drive as the servants rushed forward to help with luggage.

At the sound of a high-pitched cry, Serena looked toward Jonathan's house.

A brown-haired little boy, perhaps six years old, ran toward them, his arms outstretched, crying, "Oh, sir, it's been so long since you've come to see us. Where have you been?"

He trundled across the drive, headed straight for Jonathan. Everyone froze. Even Jonathan stood there, statue still, as the boy rammed into his legs and threw his arms around him.

Again, Serena looked toward Jonathan's house. A beautiful, dark-haired woman hurried toward them, hands twisting, voicing some apology Serena hardly heard.

She glanced back at Jonathan. His eyes were riveted to the child. Sensing this, the boy looked up at him, a questioning expression in his blue eyes.

Serena took a stumbling step backward. Jonathan's child. The rumors were true, then, and he had lied to her. This was his son.

Jonathan's son.

And that beautiful woman—Serena jerked her gaze toward the lady once again—was the mother of Jonathan's son. The woman was obviously a lady—Serena could tell instantly from her bearing, her dress, even from her expression.

A hand clamped down over Serena's wrist. As if through a fog, Serena turned her head to see her aunt standing beside her, her square jaw so tight it looked as though it might snap.

"Eliza," Jonathan said, furrowing his brow and smoothing his hand over the boy's dark head, "what has happened? Is something wrong?"

"I'm so very sorry, Jonathan. I know you told me I mustn't come here. I didn't mean to—"

Eliza. Jonathan. They were on a first-name basis. Well, it should be obvious, Serena supposed, since the woman had borne his child. Eliza's accent was pure and aristocratic.

But if she were truly a lady, why hadn't Jonathan married her?

Aunt Geraldine's fingers tightened over Serena's wrist. "We are going inside," she said stiffly.

Serena had thought she and Jonathan had been candid with each other. He'd promised to be honest with her, he'd told her he had no children, and yet there was this boy, this child. *His.*

It all came crashing down. He'd built her a house of cards, and now it tumbled into ruins all around her. If he had lied about this, he could've lied about anything. Her logical mind—it had been right all along. She never should have believed a word he'd said to her.

Eliza had reached them, a flush washed over her delicate, aristocratic cheeks. She curtsied toward Aunt Geraldine and Serena. "Please forgive me. I'm so very sorry for the interruption."

Aunt Geraldine wouldn't even look toward the lady. Instead, she tugged on Serena's arm again. "Come along, Meg."

Jonathan didn't seem angry to see his mistress and her child, only perplexed and concerned. Casting what looked like a guilty look at Serena, he wrapped his arm around the little boy, who smiled up at him.

Obviously the child knew him well and they were fond of each other.

No, he hadn't changed, after all. Moisture stung at Serena's eyes as she turned away.

What else was there to do but go inside? She was an intruder to this familial scene. Numbly, Serena followed her aunt, leaving the awkwardness of the reuniting family behind her. She caught one last glimpse of them as the door closed behind her. Jonathan wasn't looking after her. Instead, Eliza was grasping his hand, and he leaned toward her, his blond head contrasting with her dark curls in the sunlight as he spoke to her in low, gentle tones.

Chapter Nineteen

In no time at all, the scandal of Phoebe's marriage to Sebastian Harper became the talk of London.

Serena retold the event in a flippant manner, waving her hand as if to say that young people did what young people did. She relayed the story as if they were a group of people having fun—irreverent and scandalous without being overtly shameful.

Aunt Geraldine still did not approve of Sebastian, but there was nothing that could be done about that now. It was far too late for her disapproval. When Mother received word, she'd be scandalized and furious, but again, it was too late.

Then there was Jonathan. After Serena had left him on the street the afternoon of her return, he had disappeared from London and she hadn't seen him in the three days since.

If he had wanted to allay her fears, then he'd have said something, done something, by now. Yet he had made no effort to see Serena. He had serious business to attend to. Business that had nothing to do with her.

She'd seen the way he'd looked at that little boy and that lovely woman, Eliza. She'd observed the tenderness in his expression. He cared for both mother and child. It hurt to remember the little boy's worshipful expression when he looked up at Jonathan.

The only person who was there for Serena—her constant support and her stability—was Will. He'd come as soon as he heard she'd returned home from Bath, full of disgust at himself for not having been there to be of any help with Phoebe and Sebastian.

She hadn't been able to tell him the truth that day, or in the days since. She was searching for a time when they were alone, when she could speak freely to him. Yet Serena knew that each day she delayed made things worse for everyone involved, and every day that passed was one day closer to the wedding date, now only a little over two weeks away.

Jonathan's lies and subsequent disappearance didn't make it right for her to continue deceiving Will. It was no longer enough to continue the ruse for her mother and two remaining unmarried sisters. Serena knew that her decision to tell Will the truth would result in consequences—dire consequences, at that. But there was no other choice her conscience would allow her to make.

Earlier this evening, Will and Serena had dined with Aunt Geraldine. They'd eaten roasted beef in pleasant companionship, talking about Will's business in trade, his hopes to redecorate his London town house, his intention for them to travel to his house in Northumberland later in the year.

It was easy; it was peaceful—or, at least it would have been if Serena weren't so tied up in knots about her plans.

Aunt Geraldine retired shortly after dinner, leaving Serena and Will alone in the drawing room. Apprehension thrummed along Serena's nerves, bunching her muscles tight. Tonight would be the night. She must be brave enough to tell Will the truth. Tell him that they couldn't stay together. Couldn't go through with this marriage.

They'd sat for some time in silence when Will, rotating his glass of port in his hands, looked up beyond the rim at her. "Why, Meg?"

"What do you mean?"

"Why did you allow them to go through with it?"

"Who?"

"Harper and your sister."

Will's disapproval of Sebastian hadn't softened with his marriage to Phoebe. Until now, Will had said nothing, but Serena had felt it in him—that solid stiffness of disapproval that lurked just beneath the surface of his outward calm.

"Well..." Her voice dwindled. How to begin?

How to explain how Sebastian and Phoebe reminded her so much of Jonathan and herself six years ago, but even better? Stronger? Sebastian Harper, she supposed, had grown into maturity more quickly and more solidly than Jonathan ever had.

"You know they're wrong for each other."

"Not at all," Serena said. "On the contrary, I feel they're quite a perfect fit."

Will frowned into his glass. "How can you say that?"

"They love each other."

He gave a low scoff. "What does that matter in the face of such a mismatch?"

"But why must you keep insisting they're mismatched?"

"She's a lovely girl. If she played her cards to her advantage, she could have had her pick from the young bucks of the ton. She could have chosen someone rich, titled, someone with *morals.* Instead, she chose a scoundrel of low birth."

Serena went stiff all over. "I don't believe he's such a scoundrel. Not anymore."

"He's an upstart who enjoys pretending to be something he's not. At this moment, he's probably congratulating himself on his great coup at winning your sister."

Serena clenched her teeth, bemused by her protective instincts, which now, apparently, had grown to include her new brother-in-law. "I don't think so, Will. She had no dowry, remember?"

Will stared at her. "She is in possession of a far superior bloodline than he has."

"Why on earth should that matter? They're not horses."

He ignored the horse comment. "It matters a great deal. Without rank, where would our civilization be?"

"Perhaps you are too deeply enmeshed in the hierarchical systems of our military and our society."

She shouldn't have said that. Or maybe she should have. She'd bitten her tongue too often in Will's presence.

Will hesitated, then set his port on the side table. "Perhaps I am." Slowly, stiffly, he rose. "I should take my leave. The hour is late."

She glanced at the mantel clock. He was right—it was after midnight. Yet it was time for him to know the truth. She rose, too, and set a placating hand on his arm. "Please stay, Will. For a little while longer. There's something I . . . well, there's something I must tell you."

He hesitated. She could practically see him debating with himself whether to stay.

She was petrified of the truth. Afraid of what it would bring her. Her future in Antigua loomed before her, harsh and lonely. Even though Jonathan had shattered all her hope about a future with him in one fell swoop, her decisions regarding Will hadn't changed. No matter how dismal her future would be in Antigua, she could never marry him. She was a fool to think she could have succeeded in playing Meg to him for the rest of her life.

"We've that afternoon meeting with the draper tomorrow," Will said. "We could speak then, perhaps."

The draper. Will was redecorating his house with her in mind. With their marriage in mind.

"Please." She tried not to flinch, hating the sound of dread in her voice. "I must speak with you now, Will. It's important."

Will studied her closely. Then, with a tight nod, he lowered himself onto his chair.

"Very well." His quiet voice had seemed to take on some of the dread her own had held.

They stared at each other. Will looked beautiful tonight, in a black and gray pin-striped tailcoat, gray trousers, and a crisp white cravat. But his beauty, unlike Jonathan's, did nothing to prickle her flesh and turn her insides molten.

He cleared his throat and spoke softly. "I want you to be comfortable, Meg. With me. Always."

Will Langley, ever the gentleman. For some reason, her eyes stung, and she blinked hard, remembering the feeling that had swirled through her when she'd watched Jonathan with his son. She was certain she'd never feel comfortable with Jonathan again.

Perhaps she'd never feel comfortable with anyone. Perhaps she was destined to be alone.

She pushed those dismal thoughts aside and swallowed hard. "You don't have any children, do you, Will?"

That was an impertinent question beyond any other—she realized that right away. He stared at her, frozen, and she instantly flushed. "I'm sorry."

Will's Adam's apple moved as he swallowed. "You were the first woman I ever..." He cleared his throat, hesitating, but he'd made his meaning clear enough.

The truth sucked the air from Serena's lungs. She stared at him, mouth agape.

This couldn't be! Will and Meg had made love? When? How? Sweet, wholesome Meg, and honorable, gentle Will? How was it possible?

"Oh, Lord," she murmured, hardly knowing what she said. Her face was on fire.

He and Meg had had carnal relations. And she'd behaved like such a fake innocent with him, making assumptions that were entirely untrue. What on earth did he think of her odd reactions to his advances?

"I wanted to wait for you," he said, not meeting her eyes. "For us to be together again. I couldn't bring myself to want anyone else."

"Oh, Will."

Still not looking at her, he winced. "And yet..." Serena stopped breathing altogether as he met her gaze. "I have an idea what it is you wish to tell me."

He reached forward, took up his port, and drained

his glass. Serena didn't move for fear of betraying her own emotions.

Finally, he looked up at her. "You're not Meg."

Serena went still all over. "No."

His eyes turned glassy. "You're Serena. Aren't you?"

"Yes," she whispered. A part of her registered that he'd said the words for her, made it easier on her, but the rest of her cringed in wretched shame.

"Is Meg . . . ?"

"Yes." Serena nodded and swallowed hard. "She was lost at sea."

Will looked down at his knees. After a long, loud silence, he spoke in a soft voice. "I always knew. I didn't want to believe it. At first, I wondered why things had changed. It was more than the changes wrought by time and tragedy, though I tried to convince myself it wasn't. I struggled against the truth of it, but it was there, staring me in the face, ever since I kissed you in Hyde Park."

"I'm so sorry," she whispered.

"I've buried myself in work, even when it wasn't necessary, so I could avoid you. Avoid what I knew was the truth."

"Why didn't you confront me the minute you suspected?"

"A part of me didn't want to know . . . didn't want to hear that Meg . . ." Pressing his lips together, he looked away, seemingly unable to continue.

"That Meg is gone," Serena finished for him.

"Yes."

She couldn't speak; she simply stared at him through blurring eyes.

"Why?" Anguish leeched into his voice, ever so subtle but wrenching her heart nonetheless. "Why did you do it?"

"I..." Her voice trailed off. It seemed too overwhelming, too complicated to explain.

"I always liked you," he said quietly. "But this—this kind of a lie...it is so destructive. You are so different from Meg. How could you ever have believed...?"

Pain squeezed like a fist in Serena's chest. "I'm sorry, Will. So sorry."

"Why?" he repeated.

"I didn't know...at first." She gazed at his grief-stricken face through watery eyes. "I'd no idea my mother had sent word to England that I was the one who'd died. I didn't know she was writing letters to you—"

Will closed his eyes. "Good God. It was your mother."

"I was ignorant of the scheme until you sent your proposal. I don't think my mother knew exactly how it would end. But when you suggested we marry, it all became clear in her mind. I would be Meg, and I would marry you to secure my own future as well as my sisters'."

Will opened his eyes. They glistened in the feeble light.

"I'm so sorry, Will. I've felt so trapped. No matter what choice I made, I would end up hurting someone who meant a great deal to me." And she had, of course. "But that is no excuse, is it?" she continued in a near whisper. "I've hurt you, and I'm sorry."

There was a long silence. What more could she say? She wanted to repeat her apology again and again, but that would certainly do no good. She bowed her head, awaiting his condemnation.

"I have something else to ask you, Serena," he said finally, his voice quiet and steady.

"Of course."

"Do you love Stratford?"

The question slammed into her so hard, it left her breathless. She stared at him, groping desperately for something to say, finding nothing.

Grabbing his glass, he stood and prowled the length of the room before refilling his drink at the sidebar. Finally, he turned back to face her. "I see. You still love him. You would never have been happy with me. You agreed to marry me only because you felt you had no other choice."

"I am very fond of you. I always have been. Meg—"

"Serena…" His voice cracked, then trailed off, and he shook his head. "You love Stratford, and he's never stopped loving you. You must go to him."

No. She couldn't. Not now. "You don't understand. It's not because of him that I—"

"Meg is dead," Will pushed out, his voice harsh with anger and grief.

"Yes," she agreed. "She's dead. She's been dead for six years." Six interminably long years.

His eyes dulled. Setting his glass down, he stared past her at the silk wallpaper covering the wall beside the hearth, his fists bunched at his sides.

She watched him in silence. She'd lived with Meg's death for six years, but to Will it was a fresh, open wound. She rose and went to him, tentatively wrapping her arms around him. To her surprise, he responded, drawing her close and sinking his face into her hair.

"Do you miss her?" he whispered.

"So very much."

They stood for long, silent minutes, holding each other, awash in their grief.

A rapping noise came from the window, so close that Serena jumped away from Will. She spun toward the window. Darkness obscured whoever lurked behind the glass.

"Let me in, damn it!"

The voice was muffled, but it was deep and low and masculine and sent a ripple of recognition through her body.

Jonathan was outside.

The blood froze in her veins. Serena felt like a

piece of crystal. If she moved, she would break. She didn't want him to be here. Not now, not to disrupt the fragile peace she'd made with Will.

"Do you want him to come in?" Will asked in a gravelly voice.

"I..." She closed her eyes and pressed the bridge of her nose between two fingers. "No. Not really."

"Stay here. I'll speak to him."

She watched him move to the door, open it, walk out, close it behind him. All her senses attuned, she heard his footsteps down the corridor and the creak of the front door as Will opened it. Then there was a soft murmur as he spoke to Jonathan.

Her feet moved of their own volition. She stepped out of the drawing room. Will stood in the entry hall, his back to her. Just beyond him, Jonathan stood on the landing, wearing buckskin breeches and black, muddy boots, his face pale and drawn, his coat soiled, his hair tousled. Something electric buzzed through her limbs.

His gaze caught hers and held, his eyes narrowing. "I saw you in the drawing room. I thought... What the hell were you—?"

"For Christ's sakes, Stratford," Will said. "You're going to wake the whole deuced neighborhood."

"I don't care!"

"It's all right," Serena said, feeling as exhausted as Will looked. All they needed now was yet another scandal. "Come inside."

Jonathan strode in and threw the door shut behind him. The butler approached from the direction of the servants' quarters and paused in an archway, candle in hand, surveying the scene with wide eyes.

"In the drawing room," Serena said. She didn't want Jonathan to be here—didn't want to talk to him. But she didn't want to create a scene, either. She nodded at the butler, dismissing him.

The two men followed her into the drawing room, ominously silent. She closed the door behind them and turned to Jonathan, crossing her arms over her chest. "Now what's this about? Why are you here?"

"You were embracing him," Jonathan accused, his gaze swinging from Will to her. "Kissing him. I saw you from outside."

"No!" both she and Will exclaimed in unison.

"For goodness' sakes, Jonathan," Serena added, gritting her teeth, hating that he was making her explain. "I just told him everything. He knows about Meg. We were *comforting* each other."

There was a long moment of silence. Jonathan looked between the two of them, evidently trying to ascertain whether Serena was telling the truth. Eventually, he sighed. "I saw the two of you through the window... I thought..."

"Your thought was wrong," Will said quietly.

Jonathan shoved his fingers through his tousled hair. "Damn. I have no right to feel this way. But when I saw you embracing him..." He winced. "Seeing you two like that, I felt... God, I felt like something was exploding inside me."

"Oh, good Lord," Serena snapped, unable to mask the sarcasm in her voice. "You're one to talk, aren't you?"

"What are you—?"

"Oh, don't look so incredulous. You know I saw your mistress. I saw your boy."

Both men stared at her, mouths agape. Jonathan's gaze swung to Will. "You haven't told her."

Will didn't respond.

"Tell her now, Langley." There was a threatening note in Jonathan's tone.

"It has nothing to do with her." Will turned away to gather his glass of port.

Serena watched the exchange between the two men, completely befuddled. "What are you talking about?"

They ignored her.

"She's mine, now." Jonathan took a menacing step toward Will. "I'm deeply involved, and therefore she is, too. She needs to know the truth, and it needs to end. I can't lie for you anymore."

Will's mouth pressed into a flat line. He wouldn't meet either of their gazes. A muscle moved in his cheek as he clenched his jaw.

Jonathan curled his fingers into fists. "Tell her," he said again.

Not looking up at Jonathan, Will gave a jerk of a

nod. He strode to one of the armchairs, dropped his body heavily into it, and took a healthy swallow of port.

The drink seemed to fortify him instantly, though he still wouldn't look at Jonathan or Serena. He set the glass down, and straightening in the chair, his hands clasping tightly over the chair's upholstered arms, he spoke quietly. "Very well. I'll tell you everything, Serena. After all, what does it matter now?"

He gave a bitter laugh. Serena stared at him, utterly confused.

"It goes like this: After you and Meg left England, I'd planned to go to sea. There was a delay in the departure of my ship, so I remained in London for several weeks longer than I expected. It was then that I grew to know Stratford better."

Will's dark brown gaze found her standing across from him, and his eyes met hers. "Stratford was full of regret for what he'd done to you...He was determined to cut all ties from his family and follow you to Antigua, where he would plead for your forgiveness and ask for your hand in marriage."

Serena glanced sharply at Jonathan, but he was gazing at Langley, nodding as if encouraging him to continue.

"This plan required some forethought, however, and he was making his final arrangements for the journey when his brother gave him the news of your death."

"Oh, Jonathan," she whispered. "Why didn't you tell me?"

"It never seemed to be the right time," he said. "At first, you wouldn't have believed me. Later... I don't know. It seemed like an excuse, and I knew you didn't want excuses from me."

Will's fingers curled around the top of the chair arm, gripping tightly. "It was rumored that Stratford went wild after that—"

Jonathan snorted.

"—but in truth, he'd lost his mind with grief. He blamed himself for your death, thought himself a murderer. He left London and went to Bath. Since my ship wasn't due to depart for some time yet, I accompanied him."

Will rose abruptly and walked to the window, clasping his hands behind his back and staring out into the darkness. "We'd found lodgings at an inn, and that evening, we were in the tavern drinking when a young lady drew my attention. I assumed she was a barmaid."

Will swallowed hard. As if he couldn't look at either of them, he kept his gaze firmly fixed outside. "Her name was Eliza Anderson. Stratford later discovered that she was the daughter of a town magistrate. She'd climbed out the chamber window of her father's house that night to come to the tavern for a daring bit of fun with one of her friends—the innkeeper's daughter. We were eating dinner when she and the barmaids broke into a raucous song. They had fine, lovely voices, and everyone in the tavern stopped to listen."

Silence descended. Will strode to the sidebar, poured himself a glass of brandy this time, and drank deeply. Serena sank into the nearest armchair and clasped her hands in front of her, not understanding why he was telling her all this.

Will resumed the seat across from her, his expression more troubled than she'd ever seen it. "When the song was over, Eliza brazenly gestured to Stratford and, half-drunk, he approached her. They spoke for a while, and then he gestured to me. Bewildered, and very drunk on my own account, I went to them. When Eliza spoke, I assumed from her accent that she must be the jaded young widow of some country gentleman."

Will looked down at the glass he clasped in both hands. "She was only eighteen years old."

Serena nodded, but nausea swirled in her belly. Eliza Anderson was a beautiful lady, only eighteen, so why hadn't Jonathan married her after he'd compromised her? Did Eliza have a similar story to her own, but even unluckier since she'd ended up with child?

"Stratford said... Well, they'd spoken about me. Eliza took my hand and led me upstairs." Will swiped a hand over his eyes. "Rather bewildered, I staggered after her."

Serena froze as realization dawned. Not Jonathan. *Will.*

Oh, God. She'd judged and condemned Jonathan, but she hadn't heard the whole story. Still, why had Jonathan looked at Eliza and the child like that? Why had he left Town for three days? It didn't make any sense.

"Confused, I looked back at Stratford and he gestured for me to go with her." A desolate look crossed Will's face. "This was only weeks after I'd last seen...Meg. After we'd last lain together."

"Oh, Will." Serena sat very still, unable to tear her gaze from him.

"When we entered my room..." Again, Will hesitated. "She..." He blinked hard. "I said no, but my defenses...No, there is no excuse. I compromised her. Only when I saw the flash of fear in her eyes and then heard her cry of pain did I understand what I had done." Will sank his face into his hands, his expression awash with anguish. "When I sobered, early in the morning hours, after I'd emptied the contents of my stomach in the basin while she slept, the guilt nearly crippled me. I'd not only compromised an innocent lady, I..." He blinked hard. "I'd betrayed my Meg."

"Oh, God, Will—"

He raised his hand. "Please. Allow me to finish." He inhaled shakily, and when Serena didn't say anything further, he continued. "I left her the contents of my purse. Though it was not yet dawn, I summoned Stratford and we left town at a gallop with me in the lead, full of regret and berating myself violently for what I had done."

How did the story of Jonathan cuckolding the curate fit in with all this? Serena glanced at him. "What about the curate's wife?"

"A fabrication," he murmured.

Will looked at her bleakly. "After a few days, I came to my senses and decided to go back for Eliza. If word had spread about our assignation, I'd do what I could for her. I was certain word had spread—all the patrons of the tavern had seen us mounting the stairs together. Yet I couldn't abandon Meg, either. I wasn't certain that she hadn't conceived when we..." He shook his head. "I wanted to be certain Meg wasn't in any trouble before I offered for Eliza. I knew I'd hurt Meg, I knew she'd be devastated, but she had other options. She could do better than me."

"Oh, Will, she didn't want anyone but you. Ever. She loved you so much."

He flinched, then closed his eyes for a brief moment before resuming his story. "The night before I planned to return to Bath, I told Stratford my idea."

Will drained his glass of brandy.

"I didn't agree with the plan he proposed," Jonathan said, "because I knew how much he'd cared for Meg, and I knew that this would destroy everything between them. So I formed a new plan. I'd go to Bath in Langley's place to take care of Eliza's needs—if, indeed, she needed anything. For all we knew, she had no use for us. But I knew I held a great share of the responsibility for what had happened."

"We both wanted to be sure we'd done right by her," Will added.

"So you went to Eliza and—oh, Lord." In a sudden panic, Serena looked back and forth between both men. "Do you know the identity of the father?"

"It wasn't like that," Will said, a harsh, raw edge to his voice. "Stratford never touched her."

"In Bath," Jonathan continued, "I learned that her father had found out what had happened between her and Langley. The man tossed her out onto the street, saying daughter or no, whores were not welcome in his house."

"She had taken the coin I'd left her and made her way to London. She was young and naïve, and didn't understand how expensive London is," Will said. "I only discovered all of this much later, for soon after Stratford and I went our separate ways, I was called to service on my ship. But he searched for Eliza for months, until he found her in a workhouse, several months gone with child."

"Oh, no," Serena breathed.

"I set her up in a house," Jonathan said.

"And he took responsibility for both her and the child."

"It was better that way. Better that Langley keep his reputation untarnished, for Meg's sake. I *wanted* to tarnish my reputation, to blacken it as much as possible. It was my revenge on my father and my brother for their part in your death."

Serena released a harsh breath. The child wasn't Jonathan's. He was Will's. It seemed impossible... but she saw the truth of it in Will's anguished eyes and Jonathan's clear ones.

"I ultimately agreed to the scheme because I didn't want to hurt Meg. I didn't want to reveal to her how low I'd fallen." Will shook his head, his lip curling in self-disgust.

"Until now, the only three people who knew the whole truth were Eliza, Langley, and myself," Jonathan said. "My cousin Jane knows the boy isn't mine, but she doesn't know whose he is."

"Even the boy doesn't know—" Will's voice cracked, and he bowed his head.

They sat in silence for long, torturous minutes. Will wasn't exactly the man Serena had thought he was. Neither was Jonathan, for that matter.

"The way the child was looking at you," she murmured. "The way Eliza went to you. The familiarity between you all...I made assumptions I shouldn't have. I assumed you'd lied. I thought you'd run off with your mistress and child."

"I didn't, Serena. Some part of you must have known that I didn't."

"Still, seeing her... and the way the boy clung to you..."

"They're my responsibility—they have been for years. She had nowhere else to go." He released a shaky breath. "I am sorry I didn't tell you sooner. But it wasn't my secret to tell."

"I understand that much." Serena tilted her head, thinking. "But the child could just as easily have been yours, couldn't he? It's just by chance that he happened to be Will's instead."

Jonathan closed his eyes. "No doubt you're right. But I'm here with you now. I'm not going anywhere. I'll never leave you again." Kneeling beside her chair, he clasped one hand on each side of her face and tilted her head to face him. His voice was torn, ragged. "Forgive me."

Heat washed over her face as she stared at him, his hands rough on her cheeks.

"I wish I could go back," he murmured, "and relive the past six years knowing you were alive. Apologies seem so insignificant... but I'm sorry. I'm sorry for the past years. I'm sorry for the last three days. I should have told you. Should have made you understand before I went with Eliza."

"Why didn't you?" she whispered.

"When I saw Eliza and the boy when we returned from Prescot, I knew something drastic had happened, for I'd told her to come to my house only in the event of an emergency. I was surprised and concerned, and by the time I turned around to look for you, you and your aunt had gone inside. I knocked later, just before I left Town, and the butler said you were not at home."

"What had happened to her?" Serena asked. "What was the emergency?"

Jonathan grimaced. "Her landlord attempted to foist himself upon her. After she turned down his advances, he threw her out, citing her bastard child as the reason.

"It happened over a month before she turned up at my door. I saw her at the theater a few weeks ago, but I was distracted and it slipped my mind. She and the boy were staying with her older sister, but when the sister's husband returned to London, Eliza was forced to leave. He has always refused to shelter her, due to her reputation as a fallen woman. Having nowhere else to go, she went to my house only to have my butler turn her away. Fortunately, we returned from Prescot that very day, otherwise I'm certain she'd have spent the night in the streets."

"She has no friends?" Serena asked softly.

Jonathan ground his teeth. "Ladies of her class are loath to befriend her because she is the mother of an illegitimate child. Other women shun her because of her class."

"She has nowhere to turn, then."

"She's always had Stratford," Will said. "He has taken good care of her."

"Where is she now?" Serena asked.

"In Guildford, where she has lived for the past few years. I took care of the landlord. He won't be trifling with her any longer."

Will looked at Jonathan, who'd taken the seat beside Serena. "They are my responsibility. They always have been, but I've avoided it for far too long, due to my absence at sea, due to the fear of hurting Meg. Neither of those excuses are valid. I must do right by her. By them both."

"What do you intend to do?" Serena asked.

Will's face was pale in the lamplight. "First, I must make sure the boy knows who his father is." He swallowed hard. "Then I shall see to their comfort and their happiness."

For a long moment, the three of them stared at one another.

" 'What a tangled web we weave, when first we practice to deceive,' " Serena quoted under her breath.

"I must go." Will stood abruptly. Side by side, Serena and Jonathan rose as well.

"But—"

Will came toward her. He took her hand, and lifting it to his lips, he kissed it. When he raised his eyes, she saw they were shining. "For now . . . I think I must be alone for a while."

"Will you stay in London?"

"I don't know. I've a ship leaving for Siam sometime in the next few weeks. Perhaps I should be on it."

Serena didn't want him to go. His leaving tonight... it would be *final.*

She bowed her head, tears stinging at her eyes again. "Thank you, Will. Thank you for telling me the truth. And I'm so sorry—"

His palm cupped her cheek, raising her face to look at him. "I want you to be happy, Serena. I want you and Stratford both to be happy. I always have. It's what Meg would have wanted, as well."

She pressed her hand over his on her cheek. "I'll miss you so much. I wish nothing but happiness for you, too."

Gently removing his hand from her grasp, he turned his attention to Jonathan. "I assume I can count on you to take care of her this time?"

"Nothing could stop me," Jonathan said, his voice sober.

Will hesitated, pressing his lips together, then he seemed to come to a decision. "Don't reveal your true self to anyone, Serena. You must continue on as Meg."

"But why?"

"I fear what will happen if the world should discover your true identity. You'll face the fury of the ton, for they'll be embarrassed for having accepted you into their fold only to later learn that you're the notorious Serena Donovan."

"I don't care about any of that," she said. She'd already braced herself for the worst.

"But I do," Will said quietly. "Let us face the scandal of our broken engagement head-on. It'll be nothing compared to the misery we'll both have to face if the truth about your identity was exposed."

And Serena suddenly understood. It wouldn't only be her that would be punished, it would be her mother and her sisters, too. Most of all, it would be Will. He'd be ridiculed as the man who'd been duped by the wicked twin of his beloved.

"Very well," she acquiesced, finding it impossible to explain how difficult it had been for her to bear her sister's name, how difficult it would continue to be. "I'll continue on as Meg."

She glanced over at Jonathan, who nodded in agreement.

Will nodded, too. "Then I'll take my leave."

He bowed his good-bye. She watched him as he left, closing the parlor door behind him, as tears, and so much regret, stung her eyes.

Chapter Twenty

As Serena finished breakfast the next morning, a footman entered the breakfast room bearing a sheet of stationery on a silver salver.

"For you, miss," he said to her.

Raising her eyebrows at Aunt Geraldine, she took the note from the tray, broke the seal, and read.

I miss you. Will you come see me?
Now?

J.

Smothering a smile, she excused herself from the table and rushed upstairs to don her bonnet and pelisse. Then, she slipped into the bright, cloudless morning and walked the few steps to Jonathan's door.

Pausing there, she tilted her head back and faced the sun. Heat washed over her cheeks and warmth touched her shoulders through the muslin of her pelisse. Finally, she took a deep breath of clean morning air, raised her fist, and rapped lightly on the door.

She expected his butler to answer, but it was Jonathan himself. His lips curled up when he saw her, and she gazed into his smiling blue eyes for a long moment.

"Won't you come in?" he finally murmured.

He moved back to make room in the doorway for her, and she stepped inside. He took her hand and led her into his drawing room, an austere, elegant space, with the focal point of a large window framed by two Grecian columns.

As soon as they entered, he closed the door behind them and enfolded her into his arms. "I missed you so much."

"It's only been a few hours," she protested. Yet she wrapped her own arms around him, feeling her limbs and muscles softening in his embrace. How desperately she'd missed his touch.

"I meant I missed you in these past few days. And"—pulling back a little, he gave her a wry smile—"in the past few years. We've been separated for far too long. Even the past few hours has been too long. It's time for us to be together, Serena."

"Yes, I agree. We've spent far too long apart."

He drew back at that. "Really?"

A laugh burst from her chest. "Does that surprise you? Honestly?"

"Well..."

She pressed her palm to his chest. "Don't you understand, Jonathan? I can hardly keep myself away from you. I can hardly keep my hands off you. I've felt that way, struggled against it, ever since I first saw you at Will's soiree."

Some of the tension seemed to drain out of him. "It's the way I've felt about you, too, ever since then, even though at first I thought you were Meg." His lips twisted. "I'd no idea why I was having such perverse thoughts about my beloved's sister."

"Oh, no," she murmured, fighting a grin. "I can only imagine how confusing that must've been."

"It made sense when I discovered the truth." His smile faded, and he stared at her, cupping her shoulders tightly in his hands. "But we don't have to fight it anymore. Do you understand, Serena? That I love you? That I always have?"

She blinked hard. "I've always loved you...even when I didn't want to. Even when..."

He pressed his fingertips to her lips. "Shhh... Let's not speak of the past."

"You're right. I don't want to speak of the past. I only want to speak of the present. And," she added tentatively, "of the future."

He smiled again, and the glint in his eyes turned

wicked as he stroked a fingertip around the shell of her ear. "May I suggest we don't speak at all?"

He pressed his lips to hers, at first gentle and then gradually with more authority until he seemed to kiss her with all the pent-up desperation and frustration of the past days . . . weeks . . . years.

She felt it, too, that powerful need inside her, surging against the walls of her constraint, demanding to be set free.

She didn't fight him, made no attempt to continue their conversation. She wanted him, now more than ever. There was no prior commitment, no responsibility holding her back anymore. There was no longer anything to keep them apart. She could give herself freely and take everything she needed.

She thrust her body against his, took handfuls of his coat in her hands, and kissed him.

Jonathan staggered back against one of the columns. His hands shook as he stroked the soft skin of her jaw.

She loved him as he loved her. They'd always loved each other. After all these years, after all the anger and pain and loss, their love for each other hadn't died. It hadn't even faded.

He yanked at the ribbon ties of her bonnet, flung it aside, and plunged his hands into her silky hair, loosening the pins holding it in place. She was so soft, so warm.

He spoke against her sweet lips. "I love you."

She entwined her arms around his neck, taking a fistful of hair at his nape, hungrily kissing his cheek, his jaw.

He splayed his hands, moving them over her silky tresses, gently down her neck and across her collarbones and shoulders, her skin a satin whisper against his fingertips.

How long had it been since he'd touched her like this? A fortnight? Far too long.

He dragged his lips over her cheek, tasting her sweet skin. She smelled of sunshine, of promise, of salt and the sea.

He lifted her in his arms, but she didn't seem to notice. With her eyes closed, she took his mouth again.

He didn't submit nor compete, rather answered her with equal passion until he didn't know who gave and who took, but the power of their exchange thrummed between them.

He went down, pulling her with him onto the carpet. She clung to him as if her life depended on it, whimpering, ravishing him with her mouth.

Serena.

She gripped him, her eyes squeezed shut, her lips grazing his nose, swiping across his forehead.

He threw up her skirts. The need to touch her overwhelmed every rational thought. He had to feel her, worship her with his hands and his mouth. Nothing else mattered. Serena was here, his. He was hers.

She had enslaved his heart all those years ago and had never released it. He couldn't stop touching her. He didn't want to stop.

He tore open her pelisse, ignoring popping buttons, and yanked down her bodice. Something ripped. He dragged his mouth over the curve of her breast, nudging the muslin downward. He needed her breast in his mouth.

Still, when her breast was fully revealed, he paused for a moment, staring. So round. So perfect and plump, topped with a taut pink nub. With a small groan, he took it in his mouth and suckled, vaguely hearing her gasp.

He ran his hand up the silky warmth of her thigh. He had to touch her, all of her. Every inch of her was alive, resonating with an energy he felt beneath his fingertips, sensed in the air.

Jonathan found the ribbon tie of her garter and tore it free. Grasping the edge of her stocking, he thrust it down her leg. He stroked her thigh, moving higher until he found the slit in her drawers and cupped the soft mound between her legs.

She shuddered. He shuddered. He swiped his tongue over her budded nipple. His cock strained painfully against the falls of his trousers.

Someone knocked on the door. Jonathan looked up from her breast as the knob turned.

"Go away!" he said, his voice harsh and ragged.

Silence. He turned to Serena. Her large, gray eyes focused on him.

"Please," she whispered.

He doubted she'd noticed the near intrusion. It was so like her.

He moved between her legs. Now, he saw the soft nest of blond curls that hid her core. He pressed her knees apart.

Gasping, she opened to him, exposing the pink cleft of her womanhood.

"Please," she said again, her voice strangled.

He glanced up at her face. She was flushed, panting, her eyes a gray sea he could fall into.

"I'm going to love you," he said, though he could hardly speak. There wasn't enough air in the room. He ran one fingertip down her slick cleft, teasing her entrance and making her squirm. "Like I've always wanted to."

He sank his head between her legs, using his fingers to open her soft, dew-slicked folds.

She gasped, groaned, tried to twist away. He held her hips firmly, pressed his mouth over her body, hot and smooth and ready.

Her hands tangled in his hair. He grasped her thighs and devoured, taking in her essence until it sang in his blood, and he knew she loved him because her limbs trembled and she moaned his name over and over.

Her thighs tightened against his shoulders. He slipped one finger inside of her and then two, and he stroked her with his fingers and his mouth.

Serena squirmed, cried out, gasped out his name, and her slick walls clamped down over him. He pushed his tongue flat. All around him, she pulsed—against his face and fingers, over the back of his head and shoulders.

The tremors slowed, subsided altogether. His cock raged and throbbed, demanding release. He withdrew his fingers and began to work the buttons of his falls, but kept his mouth on her, covering her inner thighs with kisses.

She stroked his head lovingly now, and when he finally moved beside her, he saw that her eyelids were heavy.

"Tell me you won't turn away from me," she whispered, cupping his cheeks in her hands, her fathomless gray eyes shining.

"I'll never turn away from you, Serena."

"You won't be unfaithful?"

"Never."

Jonathan looked at her lips, red and swollen, her freckled nose, her gray eyes, their lashes clumped with moisture.

"I only want you," he whispered. "Forever."

A single tear carved a trail down her cheek. "I think you'll kill me, Jonathan Dane."

"No," he soothed. "I will make you happy. There's nothing I want more." He kissed her eyelids, her brows, the tip of her nose. "You're so beautiful."

"I want you," she murmured, closing her eyes.

"Only you. Even if it kills me. I can't seem to help it. I never could. Even when I knew I was a fool."

"You're not a fool. You're mine and I'm yours, and I'll prove that to you, over and over, for as long as it takes."

He finished with the last button of his trousers as he rose onto his knees and gathered her against him, her hip rubbing against his aching cock. He kissed the silky column of her throat, the curve of her jaw, the plump bow of her lips, trying not to let his desperate need shine through.

"Will you have me, Serena?"

Her bosom moved with silent laughter. "On the grass, in the stables, at a duchess's ball, in your drawing room," she said, her voice low. "I could never deny you, could I?"

"Good." He held the curve of her bottom, pressing her against him. He trailed kisses over her bodice and up to her exposed breasts, so pale, so full and heavy. He moved to cup one of them, weighing it gently in his hand, stroking the pink bud with his thumb. She drew in her breath.

He licked a pale curve. So beautiful. So soft and tight, so warm and sweet. He released her bottom and, while he worshipped one breast with his mouth, he stroked the other, teasing the nipple into a taut peak.

She made an incoherent noise in her throat. He cupped both creamy breasts in his hands, rubbing his lips over the hard bud of one nipple.

He gently laid her on the carpet and shifted over her, rubbing against her silken folds. "I want you so much it hurts. Can you feel it?"

"Yes." She enfolded her arms around him, holding him tight, pressing her breasts to his chest.

Gently, he moved her skirts out of the way and kicked off his shoes and trousers. He positioned himself over her, his heavy cock brushing against her curls.

She stared up at him with wide eyes. He'd seen that look before, at the dowager duchess's ball. He'd known then, and he knew now, that nothing else mattered to her but the two of them, their need, their connection. Their love. He'd never allow anything to get in the way of that again.

He brushed a lock of hair away from her luscious mouth. "Now?"

Her arms locked around his neck. "Yes, Jonathan. Now."

"I love you."

He took her in one powerful thrust, capturing her cry with his lips. Raising himself on his hands, he stroked deep inside her, watching as she let herself go, as the complex knots he had forced her to bind around her heart unraveled. He watched as the ropes, the chains, the shackles fell away, leaving her open to him, letting the love shine through in her eyes.

"I love you, too," she whispered. "So much."

He rode her gently, deeply, and he lost himself in the sweetness, the exquisite pleasure of taking the only woman he had ever loved, knowing they were finally, irrevocably, forever one.

"I've always loved you," she said, shuddering in his arms.

Her love poured through him. It drenched every fiber of his being.

"Serena," he murmured.

"I love you, Jonathan."

She squeezed him tight within her. It was too perfect. He would not last. His cock swelled, so tight, so big, he was going to explode.

He lost his ability to think. He thrust into her, feeling her slip back on the carpet. She whimpered, clutched him more tightly, arched up beneath him, wrapped her legs around him. The world shook, then fell apart, and he burst inside her, body and soul, and then sank over her.

"Love you," he murmured. "Forever."

Chapter Twenty-one

Jonathan's fingers skittered across Serena's jaw. His lips brushed over her brow. She opened her eyes.

She felt heavy, her limbs flooded with delicious, heady pleasure.

"Are you all right?" he asked.

She chuckled. "Are you?"

He rested his forehead against hers. "Yes. I feel better than I have in . . . a long time."

She smiled into his shoulder, confidence blooming within her like a rare flower. It felt so good, it was almost unnatural. Surely she would wake in her bed in Antigua and discover this was all a dream.

"Mm . . ." She raised herself up on her elbow and pulled at his shirt, wanting to do away with the barrier between them, wanting to feel the skin of his chest against hers.

She snuggled into his chest. He held her for a long while, caressing her, murmuring words of love into her hair.

She spoke against the muscles of his chest. "Do you think Will's right, Jonathan? Should I continue to be Meg? I would hate to bring you into this lie."

He released a long breath. "He's right. If London society heard of this, it would punish you severely. I've no wish to watch the vultures try to tear you apart."

"I could bear it," she said. "I could bear anything now."

"Yet what harm will it do if the truth were never exposed? The only one it made a real difference to is Langley, and he knows everything now."

She hesitated. "That's true. But a part of me hurts every time someone calls me Meg. Each time I hear the name, I know that I'm not who or what people think I am. A part of me," she added softly, "feels as though it's a dishonor to the real Meg."

"How can you be dishonoring her? I imagine she'd understand your predicament and would approve of your choice, especially knowing how the truth would hurt the people she loved."

Serena remembered how forgiving, how understanding, Meg always was. "Yes. She would approve. And I still want Jessica and Olivia to have as many opportunities as possible. They're innocent in all this, and they deserve some happiness."

"Continue to be Meg, then. For Langley, for your sisters, and for you."

"Very well." She looked up at him. "As long as *you* know who I really am."

"When I kissed you and knew that you were my Serena"—he rolled to his back to look up at the intricate plasterwork on his drawing room ceiling—"everything changed. My life had purpose again." He spoke softly. "It has purpose now. But it has nothing to do with your name. It has everything to do with the woman behind it."

"Does it?"

"Shakespeare wrote, 'What's in a name? A rose by any other name would smell as sweet.' Remember?" Jonathan laid his hand on her thigh. "He was right, you know."

"I suppose he was." She hesitated. "I'll be Meg, then. But what will *you* call me?"

He turned to face her, pulled her hand up, kissed it, and looked into her eyes. She saw the spark of desperation there, a lingering vulnerability.

"Wife?" he said softly.

She stared at him, her breath catching in her throat.

"I am a flawed man. I've made too many mistakes in my life to count. I can only hope that you will accept me, even though I have done so many things that render me undeserving of you."

She felt the ache low in her belly, the wetness on

the insides of her thighs, a reminder that she was his, had never been anything but his. His hand clasped hers, big and solid, the trace of his lips still tingled at the back of her palm, and a peace she had never known settled over her.

"In the last three months, you've proven yourself worthy of my love... and my trust, Jonathan."

He moved his hands down to clasp hers. He squeezed them tightly. "Tell me you will make me the happiest man in the world. Be my wife. Stay with me forever."

She wrapped her arms around him and sank her face into his chest. So much had happened. Yesterday, she had been bracing herself for her inevitable disgraceful return to Antigua. Today, the man she'd always loved said he returned that love, said he wanted her to be his for life, to be his wife, and he'd wanted it even when she'd thought he'd betrayed her.

He held her close, murmured in her hair, caressing her mouth, her cheeks, her damp eyes with his lips.

"Marry me," he said again. "Be my countess."

"I will," she whispered. "I'll marry you."

He scrambled up, then lifted her, sat her on the edge of a sofa, and knelt before her. "I want to hear you say it. Say you will be my wife."

Jonathan was on his knees, squeezing her hands, staring up at her through his cobalt eyes as if she was the most important thing in his world.

She was. And he was the most important thing in hers.

Serena had never stopped loving him. Not since that first night they had stared at each other across the theater. She had tried to ignore it, tried to veil it, tried to deny it. For years, she'd tried to cover it with anger and with hate. But her love for him had always been there, an aching, dormant, forbidden thing, trying to burst out, to proclaim itself to the world.

When he made love to her today, he had released her heart and set it free. She wasn't afraid anymore. She trusted that he did love her. He always had. And she loved him.

Struggling for control, she smiled, blinked hard, and spoke in a faltering voice. "I will marry you, Jonathan. I want nothing more in the world than to be your wife."

He kissed the back of her hand. "We will be wed as soon as possible."

She knew what that meant—that they must give the scandal about the breaking of her and Will's engagement time to die down.

"I want to make you my countess in the proper, respectable way." He leaned back on his heels, looked her up and down, and gave her a rueful grin.

"What is it?"

"We're not very respectable at the moment, are we? We're in my drawing room. My upper body is sweating, my nether regions are about to freeze off, and I have my lady on the sofa with one stocking bunched around her ankles, her bodice askew, her hair down, her skirt rucked up at her waist—"

She smiled.

"I am a savage brute," he said. "I should like to take you upstairs and make love to you properly. *Comfortably.* In a bed."

She stroked his arm. "Well, I cannot say no. I promised you that you could have me anywhere."

"And anytime."

"—and anytime."

"In an alcove overlooking a ballroom. In my drawing room in the middle of the day…"

"Anywhere. Anytime."

Laughing softly, they tried to clothe themselves as best as they could. Her garter was ripped, so she kicked off her shoes and one of the stockings. Her pelisse was hopeless, and her dress had a torn seam in the back and several missing buttons. As he arranged her bodice haphazardly over her breasts, someone knocked on the door.

"Go away," Jonathan ordered.

"I am very sorry, my lord," came a muffled voice from outside, "but we seem to have a bit of a situation."

Jonathan's gaze met hers, but he spoke to the servant behind the door. "A situation?"

"Er, yes, my lord. Lady Alcott is here, and she is demanding admittance."

"Your aunt has come to save you." Jonathan's mouth quirked, trembled, and he began to chuckle. He managed to tell the man to show her in.

"You're having her shown in *here*?" Serena gasped.

She gazed down at her crumpled skirt, then at his wrinkled shirt. He had left his waistcoat and tailcoat strewn on the floor, along with her pelisse, her bonnet, one of her stockings, their shoes, and most of her hairpins. Torn buttons lay scattered across the carpet.

Her aunt would see it all.

"What will we tell her?" Serena whispered. "She'll be scandalized!"

He squeezed her hand. "We'll manage." He turned the full force of his smile on her. "You and I can manage anything, if we're together."

The implacable butler opened the door to Aunt Geraldine, who took one step inside before coming to an abrupt halt as her gaze roamed the room and her jaw lowered in increasing astonishment. By the time she spoke, her face had turned scarlet.

"What in God's name . . . ?"

Her mouth remained open as if she had more to say but the words just wouldn't emerge. Serena felt her own cheeks heating as she firmed her shoulders. She'd remain tall. Heaven forbid she show the rekindling of the shame that she'd felt so consistently and for so long.

"Tell me a hurricane—or perhaps a typhoon—hasn't struck this room and divested you of all but your most intimate clothing."

"Alas, no," Jonathan said softly. "The weather has been quite temperate, my lady."

Aunt Geraldine's icy gaze came to rest upon

Serena. "You," she said, her voice as cold as her expression, "are just as worthless as your sister."

Jonathan's hand tightened over Serena's, and steel edged his voice. "I beg to differ, madam. Neither Meg nor her sister is or ever has been worthless."

Aunt Geraldine ignored him yet again. "I have supported my sister's daughters. Done everything I could to help her find respectability through her children. But it's true, isn't it? You're all the same. You have your father's blood in you. Irish blood." She spat the last with venom.

Serena bristled. "My father has nothing to do with this. He was a good man."

Aunt Geraldine, ever conscious of listening ears, stepped fully into the room and snapped the door shut behind her. Then she turned back to Jonathan and Serena and clamped her arms over her bosom, her gaze lingering on their clasped hands.

"Explain yourselves. Immediately. You"—she raised an imperious finger to Serena—"are engaged to be married, girl."

"No, Aunt. Not any longer."

Aunt Geraldine paled. "What?"

"Captain Langley and I intend to cancel our nuptials."

Aunt Geraldine's eyes narrowed. "He must have discovered your inconstancy."

Serena hesitated. There was some truth in her aunt's accusation. But Jonathan came to her rescue.

"Indeed not, my lady. The decision was mutual and amicable. Further, Langley supports us both."

The older lady frowned. "Is that so? He supports you? Indeed, I could never quite understand the gentleman's insistence on maintaining his friendship with you, Stratford. But now you are implying that he endorses your engagement in sinful acts with my niece, and that is something I most certainly will not believe."

"Aunt—" Serena began, but Aunt Geraldine raised a hand.

"I've heard quite enough from you, young lady. To jeopardize your upcoming marriage is one thing, but to go whoring yourself out at the first opportunity—"

"Enough," Jonathan said sharply.

Aunt Geraldine's gaze snapped to him.

"You will not speak to Meg in that manner."

"She is my niece," Aunt Geraldine said. "I shall speak to her however I please."

Jonathan squeezed Serena's hand once more. "And she is my betrothed. Niece or not, I'll not have anyone speaking to the future Countess of Stratford in such a tone."

Aunt Geraldine stood still, silent and tense. Serena glanced at Jonathan from the corner of her eye. He didn't turn away from her this time. Didn't cut her, treat her as though she'd never existed. He'd never do that again, she realized. From now on, he'd support and defend her, no matter what the accusation.

He was beside her. He'd never walk away.

Serena blinked against the surge of emotion that realization brought with it. The days of her feeling dirty and soiled, looked down upon, and disgraced—those days were finished. A new day—a new life—had begun for her. It was one she hadn't dared hope for in the past six years. But here it was. It wasn't only because Jonathan stood beside her. It was because she knew without a doubt that she deserved to be loved. That she deserved to be supported, defended, and ultimately understood.

Despite the tension boiling around her, her lips curved into a soft smile.

"Is this true?" Aunt Geraldine snapped. "You are marrying?"

"Indeed," Jonathan said frostily. "As soon as the scandal of the broken engagement dies down. We've no wish to cause Langley any more distress than he's already been forced to suffer."

"This is…Well, this is utterly preposterous!" Aunt Geraldine exclaimed.

"I think not," Jonathan said.

"I won't allow it. It's a disgrace, that's what it is." Aunt Geraldine looked at Serena. "He's a scoundrel of the first order. I guarantee he'll make you miserable, as he did your sister."

Serena's smile didn't fade. "I don't think so, Aunt. I'm quite convinced of his constancy."

Aunt Geraldine stomped her foot. "This is utter

nonsense. Indeed, girl, you have taken it one step too far this time. I shall send you on the first ship back to Antigua."

"I won't go," Serena said, unable to feel a bit of anger toward her aunt. Aunt Geraldine could expostulate and protest and call her names all she wanted, but anything her aunt could do was incapable of destroying her newfound confidence.

"You've no other choice," Aunt Geraldine snapped. "I won't allow you to marry this scoundrel."

"You said yourself that you'd allow your niece to marry me. Recall our discussion in Prescot, ma'am. I am an earl, if you remember." Jonathan shrugged. "But in the end, that's neither here nor there. I'm not the man I was six years ago. I love your niece, madam, and nothing will stop me from marrying her. Not the threat of scandal, your threats, or anyone else's. No matter what the world thinks or how it protests, we will be wed."

Aunt Geraldine opened her mouth, then shut it again. Serena had never seen her at such a loss for words.

Jonathan turned to Serena. "Before our guest arrived, I was going to ask you if you'd like to accompany me to Sussex. There we can wait for the scandal to run its course. And afterward, we can be wed in the village chapel."

Ignoring Aunt Geraldine's dissatisfied grunt, he continued. "My mother will want to meet you. I know she'll love you—she suffers from none of the pretensions of my father and brother. Phoebe and Harper should arrive shortly after we do."

It was a brilliant idea. Serena already missed Phoebe, and she'd always been curious about Jonathan's mother and his home in Sussex. And he was right—it would be a good place to escape the inevitable scandal of her and Will's breakup. But there was one more thing...

"Will you mind very much if I ask my sisters Olivia and Jessica to join us?"

"Not at all. We'll send for them right away." He turned back to Aunt Geraldine and cocked his head, a polite, inquiring expression on his face. "Is there anything else I might help you with, my lady? As you can see, Meg and I have plans to make. I should like for us to be on our way to Sussex as soon as possible."

"I..." Aunt Geraldine paused, and her shoulders deflated. "No. I suppose not." She raised her chin. "I suppose I shall return home and pen a letter to my sister."

"I've heard Mrs. Donovan has been sniffing after a title for at least one of her daughters," Jonathan said with a wry smile. "Might I suggest that you inform her that her life's goal has been attained and that her daughter, Meg, is soon to be a countess?"

"Humph." With that obscure answer and a stiff bow to both of them, Aunt Geraldine took her leave.

Serena turned to Jonathan as soon as the door closed. "Thank you so much, Jonathan."

He frowned. "What for?"

"For standing beside me," she said. "For defending me."

"You shouldn't thank me, Serena. You should expect it of me."

"Should I?"

"Always." Bending his head, he kissed her gently on the lips, and she closed her eyes, sinking into the tenderness of his embrace. She spent a long minute just holding him, breathing in his spicy male scent, reveling in his touch. Finally, he whispered into her hair, "We should pack."

"Pack?" she repeated, honestly having no idea what he was talking about.

"Yes. For Sussex. I really do want for us to be on our way as soon as we can."

"Can we go now?" A part of her wanted to leave *everything* behind. To start anew. Pulling back a little, she looked up at him. "Would you mind terribly? I don't need to bring anything to Sussex, really."

"Neither do I. Nothing but you, that is." He touched his fingertip to her lower lip, and she kissed it and then smiled up at him.

"Exactly," she said. "I've no need for anything but you."

They traded a sweet smile. And without another word, they strode out the front door of Jonathan's London town house and side by side, they headed toward a new life, together at last.

Two handsome rivals;
one beautiful Donovan sister.
The stakes run high . . . and
the passion runs deep.

Please turn this page
for a preview of
*Secrets of an
Accidental Duchess.*

Prologue

She was an angel.

Maxwell Buchanan, the Marquis of Hasley, had observed many beautiful women in his thirty years. He'd conversed with them, danced with them, bedded them. But no woman had ever frozen him in place before tonight.

He stood entranced, ignoring people who brushed past him, and stared at her, unable to tear his gaze away. With her slender figure, delicate features, and a crown of thick blond hair, she was beautiful, but not uncommonly so, at least to the other men populating the ballroom. As far as Max could tell, the only head that had turned when she'd entered the room was his own.

The difference, he supposed, the singular element that clearly set her apart from the rest of the women in the ballroom, was the way she held herself. There was nothing brazen about her, but nothing diffident or nervous, either. It was as though she held a confidence within herself that she didn't feel any desire to share with the world. She didn't need to display her beauty like all the other unattached ladies present. She simply was who she was, and she made no apologies for the fact.

Max wanted to know her. He would learn her name as soon as possible. He would orchestrate an introduction to her and then he would ask her for a dance.

Her small, white-gloved fingers curled around her dance partner's, and Max's fingers twitched. He wanted to be the one clasping that hand in his own.

"Lovely, isn't she?"

Max whipped around to face the intruder. The man standing beside him was Leonard Reece, the Marquis of Fenwicke, and not one of his favorite people.

"Who is lovely?" he asked, feigning ignorance, curling the fingers of his right hand into a fist so as not to reach up to adjust his cravat over his suddenly warm neck.

Fenwicke gave a low chuckle. "The young lady you've been staring at for the last ten minutes."

Damn. He'd been caught. And now he felt foolish. Allowing his gaze to trail after a young woman, even as one as compelling as he found her, was a foolish enterprise, especially at Lord Hertford's ball—the last ball of the London Season. If Max wasn't careful, he'd find himself betrothed by Michaelmas.

The dance ended, and the angel's dance partner led her off the floor toward another lady. The three stood talking for a moment before the man bowed and took his leave.

"Most people think her sister is the great beauty of the family," Fenwicke continued conversationally. "But I would beg to differ with them. As would you, apparently."

"Her sister?"

"Indeed. The lady she's speaking to—the one in the pale yellow, is the youngest of the Donovan sisters."

Max glanced more closely at the woman in yellow. Indeed, she was what most people would consider a great beauty—slender but rounded in all the proper places, with a crown of gold hair that glinted with the barest tinge of copper where the chandelier light caught it.

"The Donovan sisters?" he mused. "I don't know them."

"The lady in yellow is Jessica Donovan," Fenwicke murmured so as not to be heard by anyone in the crowd milling about the enormous punch bowl between sets. "The lady in blue is her older sister, Olivia."

The angel's name was Olivia.

Max knew just about everyone in London. He made it a game to recognize all the faces attached to the names bandied about by the gossipmongers. From the moment he'd caught his first glimpse of the angel tonight, he'd known he'd never been introduced to her, never seen her before. He'd never heard Olivia and Jessica Donovan's names, either, though their surname did sound vaguely familiar.

"They must be new in Town."

"Yes, they arrived in London last month. This is only the second or third event they've attended." Fenwicke gave a significant pause. "However, you are acquainted with the eldest Donovan sister."

Max frowned. "I don't think so."

Fenwicke chuckled. "You are. You just haven't yet made the connection. The eldest sister is Margaret Dane, Countess of Stratford."

That name he did know—how could he not? "Ah. Of course."

A year ago, Lady Stratford had arrived from the West Indies engaged to one well-connected gentleman, but she'd ended up marrying another. Like a great stone thrown into the semiplacid waters of London, the ripples caused by the splash she'd made had only just begun to subside.

"So the countess's sisters have recently arrived from the West Indies?"

"That's right."

Max's gaze lingered on Olivia, the angel in blue.

Fenwicke had said she was older than the girl standing beside her, but she appeared younger. It was in her bearing, in her expression. Though Jessica didn't quite strut, she moved like a woman attuned to the power she wielded over all who beheld her. Olivia was directly the opposite. She wore her reserved nature like a cloak. Her cheeks were paler than her sister's, and her hair held more of the copper and less of the gold, though certainly no one would complain that it was too red. It was just enough to lend an intriguing simmer rather than a full-blown fire.

Olivia's dress was lovely, of an entirely fashionable style and fabric—though Max didn't concern himself with fashion enough to be able to distinguish either by name. The gown was conservatively cut, and her jewelry was simple. She wore only a pair of pearl-drop earrings and a chain around her neck.

Her posture was softer than her sister's, whose stance was sharp and alert. But their familial connection was obvious in their faces—both perfect ovals with full but small mouths and large eyes. From this distance, Max couldn't tell the color of her eyes, but when Olivia had been dancing earlier, she'd glanced in his direction, and he'd thought they must be a light shade.

God. He nearly groaned to himself. She captivated him. She had from the first moment he'd seen her. She was simply lovely.

"... leaving London soon."

The sudden cessation of Fenwicke's voice had Max's attention snapping back to him.

Fenwicke sighed. "Did you hear me, Hasley?"

"Sorry," Max said, then gestured randomly about. "Noisy in here."

It was true, after all. The orchestra had begun the opening strands of the next dance, and couples were brushing past them, hurrying to join in at the last possible moment.

Fenwicke gazed at him appraisingly for a long moment, then motioned toward the ballroom's exit. "Come, man. Let's go have a drink."

If it had been an ordinary evening, Max would have declined. He found Fenwicke oily and unlikable, even though they mostly ran in the same circles. Fenwicke had been a constant presence in Max's life, but he'd never befriended the man.

He glanced quickly back to the lady. *Olivia.* At that moment, she looked up. Her gaze caught his and held.

Blue eyes. Surely they were blue.

Those eyes held him in her thrall, sweet and lovely, and sensual, too, despite her obvious innocence. Max felt suspended in midair, like a water droplet caught in a spider's web.

She glanced at Fenwicke and then quickly to the floor, and Max plopped back to earth with a *splat.* But satisfaction rushed through him in a warm wave, because just before she'd broken their eye contact, he'd seen the first vestiges of color flooding her cheeks.

"Very well," he told Fenwicke. Tonight he didn't politely excuse himself from Fenwicke's company, because tonight Fenwicke seemed to have information Max suddenly craved—information about Olivia Donovan.

He turned away from her, but not before he saw another gentleman offering her his arm. Max and Fenwicke walked down the corridor to the parlor that had been set aside for the evening as the gentleman's retiring room. A foursome played cards in the corner, and an elderly man sat in a large but elegant brown cloth armchair in the corner, blatantly antisocial, a newspaper raised to obscure half his face. Other men lounged by the sideboard, chatting and drinking from the never-ending supply of spirits.

Fenwicke collected two glasses of brandy and then gestured with his chin at a pair of empty chairs separated by a low, glass-topped table but close enough together for them to have a private conversation. Max sat in the closest chair, taking the glass Fenwicke offered him as he passed. He sipped the brandy while Fenwicke lowered himself into the opposite chair.

Holding his glass in both hands, Fenwicke stared at him. "You haven't seen the Miss Donovans prior to tonight, eh?"

"No," Max admitted. "Do they plan to reside in London?"

"No." Fenwicke's lip curled sardonically. "As I was saying in the ballroom, I believe they're leaving within the week. They're off to Stratford's estate in Sussex."

"Too bad," Max murmured.

But then a memory jolted him. At White's last week, Stratford had invited a group of men, including Max, to Sussex this autumn to hunt. He'd turned down the offer—he'd never been much interested in hunting—but now . . .

Fenwicke gazed at him. The man had always reminded Max of a reptilian predator with his cold, assessing silver-gray eyes. "You," he announced coldly, "have a tendre for Miss Donovan."

It was impossible to determine whether that was a question or a statement. Either way, it didn't matter. "Don't be absurd. I don't know Jessica Donovan."

"I'm speaking of Olivia," Fenwicke said icily. If Max weren't mistaken, it sounded like Fenwicke was *jealous*. But that was ridiculous. As the man had said, Olivia had been in Town for less than a month.

"I don't know either of them," Max responded, keeping his tone mild.

"Regardless, you want her," Fenwicke said in an annoyed tone. "I'm well acquainted with that look you were throwing in her direction."

Max shrugged.

"You are besotted with her."

Max leaned back in his chair, studying Fenwicke

closely, wondering what gave Fenwicke the right to have proprietary feelings toward Olivia Donovan. As far as he knew, Fenwicke had nothing more than a civil relationship with the Earl of Stratford.

"Are you a relation of hers?" he asked.

"No."

"I was watching her," Max said slowly. "And, yes, I admit to wondering who she was and whether she was attached. I was considering asking her to dance later this evening."

The muscles in Fenwicke's jaw bulged as he ground his teeth. "She has no dances available."

"How do you know?"

"I asked her myself."

He stared at the man across from him, feeling the muscles across his shoulders tighten as the fingers of his loose hand curled into a tight fist. He didn't like the thought of his angel touching Fenwicke. Of Fenwicke touching her. The thought rather made him want to throw Fenwicke through the glass window overlooking the terrace across from them.

He took a slow breath, willing himself to calmness. He didn't even know the woman. Didn't even know the sound of her voice, the color of her eyes, her likes and dislikes. And he was already willing to fight for her.

He wouldn't want Fenwicke touching any young innocent, he reasoned. He'd protect any woman from the marquis's slick, slithering paws.

"How is your wife?" he asked quite deliberately, aware of the challenge in his voice.

Fenwicke's expression went flat. He took a long drink of brandy before responding. "She's well," he said icily. "She's back at home. In Sussex. Thank you for asking." His lip curled in a snarl that Max guessed was supposed to appear to be a polite smile.

Max remembered that Fenwicke's family home was in Sussex, just like the Earl of Stratford's. He wondered if the houses were situated close to each other.

"Ah," Max said. "I'm glad to hear she's well."

"You can't have her, you know," Fenwicke said quietly.

Max raised a brow. "Your wife?"

"Olivia Donovan."

Max took a long moment to allow that to sink in. To think about how he should respond.

"She's not married?" he finally asked. He knew the answer.

Fenwicke's tone was frosty. "No."

"Engaged?"

"No."

"Then why, pray, can't I have her?"

"She'd never accept you. You would never meet her standards. You, Hasley, are a well-known rake."

"So?" That fact had never stopped any woman from accepting his advances before.

"So, you're not good enough for her." Fenwicke's

smile widened, but it was laced with bitterness. "No man in London is."

"How can you possibly know this?"

"She told me."

Max nearly choked on his brandy. "What?"

"I propositioned her," Fenwicke said simply. "In the correct way, of course, which was quite delicate considering her innocence. I dug deeply—quite deeply indeed—into my cache of charm."

Max's stomach churned. He could never understand what women saw in Fenwicke—but apparently they saw something, because the man never needed to be too aggressive in his pursuit before capturing his prey, despite his marital status.

Miss Olivia Donovan didn't see whatever it was in Fenwicke that all the other women saw. Intriguing. Without ever having met her, Max's respect for her grew.

The thought of how many times Fenwicke had left his young wife alone in Sussex left Max feeling vaguely nauseous. How many times had he seen the man with a different woman on his arm?

Perhaps what left the sourest taste in Max's mouth was that everyone knew about Fenwicke's proclivities but continued to invite him to their social events. No one spurned him. He was a peer, after all, a member of White's, and an excellent dance partner or opponent at cards.

Max's dislike of the man threatened to grow into

something stronger. Something more like hatred. He closed his eyes, and images of his own father passed behind his lids. His mother . . . alone. The tears she'd tried to hide from him. But even at a very young age, Max had known exactly what was happening. Exactly how his father had betrayed his mother, how he'd ruined her life, ultimately destroyed her. Max would never do that to a wife—he'd never marry so there would simply never be a concern—and he'd never abide anyone who did.

Fenwicke set his empty glass on the table. "I'm afraid Miss Olivia Donovan simply isn't interested."

"So, because you failed to charm the lady, you assume that I'd fail as well?"

"Of course. She's frigid, you see. The girl is composed of ice as solid as a glacier."

Another of the many reasons Max disliked Fenwicke: If a woman rejected him, he'd think it was due to some defect in her character as opposed to a natural—and wise—dislike or distrust of the man himself. And if a woman professed no attraction to the marquis, naturally she wouldn't feel any attraction to any man, because all other men were lesser beings than him.

"I sincerely doubt she's frigid," Max responded before he thought better of it.

Fenwicke's eyes narrowed. "Do you?"

Max met the man's steely glare head-on. "Perhaps you simply don't appeal."

Fenwicke snorted. "Of course I appeal. I'm a marquis, to begin with—"

"Perhaps," Max interjected, keeping his voice low, "she's not interested in participating in an adulterous liaison, marquis or no."

At his periphery, Max could see Fenwicke's fists clenching. He braced himself for the man's lunge, but it never came.

Instead Fenwicke's lips curled into a thin, humorless smile. "I would beg to differ."

Max shrugged. "Perhaps we should agree to disagree, then."

"If she did not succumb to my charms, Hasley, then rest assured, there's no way she'd succumb to yours." Fenwicke's voice was mild, but the cords in his neck bulged above his cravat.

Max shook his head, unable to prevent a sneer from forming on his lips. "You're wrong, Fenwicke."

Fenwicke's brows rose, and he leaned forward, greedily licking his lips.

"Would you care to place a wager on that?"

THE DISH

Where authors give you the inside scoop!

♥ ♥ ♥ ♥ ♥ ♥ ♥ ♥ ♥ ♥ ♥ ♥ ♥ ♥

From the desk of Caridad Piñeiro

Dear Readers,

I want to thank all of you who have been writing to tell me how much you've been loving the Carrera family, as well as enjoying the towns along the Jersey Shore where the series is set.

With THE LOST, I'm introducing a much darker paranormal series I'm calling *Sin Hunters*. The stories are still set along the Jersey Shore and you'll have the beloved Carreras, but now you'll also get to meet an exciting new race of people: The Light and Shadow Hunters.

Why the change? There was something about Bobbie Carrera, the heroine in THE LOST, that needed something different and something very special. Someone very special. Bobbie is an Iraq war veteran and she's home from battle, but wounded both physically and emotionally. She's busy trying to put her world back together and the last thing she needs is more conflict in her life.

But I'm a bad girl, you know. I love to challenge my characters into facing their most extreme hurts because doing so only makes their happiness that much sweeter. I think readers love that as well because there is nothing more uplifting than seeing how love can truly conquer all.

Bobbie's challenge comes in the form of sexy

millionaire Adam Bruno. Adam is different from any man she has ever met and Bobbie feels an immediate connection to him. There's just one problem: Adam has no idea who he really is and why he possesses the ability to gather energy. That ability allows him to do myriad things; from shape-shifting to traveling at super speed, to wielding energy and light like weapons. But these powers are challenging for Adam: as his abilities grow stronger, they also become deadly and increasingly difficult to control.

Enter Bobbie Carrera. Bobbie brings peace to Adam's soul. Adam feels lost in the human world, but in Bobbie's arms he finds love, acceptance, and the possibility for a future he had never imagined.

But before he can reach that future, he must deal with the present, and that means battling the evil Shadow Hunters and facing the shocking truth about his real identity.

I hope you will enjoy the Sin Hunters series. Look for THE CLAIMED in May 2012, which will feature someone you meet in THE LOST. Not going to spill who it is just yet, but keep in mind I just love stories of redemption. . . .

Thank you all for your continued support. Also, many thanks to our military men and women, and their families for safeguarding our liberty and our country. THE LOST is dedicated to you for all the sacrifices you make on our behalf. God bless you and keep you safe.

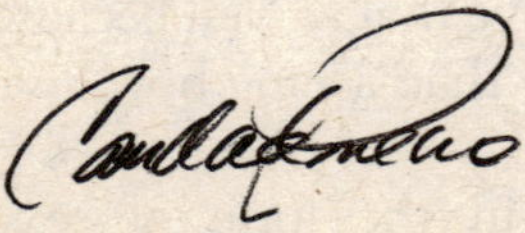

♥ ♥ ♥ ♥ ♥ ♥ ♥ ♥ ♥ ♥ ♥ ♥ ♥ ♥

From the desk of Jennifer Haymore

Dear Reader,

When Serena Donovan, the heroine of CONFESSIONS OF AN IMPROPER BRIDE (on sale now), entered my office to ask me to write her story, I realized right away that I was in trouble. Obviously, there was something pretty heavy resting on this woman's shoulders.

After I'd offered her a chair and a stiff drink (which she eyed warily—as if she's never seen a martini before!), I asked her why she had come.

"I have a problem," she said.

I tried not to chuckle. It was obvious from the permanent look of panic in her eyes that she had a very big problem indeed. "Okay," I said, "what's the problem?"

"Well—" She swallowed hard. "I'm going to get married."

I raised a brow. "Usually that's reason for celebration."

"Not for me." Her voice was dour.

I took a deep breath. "Look, Miss Donovan. I'm a romance writer. I write about love, blissful marriages, and happy endings. Maybe you've come to the wrong place." I rose from my chair and gestured toward the door. "Thanks for stopping by. Feel free to take the martini."

Her eyes flared wide with alarm. "No! Please . . . let me explain."

I hesitated, staring down at her. She seemed so . . . desperate. I guess I have a bleeding heart after all. Sighing, I resumed my seat. "Go ahead."

"I do respect and admire my future husband. Greatly. He's a wonderful man."

"Uh-huh."

"But, you see, he—" She winced, swallowed, and took a deep breath. "Well, he thinks I'm someone else."

I frowned. "You mean, you told him you were someone you're not?"

"Well, it's not that simple. You see, he fell in love with my sister."

"O. . .kay."

Her eyes went glassy. "But, you see, my sister died. Only he doesn't know that. He thinks I'm my sister!"

"He can't tell that you're not her?"

"I don't know . . ." Her voice was brimming with despair. "You see, we're identical twins, so on the outside we're alike, but we are such different people . . ."

Oh, man. This chick was in big trouble. "And you want to fashion a happy ending out of this, how?" I asked.

"But I haven't told you the whole problem," she said.

I thought she'd given me a pretty darned enormous problem already. Still, I waved my hand for her to elaborate.

"Jonathan," she said simply.

"Jonathan?"

"The Earl of Stratford. He's a friend of my fiancé

and the best man," she explained. She looked away. "And also, he's the only man I've ever—"

"That's okay," I said quickly, raising my hand. "I get it."

She released a relieved breath as I studied her. I really, really wanted to help her. She needed help, that was for sure. But how to forge a happy ending out of such a mess?

"Look," I said, flipping up my laptop and opening a new document, "you need to tell me everything, okay? From the beginning."

And that was how it began. By the time Miss Donovan finished telling me her story, I was so hooked, I had to go into my writing cave and write the entire, wild tale. The hardest part was getting to that happy ending, but it was so happy and so romantic that it was worth every drop of blood and sweat that it took to get there.

I truly hope you enjoy reading Serena Donovan's story! Please come visit me at my website, www.jenniferhaymore. com, where you can share your thoughts about my books, sign up for some fun freebies, and read more about the characters from CONFESSIONS OF AN IMPROPER BRIDE.

Sincerely,

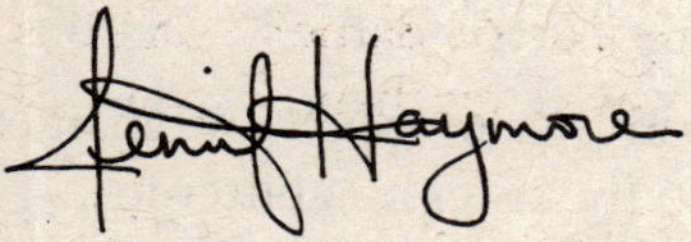

♥ ♥ ♥ ♥ ♥ ♥ ♥ ♥ ♥ ♥ ♥ ♥ ♥ ♥

From the desk of Sue-Ellen Welfonder

Dear Reader,

Does a landscape of savage grandeur make your heart beat faster? Do jagged peaks, cold-glittering boulders, and cauldrons of boiling mist speak to your soul? Are you exhilarated by the rush of chill wind, the power of ancient places made of stone and legend?

I love such places.

TEMPTATION OF A HIGHLAND SCOUNDREL, second book in my Highland Warriors trilogy, has a truly grand setting. Nought is my favorite corner of the Glen of Many Legends, home to the series' three warring clans. These proud Highlanders prove "where you live is who you are."

Kendrew Mackintosh and Isobel Cameron love wild places as much as I do. Kendrew boasts that he's hewn of Nought's soaring granite peaks and that he was weaned on cold wind and blowing mist. He's proud of his Norse heritage. Isobel shares his appreciation for Viking culture, rough terrain, and long, dark nights. She stirs his passion, igniting desires that brand them both.

But Isobel is a lady.

And Kendrew has sworn not to touch a woman of gentle birth. Isobel is also the sister of a bitter foe.

They're a perfect match despite the barriers separating them: centuries of clan feuds, hostility, and rivalries. Bad blood isn't easily forgotten in the

Highlands and grudges last forever. Kendrew refuses to acknowledge his attraction to Isobel. She won't ignore the passion between them. As only a woman in love can, she employs all her seductive wiles to win his heart.

The temptation of Kendrew Mackintosh begins deep in his rugged Nought territory. In the shadows of mysterious cairns known as dreagan stones and on the night of his clan's raucous Midsummer Eve revels, Isobel pitches a battle Kendrew can only lose. Yet surrender will bring greater rewards than he's ever claimed.

Kendrew does open his heart to Isobel, but they soon find themselves caught in a dangerous maelstrom that threatens their love and could cost their lives. The entire glen is at peril and a brutal foe will stop at nothing to crush the brave men of the Glen of Many Legends.

Turning Kendrew loose on his enemy—a worthy villain—gave me many enjoyable writing hours. He's a fierce fighter and a sight to behold when riled. But beneath his ferocity is a great-hearted man who lives by honor.

Writing Isobel was an equal joy. Like me, she feels most alive in wild, windswept places. I know Nought approved of her.

Places do have feelings.

Highlanders know that. In wild places, the pulse of the land is strong. I can't imagine a better setting for Kendrew and Isobel.

I hope you've enjoyed watching Isobel prove to Kendrew that the hardest warrior can't win against a woman wielding the most powerful weapon of all: a heart that loves.

With all good wishes,

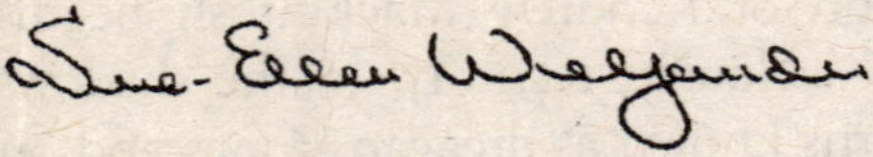

www.welfonder.com

From the desk of Sophie Gunn

Dear Reader,

Some small-town romances feature knitting clubs, some cookie clubs, and some quilting clubs. But my new series has something else entirely.

Welcome to Galton, New York, home of the Enemy Club.

The Enemy Club is made up of four women who had been the worst of enemies back in high school. They were the class brainiac, the bad girl, the princess, and the outcast. Now, all grown up, they've managed to become the best of friends. But they're friends with a difference. They've promised to tell one another the truth, the whole truth, and nothing but the truth so help them Gracie (the baker of the pies at the Last Chance Diner). Because they see things from their very (very!) different points of view, this causes all sorts of conflicts and a nuanced story, where no one has a lock on what's right or wrong.

In *Sweet Kiss of Summer*, Nina Stokes is the woman with the problem, and she's going to need everyone's help to solve it. Her brother lost his life in the war. On his deathbed, he asked a nurse to write Nina a letter, instructing her to give his house back in Galton to his war buddy, Mick Rivers.

Or did he?

How can Nina know if the letter is real or a con? And even if it's real, where has Mick been for the past two years, during which Nina tried everything to contact him to no avail? How long should she be expected to keep up the house in this limbo, waiting for a man who obviously takes her brother's last wish lightly?

So when a beautiful man claiming to be Mick roars up Nina's driveway one summer afternoon in a flashy red car, demanding the house that he feels is rightfully his, every member of the Enemy Club thinks that she knows best what Nina should do. Naturally, none of them agree. The themes of friendship, duty, and honor run deep in Galton, and in *Sweet Kiss of Summer*, they are all tested. To whom do we owe our first duty: our family, our friends, our country—or ourselves?

What I loved most about writing Sweet Kiss of Summer was that there was no easy solution for anyone. As I wrote, I had no idea what Nina would do about her dilemma. Mick struggled with an even thornier problem, as his secrets were bigger than anyone in the Enemy Club could imagine. I could understand everyone's point of view. There is just so much to consider when you're not only out for yourself, but for your country, your community, your family, and ultimately, something even bigger.

I hope you'll enjoy reading about these characters as much as I've enjoyed writing about them. Come visit me at SophieGunn.com to learn more about the small town of Galton and the Enemy Club, to see pictures of my kitties, and to keep in touch. I'd love to hear from you!

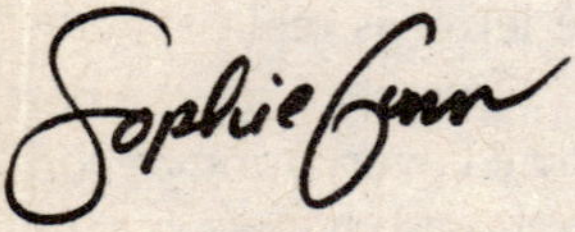

www.sophiegunn.com